THE GAME
AND THE
GOVERNESS

"Readers will adore Phoebe, a once wealthy woman who has learned to put the past behind and find happiness in everyday life. The subtle development of romance between the devil-may-care earl and the proper governess is the impetus behind this winning novel, complete with rich characters and a multidimensional plotline."

—*Publishers Weekly* (starred review)

"A fun twist on the plot about trading places."

—*Two Classy Chics*

"A thoughtful, intricate novel."

—*Smart Bitches, Trashy Books*

"A clever, tremendously entertaining tale of truth and lies, love and friendship."

—*New York Times* bestselling author Sarah MacLean
for *Washington Post Book World*

"Buy for the tortured hero, stay for the heroine who makes him grow the hell up."

—*BookRiot*

"An enjoyable and thought-provoking read. Recommended."
—*Historical Novels Review*

"This delightful romp of a story should be devoured in one sitting, if at all possible. . . . A book to be savored and reread."
—*Romance at Random*

"If you like romance that combines the light and the substantive, I highly recommend this book. I have added it to my list of the Best of 2014."
—*The Romance Dish*

"Masterful pacing, outstanding storytelling, and a deftly drawn cast of unforgettable characters set *The Game and the Governess* apart from the bounty of this summer's new releases. This magical novel is a stunning example of the transportable power of a remarkable historical."
—*The Lusty Literate*

"An amazing book . . . I can't wait for more from Kate Noble."
—*Paranormal Librarian*

"Kate Noble has woven a story that will grab the reader. I think you will fall in love with Ned and Phoebe."
—*Bookworm 2 Bookworm*

"Go grab this book. You'll really like it, I promise."
—*Little Miss Bookmark*

"Marvelous."
—*Reading in Winter*

More acclaim for KATE NOBLE and her popular novels

"Kate Noble brings the delicate elements of Regency England brilliantly alive with her prose."

—*USA Today*

"An extraordinary and unique romance worth savoring."

—*Smart Bitches, Trashy Books* on *Let It Be Me*

"The story's prologue literally gave me goosebumps—goosebumps that never went away throughout the whole book. This is the kind of deep, touching read that romance fans search for. I have a new favorite author!"

—*RT Book Reviews* on Seal of Excellence pick *Let It Be Me*

"Despite being a delight and thoroughly winning, the book is 300 pages of confirmation to what I'd suspected and now know: The Regency belongs to Kate Noble, and it's in very, very good hands."

—*All About Romance* on *If I Fall*

"If Austen were alive and writing novels today, the result might be something exactly like *Follow My Lead*, a wickedly witty and superbly satisfying romance."

—*Chicago Tribune*

"Believable and captivating . . . an outstanding and memorable tale."

—*Publishers Weekly* (starred review) on *Follow My Lead*

"Clever and graceful . . . simply sublime"

—*Booklist* on *Compromised*

ALSO BY KATE NOBLE

The Game and the Governess

Available from Pocket Books

KATE NOBLE

WITHDRAWN
THE LIE AND THE LADY

POCKET BOOKS

New York • London • Toronto • Sydney • New Delhi

The sale of this book without its cover is unauthorized. If you purchased this book without a cover, you should be aware that it was reported to the publisher as "unsold and destroyed." Neither the author nor the publisher has received payment for the sale of this "stripped book."

Pocket Books
An Imprint of Simon & Schuster, Inc.
1230 Avenue of the Americas
New York, NY 10020

This book is a work of fiction. Any references to historical events, real people, or real places are used fictitiously. Other names, characters, places, and events are products of the author's imagination, and any resemblance to actual events or places or persons, living or dead, is entirely coincidental.

Copyright © 2016 by Kate Wilcox

All rights reserved, including the right to reproduce this book or portions thereof in any form whatsoever. For information, address Pocket Books Subsidiary Rights Department, 1230 Avenue of the Americas, New York, NY 10020

First Pocket Books paperback edition January 2016

POCKET and colophon are registered trademarks of Simon & Schuster, Inc.

For information about special discounts for bulk purchases, please contact Simon & Schuster Special Sales at 1-866-506-1949 or business@simonandschuster.com.

The Simon & Schuster Speakers Bureau can bring authors to your live event. For more information or to book an event, contact the Simon & Schuster Speakers Bureau at 1-866-248-3049 or visit our website at www.simonspeakers.com.

Manufactured in the United States of America

10 9 8 7 6 5 4 3 2 1

ISBN 978-1-4767-4939-6
ISBN 978-1-4767-4942-6 (ebook)

*For my son, without whom this book
would have been completed much sooner.*

ACKNOWLEDGMENTS

Writing a novel is hard. Writing a novel with a newborn is herculean. The only way this gets done is with the support of good people. Annelise Robey at the Jane Rotrosen Agency is the best sounding board and career guardian I could have ever asked for. Abby Zidle, my editor at Pocket, has patience and good humor for days, as well as excellent story sense. And my friends, my writing group, and my family are the only reasons I manage to shower daily, let alone write. The babysitters who gave me four hours at a time in the public library to work were lifesavers.

But the biggest dose of thanks goes to my husband, who was on baby duty 24-7 over Thanksgiving with my family while I madly typed the ending of this book. He deserves all the accolades. And a drink.

 **1**

The Countess of Churzy had been in love three times.

First, when she was simply Letty Price, barely eight years old and blissfully unaware of the realities of life, she dearly loved her best friend, Joey Purser. They played together every day, until Joey's mother needed him to start working in the Price Timber Mill. And then, as the daughter of the owner, she wasn't allowed to play with Joey anymore.

The second time she was in love, she was Miss Leticia Price, sister to Lady Widcoate, and shunned by every good member of the ton. As she was only a timber miller's daughter, her father's fortune was enough to buy her sister a country bumpkin with a title, but for Leticia to think her beauty and grace would do her any good with real society was too presumptuous to endure. Then, Konrad Herzog, the Count of Churzy, crossed the room to where she was sitting and asked her to dance. He was an Austrian aristocrat, enjoying London while the last vestiges of the war trickled to an end, and Leticia fell in love the moment he winked at her during the quadrille.

The third and final time Leticia—now widowed, desperate, and needing to secure her future—knew she was in love, she had just thrown open her bedroom door to find the Earl of Ashby standing on the threshold.

"Oh . . . hello, Letty," he whispered, his hand still in midair.

"Good evening," she replied, a half smile painting her lips. "You seem surprised to see me."

"I thought you might be asleep."

"Then why knock?" Her dressing gown was by no means immodest—unfortunately. But she worked with what she had, rolling her shoulders back and showing her bosom to best advantage.

The corner of his mouth ticked up as his eyes flicked appreciatively down. He must know what she was doing. They'd been playing this game for weeks now.

The anticipation made her heart flip over. It made her blood soar.

And it wasn't the first time that evening the Earl of Ashby made her feel this way.

"Because I can't sleep. And I thought you might not be able to either," he answered.

"I was making a valiant attempt. It is well past midnight, my lord."

"Then it is lucky I caught you, my lady." Something shuttered over his eyes. Something honest and difficult. He took one deep breath, then two, before he spoke. "I wanted to make certain you were all right. I . . . I acted rashly this evening."

"Oh really?" she asked, all innocence. "How so?"

"Tonight, at the Summer Ball when I . . ." He cleared his throat.

"When you kissed me," she supplied.

Oh yes, he had kissed her. She had been standing across the room, talking to someone—it could have been her sister, Fanny, but she could no longer remember, because at that moment her breath caught and her heart started pounding out of her chest as she watched the Earl of Ashby cross the floor, stalking his prey.

Stalking her.

Before she could so much as exhale, he'd swept her into his embrace and kissed her, right there on the floor at a public ball, in front of everyone.

It was, after a lifetime of disappointment, her moment of triumph.

Even for such an alarmingly public display, it hadn't come out of the blue. She and the Earl of Ashby had been growing close over the last fortnight. He and his man of business, Mr. Turner, had come to stay at her sister's estate while he sorted out some difficulty about a property he owned nearby. That she just happened to be visiting her sister at the same time as an arguably handsome and extremely wealthy gentleman of note was neither here nor there.

That they had been inseparable almost from the moment he arrived was far more pertinent.

She hadn't expected it to be so easy. She'd been certain that to charm the Earl of Ashby, she would have to summon her most enthusiastic fawning, her best display of wit and vivacity. Walk the tightrope of being fascinating, approachable, and unobtainable all at once.

Instead, it had been like sliding into a bed after a long day. Each little look, every time he offered her his arm, all the conversations about nothing and everything . . . it all felt so, so right.

It was astonishing.

It was frightening.

And now he was standing in front of her, in the middle of the night. Still in his evening kit from the ball, his shirt open at the collar, his cravat hanging loose around his neck, revealing a tempting bit of skin at the base of his throat. Still, for all his finery his clothes fit him strangely, as if he would rather be in just buckskins and breeches—or nothing at all.

But there was something underneath that. A worry. A . . . need.

A thrill ran up her spine. Perhaps his need matched her own.

"You were very reckless," she said seriously.

"I was. I apologize for any offense I might have caused." He took another breath. "There are some things that I haven't—that is, that we haven't discussed. And I'm afraid that before anything else occurs, it is only fair—"

"Ashby," she said, her direct tone cutting through his nervous rambling.

"Yes?"

She swung the door open wide, and pulled him inside. "I can be reckless too."

෴

AND RECKLESS IT WAS. She knew it as his lips met hers. As her hands clutched the lapels of his coat, as his surprise melted into want, she knew that this was the most reckless thing she could possibly do.

Leticia had a strategy—she must, because she had very little else.

The only advantage she had in the situation was that he had kissed her. He had shown his feelings to the world. The next logical step was what that kiss implied, an even more public declaration. Preferably in a church, but she would take Gretna Green; she wasn't picky.

But to have him here, in her bedroom without any formal promises, his hands running up and down the length of her body—it was tantamount to throwing all her hard work out the window.

And she didn't care.

There was only one explanation for her actions, she decided: she had lost her mind.

His warm breath fell across her cheek as he broke free from their kiss, moving his mouth down to her jaw, her neck, to that little notch at the base of her throat. A rough gasp escaped as his hands slid their way down her back, lower, to the rounded rise of her bottom.

"You have . . . amazing hands," she said, her voice shaking, as those wonderful fingers danced over the thin linen of her dressing gown—the only thing between his hands and her skin.

But it was as if her voice broke through his haze, and his head came up.

"I have to tell you . . ." He struggled with the words. "We . . . we should not—"

She took two deep breaths, trying to calm her racing heart. Perhaps he was right. Perhaps . . .

"We shouldn't?" she asked, as her dressing gown—completely of its own volition!—slid off one perfect shoulder.

"Oh hell," he growled, and his mouth found hers again.

Clothes fell away as they groped their way to the bed. His coat hit the floor. His cravat, already hanging loose, was a nuisance. And why oh why did men's shirts have to have buttons?

But soon enough, her dressing gown was parted, exposing her breasts to the cool night air, and she had other things on her mind.

Namely him. This man who breathed out a long, shaking whistle upon seeing her.

She'd never been looked at like that before. Not by Konrad. Not by anyone. It made her feel . . .

Powerful.

His hands—such marvelous hands!—traced the curve of her high breast (although not as high as it once was) and cupped its weight before his head lowered to taste her.

"Ned. Oh, Ned." The night air echoed with his name.

His hands, making their way up her legs, stopped midway through the journey. His mouth, lavishing all possible praise on her breasts, simply froze.

Leticia stilled. "Ned?"

"Don't . . . don't call me that," he rasped, his head coming up. In the dark she could not see his eyes. Could not see what he meant.

"I'm sorry . . . I shouldn't have presumed to call you by your Christian name," she whispered. "I simply thought, since you and I . . . since tonight . . ." But not even since tonight. He'd been calling her Letty, a name she hadn't allowed spoken outside of her own head in nearly twenty years, since he'd arrived. It started as a joke. But secretly she loved it.

"No, don't apologize," he said quickly.

"Ashby . . ."

"Not that either," he bit out, so harshly it startled her.

"Then what should I call you?" she asked, worry beginning to creep into her imagination. "Darling?"

He didn't reply.

"My love?" she tried, biting her lip.

"We cannot do this. Not now," he said, moving away from her. He sat up on his knees. The cold air against her skin was almost painful. The familiar disappointment was worse.

"I understand," she said, closing the dressing gown around her body.

"No, you don't," he said, raking a hand through his dark hair. "I have to say something to you . . . before we make any mistakes. And I cannot do it now," he said, his eyes falling over her body, then quickly shooting back up to her face. "I think it's been proven I won't make it through two sentences."

"Ash—I mean, my love, whatever it is, you can tell me," she said, sitting up. She reached out to him with her free hand, caressing the side of his face. He leaned into her palm, a whimper of want escaping his throat.

But he took her hand in his, stilling it against his cheek. "And I will," he said, resolve filling his voice. "Tomorrow."

"Tomorrow?"

"Tomorrow," he promised, taking her hand and kissing the palm. "Tomorrow I will . . . say what needs to be said."

His kisses moved from her palm to the crook of her elbow, pulling her closer, drugging her. Torturing himself.

"Nmmmmmmh," was the whine as he broke free, finally this time, leaping off the bed and picking up his clothes lying crumpled in puddles on the floor.

And then he was gone.

"Tomorrow," she whispered, flopping back against the pillows. Tomorrow he would say what he needed to. And she knew what it was. His gentlemanly instincts had overtaken his baser ones, and he wouldn't dishonor her by taking what she—in a dizzy haze of sparkling love—had so very much wanted to give.

Instead, he would get down on one knee, he would ask for her hand in marriage, and she would grant it. They would be married and live in his townhouse in London during the season and at his family seat when the shooting was good and anywhere else they pleased at any other time. She would never have to worry about money again. Or her social standing, or how she was going to live now.

She would be the Countess of Ashby, and he would be her savior.

It all would begin tomorrow, she thought as her heart slowed to a lull, and she drifted to sleep.

2

"Leticia, will you marry me?"

Leticia smiled down at the man before her, arms outstretched, his hand gently holding hers.

"Oh, my darling! Of course I will!"

It was hard to believe, but she had actually done it. She had actually saved herself. It had taken almost an entire year, and pawning almost all her jewelry (she had never liked the diamond earbobs anyway, far too gauche), but it had absolutely been worth it. Because here she was, being proposed to by none other than the man with whom she would happily spend the rest of her life.

Who delivered his proposal sitting, because kneeling wasn't exactly in his repertoire.

Sir Bartholomew Babcock rose (with only minimal trouble) and smiled widely under his bushy white mustache. His girth settled and he found his balance, gripping his cane with one hand and Leticia's hand with the other.

He was the man of her dreams.

Yes. A lot had changed since last summer. Since she learned about the Lie.

"Mind if I kiss you, m'dear?" he asked, a little shy.

"In public?" she replied. There was any number of people in the museum with them. All pompously French, and none paying any attention to the couple by the center bench of the Caryatid Room, but still—Leticia knew to be cautious of public declarations.

"Just to make it official." He blushed and looked at his toes—or more accurately, toward his toes. There was no way he could see them past his belly.

In spite of herself, Leticia smiled. He was such a large, gruff man, far older than she, and yes, enjoying a particularly unfortunate flare-up of his gout, but still, he managed to be endearing.

"In that case, Sir Bartholomew—of course," she said.

He pecked her on the proffered cheek—respectably, honorably. The way a lady should be kissed in public by her intended.

"Now that I've convinced you to marry me, how can I convince you to call me Sir Barty?"

As Leticia laughed and took Sir Barty's arm, she allowed herself a small moment of personal congratulation. Who would have guessed that when Leticia walked into this very sculpture gallery three weeks ago she would be meeting the man she would marry?

Who other than Leticia, that is.

Of course, Paris wasn't her first stop. She'd tried London, but she'd had barely three weeks there before the looks started. Then she tried Brighton, Portsmouth, Plymouth, even flying as far north as Edinburgh. But everywhere she went, the whispers began before she could even gain a foothold. The only option left was to flee, chased away—by the Lie.

The Continent had been her last resort. And the biggest gamble of all.

She almost hadn't gone. Paris was a costly city. Its lodgings were expensive, its culinary treats outside the range of possibility. And if one wanted to meet and mingle with the upper echelons of society, one required a small fortune or a small army of personal acquaintances to vouch for their good standing.

Leticia had neither. But she did have just enough funds for a room at a respectable establishment for traveling ladies, and a weekly ticket to the Louvre.

And knowledge of when guides would be bringing their English tourists through.

That was the best—and most important—coin she had spent, bribing those mercenary men who loitered outside of the English hotels, looking to be hired on as guides for young gentlemen, freshly down from Oxford or Cambridge and wide-eyed with wonder on their grand tour. Those crafty guides would tell her when they were planning on taking their charges to the Louvre, thus letting Leticia know when best to be there, strolling the galleries, enjoying the Greek, Roman, and Renaissance works, and anything else that had not been returned to its home country after Napoleon had "borrowed" it.

It took a great deal of patience, of course. As fascinating as they found her (and they all found her fascinating), young men on their first adventure in the world were not keen on giving up that adventure right away—and since Paris was often the first stop on such a journey, they allowed Leticia to fascinate them (and nothing more) for the few weeks they were in France, before abandoning her for the charms of Spain, Italy, and the German provinces.

It was months of this and Leticia had been about to give up hope. Until one day she happened to sit on a bench in front of a large statue of a winged woman. And a round man with a cane hobbled up next to her.

"I hope you don't mind if I sit, my girl," the man had said, plopping himself down on the opposite side of the bench.

"Of . . . of course not—" Leticia managed, a bit thrown by the presumption of the request . . . if it even qualified as a request. After all, no gentleman would impose on a lady by forcing his company. Besides, she was waiting for a group of young English gentlemen to come through—the porter she regularly bribed was usually so punctual.

"Oh good! You're English!" he cried. "Can't tell you how hard it's been going about this city, trying to strike up a conversation, and not getting much beyond 'bonjour.'"

"I . . . can imagine," Leticia replied.

"Conversation is really all I'm good for," the man said. "If I'm even good for that." He tapped his cane against his thigh, and stretched out his foreleg across the black and white marble floor, wincing as he did so.

"It's the gout," he said, obviously seeing the direction of her gaze. "I'm afraid I can't keep up with the young lads."

"Are . . . are you here with your son?" she asked. Maybe he was part of the porter's group.

"Don't have a son! Just my little girl. But she's not here either. She's back home, in Lincolnshire. No—I'm here on my grand tour! Sir Bartholomew Babcock, at your service. But everyone calls me Sir Barty."

He gave a slight bow, then realizing perhaps that bowing while sitting might not exactly register, he tipped his hat instead. Then he realized he was conversing with a lady inside a building and whipped his hat off.

"You are on your grand tour?" Leticia asked.

"Don't exactly look like the type, do I?" Sir Barty had said. "Decades past the prime touring age, I know. But I never got to the tour before I married—that tiny frog Napoleon made sure of that—and then after the wedding, didn't really feel much like leaving home."

He winked and laughed, a huge guffaw that shook the statues in the gallery.

Leticia had smiled, warming to this somewhat coarse but obviously kind man's attentions. After all, the porter and his charges seemed to be taking their time. There was no harm in mild conversation while she waited.

"And how does your wife feel about you coming abroad now?"

He fiddled with his cane a moment, idly tapping it against his thigh. "She passed. Two years ago."

Suddenly, this Sir Bartholomew—Babcock, was it?— became much more interesting.

"I'm so sorry for your loss," Leticia said, leaning in closer.

"Thank you, m'dear," Sir Barty said. "It was hard, I grant you. But before she went, she made me promise I'd shake some of my dust off, and now I'm doing it." He winced and nodded to his outstretched leg. "Although it would be much more pleasant a walking tour if I could walk it."

"Oh, you must be in the worst kind of pain!" Leticia exclaimed, placing her hand over his. "You simply cannot be on your feet . . ."

"But neither can I be holed up in the hotel. It's the oddest place. For breakfast . . . they have oranges," he whispered to her, in the same tone one might say "they have clockwork abominations."

"I would never suggest such a thing," Leticia replied. "Not when you are on a heroic quest."

"Heroic quest? Well, I suppose I am, in a way."

"Luckily this museum has chairs for public use. We'll hire one for you."

Leticia called over to a guard or servant—they seemed to fulfill both roles—and was about to ask him to fetch one of the wicker wheeled chairs, but Sir Barty stayed her hand.

"Oh no—I can't ask for that."

"Why ever not?

"It's not . . . I don't want to seem . . . I'm used to my foot and walking on it, is all."

A feline smile spread across Leticia's face. Of course. A big gruff man from Lincolnshire would not want to seem feeble. The male ego was a terribly silly thing, and it looked as if this Sir Barty had a typical one. But it also meant that Leticia knew his weakness—his pride.

"You're likely right," she replied. "It would be foolhardy for a man as strong as yourself to use a chair. It would be taking the chair away from someone who truly needed it."

"Precisely." Sir Barty relaxed. "Besides, with such lovely company, I'm happy to wait here for the guide—some Frenchie named Gaston—who promised to show me the sights of this fancy place. Paid the man five francs, said he knew the Louvre like the back of his hand." He frowned. "At least, that's what I think he said."

Leticia's eyebrow went up. She knew Gaston—he was one of the less reputable porters. She was absolutely certain that he had indeed promised a comprehensive tour, but doubted he'd show up at the museum—he was far more likely to be drinking Sir Barty's francs away.

"If your Gaston is so late, I would be happy to show you around the museum," Leticia offered. "I come here so often I feel like I know each piece of art personally." At the quizzical look on his face, she pointed to a bronze bas-relief, a half circle hanging on the wall, with a nymph lounging beneath a stag's head. The *Nymph of Fontainebleau*—one of Leticia's favorites. "For instance—that is Nancy."

"Nancy?" Sir Barty asked, squinting at the sculpture.

"Indeed. Nancy the Nymph. She has spent all morning hunting, and finally caught a stag—which, as you must know, is exhausting work. Therefore she decided to take off all her clothes and have a bit of a sleep."

"That can't be right." Sir Barty looked from the nymph to her and then back again, utterly confused. "Oh, I see!" he then cried. "You've made up a story to go along with the statue. Jolly good!"

"I'm afraid that as much as I enjoy the museum, I'm not much of a scholar," Leticia demurred.

"Neither am I, m'dear," Sir Barty said in confidence. "Never did have much use for knowing the names of all these things. Now, what about that one over there?"

He'd pointed to a very large statue of a man with wings embracing a woman. Psyche.

"Well, he's very obviously a man who also happens to be a bird."

"Not an angel then?" Sir Barty asked.

"No, he's forever being mistaken for one, though, and it's a great burden on him. She's the only one who ever correctly guessed he was a bird man, and for that, he loved her immediately."

Sir Barty laughed his deep guffaw, this time adding a few snorts for good measure.

"If you think that's funny, there's a woman with no arms in the next room who has the most interesting history," Leticia smiled. "She cut off both her own arms," she whispered.

"How does someone cut off their own arms?" Sir Barty asked as he stood and offered Leticia his arm. "One would think you'd need your arms to do the cutting."

"That is the interesting part."

"I think the interesting part will be her storyteller," Sir Barty said with a modicum of gallantry. They'd spent the rest of the afternoon together, Leticia Scheherazade-ing her way through the galleries, making up stories for each of the statues and paintings, Sir Bartholomew Babcock falling more and more under her thrall with each new ridiculousness. She made certain to move slowly, and take some of his weight on her arm, all without him ever thinking that his gouty leg was an issue.

They parted that day without any kind of exchange of information. There were no flowers at Leticia's door at the ladies' boarding house the next morning, nor were there chocolates or a Lincolnshire gentleman of later years making formal addresses. But when she came to the Louvre that next day, Sir Barty was there, exactly where she'd expected him to be.

She learned a great deal about him as they ambled through those rooms at a glacial pace. She learned that the Babcocks had been one of the largest landholders in Lincolnshire since King Charles. She learned that the last time he'd been in London he'd been a young man, and hadn't thought much of it. If he was to go into town, he much preferred the closer York for his scene and society. She even learned why he was so aghast at a hotel that would serve oranges for breakfast.

"Well, it's like showing off, isn't it?" he'd said. "I'm a man of certain wealth, I have an orchard—but I've had an orange maybe three times in my life. To have a whole bowl of them, sitting out for breakfast . . ." He'd shuddered, and Leticia had laughed.

Sir Barty had no children other than his daughter, Margaret, who was as Sir Barty put it, "likely back home digging in the dirt, and scraping up her knees something fierce."

"I have a niece very like that," Leticia had replied. "She's nine, and mad about horses."

Sir Barty hummed in agreement. "She needs a female's guidance," he said, shaking his head. "I try as best I can, but ever since her mother died . . ."

Leticia placed a hand over Sir Barty's. "I understand completely."

And she did understand. She understood that Sir Barty needed a mother for his daughter as much as he needed a wife for himself. And luckily, she was ready and willing to be both—which placed him squarely within her power.

Of course, Sir Barty learned things about her too. But only what she allowed.

She told him of her beloved Konrad perishing in a riding accident in Brighton three years ago. She told him about her sister, Fanny, Lady Widcoate, and how dear she found Fanny's children, Rose and Henry. (She did not mention that she only found children delightful once they reached the age of being able to amuse themselves.)

And then she told him about the Lie.

Not the salient details, of course. Just what was pertinent.

"Last year . . . last year I was very nearly engaged," she'd said, her eyes falling to the stone floor between them. "But it turned out the man in question was playing me false."

"How so?"

"He lied. About who he was. Where he was from. His very name."

It was a name she had been hoping to call her own—Ashby. But it wasn't attached to the man who had kissed her on a dance floor or driven her mad with want in the dark of her bedroom. Instead, his name was rough and common, just like him: Turner. More specifically, Mr. John Turner, secretary to the real Earl of Ashby. While visiting her sister, Mr. Turner and the earl had switched places on a lark.

And on a lark, nearly ruined Leticia's life.

"Luckily, his lie was revealed in time," Leticia had said, shaking off her growing anger. "But it was very embarrassing."

"Broke your heart, did he?" Sir Barty had replied, gruff.

"I do not—" But she faltered. Because as much as she hated to admit it, to admit anyone had that kind of effect on her, it was the one thing she had never been very good at hiding. "Yes. He did. But he's thankfully in the past."

"Thankfully," Sir Barty replied. Then, with a boldness she hadn't imagine he had, let his hand fall over hers where it rested. "M'dear, I hope you know I would never lie to you like that. I would much rather take care of you."

And she glowed with triumph.

Walks through the Louvre led to chocolates drunk at small cafés along the *rue*. Then meals taken together at Sir Barty's hotel before attending the theater. All under the eyes of servants and with the utmost propriety. Sir Barty was traveling without friends and Leticia had none, so they could have very easily acted without caution. But the fact that Sir Barty was so careful with his attentions and Leticia so controlled in hers led to that moment in the Louvre where Sir Barty had taken his hand in hers and blurted out his proposal.

It was a triumph of strategy. And she could not have played it more perfectly, Leticia decided.

"Of course I'll call you Barty," Leticia replied. "If you wish it. And you must call me Leticia."

"But I already do call you Leticia." He frowned.

"Well, we'll think of some other endearment." She patted his hand sweetly.

"You've never gone by Letty, I suppose?" he asked.

A pang of regret shot through her. However, she must have looked stricken, because Sir Barty immediately squeezed her hand. "No, of course not. No one as fine as you has ever been called Letty."

Leticia forced herself to calm, to smile. "I do rather like how you say m'dear, Sir Barty," she offered softly.

Sir Barty's eyes lit up. "Then m'dear it is." He squeezed her hand, more gently this time. "Well, m'dear. I think I've had about all of the Continental travel I can stand for one lifetime. Would you like to go home?"

He did not mean back to the hotel, or to her lodgings. No, he meant home.

England.

Finally.

Yes, Leticia Herzog, Countess of Churzy, née Price, and soon to be Lady Babcock, was going back to where she belonged.

In triumph.

"Yes, Barty," she cooed. "Let's go home."

3

*L*incolnshire wasn't at all what Leticia expected.

Not that it was in any way different from any other time she had been to Lincolnshire. She was certain that she and Konrad had driven through here, and possibly spent a day or two at an inn across the Wolds by the sea when they'd had to let rumors die down. She remembered it being picturesque, if a little sparse. Expansive, but far too much windswept grain on hillsides and grazing livestock.

Then, of course, she'd passed through on her way to or from Edinburgh, trying to outrun the Lie.

She hadn't seen much of the place that time.

No, what was unexpected about Lincolnshire, Leticia supposed, was that it was going to be her home.

Strange, but home usually did not feel so . . . foreign.

"I'll warm to it," Leticia told herself as the carriage rolled across the hills.

"What's that, m'dear?" Sir Barty said, snorting himself awake.

"Nothing—simply that I am comfortably warm."

"Oh . . ." He settled back down against the cushions.

"Let me know if you need another blanket, or . . ." And he was snoring again.

She would warm to Lincolnshire, she decided. Indeed, she would find something to love about it. Such as . . . that sky. Rare was it to see a sky so blue in town!

And those fens, she thought as they crossed from the lower counties into Lincolnshire proper. There aren't fens like that anywhere else in the world! Other fens, not nearly as flat and expansive a stretch of farmland, were hardly as worthy of praise as Lincolnshire fens.

Forty minutes later, they stopped to change horses and have a bite to eat, and Leticia was introduced to the local cuisine.

"Now, what do you think of that sausage, m'dear?"

"It's very . . . sausage-like," Leticia offered.

"Indeed it is! Lincolnshire is known for its sausages. And its pork pies. And its haslet—that's a kind of pork loaf, don't you know! We must get you to try some!"

Sir Barty ordered two slices of haslet brought straight away, and as Leticia bit into it, she declared between hard swallows and in absolute truth, "Best haslet I've ever had!"

Some hours later, they crossed the Wolds, running hills noted for their beauty, and Leticia had to admit they were rather picturesque.

Loveliest Wolds she had ever seen.

While Sir Barty snored again and Leticia had pulled back the carriage curtains to allow in some air, she saw a proud, tall windmill standing at the entrance to a market town. And that made her truly smile.

Five sails, the brightest, purest white, sat regally in a circle atop a tower of red brick. The tower was attached to a long, low building—the mill itself, she supposed. Another building, smaller, was being built on one side.

It seemed so silly to find such a thing delightful—but it

seemed silly to find it at all. She was so used to cities—and when she was in the country it was at her sister's for as short a time as she could manage—that to find something as whimsical and as practical as a windmill made her feel alight.

It was the first thing that made her feel at home.

Yes, perhaps she truly could warm to Lincolnshire.

Even though something about the windmill struck her as odd.

The windmill and attached buildings proudly declared themselves (via a neatly lettered sign as they passed) as sitting at the edge of the town of Helmsley—which made Leticia gasp aloud.

"Sir Barty—we're in Helmsley!" she cried, forcing her betrothed awake once more.

But he was glad of it, she decided, because when he blinked and saw out the carriage window, his thick mustache ruffled into a smile.

"Then we are nearly home, m'dear!" he replied. Helmsley was the town nearest to Sir Barty's estate. "Next stop, Bluestone Manor."

"Home to generation upon generation of Babcocks?" Leticia asked.

"Not to mention the current generation. And then next." Sir Barty winked and then squeezed her hand. "That is . . . if you would like children. I have my Margaret of course, and the estate is not entailed, so I have no need for an heir, but . . . if children are a hope for your future . . ." His sentence ended on a mumble, at a loss for words.

Leticia knew better than to give a straight answer to such a question. "All this talk of children makes me think that you are eager for the wedding," she replied saucily. "Perhaps you should write the bishop for a special license and dispense with this wait."

Sir Barty laughed and shook his head. "Everyone in Helmsley would have my head if I denied them a wedding. No—we shall wait the proper time for the banns to be read and have a wedding the likes of which this town has never seen. Now, would you like to see the church where you'll become Lady Barty Babcock?"

She nodded and let him point out the stone spires at the center of town that marked the parish seat.

It would take nearly a month for the banns to be read. Three successive Sundays of asking those gathered if they had any objection to the union, followed by a week of waiting for the wedding itself. Then, and only then, would she consider herself secure. Until that time, however, she had to make certain there would be no objection.

She glanced at Sir Barty as he shoved his arm out the carriage window, waving to people on the street, jolly and relieved to be home again. While that month ticked down, she would concentrate on making Sir Barty happy. Making his life easier, and making a life for herself here.

A strange echo filled her chest, as if there were something askew underneath her skin. As if something were amiss.

Then she realized what it had been.

The windmill. It hadn't been spinning. Even on a day like today, with a strong, steady breeze pushing the new wheat in waves across the hillside, the sails stayed dormant.

There was something utterly sad about a windmill that didn't spin, she thought. It would live its life ultimately unfulfilled.

❧

WHILE LETICIA WAS quite decided that she would warm to Lincolnshire, she was beginning to worry that Lincolnshire—more specifically, Helmsley—might not warm to her.

Her troubles began—and some might say ended—with Margaret Babcock.

Less than an hour after rolling past the red brick windmill with the white sails, Sir Barty's carriage pulled up in front of Bluestone Manor.

It was of a respectable size—larger than her sister's home, Puffington Arms. And more graceful too—taking its name from the blue-tinted granite that made up the facade of the house. There were lovely grounds with some of the most abundant flowers and trees she'd ever seen—a worrying sight.

But what Leticia couldn't see from the drive were any servants.

No retinue of housemaids. No liveried men or stable hands coming up to take the reins of the carriage. No one at all.

"Where is everyone?" Leticia asked as Sir Barty handed her down to the drive. "Your housekeeper, butler, and whatnot?" Oh Lord, he did have a housekeeper, didn't he? "And your daughter, Margaret?"

Sir Barty snorted. "I never have them stand on ceremony when I come home. Everyone gathered around in a half circle, waiting to be inspected? Makes no sense to me—better to let them go about their business."

To Leticia's mind, waiting on Sir Barty was their business, but instead of arguing the point, she simply shrugged and said lightly, "You are likely correct, darling, but I would have thought they would have wished to greet me—this first time, at least."

"Ah, well as to that—" Sir Barty's bushy brow came down so far it almost touched his mustache. "They do not know of your arrival."

"They . . . do not know?"

"It seemed silly to write. After all, we came straight

from Paris—we would have likely beaten home any letter I might have sent."

"Yes, but"—she blinked in astonishment—"does that mean that they do not know about me at all? They do not know that you are bringing home a fiancée?"

Sir Barty bit his lower lip. "I suppose they do not. Ah well—we shall take care of introductions in no time. Hello?" he called out, opening the front door of the manor himself. "We are home!"

The bustle that she had been expecting when they drew up finally occurred, with a gray-haired man emerging from the butler's pantry next to the front door, obviously having been startled awake. He was quickly followed by two stout-looking maids peering over the banister from above and squeaking, "Lord! Sir Barty's back! Oh sir, forgive us! Quick, run and tell Mrs. Dillon!"

Soon after that, a bevy of footmen, maids, and kitchen staff amassed in the front hall, making such a ruckus that Leticia knew it was exactly how Sir Barty expected (and wished) to be greeted.

"Sir, we did not expect you for several weeks hence," the old butler admonished, and Leticia had to bite her tongue.

"Now, now, Jameson, has anything burned down? Fallen apart? Gone one minute off schedule?"

"Well, a few of the drapes are in desperate need of mending."

"Jameson . . ."

The dignified older man sighed. "No, sir."

"Then hush, Jameson. Think of what sort of impression you are making on my bride-to-be." The blood drained from Jameson's face as his eyes shot to Leticia. Leticia did her best to smile graciously, but the awkwardness of the announcement put her immediately at a disadvantage. Really, did not Sir Barty know that these first few moments in the household were crucial for establishing one's first impression? Everyone here likely thought her some interloping strumpet—not the regal soon-to-be mistress of the house they would know her to be had he written a simple letter!

The shock of the announcement had given way to titters and whispers. Leticia leaned in to Barty. "Perhaps introductions are in order, darling?" she breathed in his ear.

"Oh? Oh! Of course!" he said, taking the nudge for what it was worth. "Jameson, Mrs. Dillon"—he nodded toward the straight-faced woman whose competence bespoke her as the housekeeper—"I should like to introduce you to my dear Leticia, Countess of Churzy, and soon to be Lady Babcock."

At least Sir Barty had given her a proper introduction. She felt herself growing taller with each word of her title—and then future title—being spoken.

"It is the greatest pleasure to meet you all," Leticia said, modulating her tones, at once demure and commanding.

A particular gift of hers, putting people at ease with only her voice. It paid to have practiced restraint. When spoken, restraint sounded like grace.

"Oh, thank heavens, you're English!" the competent Mrs. Dillon cried, and came forward with a bobbing curtsey. "For a moment there I was afraid Sir Barty had brought home a foreign bride, and we would have to deal with French maids and cooks and the like."

Leticia smiled, amused. "I have lived in France, but I have little use for French hairdressers or their cuisine," she lied. "Give me good, honest English fare any day."

"She tried her first haslet on the way up here!" Sir Barty said as he squeezed her shoulder. "Loved it, didn't you, m'dear?"

To that, Leticia could only smile through her teeth.

"Then I shall have cook put it on the menu for this week," Mrs. Dillon replied. "Oh, but—I expect you'll be wanting to go over the menus, my lady? I'm sorry, it's been a bit since we've had—"

"I would love to go over the menus with you, Mrs. Dillon, but I do not wish to step on any toes. After all, we are not yet wed," she demurred.

"That'll change in a month's time," Sir Barty said proudly.

"I think for now I would like nothing more than to change my clothes and then meet Margaret. Is she in the schoolroom?"

Everyone blinked for a moment and a few glances slid toward Sir Barty. Odd. And yet no one said a word.

"Er, no. Not the schoolroom, my lady," Mrs. Dillon replied, with a perplexed glance to Sir Barty. "She's outside, I believe."

"Ah yes," Leticia smiled, trying to put everyone at ease. "Sir Barty told me she would likely be digging in the dirt, didn't you, dearest?"

"She'll make her way in before supper," Sir Barty said, throwing an arm over Leticia's shoulder and giving her a rough squeeze. "Well, Jameson—shall we go to the library? I need to put my foot up and write a letter to my steward, informing him of my arrival. And in time for the harvest too!"

As Sir Barty ambled down the hall, Jameson trailing after him in attendance, Leticia turned to Mrs. Dillon.

"My lady, I would offer to show you to your rooms, however—"

"But no rooms were made up for me, as you were not told of my existence," she finished for the nervous housekeeper. "It's quite all right. I am happy to look around the house for now."

"I'll have tea and a cold repast brought to the sitting room as quickly as possible," Mrs. Dillon replied.

"Do, but do not press yourself overly. I am happy to wait."

Mrs. Dillon eyed the maids that were standing in a line behind her, itching to give orders.

"Might I suggest a stroll in the gardens? It would do you good after all that time in the carriage."

"Oh, but I—"

"We will present ourselves to much better advantage in a few minutes," Mrs. Dillon said quietly, and the maids that could hear her nodded in time.

Leticia knew that it would be good form to do as Mrs. Dillon requested. And early favors would do wonders for their relationship later on.

But she dreaded the gardens.

"Just a few minutes, Mrs. Dillon," she said firmly. "Then you and I can have a nice long chat about the dinner menus and drapes that need mending and everything else."

"Yes, my lady," Mrs. Dillon finally said, and with a curtsy, moved at a trot to the kitchens.

Leaving Leticia free to wander outside.

Bluestone Manor was a lovely property. It was well situated, the oaks that edged the lane grown tall and thick with time, speaking to the fact that the Babcocks had been in this county for quite a long time. The house itself was a square box, three stories tall, with the entrance recessed slightly, drawing one in. As she wandered around the building, she discovered that only the front of the house was faced in that blue granite that gave it its name. The rest of the building was brick, stuccoed over in a warm yellow. As she went around the side, a terrace and glass paneled doors connected to a drawing room—one that Mrs. Dillon was madly putting to rights, setting a tea service in the exact right place. Good. She'd made the correct impression on the woman—showing her that she had some give, but was firm and worthy of being impressed.

She'd give her a few more minutes. Let her make everything perfect.

It had better be worth it, because she could feel the sting beginning in her nose, the thickness in her ears. One of the many reasons Leticia preferred the city was that flowers made her sneeze.

And the east garden was stuffed full of them.

It would be one thing if they were delicate, ladylike sneezes. But her sensitivity to flowers usually left her sneezing raw and angry, generally accompanied by a red swollen nose and eyes so puffed it could become difficult to see.

Perhaps the west garden would be better, she thought, hoping for nonflowering shrubbery, as she moved briskly to the other side of the house.

She wondered where Margaret might be hiding. In all honesty, she was anxious for them to be introduced—it might be a little startling to the poor girl to meet over supper. (And if Leticia had any curiosity about a young girl dining with the adults, it was immediately squashed—obviously, if it was only Sir Barty and Margaret here, they must be accustomed to dining *en famille*. It spoke a great deal about Sir Barty's affection for his daughter and his enthusiasm for adding Leticia to the family.)

She looked around her, but there was no sign of a little girl anywhere. Although there were signs of an incredibly skilled gardener. The hedges were trimmed into perfect cones or rounds, and all lined with violets. The orchard she spied in the distance seemed to be in full fruit. They must have a whole team of experienced men to deal with the variety of plants and flowers she saw in just that one corner of the grounds.

That seemed to be an expense Sir Barty was willing to bear, and Leticia was glad of it.

Oh, not the gardens themselves (her eyes watered just looking at them), but that he was willing to spend the money in the first place—no doubt as an indulgence to his daughter, as she loved to play in them. It made her hopeful he would be willing to splurge on other indulgences.

Suddenly, Leticia spied a greenhouse tucked back against the trees, about thirty yards from the side of Bluestone Manor.

What better place for a little girl to hide? She made her way down a sweetly curving path lined with rosebushes (trying not to breathe in as she passed) to the greenhouse door.

"Hello?" she called out, ducking her head inside. And was greeted with a whole new world.

"Oh my . . ." There was really nothing else to say. It was warm in the greenhouse—that was to be expected. But the air was heavy with damp, misting with it, like after a warm summer rain. Long trailing vines crawled all the way up to the ceiling, reaching for more and more sunshine, greedy little things. One cabinet was lined with vials of tincture in varying shades of amber and brown. An unintelligible set of numbers and letters were written on the vials in wax pencil.

There were rows upon exact rows of pots with dirt in them, each also numbered and lettered. Some had sprouts of green coming up, some did not.

Well of course, some did not—those pots that were barren were in the back row, far away from the light.

"Everyone needs a little light to grow," she hummed to herself as she picked up one of the back-row plants and moved it to the front. Even she, with her aversion to any plant, knew that.

"What in the hell are you doing?"

Leticia whipped around so fast she nearly dropped the pot she was holding.

There, in the greenhouse doorway, stood an Amazon. A mess of blond hair escaped the braid that ran down her back, the felt hat she wore flopping to the side, the brim bent back. She was wearing a loosely fitted gown on a wiry frame—one that Leticia could tell was wiry because she had the skirt tied up and between her legs, exposing her limbs to the knee. And everything, from the top of her hat to the toes of her work boots, was covered in dirt.

Leticia didn't know what was more shocking—the woman's outfit, or the look of utter murder on her face.

"I said what the hell are you doing?" the woman said again, her eyes falling to the pot in Leticia's hands. "Did you move that?"

"I . . . it wanted light."

"That's the control group! It's not supposed to have light!" She stalked forward and wrenched the pot from Leticia's hands. Goodness, the woman was as tall as most men. "You idiot," she mumbled under her breath.

"What did you just say?" Leticia gasped.

"I said, 'you idiot,'" the woman repeated coldly and clearly as she meticulously positioned the pot back in its old space.

Leticia's eyes narrowed. She drew her head up, forced her shoulders down. She may not be as tall as this person, but she could damn well make her presence felt. "I don't know what your position is in this house but it has just been seriously compromised," she said in her coolest, calmest countess voice.

"My position?" The woman's head came up as she eyed Leticia. For the first time, Leticia could see that she was younger than she'd initially thought, with a clear blue gaze that bored into her foe. "My position is daughter of the house. And I'll thank you to get out of my greenhouse!"

Leticia felt all the blood drain from her face. "Daughter?" she said, her countess voice faltering. "You're Margaret Babcock?"

Not a little girl. Not by half. No, Margaret Babcock was fully grown, and it seemed, spitting mad.

"Yes," Margaret grumbled, taking a little notebook and pencil out of her pocket. "And you're still in my greenhouse."

"I . . . I believe we've gotten off on the wrong foot. My name is Leticia—Lady Churzy, and I—"

"I do not care," Margaret cut her off as she began measuring the green shoots in the row of pots against a stick, and then writing down her observations. "This is the third time I'm asking you to leave. On the fourth I'm calling for a footman."

Oh, that's how it was to be, was it? There was no room for apology, no graciousness. And nothing even resembling ladylike manners. Well, Leticia had just had cold water thrown on her—it seemed that there was nothing to be done but throw some back.

"I'll leave you," she said, as she moved toward the door. Margaret did not give so much as a grunt as she passed. "But you should care—because my name is Lady Churzy, and I'm to be your stepmother."

She did not pause to see if there was any reaction. She simply opened the door and swept out, knowing full well that she had been heard. "I'll see you at supper."

4

 $\mathcal{S}$ upper that evening went about as well as could be expected.

Which was to say, not well at all.

In fact, as she went to bed that evening (her room still somewhat musty, having only had a few hours to air out), Leticia was kept fitfully awake by the realization that as difficult as it had been to find Sir Barty and get him to propose marriage, the hard work had really just begun.

After she marched away from the greenhouse, she went immediately to the drawing room, surprising Mrs. Dillon, who was shaking the cover off of a pianoforte in the corner.

"Oh, my lady! You gave me a start!" she said when the terrace doors shut. "Had we known to expect you, we should have had the piano tuned! Although I do not know if you play . . ."

Had we known. Those three little words caused a tiny stab of guilt to blossom in Leticia's stomach. That dreaded female guilt, taking on the weight of a man's transgressions. No matter how often Leticia tried to kill it dead, it rose from the grave, making her want to say, "I'm sorry," at every turn.

It made her feel small.

It made her feel like an interloper.

Leticia squashed those feelings down and pulled herself up by an invisible string attached to the top of her head. There. She was no longer small. She pushed her shoulders down and elongated her neck in one fluid movement, settling a calm smile across her features. She was grace and beauty incarnate once again.

"I play, but only adequately," Leticia replied. "Pray, do not make a fuss if I'm the only female who can read music." Then, deciding against making bland conversation, she said, "I've just come from the west gardens."

Mrs. Dillon froze. "The west gardens, my lady?"

"Indeed. And the greenhouse."

"You went in the greenhouse, then?" She closed her eyes against the light.

"I did. And I met Margaret."

Mrs. Dillon sighed. "I imagine that she was quite surprised by you, my lady."

"I imagine she was," Leticia said, lowering herself to a rose-colored settee. "However, I did not stay very long to find out. To be honest, I was quite surprised by her. I was expecting a little girl."

"I am so sorry, my lady—"

"It is not your fault, Mrs. Dillon," Leticia said. It was Sir Barty's fault. "Tell me, how old is Miss Margaret?"

"She's nineteen," Mrs. Dillon said. Then with a sigh, she seated herself in a straight-backed chair. "And she is sweet once you get to know her, I promise, my lady."

The dirt-covered termagant who twice called her an idiot could be sweet? Leticia did her damnedest to cover her snort of disbelief.

But . . . she was here now. And Margaret was someone with whom she was going to have a relationship for the rest of her life, presumably. Best to give the girl the benefit of the doubt.

"I'm sure you are right," she said, smiling kindly to Mrs. Dillon and watching as that woman relaxed ever so slightly. "Now, where would you like to begin? You mentioned the menus?"

"Oh yes!" Mrs. Dillon cried as she reached for the tea service and offered to pour. Leticia graciously allowed her. "When Cook heard the news, she practically wept with joy! It's been ever so long since she's had any direction, and cooking four out of every five meals with pork was about to drive her mad. Although it is Sir Barty's favorite, you know."

"Do you mean there's been no direction at all since the late Lady Babcock's death? Not from Margaret?"

Mrs. Dillon shook her head. "Miss Margaret hasn't had an easy time of it since her mother passed," she said. "She has tried, truly. But she only really has a head for her plants and flowers. Her mother, God rest her soul, tried to give her a lady's knowledge, and Miss Margaret tried to learn it, but . . . once Lady Babcock passed, I suppose she gave up trying."

"I take it Miss Babcock and her mother were close," Leticia surmised.

"Oh yes, my lady. They seemed to speak a language only they knew." The housekeeper began to fidget with her apron again, smoothing out an invisible wrinkle. Then Mrs. Dillon clammed up again, her face turning a red Leticia would guess was rather uncommon for the housekeeper.

"Mrs. Dillon—do not fret about speaking of your late mistress," Leticia said, trying to set the housekeeper at ease. "Sir Barty told me all about her. He loved her very much. They were very good together."

"They were a very happy little family," Mrs. Dillon said, letting her eyes drift to the window—where, some ways down the field the greenhouse was framed against the rolling lawn. "But now that you are here, hopefully we will find a way back to that happiness again."

For the first time since emerging from the greenhouse, Leticia felt for Miss Babcock. It was very hard to lose a mother—and at an age when one is meant to embark upon the world, perhaps needing their guidance most . . . no wonder the girl retreated into her greenhouse.

No wonder Sir Barty did not write! He would want to delay the shock of a new bride as long as possible. It was a fumble on his part, but an understandable one.

A warm spot of pity began to soften her heart toward the girl. Perhaps . . . yes, perhaps she could see the bright side in a young lady of nineteen instead of a little girl. A girl of nineteen, looking for guidance through adulthood's murky waters, whose interests in horticulture could not prepare her for the world the way a friend like Leticia could.

Yes, she could work with nineteen.

Unfortunately, that warm spot of pity did not last through supper.

After tea, Mrs. Dillon walked her through the house, showing her the living rooms, the breakfast room, the dining room, the little glass-enclosed terrace room that "was ever so pleasant in summer"—all to buy as much time as possible while maids scrambled to get Leticia's bedchamber ready.

Once the curtains were beaten out and the linens refreshed, Leticia was escorted to a lovely room, done up in heavy green silks. A number of pressed flowers hung in frames on the wall, all lined perfectly, all with their Latin names written underneath in an elegant hand.

Finally, flowers she could enjoy without sneezing.

But there was no time to dawdle. She washed and dressed quickly and made her way downstairs, to wait for supper.

Sir Barty joined her presently. Mrs. Dillon popped her head in to make sure they were comfortable and that Leticia was pleased with her rooms. Jameson came in, asking if they would like a glass of wine or port before the meal. And the clock on the mantel ticked away time.

Of course, during all this, Miss Margaret Babcock did not make an appearance.

"It's a quarter past," Leticia said, spying Sir Barty checking the mantel clock again.

"Silly standing on this formality," Sir Barty grumbled, but she could tell by the pink of his cheeks and the direction of his gaze (downward) that he was embarrassed. "It's just family, after all."

"Family should dine together, don't you think, darling?" Leticia replied softly but firmly.

"She likely was never informed—or she forgot. She's a forgetful girl, her mind on other matters."

"She was informed, dearest. I did it myself."

He looked up at that, his bushy eyebrows climbing up to his hairline. "Oh. So you—"

"Yes, I met Margaret earlier. But only briefly." She watched as Sir Barty pinked with embarrassment. "Still, even for an absentminded person, a new stepmother is not something you simply forget."

She would let Sir Barty wallow in his shame for a little bit. Not too long, but enough to realize his mistake in not giving either Margaret or Leticia fair warning about the other.

Leticia rose and cross the room to the terrace doors—thrown open to allow some of the lovely summer breeze in. She was about to subject herself to the garden again and go tramping out into the twilight to where she could see the glow of a lamp in the greenhouse—when suddenly the lamp went out and the young woman herself emerged.

"There, you see?" Sir Barty said from behind Leticia, the relief palatable in his voice. "She's on her way now."

As she crossed the lawn, Leticia could see that Margaret could be quite pretty, in the right light. Her features were proportional and her complexion was that of the English rose, typified by lovely country girls. Which was a relief, because her height made her mannish enough, and the braid swinging behind her like a cat's tail indicated her level of fury. Which at the moment was quite high.

She also was still wearing the dirt-covered dress and apron from before. However, in deference to either the company or the night breeze, she had untied the gown from the knees and let it drape to its full length—which was just to the girl's ankles.

Leticia's lips pressed into a thin line of their own volition before she forced them into a more serene, welcoming expression.

She would not have the first thing Margaret Babcock saw of her tonight be displeasure.

However, it seemed that Margaret Babcock would barely see Leticia at all. When she did appear in the doorway off the terrace, oh, she gave the proper curtsy of course, but her gaze pointedly did not even flit over Leticia's face. Instead she remained utterly focused on her father.

"Hello, Father," she said, her chin out in stubborn defiance. He held his arms open, but the girl crossed hers over her chest, unmoved. Sir Barty lowered his arms with a heartbroken little sigh, then held out a hand to Leticia.

"Margaret, I understand you have met Lady Churzy," Sir Barty said carefully. "We are going to be married."

Margaret's eyes stayed firmly on her father's, refusing to even acknowledge Leticia was in the room.

"It's a pleasure to meet you, Margaret," Leticia said. "Properly, this time. I do hope that we shall be great friends."

"I had thought she was joking." Margaret raised her quizzical brow to her father.

"Now, Margaret . . ." her father said.

Leticia kept her expression neutral, although rarely had she heard such rudeness. Even when she had been a miller's daughter trying to make a good match in London, the cuts she heard then were not comparable to the tongue of Miss Margaret Babcock.

"I thought it was a joke, because my mother is barely cold in the ground," she went on.

"Margaret, it has been two years," Sir Barty admonished harshly, but wearily. Either they'd had this fight before or they'd been afraid of having it. Both options were exhausting.

"Fourteen months," she shot back. "It's been fourteen months."

Leticia's eyes went wide. And that ball of pity began to well up in her again. For Margaret, the death of her mother must be still quite raw. But then she looked at Sir Barty's face. He was ashamed, and tired, and unsure of himself for the first time since Leticia had met him. She knew she had to wade into the fray, and that she was better served siding with her fiancé.

"I assure you, it is not a joke," she said serenely, coming over to take Sir Barty's arm, looking up at him with admiration and support. "We are quite happy."

That forced Margaret to look at Leticia.

"Well, I'm sure you are," Margaret replied, her chin wobbling. But she quelled it. "Should we get supper over with? I would like to get back to the greenhouse—I have to dissect the rhododendron roots tonight."

"Wouldn't you like to change first?" Leticia couldn't help but say.

"Why? I am going to be working again directly after, I'd much rather keep my work clothes on," Margaret replied. "Besides, it's only Father. And . . . you."

"Supper, even eaten in family, should have standards," Leticia replied gently.

Margaret shot a look to her father, and while he did not say anything, he did give a stern nod. Margaret's braid swished in consternation, but she said nothing, just simply crossed the room and headed for the stairs—presumably to change into a dress more appropriate for supper.

Although Leticia couldn't be certain. She had a feeling that where Margaret Babcock was involved, there would always be a question as to motives and actions.

At nineteen, a young lady's character should be established and steady. After all, Leticia had been married at nineteen. She'd moved from her father's home to her sister's home to her own home. What she did not do was act like she was a ten-year-old spoiled brat when faced with adversity.

At least, she hoped she hadn't.

"She'll come around." Sir Barty said, and squeezed her shoulder. "I think you'll be just the thing for her, m'dear,"

"I think so too." Leticia smiled at him. As long as she could figure out her opponent, she would have no problem winning this battle.

As it turned out, Margaret had gone upstairs to change, coming back down in a few short minutes' time in a simple day frock (Leticia was not about to quibble that it was far too much a morning dress for the evening meal), her face and hands wiped clean of dirt and her hair neatly smoothed and rebraided. (Again, Leticia was not about to quibble that her hair was not dressed appropriately for a young lady of nineteen, let alone for supper. She was much too hungry for that.)

They went into the dining room and seated themselves before a repast that Leticia was certain had been prepared in a fury.

"When Mrs. Dillon showed me the kitchens this afternoon, I had no idea that this marvelous meal would be produced from there in only a matter of hours," Leticia said, smiling at one of the serving men. "Please let Cook know that I am impressed."

"Why?" Margaret asked.

"Why?" Leticia echoed.

"Why did you have no idea? It's a kitchen; it produces food on a daily basis. Either you have little experience with kitchen staffs or you are simply trying to flatter Cook."

Leticia glanced at Sir Barty. He avoided her eyes by shoveling some meat pie into his mouth.

"It's the same food we've had here for years. Nothing special." Margaret turned to the manservant. "Correct?"

The servant, shocked out of his position at the wall, nodded and bowed.

"Still," Leticia said, maintaining her composure. "The food is new to me, and I would like Cook to know how much I am enjoying it."

Margaret shrugged—an inelegant motion for someone of her size. Leticia was certain she must have no idea how she looked, else she would never be so awkward.

Her petulance did not help, of course.

"I gather you are quite the horticulturalist," Leticia tried again as she took a bite of her own meat pie (pork, naturally). "I have only heard of rhododendrons, never seen them. I believe they hail from the Orient?"

Margaret gave that awkward shrug again. "They do," was all she would say.

"Well . . . perhaps you would show me your specimen. In daylight," Leticia added. Perhaps rhododendrons were the one plant that wouldn't affect her nose.

"If you like."

"The last time I was in London, I was told there was a fascinating display of foreign plants and flowers, grown by the Horticultural Society."

She shrugged again.

"Ladies are invited to tour their grounds. If you'd like to see it, perhaps we can arrange a short trip to London—"

"I don't think so," Margaret replied, cutting Leticia off.

"But they have excellent flower shows . . . and we could combine the trip with some shopping."

If a trip to the best London warehouses did not spur a nineteen-year-old girl's interest, nothing would, Leticia thought confidently.

As it was, an eyebrow went up, but instead of reacting with interest, she cocked her head to one side and narrowed her eyes.

"I have no wish to go to London at the moment. I am in the middle of my work," Margaret said. "But if you wish to go, by all means do so. In fact, I think it an excellent idea."

Stay away as long as you like. It was unspoken, but echoed across the dining table.

Leticia shot a smile at Sir Barty. "I wouldn't dream of it," she purred, hoping he believed her. "I only mention shopping in London because I must purchase a wedding trousseau. It is the only place to find anything worth wearing for a wedding, I'm afraid." She turned back to Margaret, serenely confident. "And I thought perhaps you would like a new gown for the occasion too."

Margaret flushed, and then turned white. Aha! thought Leticia. So she does have a care for her appearance. Even if what she cares about is looking like she doesn't care.

"I like the gowns that I have. I'm sure one will do."

Leticia took one calming breath, then two. It was infuriating dealing with someone whose bluntness put cudgels to shame. But she would not rise to the bait. No, she was the bigger—if not taller—person.

"I'm sure you are right," Leticia said, demurring. "We will find something appropriate."

Margaret's gaze shot to her father. "May I be dismissed?"

Sir Barty looked up from his mouthful of pork-based pie. "Hmm?"

"I've finished eating, I have work to return to. May I be dismissed?"

"I suppose," Sir Barty grunted over his food.

"Darling," Leticia began, but Margaret was out of her chair and out the door without so much as a curtsy before she could finish her thought, let alone her sentence.

"I had hoped to have some conversation after supper with her," Leticia said. "Listen to her play pianoforte, or what not."

"Margaret doesn't play pianoforte."

"Cards, then."

"Not much for cards either," Sir Barty replied, wiping his mouth.

"Nor is she much for conversation it seems—at least, not with me. Darling, I know you wish me to have some good influence over the girl, but I cannot if—"

"Now, now," Sir Barty interrupted, much like his daughter. "You two will find your way to an understanding. I'm certain of it."

"But—"

"Heavens, is that the time?" He glanced at the mantel clock. "I'll have to excuse myself, m'dear. We have traveled so far today, and I'm badly in need of one of Mrs. Dillon's poultices for my foot."

"Sir Barty!" Leticia exclaimed, shocked.

"Now, if I don't attend to my foot, I will wake with it swollen, and then we shan't be able to attend church in the morning. Which we need to do to have the banns read proper like." He stood—with a modicum of difficulty—travel really was very hard on his gout—and came over and kissed the top of Leticia's head. "I must beg you excuse me, m'dear. Give Cook my praise for supper—always enjoy her meat pies. I will see you in the morning."

And with that, he retrieved his cane from one of the manservants and exited in the same direction as his daughter.

Abandoning Leticia at the dining room table with enough food to feed a small army and enough worries to keep her awake and fitful all night.

Even though she hardly slept well, she was alert and at her ruthless best next morning. Today she would not allow herself to be seen at any disadvantage.

Because today, she would be meeting the village of Helmsley.

There was a very fine line one had to walk when being introduced to new surroundings. One wished to be seen as approachable, but as the Countess of Churzy, commanding a certain level of awe was expected. Indeed, some might be disappointed if she wasn't sufficiently grand—how often does one meet a real, live countess in a tiny market town off the Lincolnshire Wolds?

She chose her deep, curry-colored cambric gown—it brought out the hints of gold in her dark eyes, and paired with a gorgeous Indian shawl prompted thoughts of luxury . . . and hid the fact that the cut of the gown was a season or two behind the times. She pinned a straw hat to the top of her head—not a bonnet, no. Bonnets and their attendant fripperies hid her long neck, which was one of her best features. There were little clusters of cherries decorating the hat—just a pop of color, bringing out the red hints in the shawl and invoking the idea of warmth. Of vibrancy and humanity.

And to remind everyone that this vibrant, warm human was in fact a countess, Leticia dug deep into her trunk and pulled out the only thing she had left from that time. Her sapphire wedding ring—saved from being hawked only by Sir Barty's well-timed arrival in Paris. She put it on her right hand, polished it against her shawl, and let it sparkle.

Konrad had left her with so little, but she would now make the most of all of it.

She was downstairs ten minutes before anyone else. Ready to conquer the day and the town.

Her punctuality was observed with surprise from Margaret—who came down precisely on time, wearing the same simple frock from the night before, with a neat blue spencer over it, and a practical, unadorned bonnet—and with delight from Sir Barty.

"I knew I had chosen a good woman, but one that won't keep me waiting for hours on end before we go out? You, m'dear, are priceless." He placed a chaste peck on Leticia's cheek as he led them out to the carriage, and she was satisfied to see the shock of it on Margaret's face. But they were both widowed after all, not naive virgins blushing at the idea of holding hands. Best the girl got used to the idea.

On the drive into town, Sir Barty peppered the carriage with facts about the people they would meet at the church—people, it seemed, he had known his entire life and knew every little detail of.

"And that building there is owned by Mr. Fisher—who is not a fisherman, as you might have thought, but rather an attorney. He tried to be a puffed-up Londoner for a bit, but came back here when his father died and he inherited the building that now houses his solicitor practice. Mrs. Emory is his neighbor next door. And there's Helen Braithwaite"—Sir Barty pointed to a woman out the carriage window, but they turned a corner so quickly she missed seeing more than an older woman walking along with a man—"although she's not called Braithwaite now, but I've never been one to use her married name. Seems strange to do so when you can remember playing sticks and hoops with someone, eh? Anyway, she and her son run the grain mill—you remember, the windmill with the fresh coat of paint that we saw as we came into town yesterday? Well, they will run it, provided they get it working again . . ."

Leticia sprinkled her own *hmms* and *oh yes, darlings* into the conversation, watching as Sir Barty got more and more enthusiastic and verbose. The pride he felt in his town—and in his fiancée—was palpable.

Margaret, of course, said nothing.

When they arrived in the churchyard, it was to a large crowd of people standing in small clusters, conversing politely. Ordinarily, such pleasantries would be exchanged after the sermon, once everyone's sins were absolved for the week and they could begin anew. But ever since Sir Barty's carriage drove through town yesterday—and ever since the servants of Bluestone Manor no doubt rushed into Helmsley with the news . . .

Leticia assumed that church this morning was suspiciously well attended.

They disembarked, Sir Barty handing both ladies down. Then, pride puffing out his chest and making him walk just a bit easier, he introduced Leticia to the town of Helmsley.

Men came up to greet them, pushed forward by their

wives. As the gentlemen exchanged pleasantries with Sir Barty, the wives moved into position.

"Hello."

"Good morning."

"So pleased—"

"Charmed, my lady—"

"Where did you meet?"

Oohs and ahhs followed.

"Paris, you say? That's so . . . cosmopolitan! You must be so worldly!"

"Worldly enough to know that Helmsley is absolutely lovely—"

Titters of appreciation broke forth from the ladies.

"We are far too humble here for—"

"But beautiful, Mrs. . . . I'm sorry, what was your name again?"

"Emory," she said with a tight smile. "We are happy to welcome you to Helmlsey, my lady. And if you should ever need anything, anything at all, we have some fine craftsmen here—a market town and all." Eyebrows were raised, and hints dropped. "Milliners too—"

"Oh, but Lady Churzy is going to London for her fashions."

This last from Margaret. Leticia froze in place.

"She told me so last night. London is the only place to purchase anything worth wearing."

Every smile shut down as the ladies of Helmsley turned accusing glares on Leticia. Except for Margaret, whose small, fixed smile spoke volumes.

"For a wedding," Leticia added hastily. "I only said it in context of—"

But the ladies had begun whispering among themselves, with Mrs. Emory's voice carrying, and her stiff manners being copied by the others. "Too fine. I told you, Moira . . ."

For the second time since her arrival, Leticia felt herself scrambling. How had she had fallen into disfavor with the women of Helmsley in less than a sentence? And of course ladies go to London for their fashions! Why was this such a terrible thing to say?

But it was a terrible thing to say, and Margaret, for all her focus on her plants, knew it as such.

"We are very proud of what we make here. Do not sell the country short so soon after your arrival, my lady," said Mrs. Emory, her smile turning from tight to ingratiating. She was an imperious type, and everyone cowed around her. The queen bee of Helmsley. And Leticia got the feeling that no matter what she said, or whom she purchased her dresses from, she would have ended up transgressing this woman.

Well, it was a stumble. But at least it showed her who she was going to have to overcome, if not why.

It also showed her Margaret's cards. And she would need to address that first.

"I'm sure you are right," Leticia said, soothing. Then, "Margaret, may I have a word with you for a moment?"

Leticia and Margaret made their curtsies and moved off, finding their way to the shade of an oak tree. Leticia tried to ignore the not-so-quiet whispers of the ladies at their backs.

But she was Leticia Herzog, Countess of Churzy. There was no way an awkward country girl like Margaret was going to undermine her.

But the situation would require some finesse.

"Oh dear," Margaret said, unable to keep the snit out of her voice. "Did I say something amiss? Am I to be scolded now?"

"Heavens no," Leticia replied, her expression all innocence. "I wouldn't dare scold you. I am not your parent."

"No you are not," Margaret harrumphed.

"No I am not," she agreed. "Nor do I have any desire to be."

That got Margaret to look at her.

"I have no desire to replace your mother in your heart— if I did, I have no doubt I'd do a very poor job of it." Leticia gave her best exasperated smile. "I don't have the memories that she would have and you have of her—I haven't the knowledge or patience, and . . . can I tell you a secret?"

Margaret nodded slowly.

"I haven't a clue how to garden. In fact, most flowers make me sneeze."

The corner of Margaret's mouth ticked up for the barest second before she squashed it down.

"I have no doubt I would make a horrible mother for you, not the least because you already have one," Leticia concluded. "But I think I would be a very good friend."

"You intend to be my friend?" Margaret asked, unable to hide her skepticism.

"If you would let me. We are going to be a part of each other's lives from now on, so it would be best for us to start out on the right foot. And disliking each other would be the decidedly wrong one."

"I don't dislike you," Margaret grumbled. "I don't know you well enough to dislike you."

There was something in the way Margaret glanced at the ground. Something quiet in the way she spoke. *I don't know you.* Something that made her seem very much alone.

Then Margaret straightened her shoulders and let her gaze fall to the bark of the tree they stood under. Idly, she picked at some moss on its side. "Although I am unsure I can like someone who sneezes at flowers."

"I like flowers very much," Leticia replied. "At a distance."

"Does that mean you won't invade my greenhouse again?" Margaret asked, her eyes narrowing.

"Not unless I'm invited."

"You won't be," Margaret said in a rush. Then her cheeks pinked. "I mean, no one goes in my greenhouse. It's my . . . it's my space."

"Understood." Leticia held up her hands. "However, from what I saw you are incredibly talented. Your greenhouse could put some of those in London to shame."

Margaret pinked even further.

"You know that last night I mentioned the idea of London because I thought it might be fun," Leticia said. "For you."

"How would it be fun for me?" Margaret asked, her brows coming down.

"Margaret, a young lady should experience London!" Leticia laughed. "It's terribly exciting. The latest fashions and on-dits and the theater! Balls and parties—men to flirt and dance with! Who knows, you might even meet a man who catches your attention . . ."

She said this last bit gently. True, in the eighteen hours that she had known Margaret, she hadn't mentioned the opposite sex once. But there wasn't a nineteen-year-old in the world who didn't at least ponder the subject.

And instantly, Leticia knew she had struck gold. Because while Margaret had been blushing at the praise Leticia had ladled upon her, she turned positively scarlet at the mention of men.

"Unless of course . . . your attention has already been captured," Leticia said, a smile taking over her features. And she was rewarded by watching Margaret turn a deeper red still. "Oh, it has . . ." she said in a whisper, conspiring.

Margaret hunched over so far she looked as if she was

trying to hide inside herself. "My attention hasn't been captured. I . . . I just have no desire to go to London, that's all."

"Now, Margaret, don't be silly," Leticia replied. "Every girl wishes to go to London. And it's perfectly all right to have a beau. Or beaux! In fact, it's expected."

"He's not my beau."

"So there is someone." Leticia grinned, and Margaret covered her face with her hands, realizing her misstep. "Now, this is something for which you might find a friend useful. Someone you can talk to about him. And who can help arrange circumstances where you might meet, and flirt . . . or dance."

Margaret seemed to consider that. So Leticia decided to go for the ultimate confidence.

"Now, who is he? Have we been introduced?"

Margaret's head shot up. "I'm not telling you that!"

"Well I should like to know who it is so I don't make a cake of everything with him accidentally. Forewarned is forearmed, after all."

"Oh God . . ." Margaret buried her face in her hands again. But Leticia had the small suspicion that the girl was laughing.

"Appropriate for a churchyard, but not necessarily in this context," Leticia concluded. "All right, you don't have to tell me who he is. Instead, I will guess. I assume he's a local gentleman, given your reluctance to travel, and therefore is quite likely to be here now. Could it be Mr. Fisher? No, too old for you, I should think. And attorneys have no appreciation for growing things. The vicar is married . . . there's a young man over there by the gate, he's quite tall and looks handsome . . ."

At that Margaret turned a red so deep it was a wonder her skin remained—her insides practically being worn on her outsides.

"That's him, isn't it?" Leticia felt triumphant. "That's..."

And suddenly, Leticia felt all the blood drain from her face.

It was as if the ground gave way beneath her feet and left her grasping for purchase. Because approaching from the entrance to the churchyard, walking with the older woman they had passed on the road before (Helen, was it?), was the one man who could undo her tenuous grasp on the life she was so close to having here.

And what's more, he saw her too.

His name is Mr. John Turner," Margaret said in a small voice, her cheeks remaining scarlet. "He owns the windmill."

5

John Turner was not someone who could be easily surprised. After all, he'd spent time on the battlefield, where one was always on edge, waiting for the next surprise in the form of cannon fire. Then he'd spent several years as the secretary to his friend the Earl of Ashby—and what Ned got up to when he was bored was enough to keep a clairvoyant guessing.

Finally, John Turner had faced the accidental burning of his family business—not once, but twice. So, suffice to say, while John Turner might have had the worst luck known to man, he had the benefit of never, ever being surprised by anything.

Until now.

Because for some reason, Leticia, Lady Churzy—his Letty—was standing under the great oak tree in St. Stephen's churchyard.

What is she doing here?

"What is that, John?" He hadn't realized he'd spoken aloud.

He turned to look down at his mother, asker of the

question. Helen Braithwaite Turner blinked twice at him, expecting an answer.

"I . . . I did not expect to see Miss Babcock at church this morning. That's all."

His mother was not one to suffer lying, or indeed, foolishness of any kind. So if someone was going to call him on the oddity of his statement, it would be she. But she instead latched on to a different part of his sentence.

"Taking notice of Miss Babcock, are we?" Helen replied. "Good."

"Good?" he asked, his head swiveling back to look at her.

"It's high time you started taking notice of young, marriageable women." The stress she put on the word *marriageable* made his jaw clench, a force of habit. "Once the mill is open and running properly, you will need someone—"

"I have no need of 'someone,' I have you." Turner replied automatically, if not a little syrupy. He needed to distract her. Needed her to leave off this line of inquiry and leave him to his thoughts in peace.

What is she doing here?

But Helen Braithwaite Turner was never one to succumb to flattery.

"I won't be around forever." She snorted. "Besides, who says I want the job? I would like to take some time for myself in my old age."

"You're hardly decrepit."

"And yet, I've never been sea-bathing . . ." His mother let that thought drift off as he shook his head, a rueful smile appearing. His mother had a will of steel. She'd single-handedly kept the Turner Grain Mill alive while he was at war. When he returned to find that his father had passed and the grand windmill at the entrance to Helmsley was a proud tower of soot-stained stones, she was the one who kept the vultures at bay while he went to London to earn the money necessary to rebuild.

It had taken years longer than anticipated, and several other minor catastrophes delayed the mill's reopening, but all the while Helen Turner had persevered.

And now that she had decided it was time for her son to marry, she would persevere again.

"I'm just saying that if Miss Babcock has caught your eye, it would be a fine thing to pursue. After all, I have an inkling that the girl is keen on you . . ."

Turner did everything in his power to contain a laugh. It wouldn't do to laugh in the middle of the churchyard. But if his mother knew that the last woman he proposed to happened to be standing next to Margaret Babcock, she would perhaps dissolve into hysterics as well.

What is she doing here?

"Do you have any objection to Miss Babcock?"

His mother was not about to let this one go.

"I have no objection to her," Turner replied. He'd known Miss Babcock the whole of the girl's life. And while in her youth she had been an awkward, shy thing, she had in the past few years while he was in London become an awkward, tall thing. But that was nothing compared to her status in society as Sir Barty's daughter, and her general harmlessness. "But I do not think that interest should be given simply because of a lack of objection."

His mother snorted. "Well, then perhaps a better reason is because Sir Barty's estate produces over half of the grain in the area."

His mind was frazzled enough trying not to stare at Leticia—his Letty—and thus had no patience for games.

"What's your point, Mother?"

"My point is, even once the mill is open and running, it can still fail if we haven't any customers."

His mind swung wildly back to what she was saying, barely able to comprehend. Leave it to his mother to suggest what he thought she was suggesting. "That is terribly mercenary of you."

"I prefer to think of it as practical," she replied. "All the work . . . for all those years . . ."

Yes, all the work, for all the years that they had both done, to keep their livelihood, well, alive . . . they could have sold the burned-out husk of a windmill ages ago. They would have gotten a fraction of its worth, but it would have been enough to keep his mother comfortable for the rest of her days. And he could have earned his living elsewhere.

But he hadn't wanted to.

He'd wanted to work the mill. Own the mill. As his father had before him.

And it was about to happen for him. He was about to finally have the mill up and running again.

And now, the Countess of Churzy was standing in his churchyard, threatening to . . .

To what, precisely?

What is she doing here?

Then a thought—thrilling and desperate—bloomed in his mind.

Was she here for him?

"We should pay our respects to Sir Barty," his mother was saying. "Back from his tour of the Continent—he thought he would be gone much longer. But I knew it was foolishness—I told Barty he was going to end up lost in the first city he arrived in and spend three weeks turned around. Then he'd come home because the ship he sailed on was the only thing he knew how to find. I bet he gave Mrs. Dillon and Jameson a heart attack each."

Turner nodded absentmindedly. He was trying to keep

his eyes on Leticia, trying to see if his Letty would give him some clue as to the reason that she was here . . . other than the pale face and still expression.

If she was here for him . . . that would change everything.

"Of course I didn't expect him to come home toting some lady bride, but Barty has always managed to surprise me, even when we were young."

"What?" Turner asked, his mother's voice finally breaking into his thoughts.

"His fiancée. A countess of some kind. It was all over town yesterday." His mother eyed him. "And you've been staring at her for the past few minutes."

Turner felt something odd hit his chest.

If he didn't know better, he would have likened it to a cannonball.

"Shall we go in? It seems the vicar is finally going to start the service." His mother pulled him gently toward the church doors. "We'll greet Sir Barty and Miss Babcock after—and meet Sir Barty's bride."

ぴ

"I PUBLISH THE banns of marriage between Sir Bartholomew Babcock of Helmsley and Lady Churzy, the Countess of Churzy," the vicar droned. "This is the first time of asking. If any of you know cause or just impediment why these two persons should not be joined together in holy matrimony, ye are to declare it."

Turner could have ripped the bushy red sideburns off the vicar's head. The way he said it, as if there was nothing to it at all! I publish the banns of marriage . . .

As if there was no thought of objection from anyone! How could there possibly be? Sir Barty was a landed gentleman, the most landed in the area in point of fact. Who he took as his bride would not warrant a peep in the church. Not even from the ladies in town who were staring daggers into the back of Leticia's head. (Why were they staring daggers? Oh hell, had she already managed to offend them somehow? The ladies of Helmsley were a notoriously closed circle, and anything outside of the town was treated as suspect. He remembered when Harold Emory left to join the navy. It was feared he would come back with flippers. Hell, Turner himself was still treated with distance since he had become so "citified" in London, and his mother since the mill stopped working . . . But this digressive train of thought was neither productive nor on point, so Turner shook it off and returned his mind to the cause of his seething rage.)

It had been six months since he'd seen her. Since he'd kissed her. Lifetimes happen in six months.

Turner felt like he had loved and died every day for the last six months. When he woke in the mornings, he had a blissful few seconds of memory, still in a dream fraught with warm, soft hands and whispers in the dark. Then, the stark light of day would reach him and with it, reality. The only thing to do was to put his head down and work himself so hard that there was no room for her. To exhaust himself to dreamless sleep.

But the dream always came anyway.

If any of you know of any cause or impediment . . .

Hell yes, he knew of an impediment. The impediment was he had finally stopped dying!

The last time he had laid eyes on Leticia, she had told him she never wanted to see him again.

And he'd believed her.

They had not been on a ballroom floor, or in a bedroom, or in any of those more intimate spaces that allow for touches and whispers and persuasion. Instead, they were on a wind-whipped dock, and she was shivering against the December cold.

"Letty," he'd said.

Her shoulders tensed at his voice, then her head whipped around, eyes searching for the source of her name.

Shock flew across her face. Then fear. Both gutted him.

"Hello." He stepped forward, raising his gloved hand in a small wave, a gesture of peace. Still, she took a half step back before she remembered herself. She straightened. Her expression turned cool. She forced herself to stop shivering.

"Hello," she answered in her haughtiest voice.

He almost smiled. To hell with it, he did smile. She tried to hide herself under the cloak of a countess, but it had never fooled him. Not once.

And finally—finally—he had found her.

"What are you doing in Dover?" she asked, as casual as if they had just been introduced.

"I was waiting."

"For a ship?" she asked.

"For you."

She blushed against the raw wind. Not out of compliment, or womanly charm. But out of awkwardness and . . . embarrassment.

He'd seen her cool, seen her clever, seen her overcome with passion. He'd even seen her shocked speechless, when she'd found out . . . But he'd never thought he'd live to see her embarrassed.

In retrospect, that should have been his first clue.

"Of course," she'd replied. "You force me here, and are lying in wait when I arrive."

"Don't be foolish. I didn't chase you here."

"No." Her eyes narrowed to slits. "You didn't chase me—your lie did."

He'd hoped that when he found her she would see there

was nothing to fear from him. That her body would ache for him the way he'd been aching for her, and she'd give up this foolishness. Because Lady Churzy was many things, but foolish was not among them.

But what she was, he was quickly realizing, was blazing mad.

"Letty—"

"Don't call me that." She held his gaze—and her ground.

"My apologies. Leticia, then?"

"If you are to address me at all, it should be as Countess."

"Not long ago you let me call you many other things. Darling. Love."

"Not long ago you went by a different name entirely." She whirled on him. Advancing like a guard dog on an intruder. "Do you have any idea how I've had to live—if you can call it living? Everywhere I go, I have maybe two weeks, often less, before the rumors reach people. London first—I thought I might have a good month there, they have enough gossip of their own. But no—a countess being tricked by a . . . a secretary is too juicy an on-dit to pass up."

"I did not—"

"And then of course I tried Brighton. Then Manchester, York—I even went to Edinburgh, but everywhere, everywhere, I found myself shut out of polite society."

"They are all fools."

"They are all that is!" she'd cried. "Not even my sister, Fanny, will have me back in her house—at least not until it 'all blows over,' she says. How is a woman without funds, friends, or reputation supposed to live?"

"With me," he'd said immediately.

But she'd turned steely, her voice ice in the wind. "Wouldn't that work out just perfectly for you, then? You pretend to be the Earl of Ashby, pretend to be a man of substance . . . and used me as a pawn in your game with the real earl."

"I had to—we . . . oh hell, it's tough to explain, but we made a wager and I needed money to repair my family's business, and—"

"Yes, I'm sure your cause was ever so noble," she said, waving away his explanation. "You win your wager with him, but meanwhile you kiss me on a dance floor and make love to me—"

"That was never a lie," he said harshly, his hand coming up to her arm without thinking.

"What does it signify?" she asked, tensing beneath his fingers. "When you lied about everything else?" Her voice was a whisper against the wind now. "You lied. And you still think you can get everything you want."

"Yes, Letty, I lied," he finally said. "I lied about my name. That was all. But don't pretend you weren't lying too. You wanted me to believe you had solid ground beneath your feet, and were not desperate. That you were pursuing me for myself, and not because you thought I was an earl with money."

"I make no apologies for trying to secure my future. And a countess and an earl are natural together. A countess and a secretary"—she practically spat the word—"are not."

"Weren't we?" He stepped forward, his hand loosening on her arm, but not letting go. He let his hand trail down that arm, coming to the elbow, his fingers lightly dancing there, almost as if there were not gloves and cloaks between them. As if there were nothing between them. "The way I remember it, together we were the most natural thing in the world."

Suddenly, she was shaking again. He prayed it wasn't from the cold.

"Letty," he whispered, letting his warm breath fall against her cheek. She was close enough to taste. "I can't undo what I did. Nor would I want to. Because you would have never looked twice at me if I was plain Mr. Turner."

"We'll never know the answer to that, will we?" Her voice made his heart crack.

"We are meant for each other."

The last time they had stood this close together—in public—he had used it to stake his claim. To declare to the world that the Countess of Churzy was his. Now he would renew that claim, the only way he knew how.

"Come with me. Put this foolish running to an end. Where can you go that you think I will not follow?"

"I did not run to be chased, you idiot. I run because it is the only choice I have left!" She pulled away from him, but his hand was still on her elbow and he caught her, pulled her back. Her body slammed into his.

"Not the only choice," he said, and his mouth crushed against hers.

As cold as it was outside, as cool and reserved as she pretended to be, the warmth of her lips shocked him. Heat volleyed between them with every breath, every shiver. His hand snaked around her back, folding her against him. She gasped for air and burrowed closer. The small moan that escaped from the back of her throat sent a thrill down his spine.

And he knew he had her.

All he had to do now was get her to agree.

"Tell me to go and I will." He pressed his forehead against hers. "Tell me now and I'll go away forever, you'll never see me again. We'll be nothing more than a bittersweet memory to each other."

Her dazed eyes met his.

"But"—his voice came out a gravelly rumble—"if you

want me to stay, if you want me at all . . . you don't have to say anything."

His thumb brushed over her cheek. His heart beat faster than he knew it could go. And he watched those dark eyes as she debated. As she argued against herself.

As she . . . remembered the rest of the world. And where she stood in it. Not on a dock in Dover. No, she stood wearing the title of countess, lifting her well out of his reach.

It happened in a blink. Her face shifted back from flushed and open to icy and shuttered. "You think you can stir my blood and make me forget myself?"

"I think I can stir your blood, that's for damn certain." He felt himself getting angry . . . No, it was worse. Not anger—desperation. Because she was slipping away from him.

"That . . . is nothing," she said. "Something left over—a residue of when I could trust you. But I will never again put myself in the care of someone who lies to me."

"Letty, you can trust me—"

"No, Mr. Turner. I cannot."

Something broke over him, made his breath hitch. Because watching her in that moment, he saw the truth. The very truth at the core of his Letty.

What she said was real.

She would never let herself be with him. No amount of cajoling, no kisses or touches or heated looks was ever going to change that. And he had been the world's biggest fool to think that she would.

"Excuse me, milady?" a voice came from behind them, forcing them back outside of themselves.

A boy stood behind them, and judging by his thick oilskin coat and lack of shivering against the cold, his age belied his experience at sea. "Your trunk's been loaded, milady. Beg pardon, but Captain says we can't miss this tide."

"Thank you, I'm coming," Letty had replied before turning back to face Turner.

He held his breath.

"Go," she'd said. "I never want to see you again."

⁓

TELL ME TO go and I will. He'd spent the past six months ruing those words.

He'd thought that if he could just explain himself to her, she would understand.

Because she knew him. She could recognize him at a thousand paces, blindfolded and in the dark. And he could recognize her as well.

But it hadn't gone as planned.

She'd told him she never wanted to see him again.

And it nearly killed him.

Did he whine? Did he lock himself up and write bad poetry? Did he get angry and despair, and waste himself and any of his newfound funds in a flaming and embarrassing tantrum of feeling?

No, he did the exact opposite. He spent one night getting drunk with his friends Rhys and Ned as was proper, and then he went to work.

He lost himself in finally doing what he had spent so long planning: rebuilding the mill. The best millwrights in the country had rebuilt the structure itself. It had been rebuilt twice actually, having burned originally six years ago, and then three years later a wanderer had camped for a night in the empty building and left a fire burning—that was as best as they could determine, anyway. The first time, the fire burned so hot it smelted the iron works, shafts, and gears. New equipment had to be ordered and installed—and the expansion for the new steam engine equipment . . .

It had taken all of his energy and determination to bring the mill back from the dead in time for this year's harvest. That would be the true test—once the next harvest of wheat started being culled next month, he would know whether or not he had wasted the last six years of his life.

After a while, he began to think that he was glad that Leticia had sent him away. His work was too important. Getting his mill back, his life back on track, was too important. He didn't need the distraction.

He didn't need love.

If any of you know cause or just impediment why these two persons should not be joined together in holy matrimony, ye are to declare it.

Yes, he knew of an impediment. All he had to do was say it. Stand up and say it out loud.

But he said nothing at all.

6

"Y ou couldn't leave well enough alone, could you?"

That was what she wanted to say. Hell, that was what she wanted to scream from the oaks that lined the drive to Bluestone Manor. Instead, she settled for smiling serenely at Margaret and Sir Barty as they made their way home after church, silently berating herself the entire time for her utter foolishness.

And she was foolish. She was foolish for thinking she could live free from her past. She was foolish for feeling an ounce of security having become engaged to Sir Barty.

But she was most foolish for saying yes when Helen and Turner invited themselves over after church.

Leticia didn't know how it had happened. One minute, the vicar was reading the banns, and the next, the (rather unenthusiastic) sermon had been completed and everyone spilled back out into the churchyard, eager to get back to the real reason they had put on their Sunday finery that morning.

The townsfolk were all polite and deferential and held themselves back a bit. Leticia had hoped it was in awe, but she suspected it was more because Mrs. Emory had been spreading whispers across the pew the entire sermon.

Something that would have to be dealt with, Leticia reminded herself.

But of all the stiff bows and shy curtsies she'd received, none came from the Turners.

Because, as she was about to learn, there was nothing stiff or shy at all about Helen Turner.

"Hello!" The woman had swooped right in, her son looming behind her like a silent black cloud. "Sir Barty, back from the Continent already! Did you find there were no worlds left to conquer?"

"Hardly." Sir Barty laughed heartily at what must have been an old joke between old friends. "But I found something worth bringing home with me. M'dear, this is Mrs. Helen Braithwaite Turner, a very old friend. Helen, this is Lady Churzy."

Leticia started at her name, because she had been concentrating so hard on not letting her panic show . . . not letting her eyes drift to the figure behind Helen . . . and not letting herself wonder what he was going to say—or do . . .

She managed a dignified curtsy. There, everything was better. Calmer.

"And this is my son, Mr. Turner. John," Helen said.

Leticia looked at him.

He looked right back.

And they each made their bow or curtsy, from a distance the very picture of a pair of people just being introduced. No history between them. Nothing to draw any comment.

"Well, that was all very proper of us," Helen said, a laugh in her voice, and Sir Barty joined in. Leticia smiled, playing along, but it seemed that Turner did not have that kind of social grace. To avoid making eye contact with any of them, he'd put his attention just over Leticia's left shoulder.

"Miss Babcock," he said to Margaret, bowing. "Good morning."

Margaret gave a short curtsy, blushed, and mumbled, "Good morning."

And suddenly, everything stopped.

Helen watched the exchange closely, a queer smile playing out over her features.

Sir Barty, generally oblivious, beamed at his daughter's good manners.

And Turner . . . Turner was inscrutable. But he refused to look away from Margaret toward her.

A ball of dread began forming, solid and heavy in her stomach. What if . . . But no, that was impossible. But what if . . . Margaret wasn't the only one with feelings? What if John returned them?

No.

Utterly ridiculous.

"Miss Babcock, I am so glad to see you this morning," Helen began. "John was just telling me last night that you are exactly the right person."

"I am?" Margaret asked, her eyes going wide.

"I did?" Turner muttered.

"Indeed," his mother said, her smile firmly in place. "My daisies, in my window boxes . . . they simply aren't blooming anymore. I have no idea why all the blossoms fell off, and you are the only person John thought to ask."

"I've seen them." Margaret nodded fervently. "I believe they are too crowded. If you split the contents of the boxes into two, you would get blossoms again, I'm sure of it."

"Of course!" Helen crowed, as if Margaret had just given her the secret for spinning gold. "I don't know if you're aware, my lady, but Miss Babcock has quite the green thumb. She inherited it from her mother."

"I am aware," Leticia replied, trying to keep her voice even. "What I've seen of the grounds are . . . full of life."

"Oh, the grounds are especially lovely," Helen was saying. "Also done under Margaret's care. Although I have not yet seen them this summer."

"Yes, they are . . . at a distance," Leticia agreed hesitantly. "I have no talent for growing things, but a fond appreciation for their beauty."

"It occurs to me, Miss Babcock," Helen said suddenly, "that now that it's summer, you must have some very interesting species flowering. How are your violets? In bloom?"

Turner cleared his throat. "Mother, we should—"

"They are," Margaret replied, matter of fact, then her gaze averted again, either distracted or embarrassed.

"My son," Helen continued, her fingers biting into her son's coat, "was expressing an appreciation for your violets just the other day, Miss Babcock."

"He was?" asked Margaret.

"He was?" echoed Leticia, forcing his eyes to fly to her face.

"Yes," Helen replied, her smile telling him to not argue. "He was. He simply loves violets."

If Turner had ever expressed an opinion on violets in his life, Leticia would eat her hat.

"He can come see them," Margaret said suddenly. "If . . . if you would like, that is." Then, her eyes turned to Sir Barty. "Father?"

"Yes of course! You all should come and . . . see the grounds. Margaret always has them, er, blooming. And you and I still have a game of cribbage not yet won." Then he glanced to Leticia. "M'dear?"

She blinked twice before smiling. "Of course. It would be wonderful to have you."

"Excellent—we shall run home and follow you in our cart, then."

"Oh! Today. Of . . . of course."

"Wonderful!" Helen exclaimed. "Isn't that wonderful, John?"

For the first time all morning, their eyes met.

Anger. Heat. Hate. Reserve. Longing. Everything swirled there, in those hard brown depths. She wondered what he saw. What of his she reflected back. What she could possibly say to get him to heed her warning. *Please don't,* her eyes pleaded. *Don't intrude on my life.*

"Indeed," he'd finally said. The first words he'd said to her. "It shall be wonderful."

So now Leticia was going to have her ex-lover and his mother over for tea with her new fiancé and his daughter.

Wonderful.

It was times like this that Leticia wished she had a confessor. A friend that she could confide in, who knew all her secrets. A lady's maid would be ideal. But Leticia refused to press Sir Barty for a lady's maid until the wedding was closer and she could argue the need for one.

Perhaps she should argue for one now. She dearly needed a confidant.

As soon as the carriage pulled up to the front of Bluestone Manor, Leticia called out for Mrs. Dillon.

"We are having guests for tea, Mrs. Dillon, and . . . where do you think you're going?" she called out.

Both Babcocks made identical turns.

"I need a cushion for my foot, and to dig out the cribbage board." Sir Barty toddled over and kissed the top of her head. "I'm sure you and Mrs. Dillon will take care of everything, m'dear."

As he wandered off, Leticia turned her attention to Margaret.

"I need to attend to some pruning in the greenhouse," the girl replied with a shrug. "It cannot wait."

Sir Barty she might not be able to argue with, but Margaret was another matter entirely.

"It will have to wait. You have invited guests for tea and you must be in charge of their comforts."

"I . . . I am?" Margaret looked vaguely panicked. "Usually, my mother . . . that is to say, I usually have far too much work to do in my greenhouse to be entertaining."

Thankfully, Mrs. Dillon stepped in. "My lady, if I may—who is going to be visiting?"

Leticia tried to keep her face impassive. "Mr. John Turner, and his mother, Mrs. Turner."

"Miss Helen—you'll forgive me, Mrs. Turner—would probably prefer the sitting room, it being a bit on the warm side today."

"Then the sitting room it is," Leticia replied. And with a pointed glance to Margaret, had that girl nodding in approval as well.

Mrs. Dillon nodded to a footman, who moved quickly off, a silent order given.

"Now, I know you must be thinking that Mrs. Turner and I will get to know each other while you and Mr. Turner go off to view the violets, but I have to tell you I don't think that would be the best idea. As your friend, that is." Leticia would be run through with a serving fork before she allowed Turner to be alone with Margaret.

And it had nothing to do with the silly notion that he and Margaret were meant for each other, as his mother seemed to desire. Of course not. She simply did not trust Turner with her secrets.

He would not have the chance to tell Margaret—or Sir Barty, for that matter—anything in confidence. He wouldn't have the opportunity to ruin her life. Again.

God help her if he'd told his mother anything. Although, while he seemed to esteem her greatly, she just couldn't imagine John Turner telling his mother much about his love life.

"Oh, but . . . I never thought . . . that is, I'm sure Mr. Turner will be fine touring the violets on his own." Margaret, for once, met Leticia's eyes—and in them was stark horror.

Leticia froze midstep. On the one hand, she was extremely glad that Margaret had no plans to be alone with Turner. On the other hand, she did not want to be left alone with the Turners either.

"No, Margaret. They are your violets. Your gardening. I am sure Mrs. Turner and her son are expecting that you would want to show them off proudly."

Margaret looked panic-stricken. "Why?"

Because this entire afternoon is a theatrical farce. "Because you invited them over specifically to see them," Leticia replied through clenched teeth.

"Oh no," Margaret said. "I should much rather be in my greenhouse."

"Margaret—" At this point Letitia's patience was wearing a bit thin. "How much time have you spent with Mr. Turner? Alone?"

"None," she replied.

None. Well, at least that meant that John Turner was perhaps not as interested in Margaret as she was in him. It was a laughable notion that he'd be interested in her at all. Wasn't it? But still . . .

"If you haven't spent any time with Mr. Turner, how is it that you know you like him?"

Margaret's eyes whipped up, blazing. "I just do."

"I know, but—"

"I don't have to explain my feelings to you."

"I never thought that—"

"Because if I didn't like him, why on earth would he make me blush?"

Now it was Leticia's turn to blink in astonishment. "He makes you blush," she repeated.

"It's a physical indicator of attraction," Margaret answered matter-of-factly.

"Yes, that's true," Leticia answered slowly. "He makes you blush. Therefore, you are attracted to him."

It did make an odd sort of sense. After all, Leticia had been prone to those same blushes courtesy of Mr. John Turner. Once. Not anymore, of course.

"If I am to give a tour of the gardens, I should change clothes," Margaret said after a moment.

Leticia was about to nod in agreement, but then she remembered with whom she was speaking.

"What do you intend to change into?" she asked instead.

"My gardening clothes, of course," Margaret replied.

"Not that ragged thing from yesterday!" Leticia positively gasped. "It's completely unsuitable."

"But I cannot wear this—it's my best gown, it will get dirty." Margaret indicated her current dress; the white muslin with a blue spencer was not much better when it came to fashion, but at least it was clean, and fit her frame appropriately. Even though it was a hair shorter than proper and exposed a bit too much ankle—but that was the difficulty with being so tall, Leticia surmised.

"That's your best gown?" Leticia goggled, unable to stop herself before realizing her mistake.

"Yes," Margaret said, defiantly crossing her arms over her chest and looking down her nose. "What of it?"

Leticia threw up her hands. "Then it is what you will wear to receive guests." Addressing the obvious lacks in Margaret's wardrobe would have to come later—right now, the Turners' arrival was imminent, and she would be damned if John Turner saw that her soon-to-be stepdaughter was a complete mess.

"I just told you—it will get dirty," she argued, her cheeks becoming redder and redder.

"Margaret," Leticia said, her voice stern as a dictator's, "if I can walk through the gardens in a clean gown so can you."

"But you're not going to get near the plants—you don't even like flowers!" Margaret flat-out yelled. "My mother would not—"

"If you had a gentleman call while your mother was alive I am absolutely certain she would—"

"You can't simply come in here and change everything!" Margaret exploded.

Leticia recoiled as if struck. Her face flushed with the argument, and her horrified realization that they had an audience.

"If I may," Mrs. Dillon said after clearing her throat. "Perhaps an appropriate compromise would be that Miss Babcock wear her current gown for tea, and then put on an apron or smock when you tour the grounds. For protection."

"That . . . would be acceptable," Leticia replied after two deep breaths. "Margaret?"

She nodded slightly. But added, "It's your fault if my gown gets ruined." And with that, she flounced off (as much as someone of her height could flounce), presumably to splash some water on her flushed face.

As Margaret bounded up the stairs, Leticia was left to wonder about the girl's upbringing. While last night she had thought the child angry and spoiled, now she was beginning to wonder if she had been neglected. After all, her mother died less than two years ago, when Margaret would have been seventeen—surely she had taught the girl something of social niceties?

And how had she let the inquiry—a perfectly polite, utterly restrained inquiry about Margaret's feelings for one known liar—turn into a heated argument so quickly? She'd thought she'd made some real progress with the girl in the churchyard. She'd managed to get her to smile. To stand on somewhat equal footing.

But now Turner was coming to Bluestone Manor. It upset absolutely everything in her mind, and robbed her of her ability to reason and of her patience, which resulted in a fumbled handling of one Margaret Babcock.

"Thank you, Mrs. Dillon," Leticia said, giving credit where credit was due. "I was on my way to making quite the cake of things, wasn't I?"

Mrs. Dillon gave a pitying smile. "It will take some time. For everyone. Now, I believe I have just the smock for Miss Babcock—I'll have it pressed and ready once tea is served. My lady?"

Leticia nodded and Mrs. Dillon was dismissed.

Strange, when the older woman was not overeager to please, she left off her nervous affectations and wore all her knowledge comfortably, like a grandmother. Perhaps Leticia had an ally in the house after all.

But at that moment, Leticia had little time to reflect on such things. For any second, John Turner was going to arrive on the doorstep.

And when he did, the farce began in earnest.

The vast majority of the afternoon was rather pleasant—or would have been, had it simply been an old friend of Sir Barty's getting to know his affianced bride, while said old friend's son made gestures of courtship toward Sir Barty's daughter.

But of course, it wasn't that simple.

Being in the same room with John Turner never was.

They assembled in the sitting room at Mrs. Dillon's suggestion and began their intricate dance.

"How did you and Sir Barty meet, my lady?" This from Helen.

"Now, Helen—" Sir Barty began from his position next to the window—he was precariously balanced in a spindly chair with a tuffet beneath his bad foot, which was newly wrapped in clean linens. "Don't go interrogating my bride."

"Darling, it's not an interrogation." Leticia smiled and patted his good leg. "We met in a museum in Paris—and you simply must call me Leticia, Mrs. Turner."

"Leticia then, my lady. And how did you come to be in Paris?"

"I was traveling."

"Alone?"

"Since my first husband's unfortunate death, I am a woman of independent means." Leticia judiciously ignored the coughing coming from the corner where John Turner had planted himself. No, not planted. He sprawled. Sir Barty may have been wider, but Turner had the advantage of height, so they were both oversized in this overly feminine room. But while Barty made an effort to confine himself to his small chair, Turner let his masculinity loose, unabashedly taking up a full half of a blue velvet settee.

Oh God, she was staring. She must stop that.

"And you, Mrs. Turner? I understand you and Sir Barty were friends from childhood."

"If you are Leticia to me, I must be Helen to you," Helen answered, keeping her smile bright. It was a smirk, really. A smirk of triumph. And it was so like her son's.

Although Turner was not currently smirking. His face was made of stone.

And of course, from her corner, Margaret said very little—just kept sneaking glances at Turner's face and blushing.

Suffice to say, the weight of the niceties landed on Leticia and Helen.

"Yes, we grew up together in Helmsley—Sir Barty, although he was simply Barty then, Hortense, and me."

"Hortense?" Leticia asked.

"My mother," Margaret said, before going back to blushing.

A silence fell over the room. Helen and Turner glanced at each other. Sir Barty's mustache twitched, as if he intended to say something, but couldn't think of what. Margaret seemed oblivious to the awkwardness—or perhaps, she was so used to awkwardness that it didn't faze her.

"Hortense is a version of Horta, isn't it?" Leticia finally said. "The Greek goddess of plants and growing things. No wonder Margaret excels at gardening."

"I thought you said you were no scholar," Sir Barty said, his bushy brow coming down, while Turner's brow went in the opposite direction.

"I'm not!" Leticia laughed. "I just happen to remember a little bit from all our time in that museum, darling." She smiled and placed a hand on his good knee.

As Sir Barty warmed under Leticia's attentions, Helen's shoulders relaxed, and conversation turned to the gardens and the flowers they would amble past after tea.

Helen struck Leticia as a very practical woman—very much like the women in Manchester, where Leticia grew up. Wives of merchants and millers could not afford to be silly, and those that were quickly sank their husbands' prospects. Practicality was prized. Shrewdness even more so.

But it wouldn't be until much later in the afternoon that Leticia realized she was playing chess with a master.

To be fair, she was distracted. After all, it wasn't every day that John Turner sprawled in one's fiancé's sitting room, his face and voice (when used) giving nothing away.

They gabbed in this manner for what felt like hours, but was likely only ten minutes, before Sir Barty had gobbled up the last of the tea cakes and rose to his one good foot.

"Well, shall we take in the violets?" Sir Barty asked the room, shoving a last watercress sandwich into his mouth.

"Darling, your foot—" Leticia began, keeping her voice low, but was put off with a wave of Sir Barty's hand.

"I will manage to walk in my own park, m'dear," he replied, brusque. "Besides, violets were the point of this, after all."

"Right you are, Sir Barty," Helen said, rising to her feet, forcing her son to do the same. "Margaret, I am very much looking forward to seeing what you've done. But no one is more enthusiastic than my John."

The words *enthusiasm* and *John* seemed antithetical, at best. But with a rueful glance toward his mother, he bowed to Margaret and offered his arm.

Margaret shot a glance to her father, who nodded. She took the proffered arm and led them all outside.

The rest of the party went ahead, while Leticia kept pace with Sir Barty—thankful for the protection of his presence. Right before they got to the front doors, however, Jameson appeared.

"Sir, there is . . . a bit of business that needs to be discussed," Jameson said to Sir Barty.

"Oh yes, of course," Sir Barty said, releasing Leticia's arm. "Forgive me, m'dear." And with that he left.

Leaving Leticia to catch up to Margaret, Turner, and Helen, all by herself.

And she did, finding them in the side garden, gazing at the flower beds that lined the walk to the greenhouse.

"Where is Sir Barty?" Helen asked as soon as she arrived.

"I daresay the countess has been abandoned, Mother. I'm sure she's used to it," John Turner said. It was practically the first thing Turner had said all afternoon—and it was certainly the first thing he had said to her.

But no, he hadn't said it to her. He'd said it about her. And from the smirk (so like his mother's!) he'd meant it cruelly.

"John!" Helen admonished before coming over to take Leticia's arm. "He thinks he's so clever, doesn't he?"

Leticia's eyes zipped to Turner's. "It seems he does."

"I wager he had Jameson do it, am I right?"

"Jameson?" She turned back to Helen.

"Sir Barty has always been too proud. He knows full well the apothecary says to keep off his foot, but instead of using that as his excuse for not coming out to walk with us, he has Jameson pull him away."

"Oh. Yes. How did you know?" Leticia replied.

"He's been doing it for ages," Helen said. "Tell me, what excuses did he use in Paris?"

"Usually that he was waiting for his guide," she said, earning a startling cackle from Helen, causing Leticia to smile.

"If it weren't for you, my dear, I'd be tempted to stay inside with him and play out another hand of cribbage—we are very close to declaring a winner—but to have you be forced to chaperone the children on your second day on the job? Leaving you would be unconscionable."

Leticia decided to ignore that. "How long have you and Sir Barty been playing cribbage?"

"This current game? About twelve years, I should think. And soon enough, he'll admit defeat. Come now, let's catch up to the others."

Leticia had to admit she liked the intelligent, pushy woman. If circumstances had been different, perhaps Helen could have been the confidant that Leticia would find herself longing for. But as it was, Helen was not quite the ideal person to whom to confess secrets of her son's romantic life.

Especially since she was far too preoccupied by that son's romantic life already.

"Tell me, Leticia," Helen said, whispering a confidence, "what do you think of the two of them?"

She nodded toward where Margaret and Turner were walking ahead of them. Thankfully neither seemed to be angling to be closer to the other than propriety allowed.

Margaret had at some point acquired a plain starched apron, whose use Leticia was surprisingly glad of, since at that moment the girl dropped to her knees, reached between Turner's ankles, and began digging out a root, making better space for her violets.

Turner simply watched.

"I . . . am not certain what to think," Leticia said cautiously, her eyes uncharacteristically glued to the back of Turner's head. "I only met Margaret yesterday."

"And you only met my son this morning," Helen replied. "But surely that is enough time for someone shrewd, who has lived in the world as you have, to see if two people have a spark of interest between them."

Leticia kept the smile on her face. She was getting markedly better at keeping that bubble of hysterical laughter down in her belly. Soon she would be able to sail through Helmsley, convincing even herself that she had never met Mr. John Turner before.

But Helen was waiting for her answer. "I see nothing untoward in their manner. But on the man's side, that is not always a good thing."

"How so?" Helen asked.

"A man who was enamored would make it known. He would find an excuse to be in her presence, to touch her ungloved hand . . ." To kiss her, claim her in the middle of a crowded ballroom.

To come to her room later that night . . .

Helen's brow came down. "My son is simply reserved. He is respectful of Margaret because he is utterly respectful of Sir Barty. But what about the girl? Do you observe some interest on her end?"

Aside from the fact that Margaret had told her of her interest? Well, at that moment she was showering Turner with a rendition of her growing practices, using more words in a single breath than Leticia had heard from her in twenty-four hours.

"And these barrels here, they are filled with my own special formula—they irrigate down into the beds, you see . . . And this set I grew from cuttings . . ."

But instead of admitting it, Leticia simply shrugged.

"I think that Margaret is a lovely young woman, but she does not know much of the world. If she spent a season in London, perhaps she would find her eyes opened to many new things." Eyes opened to see that a gentleman's daughter does not marry a mill owner, perhaps. "But she seems to have no interest in it."

Helen's eyebrow went up. "No, I daresay not. Miss Margaret has always been a bit of a homebody—her mother understood her, and indulged her. Ever since Hortense passed, I've tried to act as the girl's friend, but she seems to prefer solitude. Always has."

"Yes," Leticia said on a sigh. It was somewhat worrying that Margaret's shyness had fixed her character as "odd" in the town she'd grown up in. There was little chance she'd ever outgrow it.

Helen's voice became low, confiding. "I know you will be good for the girl. And Hortense would have liked you, of that I'm sure." Helen patted her hand. "I'm also sure it must be uncomfortable to be here suddenly, thrust into a new role, but the awkwardness will pass."

"I'm sure it will," Leticia replied, a bit clipped. Although she was more certain that her comfortableness was inversely relative to her proximity to John Turner, but Helen didn't need to know that.

"For you, for Sir Barty, and for Helmsley. I'd be more than happy to pay calls with you to the ladies of the town, and show Mrs. Emory that she's making a complete cake of herself setting herself up against you—oh! Oh, look at that!"

Helen grabbed Leticia's arm so hard she jerked to a sudden stop. She nodded in the direction of Turner and Margaret. There, she saw that Margaret had picked one of the violets and was pointing to its petals. She was giving some kind of dissertation on the petals—likely the shape or color was of note—but in the process, she invited Turner to lean very close. And in leaning so close, his hand fell to the small of Margaret's back. A gentle touch. An intimate touch.

Margaret started when his fingers landed. And if possible, she blushed deeper than ever.

"There!" Helen crowed. "You were right, Leticia. Any excuse to be closer."

While Helen kept her triumph to a whisper, something violent coursed through Leticia.

He should most certainly not be touching Margaret in that way! A miller? She, a gentleman's daughter? Leticia had to do something—to protect Margaret, of course.

And her toe hit upon the answer. One of the potted trees that lined the gravel walk through the flower beds.

Leticia eyed the tree. "Oh my—Margaret!" she called out. "It seems someone left a bottle in this—"

"No, don't!"

But it was too late.

Leticia had picked up the bottle, which for some odd reason was buried neck down in the soil—not realizing it was filled with liquid.

Brown liquid.

Brown liquid that spilled all over her favorite curry-colored dress.

Everyone froze. Everyone except . . .

"Oh dear!" Margaret cried. "My tea!"

"Tea?" Leticia asked, unable to look up from the splash on her skirt.

"Yes—well, that's what I call it, anyway. That bottle is my gravitational fertilizing system. The vacuum created by the dirt and the bottle allows the tea to seep into the soil only as needed. It's the same as I have in the barrels that feed the flowers."

"Margaret—" Leticia asked, still as a statue. "What precisely is in your . . . tea?"

"It's a specific formula. I soak a burlap sack full of compost in water for several days. I'll have to get more horse dung from the stables, whip up another batch . . ." Margaret cocked her head to one side, a whisper of a smile on her face. "I guess it is not possible for either of us to walk through the gardens without ruining our gowns, is it?"

Leticia stopped listening to Margaret. Because a different sound filled her ears. The distinct rumble of male laughter. Her eyes rose and met Turner's. He was struggling to contain his mirth. No, not struggling—absolutely relishing it.

"Well, I think perhaps we should return to the house," Helen said.

"Quite—" Leticia replied, planting the bottle back in the potted tree's soil. "Margaret, come along."

"Oh no," Helen began to protest. "Surely my son can—"

"I think it best—" Leticia interrupted. At least she could find a silver lining to this situation, and use it to separate Margaret and Turner.

"One moment," Turner said, clearing his throat of laughter. His face moved not a muscle, but his eyes locked on to Leticia's. And they lit with an angry mischief.

"May I, Miss Babcock?" he said then, with a flourish worthy of the audience. Then he took the forgotten violet from her hand and tucked it into the ribbon across the crown of her bonnet.

"Violets become you," he said with an easy nod. Then he raised her hand to his lips.

"I . . . I . . . thank you." Margaret managed this basic politeness without jumping out of her skin, as it seemed she very much wanted to.

Turner's gaze found hers again, and the blank stare he gave her made her veins go icy.

He was determined to hate her.

He was determined to not care about her.

In that instant, she determined the exact same thing.

7

*Y*ou couldn't leave well enough alone, could you?"

Turner found himself pacing the sitting room, that same space in which they had passed a ludicrous interlude of teacakes and tepid conversation just a few hours ago. Why the hell was he still here, listening to his mother jabber and confined to this tiny room, when he could be at the mill, doing work, calibrating weights, and pounding his fists against the walls?

That was unfair. He knew perfectly well how he had ended up in this situation. He had provoked Leticia with that violet and by kissing Margaret's hand.

And Leticia had provoked him right back by insisting everyone stay for dinner.

John didn't quite know how it had happened. One minute he'd locked eyes with Leticia and the next Margaret was whipping her hand out of his and declaring, "I think it's time to go back to the house!" with a voice so high and cheeks so pink that there was little else to do but follow the girl back to the house.

He'd nodded as he passed his mother and Leticia, barely

pausing to enjoy (or rather, not enjoy) the stench covering her gown from Margaret's "tea" formula. He could feel her eyes boring into the back of his head as he moved.

"Well that is certainly promising!" he'd heard his mother say in happy tones. "Although, 'tis a pity it comes at such an inconvenient time!"

He was likely the only person who could hear the slight hesitation in Leticia's voice. "How so?"

"We are so close to the next harvest," his mother explained. "The mill is nearly complete, and John is determined to be open for business when the first crop of grain comes in. Usually, the crops from Sir Barty's estate are among the first to be produced, did you know? Previously, he's had to take his business to Blackwell's mills—some as far as ten miles away. But with the Turner mill reopening surely he will be happy to move his business closer to home again, don't you think?"

Turner picked up the pace. He did not need to hear his mother's subtle-as-a-sledgehammer sales pitch for Sir Barty's business to Leticia. He had known his mother's true object in wedging them into Sir Barty's hospitality today. Certainly, she would like to see her son settle down with an eligible young lady, but . . .

Sir Barty's estate produced more grain than any other landowner in the county. Being the processor of said grain would mean the Turner Grain Mill would not only survive, but thrive. And courting the daughter of Sir Barty would certainly make him look favorably on their business.

Turner told himself that he would be happy—thrilled!—to go along. After all, there was some chance he would like Margaret. True, he'd known her for years and hadn't found himself madly in love as of yet, but perhaps he would find something new to pique his interest.

It wasn't as if his heart was engaged elsewhere.

Coming to Bluestone today had absolutely nothing to do with seeing Letty in the churchyard.

Letty, who looked like a dream and a ghost and all those things he thought he'd lost.

As it was, he'd done his damnedest to hold himself together while it felt like all his seams had come undone. So while he was internally reeling, he did the only thing he could do: he played along.

Along with Leticia, who decided not to know him.

Along with his mother, who wanted him to attach himself to Margaret.

And along with Margaret, who painfully tried to tell him all about the cross-pollination required to have that specific color blue at the heart of the violets.

He'd been cordial, kind, and conscientious, no more. To his mind, he hadn't paid Leticia or Margaret any special notice.

Except for those moments that he had.

He caught up to Margaret just as she reached the front steps, where her father was waiting for them.

"Well, Mr. Turner!" Sir Barty said. "How are the violets? And where is my bride-to-be?"

"Beautiful," Turner answered. "The violets, I mean. Your daughter has quite the talent."

Margaret, true to form, blushed furiously at the compliment.

"And Let—that is, let your bride-to-be tell you herself."

He was saved at that moment by Leticia and his mother rounding the corner from the gardens.

Sir Barty's eyes widened when he saw Leticia—or more important, her dress. Then he turned red-faced to his daughter.

"Margaret . . ."

"I didn't do it!" Margaret cried, wide-eyed. "I swear. It

was an accident." She turned her eyes up to him. And for a moment, John felt bad enough for the girl to take her hand and place it on his arm. Present a united front.

"It was an accident," he confirmed. "Margaret in fact did her best to warn the countess."

Sir Barty's mustache twitched, but his shoulders relaxed. Good.

That was how they were standing when Leticia and his mother approached. Margaret's arm through his, Margaret looking at him with relief, and Sir Barty smiling down on the whole party.

They must have made quite the picture. Enough for Leticia to go white and narrow her eyes.

And that made his blood rush in his veins.

Dammit, but it felt good to know that she felt something. She'd been so cool and calm, not giving away anything, even to him, who knew her better than anyone. So to know that he could still affect her the way she affected him . . . it was enough to have his body reacting in ways it shouldn't.

"Back already m'dear?" Sir Barty had said, his voice booming out. "Pity, I was just about to join you. Goodness, what happened to your dress?"

"Gravity," she answered, raising an eyebrow. Then she shot a conspiratorial smile to his mother. "And we can take another circle of the park, if you like, darling."

"Oh no, no, no . . ." Sir Barty protested. "You would obviously like to change, I think."

"Yes, I would," Leticia answered. And his mother—thank Christ—took that as a cue.

"Thank you for the lovely afternoon! I hope this is only the first of many pleasant afternoons spent together. After all," she said, waggling her brow, "our families are long intertwined. Perhaps more so now."

He resisted rolling his eyes. He would cut his mother down to size later for her not-so-subtle ambitions, but right now, Turner was ready to leave. Dying to extricate himself from this insanity and lock himself away until his mind and body were back under control and he could pretend ignorance just as well as she did.

"Miss Babcock, thank you for the tour. You know your plants."

Margaret blinked at him. Well, it was better than blushing at least. "Of course I do. I have studied them for years."

Then he turned to the rest of the party.

"Sir Barty." Then, quietly, "Countess."

It was the most he had said to her all day.

And perhaps it was too much. Because in that one word, she must have deciphered his discomfort. His unwillingness to be there a single second longer . . . and decided to prolong his torture.

"You can't be off yet!" she said suddenly. Turner and his mother pivoted. Helen smiling, anticipating.

Turner's anticipation was less excited.

"Helen, we would be delighted if you and your son would stay for dinner." She moved to retake Sir Barty's arm, and pecked him on the cheek. "Wouldn't we, darling?"

Thus, he was still here. There was no way his mother was going to turn down the invitation—and God knows what trouble Helen would get up to without him. So there he was, waiting in the same fluffy and feminine sitting room, waiting for Leticia and Margaret to change for the meal, and listening to the clatter of china and silver as the servants in the dining room beyond worked madly to set the table for the two unexpected guests.

It was still light outside. Since it was summer and they kept country hours, it was no surprise the evening meal was being served when the sun still shone, but to Turner it felt like he still had time to escape.

If only.

Sir Barty was left to sit with the guests, and he and Helen reminisced about their youth, but as soon as Helen mentioned the mill in the most oblique way, it served as a reminder to Barty that he had some papers in his library awaiting his attention.

Now the clock ticked, and Turner paced.

"I didn't say anything, I promise you," his mother replied. "The invitation to stay for dinner was completely spontaneous, and to my mind, an excellent sign." She was inspecting the little ceramic pots on the shelf by the window—women's knickknacks that served no purpose than to give maids something to dust. She picked one up, her eyes falling over the little flowers painted on its side. "Do you think she'll make many changes in here? I always liked this room—except I might get rid of all these pots."

"What are you talking about?" Turner said, sharp. His mother gave him that stare that made him feel like the littlest of children.

"Has something displeased you, John?" his mother asked. "I would be careful of showing it to our hosts."

There was very little he could say to that, other than bloody hell yes something had displeased me, but he doubted his mother—for all her intelligence—would even be able to fathom the reason.

"It is a woman's prerogative to make changes to her home," his mother was saying. "And Leticia is so very polished. Even when she spilled that bottle on herself, she was still perfect as a princess. I can't imagine that she would let this room stay the way it is. She'll likely want Italian marble and French silks everywhere."

Turner couldn't help snorting. Yes, Leticia was regal.

But not a princess—an ice queen. And yes, she would want French silks and Italian marble and everything fine. He had no doubt she would drape this entire house over in extravagance, he thought bitterly.

"God help Sir Barty," he mumbled under his breath. Letty had no idea what it was to live by the skin of your teeth.

Except . . . hadn't that been what she had been doing when he caught up to her in Dover?

"Oh, Sir Barty knows what he's in for," his mother replied. "And he'll be pleased as punch with it—for the first few months, at least."

He snorted again.

"That is a most disturbing habit. Don't tell me snorting is now fashionable in London."

He snorted yet again—but this time, covering a rueful laugh with it.

"I just don't understand what we are doing here. You weaseled your way over for tea—"

"Our way."

"I did the pretty by Miss Babcock, and now I need to get back to the mill."

"It's Sunday, the mill can wait," his mother argued.

"After all the accidents that have befallen it, I'm taking no chances. I want it up and running as soon as possible," he countered. "That means testing the new equipment every day—even on Sundays."

He was practically itching to get back to the mill. To climb the tower and lose himself in the mundane but all-too-important tasks of checking the weight of the grindstones, the pulleys and gears that regulated the speed of the sails, and getting into the new building, to fiddle with the pipes that would transport the steam from one end of the space to the other.

Because the wind did not blow every day. And he had big plans for the Turner Grain Mill.

"It would be just as devastating to the mill if you went home now." His mother cocked her head to one side, considering him. "You seemed to be enjoying your stroll with Miss Babcock."

Turner stopped pacing. Here we go, he thought.

"I told you, Mother, I have no objection to Miss Babcock, but I also have no designs on her. She's a child."

His mother's eyebrow went up. "You did not give that impression when you were tucking a violet into her bonnet."

He could feel the heat of color spread across his cheekbones. Yes, he had done that. And touched the girl's back. And kissed her hand. He knew it was misleading. Regret had settled into his stomach immediately upon those actions, but he hadn't paid any attention to it. He was too busy watching for a reaction from Leticia.

"You could hardly do better than Sir Barty's daughter," his mother mused. "She could use a bit of polish, of course. Some social lessons, but that's what Leticia is here for."

"I will not marry simply to secure business, Mother. I have some morals." Turner growled. "And would you stop calling her that?"

"Calling who what?"

"The Countess—Leticia." Letty, his mind said, unbidden.

"She told me to," his mother replied, astonished. "I will call her what she wishes to be called. What is wrong with you?"

"Nothing," he replied, but the look his mother gave told him she knew it was not nothing. "I just don't like being . . . in this situation."

In this situation. In this house. With Leticia just upstairs. Engaged to Sir Barty, of all people.

"If you truly object to courting Miss Babcock, I will not press it." His mother threw up her hands.

"You won't?" He stopped pacing. His eyebrow went up, an echo to hers.

"Of course not, John. I want your happiness as much as I want the mill's success. And if Miss Babcock won't make you a good wife, then she won't. I have 'morals' too."

"Oh," he said. It was really the only thing he could say. Sometimes he forgot that his parent was just that—a parent. Her priorities were manifold, but ultimately centered on his happiness. "Thank you."

"You're welcome, my boy."

"Then we can give our regrets and go home," he said, straightening his coat.

"Are you mad? Not when we have already accepted." His mother laughed. "The meal will be in truth what it is on the surface—that we are simply passing the evening with old friends. I will not have your bad mood over your 'morals' ruin what is turning out to be a lovely day and a promising relationship with Leticia."

Turner grew still. "Relationship?" he managed on a cough.

"Yes. I think she and I will be great friends. After all, she will need someone to guide her through the morass that Mrs. Emory is sure to create in her stupidity," Helen said, preening.

"The same morass Mrs. Emory has created for you?"

His mother had endured a great deal while he had been away in London. When she was the miller's wife, and the Turner Grain Mill employed dozens of men in Helmsley and brought people and business from all around, Helen had been one of the leaders of town society. But then tragedy came—and with it, the town's pity.

His mother did not do well with pity. Mrs. Emory, having just purchased her shop, took advantage of her lowered place in society.

"That woman is idiotic thinking she needs to defend her

position in town. The wife of Sir Barty, and a countess to boot, owns a higher place simply by existing. Mrs. Emory is barely better than a shopkeeper. She should be kissing Leticia's feet, begging for her favor. But Louisa Emory never did think long term. So she misses an opportunity I am more than happy to pick up. Besides, if you are so against courting Miss Margaret, then this is perhaps a better way to approach the situation."

He began to pace again—between his mother's calm machinations and having the works-ruining wrench that was Leticia back in his life, he was beginning to feel like a caged animal. He needed to drink something. He needed to hit something.

He needed to know why the hell Letty had asked them to stay for dinner.

"I don't know why you feel the need to manipulate Sir Barty for his business. He will see that the Turner Grain Mill will serve his and his tenants' needs best as soon as we get the new equipment operating and open for business. Besides, he's your old friend."

Helen harrumphed at her son's naïveté. "I do it precisely because he is my old friend. Didn't you see him run out of here as soon as the mill was mentioned? I know very well that he will only change his business to the Turner Mill if there is something in it for him. Right now, Palmer Blackwell can offer the steady service he's had for the past five seasons, and likely at a discount."

"And Palmer Blackwell has enough mills and money to undercut us for a year, or two, or however long it takes for us to go toes up," Turner grumbled. He could offer a discount for so large a contract, but not nearly what Blackwell would to retain Sir Barty's business.

"Yes," he mother replied. "But Sir Barty can be influenced. And if not by his daughter through you, then possibly by his wife through her friendship with me."

This time he gave in to the desire to laugh. "If you think the countess is going to do anything you wish, prepare to have your illusions shattered."

His mother's eyes narrowed. "You are in a mood."

He took a deep breath. She was right. But she did not know the reason.

"If you are going to be in such a foul temper, I would ask that you take it somewhere else," she replied. "And then leave it there, because Sir Barty, Miss Babcock, and the countess will be down within minutes."

And within minutes he would see Letty again—but in the role of Sir Barty's fiancée. It was a role she played well, but a role it was.

It must be.

"I think I'll take a stroll around the grounds," he said. "Clear my head."

"Excellent notion." His mother nodded. "But be back before the meal is rung—I will not make any excuses for you!"

Her voice was an echo, calling after him as he went out the door. But once in the foyer, he did not turn toward the main doors, leading to the twilight outside.

Instead, he made certain no eyes were on him, and no footsteps were coming, before he made for the grand staircase at the other end of the hall.

He did need to rid himself of this ill temper. And there was only one way to do that.

Give it to the person deserving of it.

⚬⚬

HE FOUND HIS way with little trouble.

Oh, all right, there had been some trouble. It wasn't easy trying to figure out which room was Letty's—and considering the fact that he had never been on the second floor of Bluestone Manor, let alone in the family rooms, he was mostly guessing at this point. He dreaded simply opening a door and finding Margaret (or worse, Sir Barty) in the middle of getting their kit on for dinner. But just as he was about to try one doorknob, it turned, sending him scurrying to hide behind what had to be the oldest (and largest) suit of armor in all of Lincolnshire.

Sir Barty, it seemed, came by his size honestly.

At that moment, Turner was grateful for the Babcock family's penchant for portliness, because it hid him from view as a mousy young maid opened the door and stepped out of the room, carrying soiled and wrinkled linens in a basket.

The maid turned and thankfully walked in the direction opposite him. Then, with even more luck than Turner had ever had in his life, she knocked on a door a few yards down the hall.

"Yes?" Leticia's voice floated, muffled through the door.

"My lady?" the girl squeaked. "It's Molly. The laundry maid?"

A muted shuffling could be heard, then Leticia threw the door open. She was wrapped in a dressing gown, her hair still frazzled from being out in the fresh air, her cheeks flushed from some emotion he couldn't identify.

She looked perfect.

In her arms was the offending garment—now drying into a splotched mess. She held it out to little Molly. "Here. Do try to save it. It's my best—I mean, it's one of my favorites," she said, correcting herself.

"Yes, my lady."

"Please tell Sir Barty and . . . anyone else who might be waiting, that I'll be down in a few minutes."

The maid nodded and curtsied. But then hesitated.

"Yes?" Leticia asked.

"I . . . I was just wondering, my lady, do you need anything else? Water, or . . ."

"No, thank you. I'm fine."

"What about help getting dressed?" Molly was unable to hide her eagerness. "I've been learning to do hair—"

"No, I can do it myself," Leticia replied before closing the door in the girl's face.

The click of the door handle echoed through the hallway.

"I'll never be a lady's maid," the little maid grumbled under her breath, and the loss of her dreams would have been heartbreaking if it hadn't been followed with, "Wendra will never believe this."

There was only one Wendra in town, and she was Mrs. Emory's live-in maid, if Turner's recollection of his mother's long speeches on the politics of the ladies' circle was accurate. Which means that Leticia had just dug herself a slightly deeper hole with the women of Helmsley.

Turner let out his breath, which he had been holding in order to not make a sound, but also to avoid coughing. The old suit of armor could use a thorough dusting.

When Molly had disappeared down the servants' staircase, Turner crept forward and knocked on the door.

"I told you, I wish to be left—" Leticia's voice died as she threw open the door, and expecting to see the maid, was instead assaulted with the sight of his torso. Her gaze rose slowly to meet his face.

"We need to talk," he said.

"What are you doing here?"

"You asked us to stay for dinner," he drawled. "My mother is quite pleased by the invitation."

"At my door. What are you doing at my door?"

His mouth opened to answer when a shuffling sound at

the other end of the hall had their heads whipping around to pinpoint the noise.

The shuffling, wherever it was from, was getting louder.

"Go." She put her hand out, shoving him back. "Get out of here—you cannot be seen here."

"No."

His hand went to hers, holding it in place against his chest.

"Either I can be seen standing in your doorway while you're in your robe, or we can talk privately in your room."

She was frozen, except for her bosom, which rose and fell with the pounding rhythm of her breath.

Her eyes never left his face.

"Invite me in, Letty."

8

"Hello, Letty."

They were the words she had been dreading all day—and the ones that echoed in her head, the deep rumble of his voice like a memory not yet had. She knew that he would come to her. She knew that they would find a way to talk—they had to, obviously.

But she was not expecting it to be here.

In her robe. In her room.

Her bed mere feet away.

She'd assumed she'd put all those thoughts away. Enough time and anger had buried them. And while they had been forced to spend the day in proximity to each other, thoughts of bed and soft sheets and softer skin had never entered her mind.

Until he entered her room.

Now, no matter what discipline she imposed on herself, her bed was where her mind ended up.

Don't be a fool, she told herself. It's not as if you and he ever—

But they had gotten so close. Closer than Leticia had ever allowed anyone.

A flood of memories filled her body. His skin next to hers . . .

Her fingers, exploring . . .

His eyes, the next day, when she found out about the Lie.

"I must ask that you refrain from calling me by a diminutive," she said, bearing herself upright while putting as much distance between them as possible. Which wasn't easy—he seemed to take up every bit of air in the room. "We are, after all, strangers."

A wry smile twisted his lips. "And I must ask that you refrain from calling us strangers. At least while we are alone."

"I have no intention of ever being alone with you again after this," Leticia replied. "Tell me, do you often force yourself into ladies' bedchambers? If so, I must put some locks on Margaret's doors."

"Now, now. You invited me. Both times."

"That was different," she replied quietly. "We were different."

He held up his hands in surrender. "Fair enough," he said. "Why are you here, Letty?"

"I'm marrying a man I adore and living happily ever after," she answered.

Now he folded his arms over his chest. "Do me the greatest of favors. Since this is the one and only time we will be alone together, don't lie to me. And I won't lie to you."

"You, not lie?" she said. "How very novel."

He said nothing, but his eyes narrowed, just barely. Enough to show his displeasure. Good, Letty thought. He should feel something about that—the impassivity of his expression was bound to drive her mad.

"Do you know, I'm not entirely certain how to proceed," she said, trying to keep her tone light while her heart beat like a hummingbird's. "Do I say, 'It's such a pleasure to see you'? Or what about, 'What a happy surprise!'"

"I can't imagine it's a pleasure for either of us," he answered with a growl. "But I have to wonder whether it is actually a surprise to you."

Her head whipped up.

"What do you mean?"

He looked her dead in the eye. "Did you come here for me?" he asked, direct.

She couldn't help it. She laughed. A long, drawn-out peal of disbelief.

"Letty—" he said. "If you're in trouble or need help, I can—"

"No," she answered. "Of course not. I didn't even know you were here. How could I possibly?"

He hesitated for a moment—as if her logic caused more pain than her answer did. If her answer had caused any pain, that was. His walls were up, those guards in place that she had so carefully taken to breaking down last summer.

Back when the Lie was still being told and they were both very happy to be fools.

"You could quite possibly because I told you," he answered.

"No you didn't."

"I told you about the town I grew up in, I told you—"

"You let me believe it was the town the Earl of Ashby grew up in. Hollyhock. You mentioned no names."

"Then why are you here?" he asked again.

"Because I'm surviving."

He held her stare as she watched for any sign of anger or regret on his part. But true to form, he gave nothing away.

She used to be able to read him so much better.

"I'm here to marry Sir Barty. He's an eligible widower and I, an eligible widow. It's a perfectly eligible match."

"Where on earth did you just happen to meet the man who owns half the grain in the village where I happen to own the local windmill?"

"Paris," she replied. "Remember? I had to go to the Continent to find somewhere people weren't laughing at me."

He ignored the jibe. "And how was Paris?"

"Expensive."

She broke eye contact, moving lightly over to a little table, her fingers falling across some trinkets she had placed there—small things, personal things. A book she'd loved as a girl—*The Odyssey*. A ribbon she wore when she was making her debut. Suddenly, she felt the urge to hide them from his gaze.

"So you own the local windmill," she said lightly, trying to temper the conversation from growing too . . . something.

"I do. My family business."

"I'm sure it's a lovely windmill; I know very little about them."

"I'll give you a tour sometime."

"No you won't—never alone, remember?" she said.

Her eyes met his—and that was yet another mistake.

For minutes, seconds, hours—she was lost. Who knows. But the bed remained in her peripheral vision, a looming specter reminding her that there were actually three parties in the room: him, her, and them.

"No, I don't suppose we will." Then he cleared his throat, brushing away any regret that may have creeped in, and folded his arms in front of his chest. Somehow it only made him appear larger, more imposing.

"You expect me to believe this is coincidence?"

"It's not a coincidence," she said, and saw his eyes light with *aha!* She moved closer to him. Just a half step, but enough for her to lower her voice to a whisper. "What this is, is bad luck shaking hands with unkind fate. And we simply have to deal with it."

"And how do you suggest we do that?" he whispered back.

She was just about to open her mouth when a knock on the door echoed through the room.

Fear filled Leticia like a startled bird. She held up a hand, begging Turner to be silent.

For once, he relented.

"Who is it?" she called out.

"M'dear?" came Sir Barty's voice.

Oh hell, she thought. Oh hell.

"One moment!"

Desperately, silently, she reached out and pulled Turner's arm. At first he resisted, fire in his eyes.

"Being found here does you no good either," she said, her voice barely a breath. His resistance faltered. Then she dragged him by the arm behind the changing screen in the corner of the room.

Two short breaths. That was all she allowed herself. Then forced a yawn.

It was on that yawn that she opened the door a crack.

"M'dear, I was—oh! I was hoping to escort you down to dinner, but you're not dressed." Sir Barty exclaimed. The sight of her in her dressing gown was enough to make the man goggle. Confirmation that she still had her figure, at least. "Is something amiss?"

"Oh, darling, I'm so sorry," Leticia said, covering a yawn. She glanced down at her robe. "I was getting ready when I dozed off for a few moments."

"Dozed off?" his bushy eyebrows lifted in consternation.

"I know, it's so unlike me!" She let herself get a little teary-eyed, hating to be such a bother. "But the travel of yesterday, and all the excitement of today must have caught up with me . . . I feel so very foolish . . ."

"Quite understandable." Sir Barty nodded, looking a little relieved. Leticia remembered how pleased Sir Barty had been that morning when she had been on time for church. He did not indulge the feminine trait of tardiness, and she would have to be careful to avoid it in the future. "Do you . . . need any help getting ready?"

He looked so hopeful Leticia almost felt sorry for him. Almost . . . but it was bad game play to allow him any intimacies before vows were spoken. She knew that much, at least.

Not to mention, John Turner was currently hiding behind her dressing screen.

"Oh, darling, no—but thank you." She smiled sweetly and laid a hand on his arm.

"I could call for a maid, I mean." Sir Barty blushed like a schoolboy. His mustache twitched, as if chewing something over. "Come to think of it, you should have a maid . . ."

"Darling, I should adore a lady's maid, thank you!" She watched his expression go from startled to pleased. Excellent. "But we shall have to discuss who to hire later. Right now you should go down. I'll follow in a few moments. Helen is waiting." She blinked, and then remembered where Turner was supposed to be. "Her son as well," she added, then lowered her voice. "Probably best to not leave Margaret alone with them."

"Yes—of course," Sir Barty agreed, seeming to remember he had a daughter. "Don't take too long now—there's no need to stand on ceremony with the Turners, after all."

"It won't be but a blink of your eye," Leticia said, and with that, closed the door on Sir Barty.

The moment the door clicked into place, John Turner was out from behind the screen.

"I feel as if I should applaud," he said. "Funny how you are not willing to forgive me for the lie, yet you lie so easily to your intended."

"A little discretion is not a lie, so save your applause," she replied as breezily as possible. "I need to get dressed."

"Now, that I will most certainly applaud."

"Meaning you must go."

"Not until we find some solutions to our current predicament." He leaned his shoulder up against the poster of the bed.

Her bed.

He must have had no idea he was doing it, or of its implications. And as such, Leticia would not, could not let herself be affected by it. Instead she rolled her shoulders straight and brought her chin up (the better angle by which to look down her nose at him). "Fine." It wasn't fine. "By all means stay. But I have to get dressed."

She swept past him and behind the screen.

She moved as quickly as possible, ignoring the smell of wood and man that had invaded this small space in the few minutes he had hidden back here.

Really, she thought, throwing the robe over the top of the screen. It was highly annoying.

"I have an idea for how to 'deal with it,' as you say." His gruff voice floated to her.

"Do tell," she replied. Damn. She'd been in such a hurry to hide back here that she forgot to grab something to change into. "And while you do," she called out, "hand me my blue gown from the wardrobe, with the gold trim?"

She heard a bit of shuffling, the creak of the wardrobe

door opening. The unmistakable sound of someone man-handling fine silks making her want to cringe.

"Please be careful!" she said. The blue silk gown was flung over the top of the screen without so much as a by-your-leave. Well, that was her answer, it seemed.

"Do let me know if you need any help with the buttons."

She could hear the smile in his voice and it made her want to pummel him. What a terribly unladylike impulse he inspired.

"If I refused my fiancé's help, you can rest assured that I will refuse yours." She threw the dress over her head and pulled it on.

Over the course of the past three years, since the loss of Konrad and her fortunes, she'd had to become creative in her practicalities. One of which was discreetly altering all her clothes so they could be put on without the assistance of an expensive maid. (Ooh . . . she would have to discreetly alter the clothes back before Sir Barty hired a new maid—she didn't want anyone gossiping about her strange aversion to buttons up the back.)

"Ah yes. And that brings me back to the subject at hand. My idea for 'dealing with it,'" he said. She could hear the creak of his weight settling into the little chair of the escritoire.

At least, she hoped he was sitting on the chair. The other option was far more disconcerting.

Once she did up the hidden buttons on the front of her gown, she straightened her skirts as she stepped out from behind the screen.

He was sitting in the chair. Thank goodness.

"You could leave."

He said it so simply. As if it was a direction in a recipe for baking bread.

"Leave," she repeated. "Just up and disappear?"

"It's not as if you haven't done it before." He started to smile, then seeing the look on her face, stifled it. "If you leave now, it will save Sir Barty a great deal of heartache—"

"I have no intention of causing Sir Barty any heartache."

"I can't imagine he would not be heartbroken if he learned of our . . . past."

She froze in the middle of the room. Let the cold, oily feeling slide down into her belly. And she was actually glad about it. Because whatever effect he'd been having on her—his very presence, the way he'd leaned on the bed—slipped away when he played what he thought was his trump card. She could hate him now, even as she played one card better.

"He was heartbroken—for me." Triumph danced along her skin as she watched his face shutter. "I've been lied to in marriage before, I know it is no way to build a life together. So I told him. Oh, not about you specifically. But he knows some underhanded man lied about who he was, and made a fool of me in a very public way," she said simply. "It was easier. If the last year taught me anything, it is that I cannot outrun the Lie."

He heaved himself out of the chair and paced, seeming to ponder what she said. Opened his mouth to say something then closed it again.

"Still, if you feel it necessary to inform him of your involvement in the scheme, go ahead, by all means. But I have a feeling that it would do you more harm than good, especially concerning your interest in Margaret."

"I'm not interested in Margaret," he said bluntly. It must have just popped out, because he certainly didn't look like he intended to give that card away. Of course he wasn't interested in Margaret. He didn't even like her, not in the way needed for marriage. Of course everything he had done today—kissing Margaret's hand, touching her waist—had simply been to provoke Leticia. But still, relief flooded through her. She could not help but be glad to know it.

"Really?" she asked, relieved her voice came out steady. "I imagine Sir Barty might be more willing to give his grain business over to you if you were his daughter's intended."

"You figured that out too?" he replied, closing the distance between them with little more than a lean. His voice was a whispered growl. "Don't worry. Despite my mother's best intentions, I'm not so mercenary that I would toy with someone's affections for material gain."

She flinched back, as if struck. "Oh, I see. You think I am."

"Can you deny that you are marrying for reasons other than love?"

"No. And what on earth is wrong with that?" she asked. "Just because Sir Barty can offer me security does not make me a bad person. In return I will be a good wife to him and a friend to Margaret. You seem to think I will stand up in church one morning and by the following week spend through Sir Barty's fortune while I take a string of lovers."

"A string of lovers?" he repeated, his eyes narrow slivers of heat. "Not even I think you would have a string."

Just one. The words hung unspoken in the air. One man, one temptation living just in the village, with the memory of how his hands felt on her skin looming at every moment.

She would be damned before she let that happen.

"I am making vows, Mr. Turner. I fully intend to honor them. Sir Barty will never lie to me, and I will never lie to him. Certainly not on our wedding day."

He turned and paced the room, as if trying to reconcile her words to what he thought he knew of her. Perhaps they weren't so attuned to each other as they thought. Or rather, perhaps he did believe it, but just didn't want to.

"However, that leads me to my counter to your suggestion on how to 'deal with it,' as you said."

He continued pacing, but cocked his head, listening.

"You leave."

"You want me to leave my hometown? My mill?"

"It's not as if you haven't done it before," she replied. His cheeks burned at the retort, a sight she enjoyed just a little too much.

"And it's precisely why I cannot leave now. The next harvest will be here in a mere month. The Turner Grain Mill is for the first time in nearly six years operational." His gaze dropped from hers, and his eyes sought the window. "I spent too long away."

She moved forward, stood toe to toe with him. Went in for the kill.

"And you need my darling fiancé's business."

"Yes," he replied, blunt.

"Then you have a choice to make. Either you leave town, or you apologize for your actions and we can go back to pretending to not know each other. Very soon that will be the case anyway."

"You wish me to apologize?" he asked. "For what?"

She just looked at him like he was stupid, because in that moment he had to be to ask such a question.

"Why the hell should I?" he asked.

"Because this whole thing is your doing!" She rounded on him, exasperated at his stubborn, male obtuseness. "If you hadn't lied, I would not have fallen for you, and I would not have had to run when the truth came out. I would not have met Sir Barty and I would not be engaged to him now. This entire situation—which you seem so eager to blame on me—is actually all your fault."

John blinked twice, struck by her speech. "Well," he said after a moment. "I . . . ah . . . I do owe you an apology then. Hell, I owe us all one."

He caught her hand and held it still with a firm, soft grasp.

"If it means anything—anything at all—I am sorry. For your situation. For the lie itself."

"Six months ago you said you could not be sorry for lying."

"That was before I spent six months knowing you would never trust me again."

Now it was Letty's turn to blink and reel. She could handle Turner angry. She could understand him shocked and upset. But this resigned man before her, allowing a peek at his vulnerability . . .

It made the space around her heart feel queer—like a void slowly filling with a painful warmth.

No. No, stop it, Letty, she told herself. Such feelings are not allowed. Not with this man, and certainly not with the good man you are engaged to marry awaiting you downstairs.

"Thank you," she said, clearing her throat and extracting her hand. "But don't fret. Everything turned out better for me than I could have possibly hoped. It always does."

He sighed deeply and rolled his shoulders, one catching in a twinge of pain—a wound healed, but never entirely. "You won't go," he stated finally.

"And neither will you," she replied.

It hung in the air between them, echoing off the fading wallpaper. Her eyes met his, and for the first time since he'd blackmailed his way into her room, she saw something other than anger or defiance there. Something had opened in him, without him knowing it. She saw regret. She saw resignation.

She saw the question that had no answer:

What if . . . ?

Leticia was not one to contemplate the what-ifs of life. To reflect on the past wondering what could have been was an utter waste of time—and women in general did not have as much time as men to begin with. So she rushed ahead, dealing with what life threw her way, and not bothering with the road not taken.

But now, there were so many what-ifs, each one flashing across the dark brown of his eyes, it overwhelmed her.

It made her forget where she was.

Luckily, time refused to forget for her, and the little mantel clock struck the time, jumping them both back into her bedchamber.

"We are due downstairs," she said, forcing her eyes away from his.

"We still don't have a solution," he said after a moment.

"Do you honestly think we'll find one?"

He swore under his breath. "No. We will simply have to do our best to avoid each other."

"Meaning you will not interfere in my marriage to Sir Barty?" she asked, arching a brow.

"As long as you do not interfere in my business," he said. "Even if that business involves Sir Barty."

"Somehow I cannot imagine that Sir Barty will consult his bride on grain futures. But"—she held up her hand, stopping him from interrupting—"I will not influence him either way. I won't even mention your name."

He smiled. Even though she could tell he was angry, and exhausted, and a million other emotions moving over his face faster than she could count, he still managed to send a zip of feeling straight through her.

"I hate that you're here." He extended his hand. "I don't trust you."

"Likewise," she replied.

"So we avoid each other as best we can. Do we have a deal?"

She took a long, calming breath. Then took his hand and shook it. Hard.

"I think I can manage that."

9

Dear Rhys—

It is with a matter of some urgency that I write to you. Your medical knowledge is required in Helmsley, as well as your friendship. I am afraid I cannot tell you what is wrong, but make no mistake, it is serious. Please come as soon as you are able. I ask not only for your assistance but for your discretion, as matters here are of a delicate nature . . .

Turner penned a letter to his friend Dr. Rhys Gray immediately upon returning home after Sunday dinner at Bluestone Manor. It was without rancor that he wrote it. Without malice, and in fact, in the spirit of doing a good deed.

That his intent was perhaps a bit more calculated did not need to be mentioned.

Oh, the meal went well enough. After he'd left Leticia's room and found a back way to the gardens, he spent a good ten minutes there walking in circles, trying to calm his mind by remembering the Latin names of the particular violets that Margaret had pointed out (although he had been too busy straining his ears to eavesdrop on his mother and Leticia's conversation to really pay attention to the poor girl) before Margaret herself appeared, sent to fetch him in for dinner.

And all throughout the meal, he and Leticia acted with the utmost decorum, politeness, and deceit. The faces they put forth to everyone else held no hint that they knew each other, let alone that they had been in her bedchamber not twenty minutes before.

While she changed her clothes behind the world's most stubbornly opaque dressing screen and they struck their devil's bargain.

But distracting thoughts aside, Turner had to admit that Leticia seemed more than capable of holding up her end. She kept conversation to innocuous topics—the weather, their travel. Even praised Margaret for the gardens and her innovative fertilization techniques. And when the topic of the mill was brought up (as was bound to happen: as first, it was his livelihood; and second, his mother was in the room and she made damn well sure it was mentioned), the Countess of Churzy kept her smile kind, and her questions basic to keep conversation flowing before gently steering them back to more palatable topics.

Yes, she was capable of keeping up her end of the bargain.

It's just that he didn't trust her to do so. Not one bit.

How was he supposed to make certain that she didn't undermine him with Sir Barty? Other than courting Margaret, which he had no intention of doing (much to his mother's chagrin), he was not in a position to influence the man at all. But she was. And once he and his mother left that afternoon, how would he know that Letty wouldn't turn to her fiancé and immediately begin an insidious campaign against his future? He simply needed to know what was happening at Bluestone Manor at all times.

He needed a spy.

Turner had hit upon the idea midway through the meal.

"And the steam equipment—oh you should see it, Sir Barty." His mother was waxing rhapsodic. At the dining table, Sir Barty was unable to escape his mother's talk of the mill as easily as he had in the sitting room. "The furnace burns hot enough to keep all of Helmsley warm in winter . . ."

"Don't know why you bothered with steam equipment, young man," Sir Barty grumbled through bites of pork. "It's going to be nothing but a nuisance."

"Anything that makes it so I can operate every day of the year as opposed to only the windy ones will not be a nuisance, I assure you, Sir," Turner answered.

"It will be noisy and smoky, I'm told," Sir Barty replied. "No one wants that in Helmsley."

"Who on earth told you such silliness?" Helen said, trying to hide her alarm in a laugh.

"Mrs. Emory was talking about it this morning in church," Margaret had piped up. "I heard her. She wondered if coal would get into the flour, and how that would taste." She frowned. "It probably wouldn't taste very good."

"Likely not," Leticia added, before meeting Turner's eyes. "But such is the march of forward progress. Do you recall, on our way north, those young men at the inn who said they were going to Stockton to see about the railway they are building there? They use steam machinery as well, I believe."

"If I were Mrs. Emory," Margaret added, "I should not worry about coal getting into the flour."

"Quite right," Turner said.

"I should worry about the steam getting into the wheat. Nothing rots a crop faster than moisture."

Sir Barty's bushy brows went up. "She's right. That is somewhat concerning."

His mother laughed, her voice showing none of the strain Turner suddenly felt.

"It shouldn't be," she said. "Why do you think we went to the trouble of building a whole separate equipment house on the other side of the mill tower? The steam engine will never come into contact with the grain."

"It's lamentable." Sir Barty's mustache twitched in consternation. "Use a pony to pull a wheel if you need more power than the wind can provide. Why ruin what is already in place?"

"Grain mills in other parts of the country don't use wind power, they use water," Turner said abruptly. "And it has no effect on the product—"

"I'm sure you are right, darling," Leticia interrupted, smiling at Sir Barty. That smile set Turner's blood to boil. And then, in the act of smiling back at her like a lovesick puppy, Sir Barty leaned forward—and winced.

"Darling, are you all right?" Leticia immediately asked.

"Fine, m'dear, fine. Nothing remiss," he said, smiling through the furious, embarrassed flush on his face. "No need to fuss over me."

"Perhaps I like fussing over you," Leticia said. "Every man needs a woman to fuss over him, after all."

Turner nearly heaved.

"If it's your foot, you should have it on a pillow," Margaret said. "That's what the apothecary said. We should call for him."

"Margaret," her father had warned. "I can stand one woman fussing over me, but not two. And I cannot stand the apothecary. Keeps telling me to drink powders—as if something I eat or drink could do anything to my foot."

And suddenly, it popped into his head. A simple idea.

He needed someone to keep an eye on Leticia. And Sir Barty needed someone to see to his foot (which definitely needed a new dressing—Turner could smell it from down the table).

"Quite right, sir," he said. "You shouldn't trust apothecaries. Pull all your teeth out of your head before you can tell them your elbow hurts."

That garnered a bark of laughter from Sir Barty.

"I have a very good friend who is a preeminent physician, however. I'm more than happy to write to him on your behalf."

While Sir Barty politely protested, and Leticia protected his pride by saying that Sir Barty was in the pink of health, and Margaret disputed point by point how Sir Barty was not in the pink of health, the meal was somehow brought to a reasonable conclusion, with a bit of cake, minimal after-dinner conversation, and promises by the ladies to call on one another.

His mother took that as gospel, and planned to call on the countess the next day to see if she could persuade her to walk into Helmsley and meet with the local ladies—facing down the annoying Mrs. Emory in particular.

Meanwhile, his mother lamented the fact that he did not take the ladies removing themselves after dinner as an opportunity to speak privately with Sir Barty. But as Barty had not shown himself to be amenable to any more conversation about the mill, and he had no designs on Margaret, Turner was a little unsure what they would talk about. *Your fiancée is very lovely—especially that mole just above her knee. Oh, you don't know about that?*

And that would just about be the end of trying to convince Sir Barty of his mill's worthiness. Besides, Leticia had shot him a look of such condemnation he dare not dawdle with Sir Barty after the meal.

So, with his mother determined to befriend the countess, and with a pressing need to make sure that he was not being undermined . . . yes, Turner buckled under the pressure and reached out to a friend, writing Rhys a letter.

Four days later, Rhys answered it.

"What is it? What is wrong?"

Turner was on the fourth floor when he heard the voice of his old friend wafting up from below. The mill yard was awash with workers, a half dozen men putting the final bricks into place on the engine house, on the other side of the mill from the granary. They'd had the engine itself brought in first—a horizontal compound engine with pistons and cranks and flywheels—all manner of modern machinery. Once it had been assembled, the men set about building the engine house around it.

Thus Turner was the only one in the mill tower proper today. But he liked it that way. He liked tinkering with the gears, making the smallest of adjustments and checking to make sure everything was as it should be. A man who'd had his livelihood burn down twice could not be too paranoid.

The windmill tower was seven stories tall, with each level accommodating and accessing different parts of the mill machinery. From the top floor, for instance, one could access the wind shaft—the long iron bar attached to the wind sails outside—and the grooved gears of the break wheel and crown wheel, which turned with the wind. The cap of the tower would rotate, pushed by the fantail to best catch any breeze. The shafts drove power down to the millstones on the fifth floor—three different sets of sandstone and quartz, grinding against each other day in and day out, fed by the bins of grain from the sixth floor.

Or at least, they would be, when they had grain to grind. The first, second, and third floors were where the now-ground grain was separated by grind and weight, wheat and chaff. And suddenly, the bags and barrels that had brought in hard kernels of grain were full of white and brown flour.

Yes, it would be marvelous. Once they had customers. And once the sails were positioned properly, so they would turn in the wind at optimum speed. Which Turner was attempting to do from the fourth-floor balcony via the rope-and-pulley system when he heard his friend's voice.

He glanced down, and for the first time in God knows how long, smiled a true, broad smile.

Rhys was climbing down from a carriage, whose horses had been ridden very fast, if their sweaty coats were anything to judge by.

"Hello to you too, Rhys!" he called out.

"What the hell are you doing up there?" his friend called back.

Turner thought briefly about launching into an explanation about wind direction and sail positioning, but thought it might not be audible from four stories up. "I'll be right down!"

He tied off the ropes and let the windmill spin. Even when the sails were positioned into the wind, they would still turn a little bit if there was a strong enough breeze. But since they didn't have any grain to grind just yet, it was detrimental to the grindstones to have them working, so the break wheel and cross wheel were at present unattached and unturning. If they had been turning, the sound still wouldn't have been loud enough to spare Turner the scolding he was subject to now.

"John!" Rhys grabbed his arms and pulled him into a bear hug. Then he pulled back and began feeling his limbs. "No disjunction. Nothing broken, no breaks, no sprains." His hands started feeling his neck. "No swollen glands."

"This is a very odd greeting."

"No visible sores or wounds—is it an infection? Something new, perhaps?"

"Rhys, stop!" Turner said. "I'm fine!"

"Don't worry—whatever it is, we'll discover it and find the cure. There is—" He stopped suddenly. "What did you say?"

"I said I'm fine." Turner smiled. "It's very good to see you."

Turner was a different man when he was with his friends. He was allowed to be loose with Rhys. He was allowed to smile and grumble in equal measure. Only recently had he felt he could do so with his other best friend, Ned, since, when he was in the man's employ, he was forced to squash his opinions and true feelings into the role of hard-nosed secretary. And since he'd been back in Helmsley, he'd felt the weight of the town's expectations and speculation so heavily he'd automatically retreated into that same persona.

But now Rhys was here, and with him, he could be at ease. Hell, he hadn't felt this much like his true self since . . .

Since he'd sparred with Leticia in her bedchamber a few days ago.

But Rhys was talking, and turning a rather unhealthy shade of red, so perhaps he'd better pay attention to his friend.

"You're fine?" Rhys was saying.

"Fit as a fiddle," he replied. "Is that your trunk?"

Rhys glanced down at the trunk that landed next to his feet. He turned back to the driver, who had been the one to unceremoniously dump it there.

"Careful! There are several breakable glass tubes and bottles in there!"

The driver simply shrugged and climbed back onto the carriage. "Oi! Nearest place my horses and me can get a drink?"

"No, don't go yet, if you plea—"

"The Drum inn and post house, about a quarter mile back down the road," Turner replied, and stepped over to the driver, fishing a coin out of his pocket and flipping it up to the man.

The driver tipped his hat and flicked the reins, taking the poor horses toward the Drum at a blessedly slower pace than that at which they'd arrived.

When he turned back, it was to face a now-sputtering Rhys.

"You're fine."

"Physically at least," he joked. "I did not expect you to come so quickly."

"I'm afraid I'm not in a position to help with any mental problems you may have," Rhys bit out. "And what the hell else was I supposed to do? You wrote me a letter saying you were gravely ill!"

"I did not," Turner replied. Then he conceded, "Perhaps I implied it, but—"

"I thought you were dying!" he yelled.

"How else was I supposed to tear you away from your laboratory?"

"John—I wrote to Ned. And when he gets that letter he'll be on the first packet back from France."

Turner's eyebrow rose. Ned was touring the Continent with his wife, Phoebe. Phoebe wanted to see some of the world before any little Earls of Ashby were conceived and inconvenienced the ability to travel, and Ned was utterly smitten by his bride and happy to indulge her.

It's a wonder Leticia hadn't run into them in Paris. Perhaps their paths crossed in the English Channel. But no matter—the Earl of Ashby showing up in Helmsley was the last thing he needed.

"I'll write him immediately, send it express. If we're lucky it will arrive before your letter does."

Rhys scoffed, but added nothing. Then he looked about the yard, as if realizing for the first time that the carriage was long gone, and he was stuck here.

"You said you needed my help. My medical expertise."

"And I do. Just not for me," Turner said as he picked up Rhys's trunk. "What's in here?"

"Equipment. To hopefully diagnose and treat an undefined illness I thought my best friend had contracted," Rhys replied.

"It's heavy . . . oof!" Turner adjusted his weight to one foot and the trunk bobbled, sending a visible shock of panic through Rhys.

"Please be careful! Everything is custom-made to my specifications. I'll never get replacements out here!"

"Well, then, perhaps you should help me before I fall over," Turner grunted. Rhys came over and took one end of the trunk, and together they carried it across the bustling mill yard. "Come on," Turner said as soon as he was able to catch his breath. "I'll explain everything at the house."

They headed past the granary and toward the Turner home—a two-story brick structure with a slate roof in the far corner of the mill yard. The home he'd been raised in had thankfully survived two fires (the fact that it survived said fires was the reason that Turner insisted that the windmill be rebuilt with brick this time around). However, Rhys was not content to wait for explanations.

"Is someone dying, at least?"

"I'm afraid not."

"Oh," Rhys sighed, disappointed. "Then what do you need my expertise for?"

"A case of gout."

"Gout?" He glanced down at Turner's legs, his confident strength carrying his side of the trunk. "You don't have gout."

"No, but Sir Bartholomew Babcock does. And he needs your help with it."

Rhys's eyes narrowed. "Sir Bartholomew Babcock."

"Everyone calls him Sir Barty."

"Uh-huh," Rhys replied. "And Sir Barty is . . . related to royalty? A man of great importance? A man whose gout is interfering with his ability to run small nations?"

Turner barked out a laugh. "No. Local gentry."

"I've attended the queen, you know."

"I do know. And we are all impressed."

His shoulders slumped—either in resignation or from the weight of the trunk, Turner couldn't tell. "Is it at least an interesting case of gout?"

"I have no idea what an interesting case of gout would look like."

"Neither do I, and I've seen hundreds."

They reached the door of the house and were about to struggle their way through, but before they could, Turner's mother emerged, pulling on her gloves.

"What on earth are you carrying into my house?" Helen said, before looking up to see Rhys at the other end of the trunk. "Dr. Gray! What a joy to see you!"

"Lovely to see you as well, Mrs. Turner," Rhys replied, shifting the trunk so he could tip his hat. "Although why do I think it's not much of a surprise?"

"Because you always were the smartest of the lot," Helen said, reaching forward to pinch his cheek like a schoolboy. "Are you staying with us, then?"

"For tonight, yes," Turner answered for him. "But with any luck, he'll be staying at Bluestone Manor after that."

His mother's eyebrow went up, but she said nothing. "Well, then tell the girl to fix up the best guest room for him—the one that faces north. I'll be back before tea. I'm meeting Leticia in town. I never would have thought a countess would have this much trouble winning over the women of Helmsley, but they are a stubborn lot."

Before Turner could once again warn his mother against trying to be friends with Leticia, Helen maneuvered past them with a little wave, then pulled her bonnet forward to shield her eyes from the sun as she marched toward town.

"Did she just say Leticia?" Rhys asked. "A countess named Leticia?"

Turner nodded.

"It wouldn't happen to be your Leticia, would it?"

"Shockingly, it would. Leticia Herzog, the Countess of Churzy, happens to be engaged to Sir Barty. Who needs your medical expertise."

Rhys considered him for a long moment. Then he raised a hand to his chin, thoughtful.

"I think that this is going to be an interesting case of gout after all."

10

For her first full week in Helmsley, Leticia had two specific goals. Unfortunately, she had thus far failed spectacularly at both of them.

First, she was of a mind that the only way out of this predicament with Turner was through it. To that end, it would be best to move things along as quickly as possible. Which meant moving up the date of the wedding.

But here she met with her first failure. For when she attempted to talk to Sir Barty about it, he simply laughed.

"Special license? There's no need for that!"

"But darling, if we got a special license we wouldn't have to wait to be wed." She tried to say it as seductively as possible, but considering it was first thing in the morning and Sir Barty was enjoying his breakfast ham, there was little that would distract him from it.

"M'dear, to get a special license we would have to apply to the bishop, who is miles and miles away. Then, if he says yes, which he wouldn't do without inducement, the paper has to be delivered back to us! So even if we went to the trouble—and expense—of a special license, chances are the banns will be finished being read by the time the license arrives."

She could not fault him for his logic, as much as she wanted to.

"Well, what about Gretna Green?" It would only take a day or two from here to get to Scotland . . ."

"We just got out of the carriage, I cannot fathom getting back into one," Sir Barty said with a sigh. "Besides, by the time we pack to go, and get on the road, and then get married and get back, it will be our original wedding day! It seems so silly."

He came over to her chair, leaning only slightly on his cane as he did so, and placed a hand on her cheek. "I know you are eager, and so am I," he assured her with a little brow waggle. "But the wait shall be worth it, I promise."

And he returned to his ham.

Well, that was that, it seemed. But Leticia would not be cowed. Instead she moved on to her second challenge: Margaret.

"Are you headed into town?" Margaret's voice carried as she came thumping down the hall, still covered in dirt from the garden where she'd been since dawn.

"Yes. Would you like me to get you anything?" Leticia replied.

"No," replied Margaret. "In fact, you should wait until tomorrow, when it's market day."

"I'm returning a call, waiting until market day would not do."

While Turner seemed happy to avoid her like the plague, Helen had pestered her where her son had not. She had called on Monday, and sent a note on Tuesday, inviting Leticia to tea with her on Thursday. Really, Leticia was afraid the woman would turn up and force her to join a tatting circle if she didn't show.

"But if you went on market day I could go with you and . . . run into people."

"Run into people?" Leticia asked, and watched as Margaret blushed furiously, shifting from foot to foot in an awkward dance. "What, with a cart?"

"No!" Margaret cried, her brow coming down. "Just, run into people, on the street. People that we know, and that would tip a hat to us . . . or, or . . . kiss a hand possibly."

Ah. Now Leticia understood. "Someone like Mr. Turner, perhaps?"

The blush that burned on Margaret's face was all the answer she needed. And while Turner had said he had no interest in Margaret, the fact was, Margaret was utterly unaware of it.

There would be several intricate dances necessary to make Leticia and Margaret's relationship what she hoped it would be, but right now, the most important was to convince Margaret that Turner was not at all an appropriate match.

Luckily, Leticia had just the right kind of finesse.

"The call I'm paying is on Mrs. Turner," she said. "I'm sure her son will be there." In truth, Leticia prayed he wouldn't be. "If you would like to join me, you could change and—"

"*No!*" Margaret cried. Then, calmer, "No. I, ah . . . I will see her on market day, I'm sure."

"There's no reason you could not see Mr. Turner two days in a row, Margaret. After all, for affection to flourish, a young couple needs to be near each other."

"I know that, but . . ." She bit her lip. "Well, men go to war or to sea all the time and they still have sweethearts."

"Yes, but . . . their affection is already established."

"So is mine for Mr. Turner."

"Because he makes you blush."

Margaret nodded.

"But do you make him blush?" she asked, for once seemingly giving the girl pause. "An indicator of affection from a young man would be calling on a lady quite often. And Mr. Turner hasn't called on you since Sunday. He is . . . conspicuous in his absence."

Margaret seemed happy to ignore that statement, as she simply said, "I'm sorry, but I have things to do today," and trotted out the door to the gardens and her beloved soil.

Or so Leticia had thought.

It was after dinner that evening. Sir Barty had claimed that his leg was bothering him, and thus once the pork stew was consumed, made for his library, his footstool, and a bit of brandy by the fire. Leticia fully expected Margaret to stand and leave without more than a perfunctory "excuse me," as had been her custom. So when Sir Barty made his exit, Leticia made hers to the sitting room.

She was just about to begin drafting a letter to her sister (she would say everything was utterly wonderful, and absolutely nothing else) when a voice from the doorway stilled her hand.

"Theoretically," Margaret said. "If one wanted to make Mr. Tur—I mean, someone blush when they saw one, how would one go about it?"

Margaret had her arms crossed over her chest, her tall frame hunched over and protective. But she was here. She had opened up to her in a way that warmed Leticia's heart.

It made her almost sorry for what she had to do.

But really, it was in everyone's best interests. Especially Margaret's.

"You've come to the right place," Leticia said, smiling

widely, turning away from the desk and moving to the settee in the center of the room. "When it comes to matters of the heart, I have had some experience."

"Not experience with Mr. Turner," Margaret grumbled.

Leticia became very still. "No, of course not. I never met him before this week."

"I mean with men like Mr. Turner. He's . . . different from Father."

"Yes, it is true that I am used to dealing with men of a certain refinement. But most men, I've found, are the same."

"He's not," Margaret said defensively. "Most men ignore me. He gave me that violet."

Yes, he had given her the violet. And done more harm than good, she thought jealously.

No . . . not jealousy. Of course not jealousy. That was ridiculous.

"But . . ." Margaret had continued. "I haven't seen him blush. Ever. Such a physiological reaction should be as important if not more so than a voluntary action like giving a flower. One can have ulterior motives for flower giving, but not blushing. Although, he did seem to go excessively pale upon seeing us at church this past Sunday—"

"Be that as it may," Leticia said loudly, interrupting. "Men do not blush as readily as women. That is simply how it is. But there are other ways to be certain of a man's regard." She paused. "And ways to increase a man's regard."

Margaret's eyes were wide, as if Leticia were revealing the secrets of increasing an orchard's yield threefold. "I have a hypothesis as to what it is."

"By all means, tell me."

"In this scenario, we meet entirely by chance in a public place. Possibly market day or church. And then while in conversation with someone else entirely he'll come up to me and . . ."

"Yes . . ."

"I press a hand to my forehead . . . and I faint."

"What?" Leticia cried. "No!"

"But . . . I was told that fainting, when done right, is a way to attract a man."

"Whoever told you that is a fool," Leticia replied.

"Oh . . ." was the only sound that came out of Margaret's mouth, small and broken. Immediately, Leticia reached out her hand to cover Margaret's. But the girl just shifted out of reach.

"Perhaps fainting worked once for your friend, but it is not something that works for ninety-nine out of a hundred. It's terribly hard to do without looking like it's faked, and that just makes the man think of the lady as possibly ill. No man wants a woman who is ill, not matter how romantic the books make it seem."

"Really?" Margaret's eyes were still downcast. Leticia suspected there was something slightly watery about them. But really, if she went and fainted in front of Turner—crumpled to a heap in front of him, because goodness knows she would not have the elegance to swoon with grace—then it was very likely he would act, and then Margaret would really be in his thrall.

So she softened her voice, and held up her hands.

"Look at me. I have never in my life fainted, and I do not intend to ever do so. And certainly will not in front of any man."

Margaret looked up, one suspicious eyebrow raised.

"And I've still managed to attract two very eligible husbands . . ." Leticia let the idea hang in the air. "But by all means, if you think fainting is the right course of action, shall we implement it in the churchyard next week?"

Margaret chewed that over for a few seconds. Leticia counted in her mind. Three . . . two . . . one . . .

"Just for the sake of argument, what would your suggestion be?"

Leticia tried very hard to not smile like a cat that got the cream.

"Ignore him."

Margaret jerked back. "Ignore him?"

"Yes. Assiduously avoid him. If you seem him in Helmsley, barely glance his way. At church, no more than a nod. And never invite him to view your gardens, or to take tea with us."

Margaret's brows were a pyramid of skepticism. "I thought you said that if I wanted to make him like me I needed to spend time with him."

"It's not about making him like you. It's about making him think about you. He will see that you are utterly uninterested in him, and he will be mad with curiosity trying to figure out why. All men think of themselves as inherently interesting. So interesting that we poor women cannot help wanting to be in their presence."

For young ladies skilled at flirtation, this was actually a well-used tactic. But as Margaret was not skilled at flirtation, it was doomed to failure. Not to mention, Turner would barely give the girl a second thought. "You can even show interest in other men—that would really set his blood to boil."

"What other men?" Margaret asked, her nose wrinkling.

She put her chin in her hand, pretending to think. "Perhaps eligible gentlemen in Helmsley are thin on the ground, but there must be some of your acquaintance . . . Usually young ladies take a trip to London for cultivating said acquaintances."

Margaret, deep in thought, still managed to shake her head decisively. Well, it really had been too much to hope for, but she'd had to try.

"Regardless, if you ignore him, he will spend ages trying to figure out why, and then his mind will be consumed with you. So much so that he will be unable to stop himself from approaching you. Wherein you ignore him again, and again . . . until he professes his love for you."

That bit might have been pushing her luck, but Margaret seemed to absorb everything she said.

"For how long? Do I ignore him, I mean."

"For as long as it takes," Leticia answered with determination. "It might take a week, it might take a month . . . it might take several months. But if you hold tight to your resolve, it will work. He will come to you. And . . . he will be blushing when he does so."

"Has it . . . has it worked for you?"

Leticia's grin widened. "It has." Not with Turner though. He would have seen straight through her, as he always did. Instead, she thought back to how well she had played the scene in Paris with Sir Barty. Being open, approachable, and then, not giving him her direction. Not being pushy. Seemingly happy on her own. Granted it wasn't exactly ignoring, but the principle was the same. "And it took less than a day."

Margaret had nodded, her face taking on that concentration reserved only for when she was headed out to the gardens, contemplating a particular problem and its potential solution. And Leticia knew she had made an impression on the girl.

But she couldn't be certain. Either that Margaret would choose to not faint into the dirt in front of God, Mr. Turner, and Helmsley, or if she did ignore him, that its effects would be as abysmal as Leticia hoped. Therefore, she would have to break her word to Turner and involve Sir Barty in the matter.

It's not as if this had anything to do with business, she thought by way of justification. This was about matters of the heart—specifically Sir Barty's daughter's. And if there was anything the man should know about his daughter, it was her duty as his future wife to tell him.

"I'm going into Helmsley tomorrow. Helen is taking me around for market day," she said, approaching Sir Barty in his library. The plan had been formed while they drank tea in Helen's small parlor. Well, Helen formed the plan and Leticia could think of no way around it, as Sir Barty would not go and Margaret was not one for making introductions.

True to form, he had his foot up, and a second helping of dinner balanced on his stomach. Cook, having been pleased by pleasing the countess, was trotting out every single local Lincolnshire recipe she could find. There were pork chops, pork loin, pork sausage, pork pies, and even the occasional pork in cream sauce. Leticia ate them all enthusiastically, while secretly determining the need to find and hire a good pastry chef, to provide some lighter fare (and yes, sweet tarts would be lighter compared to this).

"Hmm," Sir Barty said as a reply. "Good. Helen knows everyone in town."

"I confess, I am looking forward to making friends with new people. I do not think our society should be limited to the Turners."

"It's not, my dear," Sir Barty said. "But Helen will be able to introduce you to others. Properly. I know that ladies have their own way of doing things."

"Yes . . ." she mused, putting her finger to her chin. "It's simply that we see so much of Helen. And of course you know why."

"Yes," Sir Barty sighed. "The mill. Helen is determined about it. Truth is, I'm more than happy to have my tenants take their business there if it's more profitable, but I hear such terrible rumors about this new equipment . . . m'dear, you shouldn't worry your head about such business. You should be focused on the wedding, and getting to know the town. Helen is your friend and mine, regardless of the mill. Her son too."

"Yes. Her son too." Leticia nodded in agreement. "Although there should be no need for them to call so much if that is the situation with the mill."

Turner of course hadn't called at all, but that didn't bear mentioning.

"Hmm," Sir Barty replied. "Whatever you think, m'dear."

"I just hope this doesn't affect Margaret. She's bound to be disappointed."

"Hmm," Sir Barty hummed. Then, her words penetrated his ear hair and made their way to his brain. "Margaret? How could it affect her?"

"Surely you're aware of Margaret's feelings?" Leticia placed a hand to her breast, the picture of ladylike shock.

"Her feelings?"

"For Mr. Turner. She fancies herself in love with him."

"She does?" His white eyebrows rose in surprise, for once showing his eyes completely.

"Yes. Of course, I've tried to tell her it's inappropriate, and that perhaps some time in London would do her good, meeting new people, seeing new things but—"

"Why?" he interrupted.

"Why, what?" she asked.

"Why would it be inappropriate?" he replied.

"Well . . ." She blushed. "I hate to be indelicate, darling, but you are a gentleman of some note, and he . . . he is a simple miller."

But much to Leticia's surprise, he shrugged that off. "Mr. Turner was an officer during the war—a captain. He has the friendship of an earl—the Earl of Ashley or something."

"Ashby," Leticia said under her breath.

"And the Braithwaites are landed gentry—or were, a few generations ago. Mr. Turner's heritage is not so very low. And besides . . ."

But Sir Barty hesitated.

"Besides?" Leticia prodded.

"Well, would it be so very bad a thing to have Margaret marry someone in Helmsley? And not have to go to London?"

"Darling, if it is the expense of London that worries you, I promise—"

"It's not that." Sir Barty shook his head. "It's just that Margaret has always liked plants and books better than people. Tossing her into the fray of a London season . . . I just don't want her to be disappointed."

Leticia found her heart breaking—just a little—for her fiancé. He did love his daughter. He just had no idea what to do about her.

"Darling, surely you see that it's not at all the thing . . ."

"'The thing' doesn't really matter up here," he countered. "Why are you so against the idea?"

"Because . . ." Because it's preposterous to think that my ex-lover would be my new stepson-in-law?

But that wasn't it. Life was filled with that kind of preposterousness, and it was borne by the people involved and eventually laughed at by them too. This was different . . . having Turner so close was . . .

Disconcerting.

Sir Barty chuckled. "I think you are simply angling for a trip to London," he twinkled at her. "Don't worry, m'dear,

I think we can bear the expense of you going to London for wedding clothes. As long as the dress doesn't cost too much, of course."

"It's not that," Leticia replied, flustered. Goodness, her entire argument was falling apart right before her eyes. "It's—"

"How does he feel about her?" Sir Barty asked. "Do you have any idea?"

"I . . . I do not think he has yet formed an opinion."

"I shall have to ask Helen about it," Sir Barty mused.

"No!" Leticia cried. "Er, that is . . . I'll speak to Helen about it. It's something for ladies to discuss."

"Do," Sir Barty replied as he took and kissed her hand. "I tell you, m'dear, if I could see Margaret so easily settled, and so close to home, I should happily give over my business to the Turner Grain Mill."

And it was as if the clouds parted and the sun appeared behind Sir Barty's eyes.

Oh dear.

"Say . . . do you think that would be a worthy inducement?"

"An . . . inducement?"

"Well, the promise of my business with the grain mill . . . it would make an interesting dowry, don't you think?"

As Sir Barty began to scheme ways to mix his daughter's happiness with his agricultural ventures, Leticia resisted the urge to put her head down on the table and laugh. Or cry. It seemed even when she did try to influence Sir Barty, she managed to influence him in the wrong direction!

Perhaps she had managed to steer Margaret slightly away from Turner (only time would tell whose plan the child would enact—the suggested ignoring or her own fainting), but if Sir Barty was of a mind to hand his daughter off to the man who had once been her lover . . . well, could even Turner's morality stand up to a father-approved marriage for money?

After all, his morality had led him to make a wager to save his mill. If he decided that Margaret was what he needed for its success, they might end up closer than they ever had been before.

They might end up . . . family.

Oh hell.

11

When Leticia had initially learned about her first husband, Konrad—about his secret life—she discovered that under times of extreme duress she had the unfortunate tendency to break out in hives. She could smile serenely. She could laugh and converse and be everything outwardly a countess was meant to be. Except . . .

It began with an itch. Near the mole just above her knee, a place no lady would ever scratch in public. She suppressed it, taking long deep breaths, and in the space of a few long seconds it would go away. Then, when whispers reached her ears—whispers she couldn't make out but she was certain were about her—the itch would travel. Her elbow. The hairline just behind her ear.

And it would grow.

Just a touch, a bit of pressure with the side of her nail, surely wouldn't do any harm. And it would bring some much-needed relief. But when she did let her nail cut into that small spot, the itch grew wider. And then the red spots popped up, as if they were waiting for that one small break in decorum to declare themselves.

People would wonder if she was at all well. If she had not contracted some violent illness. Soon enough people were not whispering about her, but speaking out loud.

It was because of this that Konrad took her away to the country for the first time. He kissed her on the forehead (one of the few hive-free spots) and told her he did love her—as much as he could love any woman. But it wasn't enough of a love to make him give up everything else he loved.

Everyone else.

He told her then how it would be between them. That he would give her the best of all possible lives. His title was as old as some countries, and he was related to every great house in Europe. Even if his secret was badly kept, there were enough people impressed by his pedigree to keep them in invitations. Really, since she was a miller's daughter with little more than good looks and a better dowry to recommend her, she could hardly dream of more.

Still, the disappointment, the shift from the fairy tale to the reality, had little red welts popping up all over her body. And the desire to tear her skin off was almost as strong as the need to shed that skin for another one. A stronger one.

Konrad had married her for a reason. She was clever, yes. But more than that, she was practical. He taught her how to ignore people's whispers and bury her disappointment along with her own desires. She taught herself how to keep calm in the face of even the most alarming rumors. A storm was little more than a gust of wind, if one knew how to face it. Nothing and no one was ever allowed to cause her distress again. They could try. But they would fail.

When they went back to London a few months later, she no longer worried over Konrad's social habits, his friendships. His late-night visits to parts of town that were never spoken of among ladies. Instead she smiled, and breathed. And never felt that itch under her skin again.

Not even when her former lover appeared in the same town of the gentleman she was going to marry.

Not even when faced with the various plots Sir Barty rambled on about over his morning ham to have his daughter marry said former lover.

And not even when staring down the town of Helmsley itself.

Somehow, some way, she had gotten off on the wrong foot with the town—with its ladies in particular. Who knew one little mention of buying wedding clothes in London would destroy any chance of ingratiating herself? Didn't everyone buy their wedding clothes in London?

But no, something else had made the ladies close ranks. Made them dislike her. And why? She'd wondered, a frown crossing her brow. She was a nice person. Incredibly nice. Approachable, even being so polished. More polished than most of these country folk in Helmsley had ever seen. They were far more concerned with making sure their crops came in well that summer than they were with Sir Barty's love life, so why on earth would they bother taking a dislike to her?

"Because they're silly women who can take no adjustment to their little worlds," Helen said as they made their way down the rows of stalls. "It's why they don't like the idea of the new steam equipment for the mill either."

Leticia had met Helen in Helmsley for market day, Margaret in tow and in her second-best dress. This one was such a dull color it made dirt look boring, but at least it concealed her ankles.

Helmsley was one of a ring of market towns around the famed Lincolnshire Wolds, a particularly picturesque tract of land near the east coast of England. The town had a central square, which was flanked on one side by St. Stephen's churchyard. Around the other sides of the square were shops, pubs, and tearooms, with streets leading out at the four corners, winding down to houses, and then farther out, to farms. And one road winding out to the entrance to town and the grand windmill of the Turner Grain Mill that stood there.

Normally, Helen told her, the town of Helmsley was home to a few hundred people at most—but on market days the population swelled with the farmers who brought vegetables and livestock to be sold, their wives baking sweets and tarts to fill out their stalls. The beekeepers plied their honey, and there was even a fishmonger who brought in his catch from the nearby stocked ponds—if you got there early enough, you could have fresh fish on your table that night, and not be relegated to salted.

And of course, there was pork. In every conceivable itineration.

Add to that the customers for these goods coming from the surrounding areas, as well as a few summertime tourists, and the town of Helmsley was filled to brimming with country life. And all this country life was centered in the town square.

As, that day, were the ladies of Helmsley.

"But, as narrow minded as they may be, they are what passes for company in this part of the world . . . and you can't look a gift fourth for cards in the mouth, is what I always say." Helen smirked and upped her brisk pace through the market stalls. "Although, do not ask Mrs. Emory about her locket. She will never stop talking about it if given first opportunity."

Leticia would have rather dawdled. She found the marketplace to be charming in its way. She was not used to the quaintness of a rural community. Growing up, her father's timber mill was a bastion of smoke and sawdust, the entire scene painted gray. And while she lived under her sister's roof for her teenage years, she was ever trying to shake off the coal dust from her parentage, and Fanny was trying to stand on tiptoes above everyone else, as the new lady of the area. Thus mixing with the more mundane of town life simply wasn't done.

And with Konrad, everything had been sparkle and glamour . . . or, during their fallow periods, pain and despair.

But here in Helmsley, with the sunshine warming the red and gold bricks of the buildings, carts and hay wagons jumbling over the cobblestones, and men and women calling out their wares from their market stalls, Leticia felt both entertained and a part of it all.

Helen caught her dawdling over a stall that sold fresh flowers (and trying to keep her eyes from watering—she was determined that constant exposure would inure her to the worst of Lincolnshire's effects on her), and came back around with a smile. "You should have seen this place six years ago, when my Mr. Turner was alive . . . when the mill was up and running." Helen sighed. "Twice as many stalls, because all the farmers around would be coming into town with their wheat crop. More people to sell to. Now, people shop in Claxby or Fennish Moor or Frosham, because they have to go there anyway with their grain. But soon . . ."

Pure determination gleamed in Helen's eyes. Leticia got the impression that if the woman could turn the sails of the mill through will alone, the Turner Grain Mill would be able to pulverize all the grain in England in a single week.

She was very much like her son in that respect.

"I have a feeling that Margaret would be able to discourse quite well with the flower sellers," she said, nodding toward the flower booth they had just left. "Should we fetch her?"

"No," Leticia said, smiling. "She's already run ahead to the fishmonger."

Margaret's eagerness for market day had been twofold—to see Mr. Turner (or not see him, if she took Leticia's advice) and to get the makings for her special fertilizer tea. "Fresh fish heads," she'd said with relish, "are the most potent ingredient."

"She's a very bright girl," Helen was saying. "Did I tell you how much my son enjoyed this past Sunday afternoon's visit?"

"Yes, you have." Over tea yesterday, it must have come up only a few dozen times.

"He'd hoped to come into the village with us today," Helen said, and Leticia held back a disbelieving scoff. "However there were a few things he had to deal with. But I imagine Margaret will be seeing my son soon." Helen's eyebrow waggled.

"Hmm . . ." was all that Leticia managed. She worried about Margaret seeing Turner, but she worried more about Sir Barty hearing of it if they did chance to meet.

But before she could ask any questions, Helen had begun waving madly to someone across the square.

"What sort of things are keeping him?" she asked, trying to recall Helen's attention from whomever had her so distracted.

"A friend of his has come to visit, and he wanted to introduce him to Sir Barty."

Panic shot down Leticia's spine. Turner was with Sir Barty? Now? Without her there to stop him from saying something to him about her?

Not that he would say anything, she reasoned with herself. They had made an agreement. She just had to remind herself of that every time the fear rose in her throat.

She was about to inquire as to who this friend was

(heaven help her if it was the Earl of Ashby), but Helen continued.

"And there was the incident at the mill last night."

"Incident? What—"

"Oh, Mrs. Emory! There you are!"

Helen took Leticia's arm and dragged her through the crowd and to the door of a tearoom that stood on the corner, the Blessed Thistle. Forcing Leticia to catch up, in more ways than one.

"Mrs. Turner," Mrs. Emory said, startled. She'd had her back turned when she heard her name called, standing in a circle with three other ladies. "And Lady Churzy," she finished with a stiff curtsy.

The other three ladies stood frozen in shock. One of them began fanning herself with a straw fan (although it was a perfectly breezy day), as if completely atwitter at this meeting.

Really, if this is what passed for dramatics in Helmsley, Leticia had plenty to teach them.

"Mrs. Emory." Leticia gave a slow, gracious curtsy. A countess curtsy, she decided, was best used on the likes of Mrs. Emory. As much as she wanted to be accepted by the ladies of the town, it was always best to play from a place of power, and she preferred to move the first chess piece.

Mrs. Emory, for her part, seemed impressed. Her mouth tightening, she turned to the other ladies around her. "I do not know if you were introduced to Mrs. Robertson, Mrs. Spilsby, and her sister, Miss Goodhue."

The three ladies murmured greetings, with the overheated Miss Goodhue devolving into a flurry of giggles.

"Helen," Mrs. Emory began, making a concerned pout out of her features. "I see you wasted no time."

"No time?" Helen replied through a gritted smile.

"Well, after last night!" Mrs. Emory fanned herself. "I

should have thought that you would be pulling your things out of the rubble of your mill!"

"Rubble?" Leticia interjected, alarmed. "Was Mr. Turner— or anyone—hurt?"

"Lord no!" Helen said, her hand biting into Leticia's arm. "It was just a bit of air in the equipment. Made a loud noise is all."

"I'm surprised you did not hear it, my lady," Mrs. Emory said with a smirk. "It echoed through the entire town. I was afraid it was another fire. Like the last one—it nearly jumped the mill wall into the town. I've never been so frightened."

"Bluestone Manor's estate is so large, we are rather far from town. Like I told Sir Barty, I can hear neither row nor rumor," Leticia answered, and enjoyed watching Mrs. Emory's relish dry up like water in the desert. Luckily, before Leticia could further ruin the entire enterprise, Helen stepped in.

"I'm so glad we ran into you, though," she said, her voice affecting a breathlessness that wasn't there before. "Lady Churzy was just telling me that she's desperate to look at some of the latest fashion plates for her wedding clothes and I knew that you must have the very newest magazines."

"I . . . I have," Mrs. Emory said, blinking. "They are in the shop."

"Oh, so you are the town's milliner?" Leticia asked smiling.

"No," Mrs. Emory replied, aghast. Then, after Helen cleared her throat, her eyes flashed and she continued. "I own the millinery shop," she corrected. "But ever since my son Harold has become so very successful in the navy, I have hired my dear friend Mrs. Robertson to run the shop, not to mention purchased the entire building in which it resides." She waved a hand proudly toward the building they were standing in front of. One door down from the tearoom was a storefront with dresses on mannequins in the windows.

"That is quite fortunate," Leticia said kindly. "You must be quite proud of your son."

"Of course I'm proud of him," Mrs. Emory puffed up, her eyes getting remote and teary. "I could only wish that he did not have to find work so far away, and so dangerous. But his work in Helmsley was cruelly taken . . ." She shot a look at Helen, who barely contained a roll of her eyes. Mrs. Emory turned back to Leticia. "Would you like to see a picture of my darling Harold? Here he is, in his uniform . . ."

She opened up the locket at her neck, and showed what Leticia could only assume was a very generous portrait of Harold Emory—no son of a dressmaker could have that many epaulets without some artistic license.

"He's just so handsome," Mrs. Emory was saying on a sigh when Helen cleared her throat and Leticia forced the topic back to those present.

"Quite. I ask about the millinery because I have some wedding clothes to order."

Mrs. Emory did not take kindly to having her reminisces interrupted. Her eyes became steely as she snapped the locket shut.

"But I thought you were going to go to London for your wedding clothes," she said.

"Oh, I don't know," Leticia mused. "London is so terribly far. Besides, those dresses in the window are quite smart. Mrs. Robertson, I believe you are a hidden gem."

"Thank you, my lady!" Mrs. Robertson said, fluttering. Leticia noticed for the first time that Mrs. Robertson's dress was particularly well constructed. It was a calico pattern, but the material was lined up so perfectly at the seams the pattern remained unbroken. A hidden gem, indeed. "Those are actually of my own design."

"Are they really?" Leticia asked, her face breaking wide. "How marvelous."

"Moira!" Mrs. Emory shushed. She cleared her throat, trying to regain the high ground. "Moira, why don't you go fetch the magazines? I'm sure the countess would like to compare our country styles to what she saw in Paris."

Mrs. Robertson shuffled off, while Mrs. Emory turned back to Leticia.

"I am afraid I do not know where your people are from, my lady. Churzy is a European title, isn't it? Not proper English?"

"My late husband was Austrian, yes. But my people come from Manchester."

"Manchester!" Miss Goodhue piped up. "Do you know the Goodhues of Manchester? They are our cousins."

"I'm afraid I left Manchester quite young," Leticia replied.

"Oh." Miss Goodhue looked downcast. "Well, if you should ever go back and require a solicitor, I'm sure they would give you a good rate."

Leticia shot a glance to Helen, who shrugged. Even Mrs. Emory looked aghast at this mention of things as menial as money.

"Miss Goodhue came with her sister when she married," Helen said, providing introductions no one else would. "She is the teacher at the local school."

"I have fourteen boys and girls, up to age twelve!" Miss Goodhue said, pinking, then fanning herself again. As someone so excitable, perhaps it was good she brought the fan out even on a temperate day like this.

"And you've already met Mrs. Spilsby's husband,"

Helen piped up. "He's the vicar at St. Stephen's. He'll officiate your wedding . . . and possibly others as well!"

Leticia ignored the hopeful comment and instead turned her smile onto Mrs. Spilsby.

"If you are the vicar's wife and the schoolteacher, between the two of you I imagine you know absolutely everyone in Helmsley."

Mrs. Emory cleared her throat, but no comment was made.

"Everyone in need, that is," Leticia added. "Myself included, as I happen to find myself in need—of a good baker."

"Is Bluestone Manor's cook not up to your Continental standards?" Mrs. Emory said haughtily. "I'm sure she will be mortified to hear it."

And if it was up to Mrs. Emory, she would hear it from her. But Leticia simply smiled, knowing the board and all its pieces.

"Oh, Cook is a marvel! But she will be utterly overwhelmed with everything for the wedding breakfast, so we decided it might be best to hire someone to bake the wedding cake. But Cook tells me there is no bakery in Helmsley."

"It's quite true, my lady," Mrs. Spilsby said, as if just realizing it. "There is no bakery."

"Well, who would buy bread from a town without a working flour mill?" Mrs. Emory added, and sent a pointed smile to Helen, who barely managed one in return.

"Perhaps Rebecca . . ." Mrs. Spilsby was saying to her sister. "She's the butcher's daughter, she makes their meat pies."

"Oh yes!" Miss Goodhue agreed. "She moved on from school a few years ago, but she was always bringing in little pies and cakes for me. Trying to curry my favor instead of learning her vocabulary." Miss Goodhue giggled again.

Leticia looked to where Mrs. Spilsby nodded, and noticed that two doors down from the millinery, after a print shop, there was a butcher's on the corner. And all four businesses, including the Blessed Thistle, were housed in the same three-story red brick building along the east side of the market square. A building that Mrs. Emory owned.

No wonder Mrs. Emory was so focused on patronage of the town—she had her own tenants, and her success was tied to theirs.

"Do you think the butcher can spare Rebecca?" Mrs. Emory said. It wasn't a question.

Apparently she seemed to think she owned the people who worked in those shops too.

"Let's find out," Leticia said, keeping her focus on Mrs. Spilsby, even as Mrs. Emory turned a terribly mottled color. "Would you be so good as to introduce me to this Rebecca?"

Mrs. Spilsby and Miss Goodhue both lit up, and were about to nod, when Mrs. Emory burst in between them.

"Perhaps later would be best," Mrs. Emory said. "Look, here is Mrs. Robertson with the fashion magazines."

They turned, and saw a breathless Mrs. Robertson clutching the packet of papers to her chest. "I've put my favorite plates on the top," she said. "And I think the second one would make a truly lovely wedding gown, especially on your elegant frame, my lady. I have some lace from—"

"MOIRA."

Mrs. Robertson stopped immediately and backed away. She held out the packet of papers to Leticia. "Er, please feel free to look over them as long as you like."

And with a curtsy, Mrs. Robertson stepped back in line behind Mrs. Emory.

"We are terribly late for an appointment." Mrs. Emory indicated the tearoom behind them. "So, another time."

"We intend to stop into the Blessed Thistle ourselves in a bit," Helen said. "I know Lady Churzy wants to see more of the town, but soon enough we will be famished. Perhaps we shall see you there."

"We won't be staying long," Mrs. Emory replied, cold. "It's market day—everyone has so much to do. But perhaps you and I should enjoy a visit on a later date, Lady Churzy. I take callers in my apartments on Tuesdays." Mrs. Emory let it hang in the air. Then, with a curtsy, and a "Mrs. Turner," and "my lady," she swept away, dragging the three other ladies in her wake.

Leaving a fuming Helen and a strangely amused Leticia.

"Well, that seems like some sort of concession," Leticia mused.

"Concession my foot!" Helen fumed. "She wants you to call on her. Meeting in the street for informal conversation is not enough. This way, she can tell everyone the Countess of Churzy came to her parlor. And did you hear what she said about the mill?"

"And all the ladies of the town are in her thrall because she . . . controls their rents? You'll have to forgive me for disliking her, but . . . I really dislike her," Leticia said on a laugh.

"And what she doesn't realize is that your disliking her is far more detrimental than her disliking you. Or me."

"There seems to be more to her animosity than my mention of London fashions." In fact, Leticia mused as she thumbed through the fashion plates in her hand, Mrs. Robertson had a good eye. The second gown in the packet would make an excellent wedding dress.

"She's a jumped-up woman, aiming to rise higher, and you have unwittingly provided a ceiling."

"How so?"

"She was a dressmaker, and now she's a woman of property. She has all the time in the world to get into other people's business. She started a ladies' meeting, and appointed herself their leader. But it's hard to be the queen bee when there's a countess around." Helen laughed. "Besides, she had aspirations of a title herself, and you stole that."

"She . . . she had designs on Sir Barty?" Leticia asked, aghast.

"A rich, titled widower? Half the county had designs on Sir Barty, my girl!" Helen replied, then patted her arm. "Don't worry, you didn't steal him away from anyone. Sir Barty's been very much the lonely bachelor. And I would know—I've been his friend longer than anyone. If there was anyone who did stand a chance with him, it might well have been me, but that would never happen."

"Why wouldn't it?" Leticia asked suddenly. Sir Barty and Helen seemed quite close, for all their dancing around the business of the mill. If ever there was ripe ground for blooming affection . . .

But Helen's eyes grew inscrutable, and her gaze long. "I was . . . I was very happy with my husband. And I was very close with Barty's late wife. I suppose we thought it wouldn't feel right."

There were things unsaid, but Leticia decided to leave them that way, and not to prod further. Because she suddenly understood who Mrs. Emory was.

She was Leticia. When Leticia was nineteen, and trying to step out into the world. Trying to prove herself worthy of . . . something. And trying to hold on with both talons to her station, no matter how tenuous.

"So is that why Mrs. Emory dislikes you too? Because of your friendship with Sir Barty?"

"No." Helen sighed. "When the mill burned—for the first time—her son, Harold, lost his job. We said we'd hire everyone back as soon as we were back on our feet, but he decided to join the navy instead. Mrs. Emory has been bereft without her son since."

"But if her son has done so well in the navy, then—"

"Exactly, yet still she maintains her dislike. Her maid, Wendra, lives in, and she has two parlors. And it's not as if Harold was a particularly good worker—he was late more often than not, and lazy. I imagine it's harder to be late and lazy though if you are on a ship and will be flogged for not fulfilling your duties," Helen surmised.

Leticia's eyebrows went up. Apparently the ladies of Helmsley did grudges and dramatics better than she had initially thought.

"But just wait until my son opens the mill back up, and hires a dozen men in this town. And brings in people from far and wide on market days. Then Mrs. Emory will have to stop with her foolishness and act her age. Which is far more advanced than she'll admit," Helen said, anticipating her triumph. "But I will let him tell you all about it."

Helen nodded to just behind Leticia. She pivoted, and saw Turner approaching. No, not approaching. Nothing so timid. He was moving idly, but the path seemed to clear before him, putting him fully in her vision.

"I knew he would make time to come today. Oh, but where is Margaret?" the older woman said, casting about in the crowd.

"She's still at the fishmonger's stall," Leticia murmured, not taking her eyes off Turner. It was as if seeing him was dangerous, but not seeing him was even more so.

"Shall I go fetch her?" Helen murmured to herself. "I should go fetch her. Wait here for us, please, my lady— Leticia." And with that Helen disappeared into the crowd, hurrying toward the fishmonger.

Leaving Leticia to face Turner alone. In the middle of a crowded market.

"Mr. Turner," she said, keeping her expression neutral. Uncaring, even. Taking note of their surroundings, Turner managed a quick bow before replying.

"Already sent my mother fleeing, Letty?"

"It is not I who have her running. And I would remind you that we are in a public forum."

"Would you rather I shouted your name, or would you rather tell me where my mother went?" he said, stopping himself from crossing his arms over his chest.

Leticia sighed. "She went to fetch Margaret. She is determined to see you tuck another flower behind the girl's ear."

"Yes. I've heard more than enough talk of that today."

"From Sir Barty, you mean," Leticia concluded, and Turner nodded.

"It was . . . quite strange."

Leticia was at a bit of a loss to explain Sir Barty's sudden enthusiasm for matching his only daughter to a lowly miller, so she simply ignored his unasked question and instead asked her own. "What I find strange is that you were at Bluestone at all. Talking to Sir Barty. Without me there."

"I have spoken to Sir Barty dozens of times without you."

"Before me. And we have an agreement."

He held up one hand, causing her to stop, and remember her surroundings. She pasted her best countess smile on her face and gave him a cool nod to proceed.

"Don't worry. I wasn't there talking about you," he said. "You did not even enter the conversation. I'm a man of my word."

"Then why were you there?"

"Sir Barty's foot."

She blinked. "His foot?"

"My friend Dr. Gray is in town and he looked at Sir Barty's foot. In fact, Rhys will be staying at Bluestone for the next few weeks. Sir Barty insisted."

A trickle of cold ran down Leticia's spine. She remembered Dr. Gray. He had been at her sister's house, the day she had learned about the Lie. In fact, he was the one who brought it to light.

So there was yet another person in Helmsley who knew about their past. And he was on Turner's side. Wonderful.

Turner was looking at her with a bit too much glee in his eyes for her liking, so she shifted the topic of conversation.

"I am told that there was a mishap at your mill last night."

His gaze immediately shuttered. "A piece of steam equipment was not sealed properly and it blew apart. I would not call it a mishap."

"Oh? It was on purpose then?"

"Not on my purpose—perhaps on someone else's."

Her gaze flew up to his. "You mean . . . sabotage?" She kept her voice low. "That's horrid! Are you all right?"

He looked at her queerly before answering. "I'm fine. And the mill is fine. The equipment was easily repaired. But I did notice that you were at the house yesterday."

"Yes, I was calling on your mother. But I didn't notice anything strange."

"No. You wouldn't, would you?"

He fell silent, watching her.

"You're . . . you're not asking if I had anything to do with it!" she gasped.

"You're the only person there who I can not vouch for."

"I was at your house, not at the mill!"

"Which is right across the mill yard."

"I didn't do anything to your stupid mill, John," she said with more heat than she intended. Heat enough to make him glance around and take her arm, dragging her three steps away behind the curtain of a fruit stall that had sold out its wares.

"It's my turn to remind you of our surroundings. If you want our secret kept secret, perhaps don't call me John. Especially in public."

She took one deep breath before painting a perfect smile on her face. "You're right. My apologies. Would you please stop breathing on me now?"

He took a half step back—not easy, as the stall was so crowded with boxes there was little room for one person, let alone two.

"I did nothing to your mill. I wouldn't even know how. And I am insulted you would think that of me."

It was his turn to take a deep breath. "I know. You're right, of course. I was in the mill the entire time you were in the house with my mother so I know you couldn't. I'm just . . . I need to know why this keeps happening."

"Maybe you're not as good a miller as you think."

He shot her a look completely lacking in humor. "I could be the worst miller in the world, but not even that would explain such bad luck."

"True. But who would want to sabotage a grain mill? No one in town thinks it will even work!"

He looked exhausted, rubbing a hand over his eyes. "I know. There would be nothing better for the town than for the mill to be a success, but . . . Helmsley is a place that likes disappointment even less than change." He sighed. "Somewhere along the way I lost their trust. Second chances are rare enough, but third? Especially with that last fire, two years ago."

"Mrs. Emory says it nearly jumped the wall into town."

"That's what I'm told," he nodded. Then hesitated. "I wasn't even here for it. I rode as soon as I heard, but when I arrived, everyone looked at me like I was a criminal. Except my mother. She just looked . . . frightened."

Her fingers (stupid traitorous fingers!) wanted nothing more than to reach out and soothe his brow. They had to settle for fiddling with her own sleeve.

"I'm sorry about your equipment," she said haltingly.

"I'm sorry about accusing you."

"Good. I suppose we should exit this"—she waved her hand, grimacing—"place?"

"One moment," he said, then flicked back the curtain, just barely. Two men stood outside, arguing loudly about the price of eggs.

Which meant they had to stand there. And wait.

Close together.

Not the most comfortable of circumstances. Which was likely the only reason Turner even made an attempt at awkward conversation.

"What are you carrying?" he asked.

She glanced down at the packet of papers, clutched tightly against her body this whole time.

"Magazine plates," she replied, feeling foolish. "For wedding dresses."

"Ah. Yes." He cleared his throat. "I suppose you'll have to lie to Sir Barty about this little interlude as well." He tried to make it sound light, jovial.

Tried, and failed.

"Discretion isn't lying," she replied, sharp.

"And you've already had a marriage based on lies," he finished for her.

She looked up at him, the line of his jaw right above her.

"You made a comment the other day to that effect. I don't think you meant to," he whispered, his eyes suddenly on hers. "Your first marriage . . . You implied it was a happy one, before."

"It was," she snapped, her voice louder than she intended. "Konrad and I got along famously."

"Getting along . . . it's not the same as being happy."

"What would you know about it?" she said, suddenly hot with anger. "What would you know about anything having to do with my happiness?" She tasted bitter acid in her mouth, the rush of fear. "In fact the only way you could make me happy is if by some miracle I never had to worry about seeing you at Bluestone or in Helmsley again."

And with that, she pushed past him and threw back the curtain and marched out of the stall, not giving a damn if there were arguing egg sellers nearby (although happily there were not). It took only three steps to shake off her angry posture. Two deep breaths to restore her features to normalcy. And one corner to round before she spotted Margaret and Helen, looking about for her.

"Oh, there you are!" Helen said, breathless. "Now, where is my son? Margaret told me of just the most lovely potting method and I'd like her to explain it to him."

Margaret, who clutched fish heads in a packet dripping with what Leticia hoped was water, seemed a bit unsure.

"Oh," the girl said weakly. "But, um . . . I'm not ready to—"

"Never mind that, Margaret," Leticia interrupted. "Helen, I'm afraid your son had to go back to the mill. He begged me to apologize to you. Both of you."

While Margaret looked relieved, Helen looked crest-fallen, but quickly rallied, painting a bright smile on her face. "That's my John—the work comes first. It's something to admire in a man, and a miller. I'm sure Sir Barty would agree. So . . . where to next? Would you two care to try the tearoom? Their refreshment is . . . somewhat refreshing."

"Not yet," Margaret replied. "I need to go to Jenkins's farm. He has the best manure. Feeds his horses nothing but cabbage."

Leticia swallowed her nausea. "By all means, then. Let's go to Jenkins's farm."

⚘

WHEN LETICIA WALKED into Bluestone Manor later that afternoon, all she wanted was to kick up her feet and have them rubbed.

Until she saw Sir Barty being treated to exactly that.

"And you say it's been like this how long?" Dr. Rhys Gray was saying, his back to her, as he examined Sir Barty's swollen and putrid foot.

She had never seen his foot unwrapped before. He was usually very careful about keeping it clean and out of sight, lest he offend anyone. It was swollen, with red and purple splotches with a devastating-looking open sore on the ankle. As terrible as it looked, as awful as it smelled, Leticia knew it must have been twice as painful.

Sir Barty spotted her in the doorway and quickly threw a blanket over his foot while his face flamed.

"M'dear!" Sir Barty called out. "I should like you to meet Dr. Gray—he'll be staying with us for a time. Dr. Gray, my bride-to-be, Lady Churzy."

"My lady," the doctor said. "I'm very happy to meet you."

He gave nothing away. His face was as blank as it was open.

At first she was irked. How dare Turner install a spy! How dare he not trust her to keep up her end of their bargain! The fact that she'd spent the week trying to circumvent the terms of said bargain was beside the point.

But then she realized Dr. Gray was not a threat to her. In fact, he might be a boon.

He would keep her secret, since it was as much Turner's secret as hers, and doctors kept confidences as well as priests.

And she expected to feel the weight of his condemnation. But when his eyes met hers, she saw only nervousness, and perhaps a little pity.

The pity made her bristle. But the nervousness—speaking to a lack of expertise with subterfuge—made her worried.

Well, she would deal with this new awkwardness at another time. Now she was utterly defeated. So far that week she had failed to convince Sir Barty to change the wedding date, failed to win over any of the ladies of Helmsley, and given Margaret stunningly bad advice she could only pray the girl would follow.

When it came to Dr. Gray, perhaps it was best that she did nothing at all and instead wait to see how it played out.

So there she was come Sunday morning. Waiting. In situ. The pieces on the chessboard all holding their positions.

The townspeople of Helmsley greeted them upon their arrival in St. Stephen's churchyard much as they had the previous week. Perhaps their curiosity was less than before, but they were equally polite and deferential. Mrs. Emory kept her distance, but Leticia was gratified to get a small smile and nod from Mrs. Robertson.

Leticia was already on edge, however. This would be the first time she had seen Turner in a week, and she could only hope it would be easier than last time. If they'd had the benefit of privacy, she would have been happy to rail at him for installing Dr. Gray in the house, but hopefully a few murderous looks would do the trick, she mused.

But the vicar was waving everyone into St. Stephens already, and the Turners had yet to arrive. Would she not have the opportunity to scornfully meet his eyes? To condemn him with a glance?

What a disappointing end to a terribly disappointing week.

"Shall we go in, m'dear?" her fiancé said in her ear, and she saw that Dr. Gray had already led Margaret through the doors.

"Sir Barty!" a deep, rumbling voice called out.

A zip of anticipation shot through Leticia. She turned, and saw . . .

A complete stranger.

A man of about forty, he was of medium height with pitch-black hair, dotted with white throughout. He had his hands behind his back, and his eyes never veered from his goal as he stalked up the church steps, moving like a bird of prey.

"Mr. Blackwell?" Sir Barty said, upon turning around himself. "What brings you to Helmsley?"

"I thought it had been simply too long since I set foot in a church." The man shrugged. "And I have too many sins to atone for to lay them out at my village parish's door."

His words sent a chill up Leticia's spine, but Sir Barty simply barked out a laugh. Then, turning to Leticia . . .

"This is my bride-to-be, Lady Churzy."

"Lady Churzy," he purred. His hand came out from behind his back, taking hers before she could even offer it. "Palmer Blackwell, at your service."

Palmer Blackwell. She searched her memory for where she knew that name . . .

"I am quite pleased to see you, Sir Barty," Blackwell said once he'd released her hand. "It has obviously been too long if I was oblivious to your future happiness. My congratulations to you both."

"Thank you," Leticia replied, keeping her voice cool.

"I am also looking forward to seeing Miss Babcock," Blackwell drawled. "I hear she's grown up . . . remarkably well. Is she inside?"

"I . . . I believe so," Leticia answered, wary.

"Excellent. I hope to be able to catch up with you all after services," he said, tipping his hat. Then he met Leticia's eyes.

They were colder than ice.

"Very, very pleased to meet you, my lady."

Leticia remained quite still, lest she give off a shiver of revulsion.

"Who was that, darling?" she asked once the man had disappeared inside.

"Palmer Blackwell," Sir Barty replied, his chest puffing out with importance. "He owns six grain mills—the most in the county."

And suddenly, Leticia realized who Palmer Blackwell was—Turner's competition. The man who'd taken on his business when the Turner Grain Mill burned.

A new piece had appeared on the board—one with its own agenda, it seemed.

And then Leticia felt it. That itch. Starting on the back of her knee. Small, insistent. Begging her to scratch it. The weight of all that she had been carrying began at last to show, and it all manifested into a tiny madness-inducing itch.

Whatever Palmer Blackwell's appearance in Helmsley meant, it could not be good.

12

To Turner's mind, everything was going fine. Not perfect, not swimmingly, but . . . fine. Hiding in tiny stalls on market day aside, his interactions with Leticia were kept to a bare minimum. Even though his mother had taken to her as one would a long-lost daughter, he managed to avoid being pulled into their relationship, using work as the excuse. And the work went . . . if not well, then certainly fine.

The masons had finished the walls of the engine house. The engine equipment had been installed. There had even been a successful first test of the machinery. It was on the second test, however, the following day, that the metal ring blew apart when the steam pressure built too high inside of it.

The equipment was repaired. Adjustments were made. It was probably an accident.

Probably.

He was wrong to accuse Letty of being the cause—he knew that the minute he had said it. But in a way, she was the cause, although through no fault of her own.

She slipped into his mind at an alarming rate. The calendar no longer reminded him of the days until the harvest, but of how many days that she'd been in town, as Sir Barty's bride-to-be.

A glance into the kitchens and the insane number of tea cakes there told him a countess was coming to call, one his mother hoped to persuade into taking up their cause regarding Sir Barty's grain.

Even the thought of freshly milled flour made him think of her—specifically her skin, soft and white.

It was deeply annoying.

Surely this was why he was not as vigilant as he needed to be with the mill. Surely it was his worry over Letty being in Helmsley—more important, her influence on Sir Barty—that was causing him such trouble.

Thank goodness for Rhys, he decided. Having him installed at Bluestone Manor relieved his mind that Letty was stirring up any trouble for his business.

Or at least, it should have been.

So on Sunday when he escorted his mother to St. Stephen's churchyard he had a plan in mind. Today he would let his mother work her wiles, and invite Leticia and Sir Barty over to the mill yard for tea. Formally returning last Sunday's hospitality, she'd say. Then, while there, he would confidently have Sir Barty tour the mill and its new engine. He would see that they would be capable of taking on ever so much more volume since there would be no days without power. Then he would offer Sir Barty to work at cost for the first harvest season.

That was as long as he could afford it, he'd calculated. But if one is going to do something, then one has to do it fully, mustn't they? There was no chance Sir Barty would pass up that opportunity.

He was a man of confidence. Of determination. Yes, everything would be fine. Brilliant, even, as his friend Ned would say. Marvelous.

And then he saw Palmer Blackwell in the churchyard.

He was standing at the entrance to the church, with Sir Barty and bowing over Leticia's hand. And seeing him made Turner freeze in his no-longer-triumphant steps.

"Is that whom I think it is?" his mother asked.

"I believe so," Turner replied.

Turner figured that Palmer Blackwell would appear sooner or later—news of the Turner Grain Mill getting close to completion had to have spread, even if there was doubt about its working.

"But what is he doing in Helmsley?"

"What do you think, Mother? He's protecting his business."

"It was our business first," she said, harrumphing.

When the Turner Grain Mill had burned six years ago, Blackwell was the one to take over their contracts . . . including Sir Barty's. Blackwell's mill was ten miles away, across the Wolds, but it was the closest option for many. Grinding the grain for the Helmsley area as well as his own had kept him so busy he'd needed to purchase a second mill, this one in Claxby. Then he built another, and another, and soon enough, he'd become quite rich off of their misfortune.

Yes, the last six years had been good to Palmer Blackwell. And he intended to keep his fortunes high by securing his relationship with Sir Barty. Turner couldn't fault him for that.

But he could fault him for the way he was kissing Leticia's hand.

From his vantage point, he could see Leticia smile as her hand was released. Blackwell exchanged a few words with Sir Barty, and then positively leered at Leticia. If Turner had been the man standing next to her, he would have pummeled Blackwell, churchyard or no.

But from what he could see, Leticia just smiled at Sir Barty, completely unfazed, and they went inside.

Blackwell would do anything to secure his position. Flattering Sir Barty's new bride was nothing.

And that was never more apparent than after services ended, when they all inevitably met in the churchyard.

Having arrived later than most of the congregation, Turner and his mother were forced to sit closer to the back, which meant Turner had to watch Blackwell wedge his way into the pew right behind Sir Barty and his family, in the front. From there he could make his presence felt; he could nod to Margaret, and he could lean forward and congratulate Sir Barty when the banns were read.

Turner had almost forgotten about the banns. But there it was, directly after the first blessing, reminding him like a ball of lead to his chest. He had been shot before. Twice. He knew what to expect—the jolt of pain, the shock spreading warm, then hot, too hot through his body. And yet, this second reading of the banns was not as painful as the first. Because yes, he knew what to expect—and he also knew he would survive it.

After a droning sermon that refused to end, the doors were flung open and everyone was released back into their worlds to enjoy this loveliest of summer days. But while the people of Helmsley chattered and smiled at each other, there was a far different meeting taking place under the guise of cordiality just to the side, under the large oak tree.

"Mr. Blackwell," Turner said as he walked up to the group, Helen on his arm. "What a surprise to see you in Helmsley."

"And you, Mr. Turner," Blackwell replied. "I thought you were still in London."

"I haven't lived in London for nearly a year now," Turner replied, his gaze going steely.

"Really, has it been that long? One would have thought the Turner Grain Mill would be working by now."

"There have been some delays," Turner acknowledged. "It became remarkably difficult to get masons and mill-wrights and equipment just about a year ago. A coincidence, I'm sure."

"Hardly a coincidence. My mill in Fennish Moor was being constructed. I'm afraid if you want quick, good work, you have to be willing—and able—to pay top dollar."

"My goodness," Leticia interrupted. "When men talk business, the rest of the world melts away. It's as if we ladies are hardly standing here, isn't it, Helen?"

"My apologies, Lady Churzy," Blackwell said, bowing to her with a flourish. "You are quite right. Such loveliness that you—and dare I say, Miss Babcock—possess should not be ignored."

"Thank you, Mr. Blackwell," Margaret said, her voice a shocking squeak.

"Yes," Turner added, his eyebrow going up. "My apologies as well, my lady. And Miss Babcock, Sir Barty."

A throat cleared behind the ladies.

"And you as well, Dr. Gray."

"Good to see you too, John," Rhys said, hiding his scowl as he bowed.

"Have I thanked you yet for sending Dr. Gray our way?" Sir Barty said. "He's done absolute wonders for my foot—there was hardly any seepage this morning! Isn't he marvelous, m'dear?"

"Yes," Leticia said through a tight smile. "It's simply a wonder that he's staying with us."

"Have you had the chance to peruse the grounds?" his mother asked Rhys. "They are simply lovely, and a credit to Miss Babcock."

Turner felt his mother's toe come down hard on the top of his boot. She had rather steely toes.

"Quite," he added.

"I have heard tell of your horticultural prowess, Miss Babcock," Blackwell said, his eyes on Margaret. "I understand your violets are in full flower."

It was an innocuous phrase. True, even. Then how, Turner wondered, did Blackwell manage to make it sound so . . . oily?

But instead of being put off by it, Margaret turned a tooth-aching smile to Blackwell. "Thank you. That is quite the compliment."

Something must have been caught in the girl's eye. Because she began batting them furiously.

"Yes, the—er, violets are indeed blooming, Mr. Blackwell." This from his mother. "We were so lucky as to be able to tour them last week. And perhaps we could invite Sir Barty and Leticia," she emphasized, reminding everyone of their closeness, "to tour our grounds today? My son has just finished putting the final touches on the engine house, and you should be our first guests!"

Sir Barty shot a look between his daughter and his wife-to-be. Leticia as always remained quite inscrutable.

"That would be quite the treat," Leticia said eventually. "I think—"

Again, it was Margaret who jumped in. "But it will have to be on another day. We are having Mr. Blackwell for tea. That is, if he's amenable."

"I should like nothing better." Blackwell blinked, and then smiled. And Turner wanted nothing more than to punch his perfectly straight teeth into a more natural arrangement.

"Well," his mother said, visibly flustered (and Helen Braithwaite Turner did not fluster easily), "I could . . . did I tell you how much we enjoyed seeing the violets? I imagine they change much in a week."

"Actually, yes," Margaret said, but she was quickly silenced by a gentle hand on her arm.

"Perhaps we can arrange to see the mill this week some-time," Leticia said with finality. Then, curtsies and bows were made, and the group parted.

But Blackwell hung back for a moment.

"I wouldn't mind taking a tour of your mill either, Mr. Turner. In the future that is. After all, I'll be acquiring it soon enough." Then he called out, "Wait for me, Lady Churzy!"

And John realized, with a flash of feeling, that Black-well was going to get the advantage. Because Blackwell was going to win over Leticia.

After all, he was the answer to all her problems. If he held on to Sir Barty's business, he'd be able to push out the Turners. From the grain mill business. From Helmsley. And if he was gone from Helmsley, Leticia was free.

Turner would be damned if he let that happen.

"That was a setback," his mother said at his side. "But we'll have them come see the mill this week. You'll see. Leticia will make it happen. I'm going to go say hello to Mrs. Robertson—she's finally stepped away from Mrs. Emory . . ."

And with that his mother moved off. She'd always been more resilient than he. Able to brush off a defeat, accept the new paradigm, and start turning it back to their advantage. Meanwhile Turner stood there, still and silent as the grave.

He should really start taking a page out of his mother's book.

"Rhys!" he called out. Rhys stopped and turned. Then he said a few quick words to Sir Barty, who nodded and stepped into his carriage after Margaret and Leticia. Rhys made his way over.

"Make it quick. They're holding the carriage for me."

"I need you to keep an eye on things," Turner said.

"I thought that was the entire point of installing me at

Sir Barty's beck and call," Rhys said, crossing his arms over his chest. "I keep an eye on your countess while attending to Sir Barty's gout—which is a sadly mundane case, by the by. I was hoping for at least a small medical mystery, but no—he eats too much rich food and—"

"Not on Leticia. On Blackwell," Turner interrupted. "And Leticia. The two of them together."

"You know I don't have any experience as a spy?" Rhys said, his brow coming down. "My time in the war was spent cutting off limbs and stitching up foolhardy soldiers like you."

"Rhys . . ." Turner warned.

"Why do you need me to keep an eye on both of them now?"

"Because I'm afraid that she . . ." How could he explain? That he thought Leticia would jump at the chance to side with his greatest enemy? But he didn't think that. He was just . . . terribly afraid of it. "Just do it. Please, Rhys."

"Fine." Then, after a moment, he leaned in closer. "I haven't seen or heard anything from your countess that would give one alarm, John."

Turner's mouth pressed into a hard line.

"She's been nothing but kind and welcoming. She seems to dote on Sir Barty, tries very hard with Miss Babcock, and has never even once said your name." Rhys's head cocked to one side. "But that's what you're truly afraid of, isn't it?"

Turner stared off into the distance. "You should get going. They are waiting for you."

Rhys glanced over his shoulder and saw Sir Barty's carriage idling. "What should I tell them when they ask what we were discussing?"

"Tell them I needed a liniment or some such thing."

Rhys shot him a look of utter contempt. "Yes, because that's what I do. Make liniments."

"Well, hell, what is it that doctors of your stature do, Rhys?"

"Apparently I take care of gout and spy on friends' lovers."

"You're perfectly situated, then."

And with that, Rhys turned on his heel and walked briskly back to the carriage.

Leaving Turner standing in the churchyard . . . in the unfortunate position of having to wait.

13

*D*r. Rhys Gray was not a man used to being around strangers. Well, that was not true, precisely. He was used to being around strangers—people who were in some kind of distress, whether it be crying out in pain from being shot on the battlefield or quarantined due to some mysterious illness. Those people were in his control, and oftentimes unconscious. What he was not accustomed to was being in the presence of strangers with whom he had to converse.

It made him long for his beautiful laboratory in Greenwich. To spend the day in solitude, his main communication being correspondence with other physicians and scientists across the country (and some in Europe) where they shared their ideas, their research. Oh, he did go out occasionally. He very much enjoyed the visits he made to town to see his friends Ashby and, before he returned to Lincolnshire, Turner. He was once physician to the queen, when there was a particularly troublesome skin condition no one else was able to diagnose. And every few months, he gave a lecture at the Royal Scientific Academy.

But he preferred, on the whole, to be left to his own

devices. This, he reasoned, is why he made a terrible spy. He was not a keen observer of the human condition—unless of course, that condition was in the throes of great pain or pestilence. So he would miss subtle clues. Pointed glances. An odd phrase here and there. What's more, he lacked the ability to snoop successfully, or to think of an excuse for said snooping when caught.

"What are you doing?"

Rhys jolted. He was leaning on the side of the greenhouse, trying to keep an eye on Lady Churzy as she wandered the gardens. They had just arrived back from St. Stephen's. Mr. Blackwell was due to arrive any moment—he'd claimed the need to go back to his room at the inn and change his clothes.

"You're staying in Helmsley?" Lady Churzy had asked. "I thought your estate was not ten miles from here."

"It is, my lady," Blackwell had answered with a slick smile. "But I have business over the next few days in the area, and it's a blessing to my horses to not ride twenty miles around every day. So I'll be at the Drum for the week."

Lady Churzy seemed surprised by that. If she was conspiring with Blackwell about anything, she was very good at hiding it.

But John had seemed increasingly suspicious. He wanted Rhys to step up his spying. So Rhys would step up his spying.

When they arrived back at Bluestone Manor, Lady Churzy said she wished to take a walk, to clear her head before tea. He was about to offer to go with her, but then Rhys thought better of it.

She was too smart to think that his presence at Bluestone Manor was anything other than what it was—a poor attempt to keep an eye on her. Therefore, if he walked with her, she would be entirely guarded.

However, if he followed after her, he might be able to overhear some pertinent and dastardly information that John seemed keen to know about. (And the sooner he did that, the sooner he could leave.)

Of course, after about ten seconds, he realized the flaw in his logic. Lady Churzy, like most sane people, was not given to talking to herself aloud. In truth, the most interesting thing she had done was scratch at her knee through her skirts.

"I said, what are you doing?"

He turned around and saw Margaret Babcock standing behind him. She had put her smock over her Sunday dress, her hand on the greenhouse door's handle.

He'd been at Bluestone a few days now, and Margaret Babcock struck him as a sweet, quiet girl who liked to be left alone. As someone who also liked to be left alone, he was happy to comply.

"I'm . . . I was . . . there's a plant," he said lamely, "that might help with your father's foot. I just thought of it. I was wondering if you had one in the greenhouse."

"You want to come into the greenhouse?" Margaret asked.

"Er . . . yes?" he replied. "That is, if you don't mind."

She looked stricken. As if caught in the sights of a hunter's rifle.

"What are you doing?" he asked instead. "I should think you would be preparing for tea."

"We have a little time," she replied. "Enough to check the soil moisture of the saplings I planted earlier."

"Oh, I see."

"I . . . I have to wear this smock, to be careful of my dress," Margaret explained, awkwardly fingering the plain, but serviceable-looking apron. "Even though checking soil moisture is not particularly dirty work."

"Yes," Rhys said, trying to hide a smile. "That would make sense."

And they stood there. Rhys feeling unbelievably stupid. Because by then, Leticia had left the rows of violets, her retreating form becoming smaller and smaller as she headed back to the house.

She'd done little more than sneeze.

His first attempt at being a more active spy had failed spectacularly.

"No one comes into my greenhouse," she said finally, forcing Rhys's attention back to the conversation.

"That's all right," he said. "I understand. I have a laboratory in Greenwich. I hate having people invade my space there. It's as if they are entering the inside of my head."

"Yes," Margaret said—and for the first time, her eyes met his. The effect of that clear blue gaze was utterly startling. "That's exactly what it's like."

Rhys heard a carriage in the drive. Mr. Blackwell arriving, no doubt.

"I shall leave you to it, then." Rhys bowed. "To check your soil, that is. I have a feeling Lady Churzy would not have you be late to tea."

He turned and began to walk away back to the house, exhaling for the first time since she caught him.

"What kind of plant is it?" she called after him. "To help my father's foot?"

"It's ah . . . it's in the poppy family," he said, trying not to sound like an idiot without an ounce of formal scientific training. "It doesn't have a name yet. Still being studied."

"I don't think I have it," she replied.

"I should think not. It was just a thought."

"But you can come inside and look," she said, opening the door.

"Oh," Rhys replied, completely out of his depth. "I . . . all right. Thank you."

And Rhys was too taken aback by the offer (and again too inept a spy to notice) that as Margaret held the door open for him, a slight blush began to spread over her cheek.

❧

IT TOOK LETICIA only one day to figure out why Palmer Blackwell caused her to itch. Nay, less than a day. A mere afternoon.

The difficulty was deciding what to do about it.

"But surely we deserve one Sunday afternoon to ourselves," she had said to Sir Barty when they entered Bluestone. The entire ride back from church, Sir Barty had expounded on the delights of one Palmer Blackwell. Apparently he'd been a man of great jolliness. More than ready with a joke or a hand at cards.

"Always enjoyed running into him in Bourne or Lincoln. Quite the fellow!" he had said.

If Leticia had been at all wondering why Sir Barty would refuse to use the Turner Grain Mill, considering his lifelong friendship with Helen (not that she was wondering, because that would have implied she had some investment in Turner's business), she now seemed to have at least part of an answer. Palmer Blackwell had thoroughly charmed Sir Barty. He saw him as a chum. A compatriot, always up for fun.

Many a business deal was made in the backroom of a gentleman's club, with copious amounts of brandy and the haze of a good time.

"I know, my dear, but Palmer Blackwell is a capital fellow. What a grand idea, Margaret, inviting him to tea!"

"But . . . what about Mr. Turner?" she found herself saying, and wanting to bite her tongue. "I thought you wished to encourage his affections for Margaret?"

Margaret had hopped out of the carriage, immediately setting off to check the soil of one of her plants. As long as she didn't ruin her dress and was back in time for tea to be served, Leticia decided she didn't mind.

What she did mind was the sense of unease that settled over her when Palmer Blackwell looked at Margaret.

No one was more surprised than Leticia (with the exception of perhaps Helen) when Margaret decided to forgo the fainting scheme and ignore Turner. Leticia fairly wanted to applaud. But then she took things one step further and invited Mr. Blackwell's notice. And invited him to tea.

Mr. Blackwell, who was already making Leticia itchy with his ingratiating manner and penchant for barely veiled entendres.

Mr. Blackwell, who made obsequiousness an art.

Mr. Blackwell, who was twice Margaret's age and whose appearance was timed to coincide with the harvest season.

Mr. Blackwell, who had made Turner's blood boil.

Margaret could not have chosen a better—or worse—person to show favor to. It was almost laughable.

Then she told herself she was being silly. Overly on guard. Perhaps Mr. Blackwell was a fine man, a good miller and no threat to her whatsoever.

So why this churn in her stomach?

Why this itch just outside her knee?

"I do wish to encourage Mr. Turner." Sir Barty blinked.

"Inviting over his direct rival to the business does not seem very welcoming to Mr. Turner," Letitia remarked.

"Aha! And that's where I have thought one step further than even your beautiful mind," Sir Barty crowed, and kissed the top of her head. "I was thinking about what you said, about Margaret liking Mr. Turner, and decided that I had not seen any reciprocal feeling. Why, when he came on Thursday with Dr. Gray he barely said one word about Margaret. And I tried to induce him, believe me. So, what better way to prompt it than to show favor to Mr. Blackwell instead?"

Leticia's jaw dropped. She was certain she gaped like a fish. It was a particularly deft bit of game play, worthy of herself. Coming from Sir Barty, of all people! Perhaps she was influencing him in more ways than she'd anticipated.

How very disturbing.

"I only wish you had invited Mr. Turner and Helen over for tea as well. It would have been entertaining to watch. Besides, no one is a better partner at whist than Helen. Did you not notice me nudging you?"

"I . . . no, darling. My apologies." In truth she had noticed. Sir Barty was not particularly subtle—his elbow had likely left a bruise. But at that moment, she was not able to comprehend the idea of having both Turner and Blackwell in the same house.

She was itchy enough as it was.

"Nothing to be done about it now," she replied casually. "I'll send Helen a note."

"Ah well." Sir Barty shrugged. "Where did that doctor get off to? I need him to rewrap my foot. Oh, Mrs. Dillon! We're having a guest for tea again—and possibly dinner. I leave that up to my dear Lady Churzy."

So. It seemed as if she would simply have to wait and see how today played out. Palmer Blackwell, as much as he prompted itching on her part, could simply be a man protecting his investments. She should give him the benefit of the doubt. After all, that's all she wished for herself.

But by the end of dinner, she knew her womanly intuition had not failed her.

It started off innocuously enough. Mr. Blackwell was able to maintain easy conversation over tea. He left the sweeter cakes to Sir Barty, and didn't take up half the room the way other guests who should remain nameless had. He was equally attentive to both ladies, as well as Dr. Gray and Sir Barty.

Indeed, everyone seemed more than happy to be entertained by Palmer Blackwell.

"And that's my tale of the last time I was in London," Mr. Blackwell finished. "And it's why I avoid it now. Honestly, I doubt they'd let me back in after that embarrassing display of horsemanship."

"I'm sure the city of London misses your wit, Mr. Blackwell." Leticia smiled. "If not your horsemanship."

"As I am sure they miss you, Lady Churzy," Blackwell replied, his expression warm, but his eyes hiding something else. "You lived in London for a time, did you not?"

"I did." Leticia did her best to keep the wariness out of her voice. "With my late husband."

"Yes, Lord Churzy." Blackwell put down his cup, and a slosh of liquid had never seemed so sinister. "He was a very accomplished horseman, wasn't he?"

"He enjoyed riding, yes."

"He and Lord Vere cut quite the picture through the parks of town, if I recall correctly. They must have been very good friends."

Leticia's cup froze in midsip. For just a fraction of a second, but long enough for Mr. Blackwell to notice it. And when she lifted her eyes to his, she saw victory in them.

"Quite," she said. "He was riding with Lord Vere when he was thrown from his mount."

Mr. Blackwell's smile fell, and he affected the posture of regret. "Oh, but I must apologize, my lady. I did not wish to remind you of the sadness of your husband's death."

"Thank you, Mr. Blackwell," Leticia said, as serenely as possible. "It is difficult, but I prefer to remember happier times. And look forward to making more." She squeezed Sir Barty's hand.

"I told you I'm an embarrassment," Mr. Blackwell said. "You can't take me anywhere."

"At least not London," Dr. Gray added, from his seat beside Margaret.

And then . . . Blackwell winked.

But not at Leticia.

At Margaret.

There was nothing to indicate Margaret had even seen it. She simply went on sipping her tea, smoothing her skirt away from Dr. Gray's leg. Except . . . she blushed.

Blushed. At Mr. Blackwell? Oh no.

At that point, the itch began to move, migrating from Leticia's knee to her forearm. It took five deep breaths before she felt she'd conquered the urge to scratch it.

The rest of the afternoon proceeded much like last Sunday afternoon—just turned bizarrely on its head.

They went to tour the gardens. Sir Barty played the same little game where he claimed that his foot was well enough to allow him to come along, but then Jameson appeared with some "business" to attend to. That left Leticia, Dr. Gray, Margaret, and Palmer Blackwell to make up their foursome. But this time, there was no means by which to hang back and observe. She had to watch Blackwell compliment and Margaret blush from up close.

"He seems to be laying it on a bit thick, doesn't he?" Dr. Gray murmured at her side. The path only accommodated walking in pairs, and Mr. Blackwell had slid himself next to Margaret before Leticia could blink. Leaving her with Dr. Gray.

A man who she knew had been sent to spy on her for Turner.

It seemed she was surrounded by men with hidden agendas.

Fortunately, Dr. Gray spied very badly. And she had to assume reluctantly. Over the past two days in Bluestone Manor, he had done little more than wrap Sir Barty's foot, advised Margaret on proper microscope use (he had brought one with him from London), and eaten their pork. Nary a probing question, nor a surreptitious search of her things. And when he did try to spy on her, well . . . did he not think she saw him lurking by the greenhouse?

All in all, Dr. Gray was proving to be less of an adversary and more of a . . . presence. A reminder that John Turner existed. Merely a mile or so away.

As if she needed a reminder.

She was about to answer Dr. Gray when Blackwell exclaimed, "The beauty of these flowers is eclipsed only by the beauty of their keeper." And again, he leaned over Margaret's hand.

At this rate, poor Margaret's hand would be soaked.

"Regardless of the thickness of his flattery, it is not malicious. And Margaret is a lovely young lady," she said instead. As unassuming as Dr. Gray's presence was turning out to be, confiding in him about her current alarm would still be a mistake. Could be a mistake. Oh hell, she hardly knew anymore.

Of course, Leticia's statement had been nothing more than observable truth. Palmer Blackwell's flattery of Margaret seemed to be in no way mean. And Margaret was looking particularly pretty that day—especially since every time her face turned in their direction, she was blushing.

It appeared Palmer Blackwell's flattery was also working.

"Miss Babcock, thank you for the tour of your gardens. Rarely have I seen such loveliness," Mr. Blackwell said when they made their way back to the house. "I shall think of nothing else while I am eating my supper tonight, alone in my room at the inn."

It was a hint as broad as the English Channel. One Leticia refused to take. And luckily, Margaret did not have the social savvy to pick up on it, blushes aside.

Unfortunately, by that time Sir Barty had appeared on the steps. "Done already? And here I was, about to rejoin you!"

"What a pity, darling," Leticia replied kindly. "And Mr. Blackwell is just about to take his leave."

"What? Going already?" Sir Barty's mustache bristled. "We'll be having none of that! Mrs. Dillon—an extra place at dinner! There's enough pork for everyone!"

Mr. Blackwell smiled broadly. But while the smile was directed at Margaret, the look in his eyes was for none other than Leticia.

It said, quite simply, I win.

❧

DINNER WAS A curiously banal affair. There was nothing on the outside that suggested they were anything other than a pleasant party. The overly flirtatious air and syrupy compliments were left behind in the garden, now that Sir Barty was there. Ever oblivious, even he would likely cringe at such an overt display toward his daughter. Instead, Blackwell continued the theme established at tea, telling anecdotes of his youth—sanitized versions for ladies' ears, of course.

"I tell you, I still feel sorry for that pig to this day."

Soon enough, the ladies removed themselves after the meal was complete, allowing the men to converse.

And for once, Leticia was thankful that Dr. Gray had been unceremoniously dropped in their laps. Because Blackwell wouldn't have Sir Barty to himself.

But there was enough to deal with in the intervening time, waiting for the men. And by enough to deal with, she meant Margaret.

"I cannot believe I dropped the pork pie on my lap," Margaret was saying as they sat in the drawing room, the guffaws of her father still audible from across the hall. While most girls would have died of embarrassment, Margaret became exasperated with herself. "Water alone will not get this out."

The napkin on her lap had not been enough to save her Sunday gown, and she had a smear of brown sauce on her skirts.

"Give it to Molly," Leticia replied. "Do you think she would make a good lady's maid? She claims to do hair well."

"I do not know, but she'll be pleased to be promoted above her friend Wendra," Margaret said idly, showing for once an alarming grasp on the downstairs politics of the house. "It's my best gown. Now you're going to say that I need to wear my smock while eating too."

"Of course not. But if it is ruined, perhaps it's a blessing in disguise. Your father has granted me a surprisingly generous allowance for wedding clothes. I'm certain we can make it stretch to include a gown or two for you."

"No," Margaret answered.

"Certain things are expected of you, Margaret. At the very least for the wedding. I'm afraid your blue ball gown is too short—"

"No. I told you I don't want any new clothes. I like the dresses I have. Molly can clean this one." She crossed her arms over her chest. "Can we discuss something else please?"

"Certainly," Leticia replied, happy to move on, but not quite done with the battle. It was such a sticking point for the girl, but something really had to be done.

Another echo of laughter traveled down the hallway from the dining room, filling the silence between the ladies.

"I have never understood this part of the evening ritual," Margaret said eventually. "I should like to hear what story has my father laughing so."

"That is the reason for this part of the evening ritual," Leticia answered. "There are some stories men like to tell that are likely not appropriate for a lady—especially a young lady—to hear."

"Why?" Margaret's nose wrinkled. "It's just words. It cannot cause harm."

"Words can cause harm, no matter what nursery rhymes might have told you," Leticia replied. "All too often, they are the most cutting weapons in an entire arsenal."

Margaret seemed to take that in. "But it is a silly ritual. You have to admit that."

Leticia sighed. "Yes, at times it is rather silly."

"What are we supposed to do while the men are talking?"

"Talk among ourselves."

"About what?" Margaret's brow came down. "I really wish I could check my soil moisture again. The air was terribly dry today."

Yes, and Leticia had barely been able to hold in her sneezes.

"We can talk about our visitor," Leticia said, ignoring Margaret's concern for her soil.

"Dr. Gray?" Margaret asked.

"No," she replied. "I mean Mr. Blackwell. How well do you know him?"

"I have met him only a few times. He does business with Father."

"Has he . . . has he ever paid attention to you akin to today?"

Margaret shook her head.

"And you are aware that not all attention a man gives is complimentary?" Leticia added. "Know that if someone pays unwanted attention to you, you can come to me about it."

"Of course." She nodded. "I know that."

But as she did, that blush spread over her cheeks again.

"What if . . . what if our guest—I mean, someone pays me such attentions, and they are not unwanted?" she asked.

Leticia felt herself still. "Oh? Are . . . are you referring to Mr. Turner?"

"No . . ." Margaret's brow came down. "I . . . I am revising my theory. About human interaction and indicators of attraction as being a basis for selection of a husband."

"Oh?" Leticia's eyebrow went up. "You no longer feel that blushing is a strong indication of attraction?"

"No, it is," Margaret replied. "But I have recently— just today, in fact—come to the conclusion that one can be made to blush by multiple people. Therefore it cannot be the only indication for husband selection."

"I am relieved to hear it." And she was. Although she did it in her own peculiar way, Margaret was coming to the same realization every young lady did when their first crush disappoints them—there are many more fish in the sea. "After all, some people are not given to blushing."

The difficulty was this realization seemed to have been prompted by the arrival of a man who made her skin crawl, quite literally.

John Turner had done many things to her—many overwhelming, mind-altering things—but he had never caused her to itch.

And the way Blackwell had spoken about Konrad set her teeth on edge. There was nothing revealing in his speech, true, but she was learning that he was a master of the oblique. He merely hinted at knowledge he should not have.

Truths that if spoken aloud, could be almost as damaging as the Lie.

Yes, she thought, words were often the most dangerous of weapons.

"What would the other indicators be, then?" she asked carefully. "What would you have in a husband?"

"I don't know," Margaret said, coming to the realization that yes, perhaps she did not know. "I assumed I would never marry. But then Mr. Turner made me blush and I began to think differently."

"Never marry?" Leticia asked. "But why?"

"I just . . . I don't dance well, I don't know why other girls are always laughing and smiling at men. Or why men are gallant in one setting and brutish in another. I like flowers. I understand flowers. The male/female fertilization habits and proliferation of plants are so much more interesting. The singular pairing off of a man and a woman seems at times unnatural to me."

Leticia's brow rose, but she held her tongue. No need to let the girl know she was espousing some rather bohemian thoughts.

"I much preferred to stay in my greenhouse. My mother used to joke that unless I fainted at someone's feet, I was not in danger of meeting a husband at any rate."

"Your mother," Leticia repeated.

"It's how my mother met my father. Or rather, how she says she got his attention."

That explained the origins of the fainting scheme. And Leticia had been right. That plan would not work on ninety-nine men out of a hundred. But a man like Sir Barty, who simply wished to protect everyone? It would certainly work on him.

"What did your mother tell you about being married?" Leticia tried.

"That it's something expected of a lady. I told her that as a lady I would rather not limit myself. She kissed my head and told me someday I might feel differently and we went back to trimming a juniper bush."

"Your mother sounds very wise." Leticia's smile could not be contained.

"But now that that day is here, I don't know what would make a good husband." Margaret shrugged, as if this admission was not the loneliest thing Leticia had ever heard. "What do you think would make a good husband?"

"Well, I suppose it depends on the person," Leticia said, taken aback, but not letting it show. "There are any number of men out there who I'm sure would make you a good husband, but the question is, what would make the right husband?"

"What made Father right—for you?"

Leticia hesitated. "Your father . . . he wants to take care of me. That is his best feature. He wants everyone to be well and happy."

"So, someone that takes care of you is most important," Margaret said, nodding.

"Not necessarily," she replied, lost in thought. "You should want to take care of them as well. In fact, your partner's happiness would begin to supersede your own. But it's all right, because your happiness and his are the same. Your goals and interests would be shared. You would work toward building a life together, not giving up the one you have, but letting it become part of something bigger. Which makes choosing the right person very important."

Margaret nodded, but her gaze was toward the window. Not really understanding, but letting the thought take seed.

"So I need someone who I have shared goals and interests with," she mused.

"Yes. But more than that, you need someone you wouldn't mind spending your life with. Because you will be tied together forever. So it had best be someone you can walk besides for a while, and hold hands as you go."

"Someone I like," Margaret said.

"Yes."

"Hence the physiological response of blushing."

"I . . . suppose."

"And that's what you have with Father?"

"It's . . . it's something I hope to have with your father. Once we wed."

She couldn't tell the truth. She couldn't say that it was as much a dream to her as it was to Margaret. Sir Barty wanted to take care of her . . . but once she was taken care of, he was happy to place her aside and go back to his library and his pork.

She'd come close once. Close to thinking she'd met someone she'd like to walk beside for a while, and hold hands with as they went.

"But you don't blush."

Leticia's head came up. "What do you mean?"

"You don't blush," Margaret said. "When you look at Father. But as you said, some people aren't given to blushing."

With that, Margaret wandered over to the shelves and pulled down a small volume. Leticia could see it contained detailed sketches of various plants. There was, it seemed, nothing more to be said on the subject.

Thank goodness, she thought, letting all the air out of her body. Margaret's observation had unnerved her, as did the girl's lack of judgment when she said it. But Leticia was more than happy to judge herself.

Her loud, condemning thoughts simply jumping at the bit to begin their assault.

You don't blush with Sir Barty. But you are given to blushing, aren't you? How long do you think you can really keep up this farce? If Margaret can see it, can't everyone?

The atmosphere of the drawing room was becoming rather closed in. In fact, Leticia could do with a walk. But a turn about the room wouldn't help. She needed fresh air.

"I think I'll step out onto the terrace for a moment," she said, standing with as much grace as she could muster.

Margaret looked up from her book. "What about the gentlemen? Aren't they meant to join us soon?"

A guffaw carried across the hall from the dining room, the men obviously still enjoying themselves. "I will be back before they attend us, I have no doubt."

Leticia took a deep breath the minute she closed the door to the outside. It was a warm summer evening, late enough that the sun had just dipped below the horizon, a glow of orange and red to the west framed by the dark silhouettes of Margaret's greenhouse and the stately trees that edged the gardens.

They had just passed the summer solstice, Leticia realized. These were the longest days of the year. Every day from now on would be shorter and shorter, the edges of the night closing in on the day.

She could sympathize.

Without realizing it, Leticia stepped off the terrace and began walking west, drawn to the last of the sun. Soon enough, she was through the gardens and at the line of trees. To her left was the drive of Bluestone Manor. Follow it a half mile and it would lead to the road. The road ran to Helmsley, and from there, it ran . . . anywhere.

You could just go. She was shocked to hear her own voice echoing in her mind. But . . . she could. She could

do as Turner had asked (or demanded) and leave Helmsley. Remove herself from the insanity of this situation and
wipe the slate clean. Try to find somewhere new. Someone new.

She liked Sir Barty. She truly did. He was a decent man.
He deserved someone who blushed, didn't he?

And what did she deserve?

She deserved security. She deserved to feel safe. To no
longer have whispers dodging her heels and be afraid for
her future.

She deserved to silence the silly voices in her head that
said otherwise.

Ruthlessly she shuddered. Moments of weakness were
all fine and good. As long as that was all they were—
moments. Walking away from her situation was not an
option. She was too close to her goal. Thus she would deal
with all the peculiar daughters, all the gout, all the minis-
cule dramas of Helmsley, and all the Turners life threw at
her. She would deal with them—and she would vanquish
them.

Pulling herself up by the invisible string on top of her
head, she rolled her shoulders back and turned on her heel,
intent to go back into the house.

And ran directly into the form of one Palmer Blackwell.

"Lady Churzy." Blackwell smiled—his grin disturb-
ingly bright in the fading light. "There you are! Dear me,
you quite disappeared in these trees."

"Mr. Blackwell," she said, taking a generous step back.
"What are you doing here?"

"I volunteered to come out and fetch you." He leaned in
conspiratorially, taking back much of the space that Leticia
had tried to put between them. "Sir Barty was about come
out himself, but we both know that it would take him twice
the time to find you, and twice as much complaining."

Leticia was about to step back again, but stopped herself. Stand your ground, she told herself. She was, after all, a countess. Men like Blackwell could not move her.

"We should go in, then," she said. "My betrothed is no doubt waiting for us."

"One moment, if you please, my lady." Blackwell's hand reached out and took her elbow. She tensed immediately. "I must again apologize for my bluntness this afternoon at tea. I had no wish to remind you of your husband's death."

"It is unnecessary, Mr. Blackwell."

"Indeed, I'd hoped to remind you of his life. Lord Churzy was a man of . . . such life."

Leticia stopped. Wrenching her arm free of his grasp, she forced herself to turn to him. "You knew my husband?" she asked, direct.

"Let's say I knew of him," Blackwell replied. "After all, I am familiar with the Yew Tree Club."

Leticia remained still, her face impassive. But underneath, she was almost glad. Glad that Blackwell was finally showing the cards he'd hinted at having that afternoon.

"Your husband's tastes were . . . specific. As his wife you must have been privy to them." The moon had begun to glow in the darkening sky, allowing Leticia to see Blackwell's eyes as they raked over her body. "You must have been privy to a great deal."

"I'm sure I don't know what you speak of."

"Sir Barty is a very lucky man. I wonder, does he know how lucky?" Blackwell persisted. He leaned in again, his breath—heavily spiced with claret—hot and humid against her cheek. "You and I could be such friends to each other, I think. After all, you haven't many here, have you?"

"Mr. Blackwell," she spoke in her sternest voice. Her countess voice. The voice that sent greater men than Blackwell running for their mothers. "I'm sure as your friendship with my fiancé is so entrenched, you and I will have many opportunities to meet."

The smile died on Blackwell's face. His claret-hazed vision cleared and he spoke with the sobriety of a Quaker—and the malice of a snake.

"Sir Barty is a good man, is he not?"

"He is."

"But he hasn't seen much of the world. Not as much as you and I. If his friends, his fiancée—let alone his wife—embarrassed him . . . I don't know how he would manage."

His wife. Oh heavens, this man did know the weak points, didn't he?

She was about to answer again—dredging up that imperious voice that had suddenly found itself faltering in the red of anger—when the sound of twig snapping broke through the dark.

"Oh hell . . . er, I mean, hello!" Dr. Gray's voice called out. "Lady Churzy, Mr. Blackwell, there you are. We began to fear you had gotten lost."

"Dr. Gray," Leticia replied. "How good of you to find us."

"Shall we return to the house?" Mr. Blackwell said. "We need only follow the lights, like moths to a flame."

Mr. Blackwell offered his arm, but Leticia made no move to take it. Instead, for once, Dr. Gray showed a prescience she had not thought possible in a man of learning.

"Actually, my lady, could I have a word with you?" he said. "I, er . . . I need to ask for a favor. About my rooms. I should hate to go to Sir Barty about it . . ."

As unbelievable as that excuse was, Mr. Blackwell simply shrugged. "I leave you to it then. I should hate to keep Miss Babcock waiting. I confess I am finding her company uniquely delightful. I would ask your permission to call on her, my lady, but you're not quite her stepmother yet."

Once Blackwell was at a safe distance, Leticia found it again possible to exhale. But she dare not let her posture go slack. She could not let Dr. Gray see how unsettled she was. He was after all, here on orders.

But while the good doctor was a man of facts, and extremely bad at lying—and spying—he was also a creature of diagnosis and prescribing solutions.

"He's a problem, isn't he?" the doctor said.

There was no point in lying. "Yes," she said simply. "How much did you hear?"

"Enough, I should think. Was that what I thought it was?"

She nodded. "A warning."

"What do you intend to do about it?" he asked.

Leticia blew out a breath. What could she do about it? The possibilities were endless . . . but her options were rather limited. "I don't know."

And that scared her. Scared her into laughing. At least she knew now what it was about Palmer Blackwell that made her itch.

He was a problem, yes. But not one easily dismissed. He was too smart, too treacherous for that.

Dr. Gray hesitated. Then he took one step closer, glancing from one side to the next. "If you don't mind my saying so, my lady, Mr. Blackwell was wrong about one thing."

"Oh?"

"You are not friendless here. In fact, you have one friend in particular who, in this circumstance, has similar interests to your own."

John Turner.

She could tell Turner of Mr. Blackwell's warning— but could she? The last time they spoke, truly spoke, he'd asked her to leave town. Hell, he'd outright demanded it! He might decide that he'd let Blackwell drive her away . . . except for the fact that he hated Blackwell.

Dr. Gray must be right . . . he would want Blackwell gone as much as she.

Some proverb-spouting person in the past had said the enemy of the enemy is my friend. Leticia could only assume the speaker was a woman.

Still . . . they'd come to a fragile truce, wherein they did not see or speak to each other. To break that truce would place her squarely within his power.

And that sounded most uncomfortable.

But if he would be willing to help, it also sounded like a relief. To have someone to talk to . . . to rely on . . . she was so very tired of holding everything in.

"I doubt he has any interest in helping me," she said, tamping down the emotion in her voice that threatened to overwhelm. "In fact, he might glory in my predicament."

"He wouldn't, my lady. I promise," Dr. Gray said, with a fierceness she hadn't known the steady man capable of. "And if he did, I'd give him a concoction that would make him clutch his chamber pot in his regret."

Leticia let out a watery laugh and allowed herself to lean on Dr. Gray's arm as they began to walk back toward the house.

"I suppose it is only common sense to take one's doctor's advice."

14

John—

There is information you must be made aware of. Send a note forthwith saying you have need of a doctor's services. Leave the door to your kitchens unlocked. We shall meet there before dawn.

Rhys

John Turner was a patient man. One could not spend five years in the service of the Earl of Ashby, scrounging and saving every penny to rebuild his fortunes and repair his mill, without cultivating a bedrock of patience. Nor could one live through the struggles to raise the mill from its proverbial and literal ashes without the perseverance to do that little bit more every day to achieve one's goal.

Nor could one spend six months trying to find a single troublesome countess, on the thin hope of reconciling—and then be forced to live in the same town as said countess after she had refused him.

Yes, Turner had spent a long, long time being patient. He was damned tired of it.

These were the thoughts that crossed his mind as he sat in the kitchen, dozing off over his tea.

He had received Rhys's note just before he was about to head to the mill and his pallet there. His mother had retired a few hours earlier with a good book, leaving him with the less-good books—the account books.

After going cross-eyed for an hour on numbers, trying to see if there was any way he could offer his mill's services to Sir Barty at less than cost, and if so, for how long, he'd just snuffed out the candle when the boy from Bluestone Manor arrived, thrusting the note into his hands.

After he read it, he had only one thought: Rhys was really getting into this spying business.

Although he still had some things to learn about sneaking around. After all, the note could easily have been read by the boy (presuming the boy could read), thereby negating any subterfuge.

And why was subterfuge necessary anyway? Rhys was known to be his old friend, he could visit anytime! In fact, it would be less suspicious if he'd simply stopped by on his way into or out of Helmsley. Yet Rhys had something worth telling him, and so he wrote up a note and sent it over via his own boy, inviting Rhys for a late-night visit and a fictitious medical emergency.

Or rather, early morning. If Rhys didn't hurry up and get here, his covert actions would be useless, because their maid would be up to light the fires and start breakfast.

"This had better be important," Turner grumbled, his eyes again falling on his pocket watch, laid open on the counter, where he sat and his tea went cold.

But it must be important, and Turner guessed what it was—something to do with Blackwell. His arrival stirred up some mess. Rhys must have followed his instructions and kept a close eye on Blackwell and Leticia. And he must have seen something between them. Some conspiracy, perhaps.

The idea made Turner's blood boil.

Of course Leticia would jump at the chance to find an ally against him. Hell, when they had spoken, truly spoken a week ago in her bedroom, she told him he needed to leave. Then, when they were standing so close together in the market stall, she said the thing that would make her happiest was if he would just disappear. Leave the village he grew up in, his life's work, simply because she had staked a claim. She was likely persuading Sir Barty at that very moment (although, any persuading she was doing to Sir Barty at three in the morning was not something he wanted to contemplate and indeed, turned his vision black) that Palmer Blackwell was the only person trustworthy enough to do business with. That the Turner Grain Mill was folly, it would never be what it was when his father was alive, and considering its history unlikely to even open its doors.

And there was not a damn thing he could do about it.

But if that was the case, a tiny weed of logic popped up, why on earth would she have befriended your mother?

It was then, as the dark thoughts began to turn over in his head, whispering their insidious ideas into his ear, that he heard the rumble of a carriage. It pulled to a stop, and the dim light of a lantern appeared underneath the kitchen door.

He leapt up and crossed the room in three strides. He wrenched the door open.

"It's about damn—" But the words died on his lips.

"Hello, Turner," Leticia said from beneath the heavy hood of her cloak. "Aren't you going to invite me in?"

༄

THE KITCHEN OF the Turner house was very cozy, although one would be stretched to call it comfortable. It was a small space—although the house did not call for a large kitchen. They did not serve dinners for scores of guests here. Instead there was a large hearth, where embers from yesterday's fire still glowed. A stove stood in the corner, and shelves of china and crockery lined one wall. There were even some modern conveniences such as a well pump that at some point had been built into the wall. There was a long table in the center of the room, set high for a maid or cook to work while standing. On it was a pot of tea, long neglected, and a pocket watch.

All of these things were what Leticia decided to stare at when Turner pulled her roughly into the kitchen, fitting her against his side, hiding her from any errant light and prying eyes.

Although she doubted there were any prying eyes. This was Helmsley, not London. Country hours and all that. Still, better to be safe than sorry.

She was contemplating the lack of prying eyes and the teapot on the counter when Turner released her and came around to look at her.

"What are you doing here?"

"I can answer that," came a voice from behind her. "Would you care to invite me in as well?"

Dr. Gray lounged in the doorway to the kitchen, a bit smugly if truth be told.

"For someone who insisted on a clandestine meeting, you are making a mockery of it," Turner grumbled, cocking his head in an invitation to enter.

"Oh, a person could see me. I planned it all out," Rhys said, a smile lighting his face. "Bluestone Manor knows I received a note asking for medical help. I know this because when your note arrived I made sure to say, 'Oh dear, my medical services are needed in Helmsley!' when the note was delivered."

"How very intelligent of you," Turner drawled.

"I even left the note out in the hall, should someone pass by and see it. Sir Barty said I could take a gig whenever I please, so I had the stable lads rig one up, making certain to tell them my purported mission—"

"Of course you did."

"And drove it myself. I picked up your countess at the edge of the property, none the wiser," he finished proudly.

"No one saw me," Leticia added. "I made certain of it."

"None of that answers the question of why she is here," Turner said.

"She is here because she needs to speak with you," Leticia replied archly. "Privately. And if I called during the day there would be no way to ensure your mother would leave us by ourselves. In fact, I'd wager she wouldn't."

"Indeed," Turner agreed, his hands falling to his sides. He too seemed unable to find a suitable place to look. But while she focused on the makeup of the room, he was overly concerned with the floor.

"I thought it best that you not hear this information secondhand," Rhys said quietly. "Although to complete the façade I need to attend to someone here. Do you mind if we simply tell everyone you were laid low with a stomach complaint?"

"Actually, there is someone in need of a doctor," Turner answered.

"Indeed?"

"One of the draft horses," he replied. Dr. Gray's face fell. "He threw a shoe while pulling a cartload of wheat into the mill yard."

"I'm not a blacksmith."

"True, but then a splinter was discovered deep in the hoof. We took it out and packed it with clean mud, but poor thing can still hardly walk."

"First of all, there's no such thing as clean mud. Secondly—"

"So you'll have a look, then," Turner interrupted. "Excellent."

Dr. Gray looked as if he had another, more tart answer on his lips, but then his shoulders sagged and he picked up his medical bag from the floor. "I'll be in the stables then, when you are ready."

And with that, Dr. Gray slipped quietly out the door.

Leaving Leticia alone with Turner.

"Poor Dr. Gray," she said, in an attempt to fill the silence that had suddenly surrounded them. "He seemed so eager."

"I know," Turner replied. "It's long been my duty to crush his spirits."

"Your duty or your delight?"

"Why not both?"

She smiled, a little. So did he. And then . . .

There it was again. That silence.

Leticia found herself staring at a loose thread on her cloak.

Turner ran his hand through his hair.

"Why don't you sit and tell me what brought you here at three o'clock in the morning." Turner said. "The fire is not very warm, but I didn't wish to alert anyone to my . . . to our meeting."

He brought over a stool and placed it next to the one in front of the abandoned tea. Then he ushered her over.

"You have a very nice room here," she blurted—yes, blurted!—as if she were a naïve debutante.

"It's a kitchen." His feet shuffled against the chair. "A small one at that."

"It has all you need. It reminds me of the kitchen where I grew up," she said, and immediately felt stupid for doing so. Why on earth bring that up? Who cares what the kitchen was like where she grew up?

"Would you care for some cold but strong tea?" he said, indicating the pot in front of him. "I can get another cup."

"No, thank you," Leticia said, clasping her hands in front of her. She had no idea what else to do with them. "You are being awfully polite."

"What would you have me be?" he asked.

"Honest."

"I'm not the one here with a story to tell," he said, his eyebrow going up.

"But you don't want me here," she replied.

"And yet, you are here. And so politeness seems like the thing to do." He leaned his elbow on the table. "Tell me why you are here, Letty."

"Don't—" she began, but then let her body slump. She didn't have it in her to have their usual argument. She wasn't there to spar with him. And in the wee small hours, every defense she had—her title, her grace, her wit—was stripped away, leaving her with only the truth.

"I need your help," she said finally.

"My help?" Both eyebrows were up now. "With what?"

"Getting rid of Mr. Blackwell."

Turner was silent a few moments. Then he took a large sip of what must have been very cold tea. Once he put the cup back down, he laced his fingers and returned his gaze to Leticia.

"Now, when you say 'getting rid of,' you don't mean—"

Her jaw dropped. "Of course I don't mean that. Do you take me for a murderess?"

"I didn't think so, but I wanted to be certain."

The look she sent him spoke loud enough that he held up his hands in defeat. "All right, all right. What do you mean then, by 'getting rid of Mr. Blackwell'?"

"I mean, I would prefer it greatly if he never had cause to darken Bluestone Manor's door again."

"Why?"

It was such a simple question. But one that hung in the air above her, ready to fall like the sword of judgment.

But damn it all, she had come this far. She had let Dr. Gray write his note and set foot into this kitchen, and the moment she had done that, she'd committed to this. To this confession.

"Because of what he knows about me," she stated as calmly as possible. "Or, what he thinks he knows."

Turner sucked in his breath.

"He knows about you and me, then? And the lie?"

"No!" she exclaimed. "As far as I can tell, Mr. Blackwell has no idea that we know each other."

"Or how well," he added, and she felt her face flame.

Oh yes, she was given to blushing. Under the right circumstances.

"I find this all very strange," Turner said, idly playing with the handle of his cup. "Because after church this morning—actually, I suppose it would be yesterday morning at this point—you seemed to be very receptive to Blackwell."

"Sir Barty is quite friendly with Mr. Blackwell. And Margaret . . . well, I'll get to that. I only gave him the benefit of the doubt. But to me something seemed . . . insidious about the man."

"Really?"

"Truly. Perhaps you cannot read my feelings as well as you think," she said.

He considered her for a moment. "I read them well enough to know that you did not wish me or my mother anywhere near Bluestone today."

"That was a mistake on my part. If you had been there

today, perhaps Blackwell would have not felt the need to threaten me this evening."

Turner's face darkened. His hand tightened on the teacup. "He threatened you?"

"Warned me, rather," she replied, her voice as calm as she could make it. "That should I take it into my head to come between him and Sir Barty—and possibly him and Margaret—that he would reveal things about my late husband I may not wish to have known."

She waited.

And waited.

"You're waiting," he said finally. "But I'll not ask the question."

"Don't you wish to know?" she asked, her hand rising absentmindedly to her neck.

"Only if you wish to tell me. We did make a pact to avoid each other as much as possible. One assumes that includes a ban on prying into each other's lives."

"One that you broke already by sending the good doctor to keep an eye on me."

"And to attend Sir Barty's foot. Don't forget that."

"Mr. Turner," she sighed. "Can we please stop talking circles around each other?"

But Turner just threw up his hands. "Leticia, I lived in London long enough to be bored by most gossip, and eventually just outright ignored it. I have little care for what your late husband did that Mr. Blackwell might know, except that it is making you scratch your neck raw."

Her hand immediately froze, covering her neck with her palm. Damn it all, she had been scratching. She forced her hand down into her lap, letting the air attack her screaming skin.

Turner stood up abruptly and walked over to the larder. There, he pulled out a jug of cream.

"What are you doing?" she asked. "You don't take cream in your tea."

Instead he pulled a handkerchief out of his pocket, shook it out to make certain it was clean, and soaked it in the cream.

"Allow me," he said, bringing the cloth over to her.

Then he placed the cool cloth against the red of her neck. She closed her eyes as the relief soaked in.

She remembered this. His gentle touch. His attentiveness.

And then, just as quickly as it had come, it was gone.

"Hold that in place," he said, taking his seat again at a respectable—and safe—distance. "It will help."

"How did you—" she started to ask.

"Something my mother used to do when my father's hands would go raw from the ropes and pulleys," he replied. Then he cleared his throat, and with it any trace of softness. "Now if you're going to tell me, tell me. If I don't need to know, then don't. But if you're just going to sit in my kitchen, it's three in the morning and I have a bed calling my name."

She tried to not think about the mention of his bed, and instead took a deep breath. She was here for a reason after all.

"Actually it's not such a strange occurrence, I'm told. My husband Konrad was a man . . . who preferred the company of other men."

If Turner was surprised or disgusted or confused, she could not see it on his face. Instead he asked, "Are you quite sure?"

"Quite." She allowed a little bubble of laughter to escape her lips. "A wife knows. There were certain marital activities that Konrad was reluctant to engage in."

Both of Turner's eyebrows rose. He coughed to clear his

throat. "That may well be. But how would Mr. Blackwell—who is not a wife—know of it?"

"That's a longer story," she said, sighing. "You have to understand that Konrad . . . When we married, I was a bit more naïve than I am now."

"I cannot imagine you naïve."

"Strange but true," she said, the ghost of a smile on her lips. "I was just a rich miller's daughter, with a sister who had married well enough for the country, but for me to try for a ton connection? It was presumptuous at best. I was friendless, I had very few invitations. Then, at one ball, Konrad asked me to dance. And he was dazzling. He lit the room around us brighter than a thousand candles. I was so swept up in anyone paying attention to me that I didn't pay attention to anything else."

"But soon enough . . ." he prompted.

"Yes, soon enough," she agreed, "I made my discovery. And when I confronted Konrad about it, he didn't deny it. In fact, he was somewhat surprised that I was surprised. It was not something about himself he hid very well. Which was actually more the reason he was in London than any war. He'd caused a bit of a scandal in Vienna and his family sent him away until people's memories became shorter. He thought marriage would hurry that along for himself."

She shifted the cream-soaked cloth to the other side of her neck, where the ghost of an old itch began whispering for attention.

"After I found out we went to the country for a bit, and when we returned to town, I was no longer naïve."

Turner shifted in his seat again. But he no longer idly toyed with his teacup or let his eyes fall to the floor. Indeed, his eyes were boring into hers. But he was patient.

Always infinitely patient, her Mr. Turner.

"While our marriage was a bit of a scandal—an Austrian count to a miller's daughter—Konrad was his own scandal. He tried to keep his secret, but . . ." She shrugged. "Because of his title, it was overlooked by the less picky members of society. When there is a ballroom of four hundred people, chances are one or two of them are going to be less than paragons."

"I remember enough about London to know that," Turner said, rubbing his chin in thought. "I'm quite surprised we did not cross paths, or rather, that you did not cross Ashby's path."

"Who would have introduced us? We did not have many close friends. So we became very good friends to each other."

"Friends?"

"Yes," she said, smiling at the memory. "Konrad—in private, when he was allowed to be himself—was a wonderful person. But he could never be truly happy, and that, I believe, led him down some darker paths." She took a deep breath. "Have you heard of an establishment called the Yew Tree Club?"

"Not specifically," Turner replied carefully. "But I can guess."

"Aside from the usual vices, it caters to a wide variety of predilections. Including Konrad's. More than once I had to fetch him from the Yew Tree. I could not trust a driver or a servant to not tell tales out of school. Appearances had to be kept as much as possible, after all."

She remembered those early mornings. Yes, she did— the predawn bleariness. The knock on her door of an urchin with a note. And then Konrad, crying and unwilling to leave the debauched room of the Yew Tree in which he had barricaded himself, until his wife came and scratched on the door. He was so deeply miserable, giving in to what he wanted and knowing it wasn't permitted, that it had made everyone he'd ever loved cast him aside.

Then they would go to the country for a while, just in case there had been someone at the Yew Tree who reveled in tales of another person's misery.

"Mr. Blackwell is familiar with the Yew Tree, I take it," Turner said finally.

"Yes." She nodded. "Although his predilection—if he has one—is not something I care to know."

"He shouldn't have done that to you," Turner said, shaking his head.

"Mr. Blackwell?"

"No, Konrad." The name came out like fire. "Making you go to the Yew Tree. You were his wife."

"Yes. And as his wife I was one of the few people he trusted completely," she said.

"You were a better wife to him than he was a husband to you. You still are."

"I hate to shatter your illusions, but that is the case in most marriages," she replied. "Besides, Konrad was not a patron of the Yew Tree Club very long. Eventually he met Lord Vere."

"Lord Vere? From Northumberland?" Turner's head came up. "He and Ashby were both members of White's, if I recall. Are you telling me . . ."

"Yes—he and Konrad fell in love. But Lord Vere was much better at hiding his truth than Konrad was. And it drove Konrad mad that Vere would keep his distance in public. They couldn't even be seen as friends. And eventually it killed him."

"Killed him?" Turner asked. "I thought your husband was thrown from his horse."

"He was, when chasing after Vere in the course of a lover's quarrel." Riding was one of the few things they could do together in front of the world. Vere had been about to get married. Konrad, although married himself, was eaten up inside with it. Because Vere intended to make his a marriage in truth—he had a legacy to think of, after all. The last she'd heard of him, Vere had just had his third child with his fat wife—visiting her once a year in Northumberland, just long enough to get her pregnant again, and spending the rest of his time comfortably ensconced in a leather chair at White's.

"And he left you behind to pick up the pieces," Turner concluded. "And one assumes without any money."

"You knew me as a fortune hunter the moment we met, didn't you?" she asked quietly.

"I knew that you were desperate and cunning, and would do what you had to do to keep your place in society," he replied, his voice equally low. "And I didn't care a whit."

He'd loved her anyway. The words echoed in her head, but he hadn't spoken them. They were as much a memory as Konrad.

"Well, when needs must," she said instead, hiding any emotion under a sniffle. "I can't help but still feel my life would have been so much different if Konrad had been able to be honest from the start."

"Would you have still married him?"

"Probably. Probably not. But it's a decision I could have made with my eyes open. After he died, his family wanted nothing to do with me. We'd never conceived a child so they had no such obligations. And here I'd been a lowly miller's daughter and then a countess. Of the two, I much preferred the latter."

"Why?" he asked, unable to keep the curiosity out of his face. "Speaking as someone who owns a mill myself, I find it to be much more satisfying than living a lie."

"Because it can all go away so quickly," she replied. "My father was successful, but every penny was pinched, everything was always on the precipice of falling over.

"Then a blight ruined the timberlands that supplied his mill. Everything became so much harder for him after that . . . He tried to economize, but eventually he ended up selling the mill for a fraction of what it was once worth. Luckily Fanny and I were already married by then, but he died bitter and striving. At least when Konrad was alive, I had some security. I knew I would never live in uncertainty."

"Yes, it is hard," Turner said after a moment. "But everything worth doing is. The world is growing, and it needs to be supplied. Surely that is worth risking a little uncertainty."

She said nothing. After all, what could she say? That she was selfish and wanted creature comforts? That she had once been dressed in silks and diamonds and nothing else could possibly compare—not even a cozy kitchen and an intimate conversation in the wee hours of the morning?

Not even the look from a man to whom she could tell all her truths, no matter how hidden or small?

"You've risked more uncertainty than most," she finally said. "A mill that has burned twice? At this point, most would call it foolhardy to continue."

"Most would call it madness. Especially those in this town. But that's not the point."

"What is the point?"

"This is where I am meant to be. I could have stayed in the army, an officer. I could have stayed in London. Ned would have given me something to do. But I spent so long in other places, trying to fold myself into roles that were not mine. This is where I am meant to be, and this is what I am meant to be doing."

"Grinding grain to make flour."

"We make some very good flour," he replied, smiling. And she realized his smile matched her own.

His dark eyes held hers for a long moment, and Leticia felt something strange and foreign spread over her skin.

Peace.

She could fall asleep right there, she thought. She was, for the first time in a very long time, truly relaxed. She could put her head down on the counter and let her bones melt, having unburdened herself to the man in front of her, and trusted that he would keep those secrets safe.

After all, they had other secrets, the two of them.

It was Turner who looked away first.

"So, from what I understand, Mr. Blackwell has the means by which to expose your late husband's . . . predilection to Sir Barty. And this has you frightened."

"Frightened is a strong word," she said, blinking her way out of their stolen moment.

"You came to me, you must be frightened. But I did not think you scared this easily."

"This easily?" Her eyebrow came up.

"Yes, because you said it yourself. This is not something Konrad hid very well. Therefore in some circles it might have been considered general, if unspoken, knowledge."

"Yes, but Sir Barty and Lincolnshire are not members of those circles."

"Surely he would not hold Konrad's sins against you."

She looked at him with pity. "Surely you're not that naïve. Don't you know that a wife is judged by her husband's actions? A man may spill the ink, but a woman wears the stain."

"No woman could wear this stain," he replied, crossing his arms over his chest. "It is actually, physically impossible."

"So?"

"So . . . tell him. Tell Sir Barty. And tell him why you're telling him. Then Blackwell will have nothing to hold over you, and you can go about your life free of him."

"It's not that simple," she replied.

"Yes it is."

"No," she said. "It is not. Oh, you are right on many levels. I could tell Sir Barty about Konrad. Hopefully he would not bat an eye. Let's say I tell him too why the topic has come up. That Mr. Blackwell made veiled threats with this knowledge. That, I am afraid, he would not believe."

"Of course he would," Turner said, but looked as if even he did not trust it.

"There are a few ways this chess match could play out. In the less likely version, Sir Barty believes me absolutely and throws Blackwell out."

"Why is the best-case scenario also the least likely?" Turner asked.

"Because we are living in the real world, not a fiction," she replied dryly. "The second most likely event would be that Sir Barty believes me absolutely and confronts Blackwell with it. In that scenario, Mr. Blackwell is smart enough to explain himself, saying I misinterpreted what was said, and that he apologizes profusely. Forget for a moment that it is his fiancée who brings him this accusation. Blackwell is forgiven because he is such a good fellow."

"And the third . . ."

"The third is that Sir Barty does not believe me at all, because Blackwell is, as stated, such a good fellow. He will not even bother going to Blackwell before patting me on the head and dismissing my account." She took the cloth off her neck and delicately folded it before placing it on the counter. "But all three of these scenarios have the unfortunate side effect of letting Mr. Blackwell know that I have made a move against him. And he will not look favorably on it."

Turner's hand dropped from his chin as he considered her words.

"You must be very good at chess," he said finally.

"I am astonishingly good," she replied. "Getting rid of Mr. Blackwell will not be easily done. He is currying favor with Sir Barty. And, it seems, with Margaret—and she could very well be responsive to his overtures."

She thought back to the day of blushes and their conversation after dinner. If Blackwell was a threat, it was here.

Turner's jaw set at that. "He's angling after Miss Babcock?"

"Is it so unthinkable? After all, it's what your mother would have you do to secure your interests with Sir Barty. Heavens, even Sir Barty is all for offering up the milling of grain as dowry to you. I imagine he'd make the same deal with Blackwell. And while Mr. Blackwell is not only bad news for me, he is bad news for you, for obvious reasons. But he is utterly terrible for Margaret. Can you imagine a man like that marrying her? What he would do to her?"

If Margaret became Blackwell's bride, she'd be taken away, rendered even more friendless than she currently was. His dark and twisted soul would break hers, and quite easily. For underneath that tough spiked shell, Margaret was very much protecting something pure and vulnerable.

"We cannot allow that to happen," she said, folding her hands in her lap now. "And the easiest way to rid ourselves of Blackwell is for you to win Sir Barty's business."

He waited. He sipped cold tea as he did.

"By courting Margaret," she said.

There was a distinct sound. A low, choking sputter. It bridged into a coughing fit, and then a pounding on the chest, to clear the path for a chuckle that grew and grew into full-fledged laughter.

"Shh!" Leticia said, lurching forward to cover his laugh. "Do you want to wake the house?"

"I'm sorry," he said, taking her hand down from his mouth. "But it strikes me as odd, seeing as only a week ago you dictated that I should stay far, far away from Margaret."

"Currently, you are the lesser of two evils," she replied.

"So you want me to marry Margaret . . ."

"I did not say marry," she corrected quickly. "I said court. Return her interest to you and only to you, so Blackwell does not stand a chance there."

"So you want me to lead the poor girl into thinking I wish to marry her." Turner crossed his arms over his chest. "To keep your secrets safe."

"Yes! I mean, no!" Leticia said, exasperated. "Look, it's not a fully formed plan."

"I'll say," he said.

"Just pay enough attention to her to let her think her plan to ignore you worked."

"She had a plan to ignore me? Why do I think that idea came from elsewhere?" The corner of his mouth picked up as he squeezed her hand.

He was still holding her hand. She'd covered his laughter, and he'd taken her hand in his to release his mouth, and . . . just not let go. And it was so easy, so comfortable, so right, that she simply didn't notice. She was sitting in a kitchen at three in the morning holding hands with John Turner like it was the most normal, natural thing in the world.

But it wasn't normal and natural. Or at least it shouldn't be. She did not belong in this kitchen. She belonged in a drawing room at Bluestone Manor.

She belonged with Sir Barty.

And that thought had her pulling her hand free. And he let it go.

"You, Sir Barty, my mother," he said. "All have this half-cocked idea that my courting Margaret would solve all of our problems. Never mind my feelings on the subject. But you seem to be forgetting that Margaret is a creature of her own mind. Why don't you trust her to see through Blackwell on her own?"

"I have no doubt that she would, eventually." It was true, for as much as Margaret kept her head down and her attention firmly on her plants, she could be disconcertingly observant. "But by then it could be too late. A marriage hastily done simply because she's nineteen and does not know how to separate affection from flattery? Trust me, therein lies disaster."

"Fair point," Turner said, leaning his chin on steepled fingers. "I think you're right on one score—that the best way to rid ourselves of Blackwell is for me to win Sir Barty's business. But I would prefer to do it without playing a young woman for the fool."

"It would not be forever—just long enough to foil Blackwell's plans," she replied, leaning in with earnestness. "Margaret, I'm certain, would recover." Although she wasn't all that certain, but hoped it would be the case. "It would be for the greater good."

"Funny. That's what I told myself last summer." His eyes searched hers. "With you."

Leticia's head came up. Was that an apology? But before she could ask, he let out a long sigh.

"I'll do it," he said, his hand going to his chin again, calculating. "But you must do something for me."

Leticia knew better than to agree to a bargain when the terms were not defined. "What is that?"

"Two things, actually. First, invite my mother over for tea," he said. "She would find it very pleasant. I know she was hurt by our exclusion today."

Leticia felt that little slice of guilt go through her. "Of course. It will be strategic to invite you both. You will be able to spend time with Margaret, and with any luck Blackwell will—"

"Letty, did you hear what I said?" Turner laughed. "I would not have you invite her over for strategic purposes. My mother likes you. Not everything need be a play in a game. Lord, the two of you are birds of a feather."

He rubbed a hand over his face. "My mother does not have many friends. Sir Barty and Lady Babcock had been friends for so long, but ever since Lady Babcock's death things have been strained . . . it's hard not to notice."

Yes, things were oddly strained. On both sides. But Leticia need only remember the way Sir Barty lit up when he pointed out Helen on the way into town that first Sunday, happy to see a friend.

"I will happily invite her—for friendship as well as strategic purposes," she added quickly. "But when she comes for tea, she cannot mention the mill."

Turner looked taken aback. "She cannot?"

"That's why there is tension." At least, she thought it was. "Sir Barty practically ducks out of the room every time she comes in, because the hints she drops could level Parliament. He does not want to be pressured by one of his oldest friends. In fact, all he wants to do is enjoy her company and play cards."

"The mill is the only thing that consumes her thoughts these days. If I've been under pressure to bring it back to its former glory, she has been under exponentially more, because she's had to deal with the town and its censure by herself while I was away."

Hence the lack of friends. Oh, the town was polite to Helen, but there was no confidant. No comfort. Mrs. Emory had seen to that.

Everyone needed someone to talk truths with at three in the morning.

"What is the second?"

"Hmm?"

"The second thing I must do for you," she clarified.

"Convince the rest of Helmsley to trust the Turner Grain Mill with their business."

She stared at him blankly.

"That's all?" she asked finally. "You don't want me to fetch you the crown jewels as well?"

"I've been running over the books, and if Sir Barty cannot be won over this harvest season, we will manage to survive until the next harvest if there are enough of the smaller farms willing to trust us to mill their grain."

"Surely once the crop starts to come in, they will see that your mill is superior . . ."

"No they won't. Not if the sermon this morning was any indication."

She had to confess, she hadn't really heard the sermon. She'd been too busy watching Blackwell out of one eye and Turner out of the other. It's a wonder she didn't require spectacles.

"It was about constancy. And the old ways being the best."

"That doesn't mean it was about the steam equipment at your mill."

Turner simply looked at her like she was missing her nose. "The steam equipment is the only thing in Helmsley from this century. They don't trust anything new. Beside that, no one trusts me to run the business, since it's burned twice and hasn't ground an ounce of flour under my leadership."

"But you can lead the business," she cried. "You are!"

"I've convinced you, at least. And now I need to convince the town. With your help."

"How do you expect me to do that?" she asked. "You said it yourself, they don't trust anything new. And I am quite new."

"You are also Leticia Herzog, Lady Churzy," he replied. "You can charm entire continents. I've seen you, in the churchyard. Mrs. Robertson, the vicar's wife . . . they all want your favor, but are too proud to approach you for it."

"Or they are too under Mrs. Emory's rule. Who hates you for her son losing his job."

"God save me from another Harold Emory." Turner rolled his eyes. "But if people could simply see the mechanisms working—hell, we were going to show you today, but then . . ."

"Then Palmer Blackwell arrived." Leticia thought for a moment. If she could get the vicar's wife on their side, she could influence the vicar. And Mrs. Robertson would be able to tell everyone who came into her store . . . and Miss Goodhue would tell her students, who would in turn tell their parents. It could be done. But it would take more than finesse. It would take . . .

"You say you were going to offer Sir Barty and myself a tour of the steam equipment?" she asked suddenly.

He nodded.

"So it's all ready. It's working properly? No more explosions?"

"Yes," he replied. "At least, I've done everything I can to make sure of it."

"That will have to do." She hopped down from her stool, straightening her skirt and fitting the hood of her cloak over her head. "I suggest you have your equipment running in tip-top condition by Tuesday. This has been an incredibly edifying evening, Mr. Turner. I thank you for your assistance."

She moved toward the door.

"Wait . . ." he called after her.

"I'm sorry, but Dr. Gray must be waiting in the carriage by now and I have a great deal to do today and tomorrow. As do you." She pulled on her gloves. "I will send around a girl with a note after breakfast, asking you and Helen to attend us for tea. Don't forget what I told you to tell your mother."

"I won't . . . but, Letty." He reached her and took her elbow, gently but firmly, turning her back to him. "What on earth is going to happen on Tuesday?"

"The same thing that happens every Tuesday, or so I'm told." She dazzled at him, the sparkling plan fomenting in her mind. "Mrs. Emory receives callers."

And with that, she marched out the door, a veritable bounce in her step.

Leaving Turner behind, completely bewildered but smiling. Smiling like a daft fool.

15

"Mrs. Emory! A pleasure."

Mrs. Emory looked up from where she was surrounded by a gaggle of women from the town, including her usual retinue of Mrs. Robertson, Mrs. Spilsby, and Miss Goodhue. There was shock on her face.

There was also a piece of cake half in her mouth.

Well, Leticia thought, smiling. This is a promising start already.

"Lady Churzy," Mrs. Emory said, once she swallowed her cake. "And Miss Babcock. This is . . . quite the surprise."

"Is it?" Leticia replied. "After all, you told us of your receiving callers on Tuesdays."

"Yes, but . . ."

"She said there was no way you would actually come!" Miss Goodhue piped up, only to have her arm swatted by Mrs. Spilsby.

"Indeed?" Leticia purred. No wonder Mrs. Emory looked so shocked. She'd obviously interrupted her gossiping time—and it was not difficult to guess the subject of her speculations.

"What my sister means, my lady," Mrs. Spilsby said smoothly, covering for Miss Goodhue with the practiced peacemaking of a true vicar's wife, "is that Mrs. Emory assumed you would leave a card first, and then have the call returned. Like the fashionable ladies one reads about."

"Oh, standing on ceremony is so very dull, don't you find?" Leticia replied, waving a hand in the air as she seated herself next to the sandwiches. "Oh, watercress, lovely. Margaret, what is your opinion?"

Margaret looked as startled to be included in the conversation as Mrs. Emory was to have them in her parlor. But the girl took her cue and showed herself to be not completely inadequate in social situations.

"I—ah—I am not one for standing on ceremony either?" she replied, and Miss Goodhue scooted over to offer her a seat on the couch.

She'd had some difficulty convincing Margaret to come with her to pay this call. Leticia had arrived back from Turner's kitchen in the wee hours of Monday morning with a plan forming in her mind. It could work. It would work. But unfortunately, she had other responsibilities—one of which was making certain that Mr. Blackwell and Margaret were not alone together, for the girl's own sake, whether she realized it or not.

And also unfortunately, that seemed to be the sole aim of Mr. Blackwell, all of Monday.

He'd come over for tea, just as Helen and Sir Barty were taking out the cribbage board. Came in with all the bounding determination of a man desperate to be liked.

"Miss Babcock! I have been thinking all day about your orchard! I decided to forgo my afternoon appointments so I could ask you about it. Is there something magical you put in the soil to boast such marvelous fruits?"

"That's my tea, Mr. Blackwell." Margaret shifted in her seat to face the new arrival.

"Tea?"

"Yes, you should try some, Blackwell," Turner said from Margaret's other side. "I'm told it's most refreshing."

Turner had glanced at Leticia then, and she did her best to hide a smile. But soon enough Turner had returned Margaret's attention to him by asking about the various plants Margaret was busy experimenting with.

She'd felt safe that Turner would be able to keep himself between Blackwell and Margaret, but all it took was one moment where Turner had moved to speak to Dr. Gray, and Blackwell was at Margaret's side, convincing her to go on a tour of the gardens.

And all it took was one glance in the direction of Mr. Turner and Dr. Gray, who were deep in conversation, and Margaret accepted Blackwell's offer of escort.

Leticia had to trot to catch up to them before they got too far. And she pulled Turner along with her.

"What were you doing, abandoning Margaret to Blackwell's clutches?" she scolded though her panting.

"Blackwell has clutches now, does he?" Turner scowled. "And I had to talk to Rhys—he's been giving me questions to ask Margaret about her research. He knows a great deal more about it than I."

"Can't even talk to a girl on your own now?" she asked.

"Depends on the girl," Turner muttered under his breath, and shot her a rueful smile. She couldn't help but laugh.

This "working together" was off to an admirable start.

Of course, they caught up to Margaret and Blackwell in the orchard before anything untoward could happen. Margaret was even laughing—a bit too loudly, but for all the world seemingly entranced by Blackwell. And when she saw Leticia and Turner, Leticia thought she saw for the briefest of moments . . .

Disappointment.

Did that . . . did that mean that Margaret wanted to be alone with Blackwell? Oh dear.

Leticia decided she would berate herself later for her ill-fated advice to Margaret.

And Blackwell did glare at Leticia, as if saying that this interruption was a breach of whatever deal he'd thought he'd fostered. But after one small aside to Blackwell, noting that "Turner was adamant about following after Margaret. And I cannot have her with one gentleman alone, let alone two," the man returned to his normal, slimy sort of charm.

The rest of the day had gone well enough. Helen and Sir Barty passed a marvelous afternoon of cribbage, the game still being far too close to call. Blackwell lingered as long as he was able, trying to weasel an invitation to stay from Sir Barty, but luckily the man's foot was putting him in a bit of a temper and they decided to call it a day rather early.

The more she thought about it, the more she saw Mr. Blackwell as a danger. Not toward herself—she could handle herself—but toward Margaret. His displays of admiration were so overt, so florid, that they practically smelled rancid. In any other situation he would be laughed at, and then assiduously avoided. But Margaret did not have the experience with men to know that his overtures were foul or how to handle them. He was of the type who would use anything to his advantage, even—especially—a girl's naïveté.

Thus, Leticia knew she could not leave Blackwell alone with Margaret. And since Turner had to be at the mill on Tuesday, Leticia would have to take Margaret to pay calls with her.

"But it's not market day," Margaret protested. "There is no hope of acquiring fish carcasses. And why Mrs. Emory? You do not even like her."

"Sometimes, Margaret, I am afraid people must go into town simply to spend time in the company of people they do not like."

"Yet another social custom I will never understand," Margaret grumbled.

"And yet again I agree with you, but it must be done. For Mr. Turner's sake."

"Mr. Turner?" That brought Margaret up short, added pink to her cheeks. No matter Blackwell's influence, it seemed that Turner still had the ability to make her blush—something Leticia never imagined she would be thankful for, but there it was. "What has he to do with Mrs. Emory?"

"You'll find out today," Leticia said. "Now, I need you to do something for me. While we are with Mrs. Emory and her ilk, I need you to agree with everything I say."

Margaret again looked skeptical. "What's in it for me?"

"With any luck, an incredibly quick visit to Mrs. Emory and then a tour of a fascinating mechanical wonder."

That was more than enough to have Margaret agreeing, and as they nestled in among the other ladies in Mrs. Emory's parlour, Leticia could only hope Margaret's agreeableness would last.

"Mrs. Robertson, I am terribly glad to see you. I had hoped to find you in your shop, but it was closed."

"Er, yes." Mrs. Robertson glanced at Mrs. Emory. "We are closed on Tuesday mornings. For . . . restocking? Yes, restocking."

How the store was meant to be restocked when its sole employee was abovestairs attending to the shop owner's whims was left unresolved.

"No matter!" Leticia said brightly, and whipped the magazine pages out from the folio she'd carried under her arm. "I wanted to return these to you."

"Oh dear—did you not find anything fashionable enough for you?" Mrs. Emory's voice dripped with sarcasm. "Heaven knows we cannot approximate Paris fashions here, us simple folk in the country."

She tittered as she said this, and a number of the other ladies tittered in agreement.

"Oh, but you can!" Leticia replied, allowing a dazzling smile to smother any slight. "Perhaps you are unable to, but that is why you turned your shop over to Mrs. Robertson, whose skill with a needle is unparalleled, if those gowns in the window are anything to go by."

Mrs. Robertson blushed under the compliment, and suddenly, all attention was turned to her.

Mrs. Emory turned red for an entirely different reason.

"I thought you were absolutely correct, Mrs. Robertson— the second dress you had in the pile, the one with the lace overlay? Absolutely delightful! I refuse to wear anything else for my wedding."

"Oh, my lady!" Mrs. Robertson cried. "I knew that would look best on you. Now the drawing showed three rows of flounces on the hem, but I find myself rather against flounces, don't you? We should let the cut and the material speak for itself . . ."

"Yes, of course," Leticia said, nodding. Then she turned to Margaret. "Margaret, what is your opinion on flounces?"

Margaret's head again came up. "Ah . . . they are rather too showy?"

And she was rewarded with the broadest of smiles from Mrs. Robertson—and Miss Goodhue next to her.

"Oh yes, Miss Babcock!" Miss Goodhue said, not noticing her own dress had three flounces. "I think you're absolutely right—to appear tall and elegant ladies should eschew flounces."

Margaret looked down at the overeager (and so very much shorter) Miss Goodhue with something akin to bewilderment.

"And with an ivory silk under the lace," Mrs. Robertson was saying. "Oh, if only I had my pencils, I could sketch it for you right now! We could go down to the shop—"

"Moira!" Mrs. Emory cried. Then an uneasy smile settled on her face. "There is no need for that. It's our day for receiving callers."

"True," Leticia replied. "There is no need to go down to the shop. After all, I'll just have Mrs. Robertson come up to Bluestone and take my measurements there."

From the hue that Mrs. Emory took on, Leticia was reminded that envy indeed had a color. And it wasn't ivory silk under lace.

"That is . . . very good of you, my lady," Mrs. Emory bit out.

"Pish," Leticia said, waving that away. "It's not good of me. It's commerce. I am in need of Mrs. Robertson's services. That is, after all, the point of business."

"It is," Margaret agreed. Miss Goodhue nodded as well.

"I am surprised you have knowledge of how business works, my lady." Mrs. Emory's eyes became steely. Really, her attitude of immediate dislike was as stubborn as it was unfathomable. "I am informed that true ladies do not sully themselves with such practices."

"As a lady, I prefer not to limit myself," Leticia said, sending a wink toward Margaret, who blinked back her shock. "But really, it's simply common sense. Good work begets business, and business begets more business. And one business helps another. After all, if Mrs. Robertson's work is as stunning as I know it will be, she will have oodles of people asking her to create gowns for them. And that brings people into Helmsley, which in turn has them buying other goods here."

"Of course," Mrs. Emory agreed. "However, this is hardly a topic of conversation for this group–"

"Why ever not?" Leticia asked. "After all, there are more women of business in this room than not. And I speak as one of the not. You, Mrs. Emory, own this building. Mrs. Robertson runs your millinery shop. There are women here who manage the business of the home while men go out into the fields. Mrs. Spilsby is the vicar's wife, so while her husband attends to the spirit, she does the practical work of attending to the body through, I'd guess, half a dozen charities. Am I right, Mrs. Spilsby?"

It was Miss Goodhue who piped up from next to Margaret, however.

"She does so very much! The meals we organize for those women having their lying in, and those who are infirm or elderly. Oh, Miss Babcock, I do think they would love your flowers—perhaps we can arrange a showing or to have some sent around with the baskets . . ."

Leticia smiled. "Miss Goodhue will sing your praises, Mrs. Spilsby, even if you will not. However, praise is most certainly due for you sending me young Rebecca. She is a wonder at pastries and cakes. Cook is taking her completely under her wing—I'll be hard-pressed to give her back after the wedding!"

"Oh, thank you, my lady," Mrs. Spilsby said, blushing. "But I am not her employer, I merely knew she was looking for a situation. She is free to stay on with you if you wish."

"There! You see, the business of taking care of the town is always left up to the women."

"Er, had I known you were serious about needing someone to make a wedding cake," Mrs. Emory began weakly, "my Wendra is widely regarded as the best baker in town."

Leticia took the opportunity to let her gaze fall over Mrs. Emory's stout form. "I'm sure that's the case, but I know you simply couldn't do without her." And there was no way she was letting Mrs. Emory's tattletale under Bluestone Manor's roof. After all, now that she had promoted Molly to her own ladies' maid, and made her discretion a condition of the position, she had plugged that leak.

Wendra and Mrs. Emory must be absolutely chomping at the bit for information.

As if to emphasize the point, she reached over and took a little frosted tea cake from the tray in front of Mrs. Emory. Bit off the tiniest corner of it. Then tightened the corners of her mouth, as if hiding a grimace, and delicately put down the tea cake.

And everyone saw.

Silence fell over the room as each of the ladies in attendance contemplated their own tea cake, and one by one put them all down.

Leticia smiled serenely, hiding the fact that she had won the room.

Mrs. Emory did not hide the fact that she was livid.

"I am afraid I do not understand to what your speech tends," Mrs. Emory said stiffly. "We are simple country folk, after all. The ways of town are completely foreign to us."

"Well, then I'll talk slowly, for your sake," Leticia purred. "I grew up in a town very much like this one. And whether living there or in London or in a castle, people need each other. One cannot be prosperous at the expense of another. Everyone must be prosperous together. Especially when you live next door to them. Our fortunes and futures are all tied together."

A murmur of agreement went through the group.

"That is exactly what my darling Enoch preaches," Mrs. Spilsby said, nodding.

"And I'm certain everyone here would agree with that sentiment," Mrs. Emory hastened to assure. "Myself in particular."

"Then why are you so against the Turner Grain Mill reopening?" Leticia asked. She said it sweetly, but the bite behind the words did not go unnoticed. "After all, it would be nothing but good for the town to have the mill working again."

"I quite agree," Margaret said, without any prompting.

Mrs. Emory drew herself up in her seat, puffing herself up. Fire lit her eyes, ready to do battle.

"I would like nothing better for the town to have a working mill again," she said smoothly. "However, I have no faith that the Turner Grain Mill will ever function properly."

"Oh really? Why?"

"Other than the fact that the property has burned twice in the last six years? The explosion just last week? The current Mr. Turner never ran the mill before. His father did, but the son went off to war and left for years. And now he comes back with newfangled ideas and steam equipment—and nothing ruins wheat like steam, mind you—trying to tell us all everything will be better than before? What was wrong with the way it has been the past six years? Mr. Blackwell has kept the grain milled in a timely fashion, from what my friends tell me. If the Turners really wanted to do something for the town, they could sell the business to Mr. Blackwell and have him run it—that way we'd have a mill and someone proper in charge. Or burn the property down, since that is what will happen anyway once that nefarious machinery is turned on. And it will likely burn down the entire town this time.

"You say our fortunes and our futures are all tied together, and they are endangering mine."

"Is that so?" Leticia replied. "So you have no hope at all that the mill will work?"

"No. Although I truly wish it were otherwise. And you can tell them that, my lady," Mrs. Emory finished triumphantly. "Seeing as how you have become such good friends with them."

Leticia rose to her feet. "Actually, Mrs. Emory, I think you should tell them."

"What?" her adversary replied, astonished. "What is this?"

"You say you wish the mill were operational. Why don't we go see if it is?" She held out her hand, the offer of a bargain. In Mrs. Emory's own sitting room. In front of everyone. "Right now."

16

Getting everyone out of Mrs. Emory's apartments on the main square of Helmsley was not an issue. The ladies of the town burst out of the building like a petticoated explosion, breathlessly giggling and twittering at their Tuesday-morning excitement. Usually when a group of this size was required to move from one place to another, there would inevitably be delays, while someone needed to retrieve her gloves, another needed to visit the necessary, and yet another was not at all sure that their prescribed route was the best course.

Not this time.

No one wanted to miss this.

Leticia and Mrs. Emory walked arm in arm, the picture of friendliness—but only from the neck down. Anyone who chanced to look at their expressions knew they were opponents, forced into a truce but ready at any moment to engaged in battle again.

As the ladies of Helmsley made their way across the square and along the street leading to the mill at the entrance of town, they collected no small number of curious stares.

"We're going to see the mill!" Miss Goodhue called out as they passed the butcher's shop, to one particularly confused looking butcher. It wasn't every day a flock of women marched down the street with a goal. Women en masse, with purpose, are a fearful thing. "We are going to see if it works!"

"I want to see if it works too!" the butcher's son, about eight or nine, called back to Miss Goodhue.

"I heard it might not be safe," the butcher told him.

"Safe enough for ladies," Leticia called back.

After that, their retinue included more than one person of the male persuasion.

When they arrived at the mill yard, they resembled nothing so much as a small, very polite mob. And as was their mobbish tendency, they did not let the gate hold them back. Instead, led by Leticia and Mrs. Emory, they went directly through the yard, passing by the half dozen or so men offloading carts of coal and others transporting barrels of grain to walk directly up to the entrance of the windmill itself.

Two knocks later, the door swung open.

"Lady Churzy! What a complete and utter surprise to see you here today," Helen said as she dropped to a curtsy. "And Mrs. Emory and . . . well, everyone. What a pleasure."

"Mrs. Turner," Leticia said, returning Helen's curtsy. "We were hoping to see Mr. Turner's mill."

"Certainly. I was just bringing my son a tray for his luncheon," Helen said. "He's right upstairs."

Mrs. Emory, whose face had become more and more grim as they got closer to the mill, pounced on the opening left her. "Oh, well, we should not wish to disturb your son's luncheon . . ."

"Nonsense," Helen replied. "I'm sure he'd be happy to help you."

And with that Helen swept aside and let them in.

Well, not all at once. Because while getting everyone out of Mrs. Emory's apartments and up the street to the mill had not been a difficulty, fitting everyone inside the windmill was.

But they managed to squeeze in. Leticia looked back over her shoulder and saw Margaret at the very back—her height being a useful marker, Leticia had asked her to bring up the rear. Of course this meant she had no means of escaping Miss Goodhue, who chattered along happily beside her.

Or perhaps she didn't wish to escape. Perhaps Margaret had made a friend.

Leticia took a deep breath and led the group up the metal spiral staircase.

"Lady Churzy," Turner said as her head popped up on the second floor. "What a complete and utter surprise to see you here today."

Leticia decided to ignore his practiced speech—which was the exact same as his mother's—and dive right in before anyone could be the wiser.

"Mr. Turner. I was hoping you might show my friends and me the workings of your mill."

"I don't see why not," Turner drawled. Then he stepped over to take her hand and help her up the rest of the stairs.

"Hell, Mrs. Emory, Mrs. Spilsby, and . . . everyone. Is that the butcher's boy back there?" He turned his gritted smile to Leticia. She gave the same bright smile back.

"Well." Turner clapped his hands together. "Why don't you all come up? The best place to start learning about a windmill is not at the bottom, but at the very top."

Leticia stood next to Turner as Mrs. Emory led the pack up the spiral staircase to the top floor.

"Why is the entire town in my mill?" Turner whispered to her, nodding hello as people passed.

"Because you invited them," she whispered back.

"I thought you said it would only be a few ladies."

"They multiplied."

"I'm told ladies cannot do that on their own."

She fought every impulse that she had to shoot him a disdainful look. He fought every impulse to smirk. And soon she was fighting her own smile.

"The next time a theater troupe comes through Helmsley, you should ask for lessons," she said.

"Was it that bad?"

"You are as wooden as a forest."

"I'm sorry. I'm nervous. A great deal rides on this."

"Take two deep breaths and set yourself at ease."

He did. She could see his shoulders relaxing.

"There. Much better. You will be fine. You know this mill like the back of your hand. Besides," she said, cocking her head to one side. "I would never have thought that you would require assistance in pretense."

"Really? Why?" His gaze parroted hers.

"Consider how we met."

That made the corner of his mouth twitch.

"Are you two coming?" Margaret's head appeared above them as she leaned over to look down the spiral staircase.

"Right behind you!" Leticia called out. "Shall we?" she said to Turner.

"After you."

❧

EVERYONE STOOD WEDGED together on the seventh floor of the windmill. As the building was cone-shaped, this floor was smaller than those below it and more than one lady found a stray elbow in her corset. Added to that, the seven flights of circular stairs was a bit more than most people were used to climbing, and thus the atmosphere at the top of the mill was as thick with perspiration as it was with anticipation.

At least, that was to what she was going to attribute that little droplet of sweat she saw at Turner's temple. That was it. Not those nerves he spoke of. Because what reason did he have to be nervous?

It was only his livelihood at stake.

And in a roundabout fashion, her future in this town as well.

Heavens, was that damp she felt on her own brow?

"Hello, everyone, and thank you for your interest in the Turner Grain Mill," Turner began, his voice clear and booming. A practiced presentation, but rightly so—he had to do this well. "As you might know, my father, the late Lewis Turner, built this mill almost twenty years ago. I was a lad of nine when it opened—"

Leticia's eyebrow perked up. Considering her own passage into her thirties a few years ago, the math would indicate that she was older than Turner. For some reason, the thought was just . . . disturbing.

"And therefore I have been with her for her entire life," he continued, reaching out a hand to pat the rough brick of the walls, the smooth wooden beams of the machinery.

"Or lives, you should say," Mrs. Emory piped up from the front of the group. She maintained her straight back, her broad stance, taking up as much room in the crowded space as possible. She looked to her underlings for support, but only Mrs. Robertson (whose employment was, after all, in Mrs. Emory's hands) nodded in agreement.

"Quite right, Mrs. Emory," Turner replied with a cheerful smile. (Turner? Cheerful? Was the sky about to fall too?) "This is not the original structure. Nor the second structure. But after the first fire, we rebuilt in haste and without thought to safety—and that was my mistake.

I thought only of reopening, of providing Helmsley with a mill again. That the rickety wooden frame we'd built burned again allowed us—the millwrights and me—to take our time and build a strong, proper mill in its place. As you can see now, since there are a dozen of you, seven floors up and not a worry in the world."

The superior tilt to Mrs. Emory's mouth dropped as she realized that, indeed, she was standing inside the mill with a dozen of her closest townspeople and there was nary a squeak to the floorboards.

"It also allowed us to make improvements to the mill—but we'll get to those later." He smiled broadly, warming to his subject. "That very large iron pole above your heads is the wind shaft connected to the cap and the sails outside. It turns these gears here"—he pointed to a rather intense and heavy-looking set of large-toothed gears, attached to another long pole, this one perpendicular and running down through a hole in the floor—"and drives the energy of the wind down to the grindstones two floors below us. Where we are milling grain right now. Shall we go see?"

"But . . ." Margaret began, however, a very quick look from Leticia kept the young lady from spouting her logic. Not yet, Leticia silently pleaded. Just wait.

Everyone trooped down the same circular staircase they had come up, but this time led by Turner, with Leticia positioning herself right behind him.

As they passed the sixth floor, Turner pointed out the large basins full of grain being fed via funnel to the floor below. "We bring the grain up with pulleys in sacks," he said, pointing to behind the basins, where a pallet of empty grain sacks sat. "We use enough pulleys and counterweights that one man can pull up five hundred pounds of grain."

"That used to be my Harold's job," Mrs. Emory said

stiffly. "Why, if he'd been working here when the fire broke out, he would have been trapped."

"Actually, he would have been able to get down via the stairs, the pulley system, or by jumping to the balcony a few floors below, but perhaps it was for the best that he overslept that morning," Turner answered.

Mrs. Emory turned a particularly mottled shade of sour.

"Shall we?" Turner asked, leading the group to the next floor.

When they had all marched past the fifth floor on their way up to the top of the mill, they had spared a bare glance for all the mechanical noise and white powder floating through the air, but now they could gawk at their leisure. Here were the guts of the mill itself.

"If everyone would stay close to the staircase, please. We are not quite used to giving tours," Turner said as he moved toward the grindstones themselves. There were three sets of them. "These are granite, specially cut in France," Turner was saying. "I had to take a trip to Dover especially to get them."

Was it possible that Turner . . . winked at her as he said that? And was it possible that she blushed in response?

Heavens, she was as bad as Margaret.

"Grain is funneled from above at a steady pace—not too much at once, lest we choke the system." Everyone craned their necks up to see the grain being fed via funnel and slope to the grindstones. The butcher's boy looked like he was about to stick his head directly underneath the flow of grain. Miss Goodhue pulled him back. Then did the same for Margaret, equally interested in the mechanics.

"These tentering bottles are weights that keep them counterbalanced, so the stones can grind at different consistencies. We can make flour that's a fine grind, a medium grind, and a coarse grind, depending on how you like your bread. And that flour, once ground, flows down to the sifters on the floors beneath, which divide it all into their weights."

"Amazing," Leticia said, taking her own cue. "And to think all of it is powered by wind."

"Actually, not all of it."

"Aha!" Mrs. Emory cried, and drew the startled looks of everyone around her. "Therein is the problem, Mr. Turner. That you have a windmill is all well and good, but it's not just a windmill, is it?"

"No."

"And you haven't the experience running a mill on steam power, do you?"

The corner of Turner's mouth ticked up, ever so slightly. "No, I haven't."

"So we are to be subjected to your experimentations?" Mrs. Emory was really building to her topic, letting her passion and vehemence sway her, if not those around her. "To the smoke, the noise, the heat, the danger?"

"I don't understand," Leticia said sweetly. "What danger? We are all perfectly safe right now."

"Of course, this is safe. This is fine, running the whole operation on the wind. But Helmsley is a small town, built on tradition. Really, if you were to ever turn that machinery on, who knows what havoc it would wreak!"

"But, Mrs. Emory . . ." Turner said, his brow coming down in confusion, "it *is* on."

All the blood drained from her face. A murmur went through the ladies around her.

"Didn't you notice on the top floor?" Margaret asked, unable to keep the mechanical disdain out her voice. "None of the gears were turning. Down here . . . everything is."

They all watched the realization hit Mrs. Emory hard. Yes, when they toured the top floor, none of the poles and gears had been spinning. But when they came down to this floor, the grindstones pulverized grain into flour, powered by a wheel and shaft that redirected through the floor at a different angle, heading out of the mill itself, to the engine house next door. When everyone went to look out the small window, they could see that a plume of smoke was feeding out of the stack, calmly puffing away.

"And as you see, it's very quiet. You hardly noticed it."

"Mrs. Emory didn't notice at all," Miss Goodhue said under her breath with a giggle.

"Add to that, the steam is kept far away from the grain on the other side of the mill. The millwrights based the layout design on those grain mills powered by water," Turner said, smiling. "They are very adept at keeping the grain dry."

"And should fire ever break out, there would be a surfeit of water on hand," Margaret added, her eyes lighting up.

"True," Leticia said, sending Margaret a look, praying that she end the subject there. "And since Mrs. Emory said we were all perfectly safe . . ."

"I did no such thing!" she cried.

"Are you certain?" Leticia replied, nonplussed. "I must have misheard then. Mrs. Spilsby, do you recall what Mrs. Emory said?"

"She . . . she did indeed say that we are safe."

"I did not—"

"Do you really wish to contradict the vicar's wife—who, I must imagine, lives by a code of integrity?"

Mrs. Emory's mouth opened, but this time no sound came out.

"Then surely you have to admit, the mill—even with the new steam equipment—is perfectly safe. And running very well."

"I will do no such thing," Mrs. Emory said stiffly.

"Come now, Louisa," came a new voice from the staircase. Curiosity had obviously gotten the better of Helen, as she was standing behind them. "This little grudge is silly. We never meant to cost your Harold his employment."

"In fact, once the harvest begins in earnest, we hope to be able to hire on a dozen men," Turner added.

"Oh—I'll have to tell my brother!" the butcher's boy squeaked. "Pa says he's useless hanging around the shop!"

Mrs. Spilsby leaned over and whispered to Mrs. Robertson, who nodded fervently. "Oh yes, my nephew is looking for work too . . ."

"MOIRA!" Mrs. Emory cried, hoping to bring at least one minion back in line. But this time, it was not to be.

"It's true," Mrs. Robertson replied, her back straightening.

"Well, I . . . that is . . ." Mrs. Emory grasped for words, and for her dignity. "I believe the morning is over. We cannot dawdle all day, there is business to be done. Ladies . . ." She swept past everyone, past Helen, and descended the spiral staircase.

But for once, no one followed her.

"Well, if you all would like to see the rest of the mill," Turner said, unable to stop grinning. Enthusiastic nods greeted him.

They trooped down to the next floor, where the flour was sifted by weight and grind into different funnels, which were then funneled again into sacks beneath that.

Everyone was duly impressed with the functions of the mill. The butcher's boy and Margaret especially were peppering Turner with so many questions (Who are your millwrights? How many pounds can be milled in one day? Does one pound of grain equal one pound of flour? What does that lever do?) that Helen had to step in to put a stop to it.

"If everyone would like, I have tea and sandwiches back at the house. You are all more than welcome to a spot of refreshment," she said graciously, basking in the glow of the town's favor.

Mrs. Spilsby and Miss Goodhue claimed to be famished, since they had not eaten any of Mrs. Emory's tea cakes, and led the group down the rest of the stairs and out into the mill yard.

"That was well done," Helen said to Turner, once Margaret (again bringing up the rear) had passed by.

"Thank Le—Lady Churzy," Turner said as he eyed the bags that were being filled with flour from the sifting floor above. "It was her plan."

"You are a true friend." Helen smiled gratefully at Leticia. "If there is ever anything I can do for you, do not hesitate to ask."

"It was my pleasure," Leticia replied. She could demur, but why? It had been a pleasure, watching Mrs. Emory dig her own grave.

"Mother, I will catch up to you—this sack of flour is nearly full and needs to be changed," Turner said, unhooking the burlap from where it had been fed by the funnel above.

"How do you change the sacks?" Leticia asked, stepping closer and peering up at the workings. After their tour, she was as enthralled with learning how the mill worked as the butcher's boy.

"Wait!" Helen said, but it was too late.

Because flour was still flowing. And when Turner removed the bag, flour ended up flowing freely.

And "freely" included, in this instance, all over Leticia's face.

~&~

"HERE, THIS SHOULD HELP," Turner said as he handed Leticia a cloth dipped in water. They were back on the ground floor of the mill, where Turner had fashioned a small space for himself out of what had been a storage room. There, he had a desk and drawer, for purchase orders and the like, as well as a pallet and some basic necessities. Necessities that included a razor, a basin and pitcher, and a looking glass.

"May I see?" she asked, indicating the looking glass.

"Probably not the best idea," he said, hedging.

"Is it that bad?"

When the smoke—or rather the flour—had cleared, Leticia was left blinking the white powder from her eyelashes. And Turner and Helen were left agape.

It was his mother who sprang into action.

"Oh dear—and your dress too!" she said. "You can't take tea like that."

Leticia looked down at herself. "I can't cross the mill yard like this," she grumbled.

"John, take her down to your office—she can clean up there," Helen said. "I'll tell everyone you're visiting the necessary. Just hurry up! That butcher's boy is going to eat me out of house and home."

While Leticia was still blinking flour out of her eyes, he took her by the hand and led her here. As soon as he could, he dropped her hand. No need to tempt fate. His body was still coursing with energy, pulsing with his nervousness and triumphant showing of his mill. The contact of her hand in his only further muddled his mind.

"It can't be any worse than my imagination, so just hand me the looking glass," she huffed.

He shrugged, handing it to her. "Suit yourself."

She took one glance at herself and almost dropped the mirror. "You didn't tell me it was in my hair!" she cried. "I look like a crone."

"No," he protested. "You look lovely."

The glance she sent him was particularly effective given her artificial pallor. "Not even you can believe that."

But he did. She looked—to be honest, she looked like she had taken a face full of flour, but there was no one in the world who could have worn it as well.

It was on the tip of his tongue to tell her as much, but he stopped himself. That wasn't something she wanted to hear, surely. Not from him.

She took the damp cloth and wiped the flour off her face, the pink of her complexion bringing her to life with each stroke.

"Did I miss any?" she asked, peering at herself in the looking glass.

"Just here," he said, indicating behind his ear.

"Where?" She wiped at the spot on her corresponding ear, completely missing it.

"Let me." He couldn't stop himself. He took the cloth from her hand and ran it gently over the spot behind her ear, following the faint line of flour down her neck to the collar of her cloak.

"Ah . . . thank you," she said, her eyes dropping to the floor as she took the cloth from him and stepped back.

He nodded, the only response he could manage. Then, once she was at a safe distance, he said, "I'm glad to see your neck is better."

"Hmm? Oh yes," she replied as she slipped the cloak off her shoulders and shook it out. "It was an unfortunate side effect of not knowing what to do. When I had a plan and a means by which to execute it, it cleared right up."

She folded the cloak neatly and laid it over the back of her chair. Then she began pulling at the pins in her hair.

"What are you doing?" he asked.

"What I must."

Then, the last of the pins in her hand, she flipped her

hair forward, and shook out the flour from the long, mahogany tresses.

"You're getting flour all over my bed."

"That's the price to be paid," she replied from underneath all that hair. "God knows I'll never get it to look as good as Molly did, but this is the only way to get the flour out. Where did you get the grain, by the by? It's not quite harvest season yet."

"Purchased it last harvest, stored it in the granary."

"And not an ounce gone to rot. Another check in your steam equipment's favor."

White powder fell out of her hair—which, in her present bent position, nearly touched the floor. It took everything in him to not reach out and let his fingers slide through those dark locks.

"So you took Molly on as your ladies' maid, did you?"

"Yes," she said. "How do you know who Molly is?"

"She's how I knew which bedroom door was yours."

She paused in her motions, apparently trying to remember. But then resumed shaking her hair. "Ah, yes. Now I remember. Well, I decided it was prudent. She came cheaper than anyone else, and the position elevates her so much that she'll never tell tales out of school again, lest she risk her position. Plus, she actually is quite talented with hair."

"Your practicality astonishes me."

"Thank you," she said as she flipped her hair back and brought her head up again.

And stopped his heart.

Her face was flushed, her eyes sparkling and dark, dizzying from the movement of her head. Her hair flung back in wings from her temples, streaming down her back as if caught in the wind.

He'd never seen her look like that. So open, and young.

So free.

It took some moments for his heart to start back up and for his hearing to be restored. But when it did, his heart nearly stopped again.

"You have a bed," she said.

"What?" he replied.

"You have a bed in here. Why?"

"Oh," he replied, sighing in relief. At least, he thought it was relief. It was the residual energy from their triumph over Mrs. Emory. That was what was affecting his hearing. And his heart.

"I work late some nights. It's much simpler to lay my head down for a few hours here."

"That would make sense if you lived quite far from your work. But your real bed—which I'm assuming is much larger and warmer than this thing—is merely across the mill yard." She narrowed her gaze, contemplating him. "You're sleeping here as protection, aren't you?"

His mouth formed a grim line. "It's merely a precaution. If someone wanted to burn down the mill . . ."

"When the mill burned before, it was by accident." Suspicion entered her voice. "Wasn't it?"

"The first time, I believed it was an accident, yes. And I swelled with guilt because I was not here. But the second time, when we were nearly done rebuilding . . . I've had my suspicions. And the explosion the other day reinforced them." He could see the concern in her eyes and let his mouth tick up at the corner, just to make her feel better. "But accident or no, if I'm here, it reduces the likelihood of it ever happening again."

"You can't spend every minute of the day in the mill," she said.

"Not every day, no. Every night, however . . ." he reasoned.

It's not like he had anything else to do at night. Except for those rare occasions someone came knocking on his kitchen door.

By the way her eyes darkened, she was thinking along the same lines. Then, remembering herself, she looked away. At the floor, at the desk—anywhere but the bed—and her eyes eventually found the looking glass.

And something strange filtered through his blood. The realization that she was as affected by him as he was by her.

The question was . . . was he stupid enough to do something about it?

"I . . . I need to pin up my hair," she said finally, nodding toward the looking glass, where it sat on his desk. "Would you hold that for me?"

"Of course." He took the mirror and held it level with her face. She reached out once to adjust his hand, but then drew back as if he were hot to the touch.

Interesting.

"I still cannot believe you are sleeping in your mill," she said, by way of conversation, as she separated her hair into long sections, rolling and twisting them into place.

"It's not so bad," he replied. "At night, when everything is still and dark . . . I can go out onto the balcony on the fourth floor and see all the way down into Helmsley. And I know."

"Know what?" she asked.

"That I'm where I'm supposed to be."

Her eyes softened as she smiled. "Don Quixote. I should have known you'd own a windmill."

"Why? Because I've deluded myself into thinking this will work?"

"No. Because you're a dreamer." She stuck one of her pins in her mouth and talked out of the corner. "But that wasn't what I meant. I cannot believe you are sleeping in your mill because you think someone is going to try and burn it down."

"Is it really so far-fetched?" he asked.

"No. But sleeping in the mill seems like the very least you could be doing to catch the perpetrator. Why, if your mill was burned before, that's arson! Whoever did it should be in prison."

"I have no proof of anything. All proof would have burned at the time, wouldn't it?" he replied.

"But you have to have a guess as to who would do such a thing. Palmer Blackwell, for one."

"Of course." He could feel himself scowling. "But when the mill first burned, it was my father running it, and it was doing very well. Everyone in Helmsley loved him, he was fair and honest with his customers. I cannot imagine that Blackwell would have made a move against him. It would have been too much of a risk."

"People will do alarming things for money," she said, pinning the last strand of hair into place. Then grimaced at her reflection in the mirror. "I should know."

"Don't," he said quietly.

"Don't what?" she asked.

"Don't talk about yourself like that."

"I was making a joke, Mr. Turner."

"No, you weren't."

He let the mirror drop, forced her eyes to meet his.

She could have laughed. She could have backed away, denying the truth, and made light of it. She could have danced out of the room. But instead she met him eye for eye, honesty for honesty.

"I know what I am, John," she said, clear and forthright. "And what I am doing is not so very alarming. Women do it every day, marry for money. For most of us, it is the only option. In fact, I'm quite lucky."

"Are you?" he breathed.

"Yes. Because I like Sir Barty. I . . . I like him very much."

"He's very likable."

"I will be a good wife to him." Her voice shook, ever so slightly, as the space between them shrunk by inches, disappearing like flour in the air. "A good stepmother to Margaret."

"I have no doubt you will." His voice was a rumble of warmth. "I know what you are too."

"You . . . you do?"

"You were married to a man whom you loved but who could not love you. Now you are marrying a man you don't love for the same reasons your first husband asked you to dance."

"I . . . I never said anything about love. I'm surviving."

"You are. But there is more to life than surviving."

Her eyes flicked to his lips. Her voice rasped. "Like what?"

It was the only permission he needed. His body ignored every protest his mind painted in bold red letters as he wrapped himself around her. In fact, everything happened as if he were not the one moving his arms, his head, his lips. They all worked of their own accord.

He let his hands trail down her back, finding the small, the dip just before the rising swell of her bottom. She let out a small sigh, a sound of release, and it made his hand fist at her back, gathering up the thin material of her dress and pulling her closer to him.

She melted in his arms as easily as if she had never left them. As if the last year had not separated them.

As if she lived not in a grand manor, nor he in a mill.

The heady spice of her warm mouth flooded him with memories. But this wasn't long ago. This was here, and now, and Leticia Herzog, Lady Churzy—his Letty—was pressed up against him, and kissing him back for all she was worth.

Her hands crept up to his shoulders, hesitant at first, then winding around his neck, lifting her ribs, those sweet breasts that pressed into him with abandon. It made his fingers itch, made his hands fist all the tighter.

She fit against him so perfectly. Every notch, every bend and curve, his body cried as if it were coming home. He released her lips when her hand snaked into his hair, let his mouth roam to her ear, the fine line of her neck.

Her gasp filled the air, and drove him mad. His lips found their way back to hers; this time she was open for him, letting their tongues dance together, caught on a lifting breeze of joy and want.

"Letty," he breathed. "Oh God, Letty."

And just like that, the breeze, the joy, stopped. She stopped. Froze in place.

When his eyes blinked open, it was to see shock and horror in hers. Slowly, painfully, she untwined her arms from around his neck, unplastered her body from his.

Cool air rushed into the void between them, filling like an ocean.

"I have . . . I have to go," she said shakily, stepping as far around him as possible to grab her cloak from where she had lain it before. "I've been away too long already. Who knows what excuse your mother has had to concoct to cover for my absence."

Her fingers shook as she tried to knot the cloak around her neck. Eventually she just gave up, crying, "Oh hang it!" and letting the ribbons fly free.

Two quick steps later her hand was on the doorknob.

"Letty . . ." he said, but from the tense of her shoulders, he immediately realized his mistake.

"Don't call me that," she said quietly, her voice breaking. "You cannot call me that."

The sound of her name on his lips—the name she called herself, no matter how much she denied it—had brought her back from their own private cloud, and down to earth with a thud. And now, it sent her running for the hills.

Running back to his mother. Back to the ladies of Helmsley. Back to Bluestone Manor.

Back to her complicated, delicately balanced life.

As the door to his office/sleeping space/storage room closed with a gentle click, something else tumbled in his chest and locked into place.

And left him laughing. Laughing loud and raw and echoing against the walls of the mill.

That laughter quickly gave way to despair.

Because there was really no reason to lie anymore, was there?

The truth was, he was utterly done for.

17

The days following the events at Turner's mill were so very eventful that Leticia did not have time to concern herself with John Turner, or his presumptuous kissing.

First, there was Mrs. Robertson's visit to take measurements for the wedding gown. This took an entire afternoon. Then of course, there was every lady in Helmsley who decided to pay return calls on Bluestone Manor—with the notable exception of Mrs. Emory. As Leticia had won over the town, she had also won the allegiance of every woman who witnessed Mrs. Emory's defeat. And several others. Like chicks without a mother hen, they flocked around her, waiting to be told what next to do, who next to gossip about, and what fashion next to adopt.

It was, to Leticia's mind, her rightful place.

Mrs. Spilsby and Miss Goodhue made certain to call twice, and Mrs. Spilsby relayed that her husband's sermon that week was likely to have some very pro–steam equipment themes.

"Well, Jesus himself was something new, once upon a

time, wasn't he?" she'd said, making Leticia laugh with delight.

Helen was just as delighted. She sat by Leticia's side every morning as the women made their way into the little sitting room with the good north light that Leticia had taken as her own at Bluestone. (She really would have to create and enforce a standard day for taking calls, she decided.) And as Helen was there, one might suppose that Turner would put in an appearance as well, but no.

John Turner had not come to Bluestone in an entire week.

Considering the fact that he was supposed to be courting Margaret, and keeping her mind far away from the possibilities of Palmer Blackwell, this simply would not do.

Not that her mind was tuned to Turner's movements. But rather, it was important that he be there, especially considering that Palmer Blackwell had made himself a fixture at Bluestone, and at Sir Barty's side.

"You have become very popular in such a short period of time," Blackwell noted one morning, as another set of ladies streamed past him to Leticia's sitting room.

"Please, Mr. Blackwell, you flatter me," she demurred.

"I am told that your influence extends far in town now," Blackwell replied.

So. He'd heard about how she'd challenged Mrs. Emory, and everyone in town was now looking with more favor on her and on the Turner Grain Mill. Obviously it raised his suspicions.

"Only in small feminine matters," she assured, giving nothing away. "Matters of business are completely out of my sphere, and better left to the men. That's what I tell Sir Barty, at any rate."

"Hmm," Blackwell grunted. No matter his suspicions, he could not say that she'd placed any undue influence on

Sir Barty regarding his grain. And that was all that he'd threatened.

Although, perhaps it was time to let him know his threats were baseless. Especially if Turner wasn't here holding up his end of the bargain, something far more direct might have to be done to rid them of Blackwell.

"What was the name of that club?" she asked, causing him to draw back. "The one you mentioned to me the other evening?"

He blinked twice before answering. "The Yew Tree Club," he said, with a simpering smile. "As you well know."

"Hmm . . . only because my late husband went. But only once or twice, I believe. We preferred to travel. But if you enjoyed it so much, perhaps I'll tell Sir Barty, let him know you recommended it. Since we've skipped so many of the celebrations that usually accompany a wedding, I'm hoping to go to London for our honeymoon, and he will likely enjoy going to a gentleman's club while there. I'm sure he would take any recommendation of yours to heart."

She watched as all the blood drained from Blackwell's face. And it became abundantly clear to her that Blackwell had never expected her to call his bluff. An obsequious weasel never has to play the hand out—they let someone else do the hard work for them, and then pick up the pieces.

Well, he would not be getting any of her pieces.

"I don't know if it would be to his taste," Blackwell said, bowing. "If I recall there are a number of stairs, and walking isn't . . . that is, he wouldn't like it."

She hid her smile as she curtsied in return. "I'm sure you're right." Then she glided past him, greeting the ladies in her sitting room, and shut the door behind her.

It was a risky play. But since she had Helmsley's social circle at her back now, she felt far less alone in the country. And as such, she was not willing to suffer fools. Of course, it did mean that Blackwell redoubled his efforts with Margaret—but as Margaret was kept constantly (and chafingly) at Leticia's side, he was left with no recourse but to glue himself to Sir Barty—who half the time was immersed in his cribbage match with Helen.

"But I have to rotate the geraniums," Margaret said, looking mutinous. "They need even light. It will take me five minutes, and I'll wear my smock."

"Not until after our guests leave," Leticia said gently. She was not taking even a five-minute chance, when Palmer Blackwell was within five miles.

"But the light will be gone by then!"

"Excuse me," said Dr. Gray. Goodness, she had half forgotten Dr. Gray was there, buried underneath all the ruffles and crinolines as he tried to sip tea, surrounded by the ladies of Helmsley. "But I am deeply curious about Miss Babcock's experiments in botany. Perhaps I could accompany her?"

She met the doctor's eyes. Ever since that night he had happened upon her and Blackwell, he had become an ally of sorts. And for this past week most of his use had been in being a friend to Margaret.

Every time Helen showed up at the door without Turner, Leticia could see Margaret's disappointment in her posture. (If it was a posture she recognized in herself there was no one nearly as observant as she in attendance.) But then invariably Dr. Gray would cheer her up, by asking her about her work in the gardens, or her scientific method, or some such thing.

She never thought she'd say this, but thank heavens for Dr. Gray.

Added to that, Sir Barty's foot was much better too.

Margaret nodded fervently at Dr. Gray's suggestion. "Oh, all right. But take Miss Goodhue." Some proprieties had to be observed, even if it was only Dr. Gray. And the girl was overly eager to be friends. "And be back before the tea tray."

"Actually, Miss Babcock, if you would wait just a moment." Palmer Blackwell's voice came from the doorway. Sir Barty stood behind him, beaming from underneath his mustache.

"I know that gleam in your eye, Sir Barty," Helen said, her eyebrow going up. "Either you think you've got a winning hand at cards or you have something up your sleeve."

"And I know a leading question when I hear it, Mrs. Turner." Sir Barty twinkled at her. "But in this instance you are correct. I'll let Mr. Blackwell do the honors."

"Thank you, Sir Barty." Blackwell beamed. "And it is an honor. An honor to invite you all to my home, Blackwell Arms, for a ball!"

A thrill of excitement went through the ladies grouped around them.

"And not just any ball," Blackwell continued. "But an engagement ball, for Sir Barty and his lovely bride-to-be, Lady Churzy."

"Isn't it a treat, m'dear?" Sir Barty cried, coming forward to struggle himself into the seat next to her. "And he did it for you."

"For me?" she could not help but blurt out.

"I recalled how you said that you and Sir Barty had missed out on some of the celebrations that go along with a wedding. Well, even though this is a second marriage for both, it deserves celebration."

"What a perfect gift!" Sir Barty exclaimed. "Always thinking of everything, this one."

"Indeed," Leticia said as she kept the smile plastered on her face. "A perfect gift."

She glanced over at Helen, who gave an imperceptible

shrug, and then grinned as widely as possible at Blackwell. "How marvelous. Mr. Blackwell, I can speak for my son and say we will be delighted to attend."

"I would not have it any other way, Mrs. Turner." Blackwell's grin became predatory.

"And, Sir Barty, you had better rest up your foot," Helen continued, ignoring Blackwell. Leticia wished she had that older woman's resolve. "You've danced a reel with me at every party since we were sixteen and you get no rest this time. With your permission, of course, my lady."

"Certainly," Leticia replied. "I'm sure my darling Barty would not wish to disappoint you."

"For you, Helen, I will dig out my dancing shoes," Sir Barty added, and did a quick shuffle, not even leaning on his cane.

Dr. Gray really had worked wonders.

But Sir Barty's quickstep had the effect of making every single lady in attendance giggle and titter. The idea of a dance awakened something primal in them. Visions of fripperies, of shining ribbons and swirling skirts ran through the ladies like St. Elmo's Fire. Of men dressed in their best, and gallantry and champagne punch and lots and lots of dancing.

And with dawning understanding, Leticia realized the true genius of Blackwell's generosity. Not only did it further ingratiate him to Sir Barty, but who on earth was going to care about how well the new Turner Grain Mill was working when there was a ball to dream about?

"And Miss Babcock, may I take this opportunity to ask you for the first dance?"

Margaret's head came up. She had been the only female present not to pink with glee at the idea of a ball. But when she met Blackwell's perfectly composed look of earnestness, she blanched.

The ladies around them tittered again, seeing a love match made before their eyes. Miss Goodhue looked near to fainting from excitement.

"Of . . . of course," Margaret answered.

He'd guaranteed her answer, asking in front of everyone. He'd made it so Leticia could raise absolutely no protest, nor Margaret, if she'd wished to. But of course, Margaret didn't wish to.

Because Blackwell made her blush just like Turner did.

Or did he? When he asked Margaret for the first dance, she'd gone pale, not pink. For the first time, Leticia saw the situation with a bit of hope. Perhaps Margaret was beginning to see Blackwell's smarm for what it truly was.

Which would be a miracle, and in spite of the fact that Turner had not bothered to show up and woo Margaret for nearly a week!

And while she had been much too busy over the course of the week to think about Turner at all—or his presumptuous kissing—now she was desperate to speak to him.

Because their plan required some adjustment, given the current circumstances. That was all. No other reason.

However, when she thought about how to speak to him, she was at a loss. She could send him a note. But what on earth would it say? Please forget any kissing that may have occurred and call on me at your earliest convenience?

She could call on him herself . . . but there was no way for her to extract Helen from the room when said call occurred. And the idea of invading his kitchen again at three in the morning made her freeze with warning. It would be too different this time. Too . . . intimate. Too easy to let the atmosphere and the closeness play tricks on her.

She needed to be alone with him, but not alone. To be able to speak to him about business without anything messy getting in the way of their purpose.

Unfortunately, there was only one time and place where Leticia could think such a thing would be possible.

❧

"THERE YOU ARE," Leticia called out as Helen and Turner entered the arched gateway to the churchyard the following Sunday. "We were about to despair of you."

"It's my fault we are always late," Helen said with a smile and a wave. "I make us walk—it's good for the constitution—and I walk much slower than I remember."

"As do I, Helen, as do I," Sir Barty replied from his place on Leticia's arm. "Vicar Spilsby has just opened the doors, so you aren't too late to get a good pew."

"Lady Churzy, Miss Babcock," Turner said on a bow, his manners perfectly correct. "Sir Barty. Rhys."

"Mr. Blackwell already went in," Margaret blurted. "To save seats in the pew behind us."

"Smart of him," Helen remarked. "Perhaps you should run in and save seats for us as well," she said to her son.

"In a moment," he replied. Then, an impenetrable look passed between Turner and Dr. Gray. Nodding, Dr. Gray turned to Helen.

"I'll help you look for seats, Mrs. Turner," he said. "Sir Barty, perhaps you should come with us. If you are to spend the whole night dancing in a few days, I prescribe as much rest as possible until that time."

Sir Barty looked alarmed. "But I've been feeling so much better . . ."

"And we want it to stay that way," Helen added. "You'll not get out of your dance with me, young man." She waggled a finger in Sir Barty's dimpling face. "Come along. I'll not be stuck in the back next to Mr. Jenkins and his cabbage breath again."

As everyone in the churchyard was quickly moving

into the church itself, it would be a miracle if Helen didn't have to deal with Mr. Jenkins's cabbage breath (it seemed not only his horses feasted on the stuff), but Leticia wasn't about to mention it. Whatever got them into the church faster and left her and Turner to themselves.

Sir Barty, Helen, and Dr. Gray moved toward the doors. She and Turner had little recourse now but to follow themselves . . . albeit slowly. Still, the number of steps from where they stood by the oak tree to the door . . . Leticia reasoned that she and Turner could have a good ten, fifteen seconds of private conversation before their lagging behind was noted.

Not enough time.

Desperate times call for desperate measures, Letty thought, as she slipped her hands behind her back and pried the sapphire ring off her right ring finger, letting it fall to the grass.

"Oh dear! My ring!" she cried, bringing her hand forward. "I was playing with it while we were waiting. It must have fallen to the ground."

"Where?" Margaret asked as she began to peer at the grass and dirt. Good thing Leticia had stepped over the ring, lest the girl find it immediately.

As it was, Margaret was halfway on her hands and knees about to begin scouring when Leticia's cry of "No!" caused her to realize her mistake and straighten. "Margaret, go tell your father the reason for my delay. And don't let the vicar keep his sermon waiting. I'll find my ring."

"Allow me to assist you, my lady," Turner said.

If Margaret thought anything was amiss, she didn't say anything. Simply bobbed her head and moved with a determined stride into the church intent on her mission.

"Did you really lose your ring?" he asked.

"I strive for authenticity in all my fictions," Leticia

replied. "But I have it under my shoe. Still, better to root around a bit, in case anyone should . . . well, I guess the church doesn't have any windows facing this way, does it?"

"No. No one is watching us," he said. "We need to talk."

"Yes, we do," Leticia agreed. "And we could have spoken anytime this week if you had come to call, like you were supposed to!"

He seemed taken aback by her vehemence. Even though she kept her voice low and soft, there was no mistaking her exasperation. "Really, Turner. We had only just solidified our plans, and once I help you show your mill to good light, you renege on your part? I needed you this week."

"Did you?" he growled.

"Since you made such a good showing of the mill, Blackwell has redoubled his efforts with Margaret and Sir Barty. He's even going so far as to throw an engagement party for us. Now Barty thinks the sun rises and sets with Palmer Blackwell, Margaret is dancing the first dance with him, and no one is talking about your mill anymore."

"None of that could have been prevented by my attendance."

"I disagree. But regardless, now we need to figure out what to do about Blackwell," she said in a rush, the excitement causing her to become slightly breathless. "But I think he made a misstep."

"Leticia . . ."

"No, listen . . . I think that by inviting us to his home, he has opened himself up to a scrutiny that he does not expect. Because he cannot know that you suspect him of having burned your mill—it's been so long. Perhaps this is our chance to look for proof. Any man who runs three mills must keep meticulous records. All we have to do is find it. Then, he'll be gone, you'll have Sir Barty's business, and no one need ever worry about Palmer Blackwell darkening any of our doors again. We can go on as we are meant to."

"You think things are that simple?"

"Of course they are. Now agree with me, apologize for not having shown your face at Bluestone for a week, and come inside." She bent down and picked up her sapphire ring, none the worse for wear for being under her shoe for a minute or two. "We'll be missed if we are out here much longer."

"No."

Her head came up. "No, I promise you we will be. No matter what Margaret tells the vicar, he will delay starting until we're in the church."

"I mean to say no, I cannot agree with you. I cannot apologize for not keeping up my end of our bargain. And I cannot come into the church."

"Why not?"

He took a deep breath. "Because today, in that church, the last of your banns are going to be read. And if I hear them . . . if I hear the vicar ask if any know of an impediment to your marriage to Sir Barty, I will not be able to stop myself."

"Stop yourself . . ." Her mouth hung open.

"I won't be able to stop myself from telling everyone that I'm in love with you." The corner of his mouth tilted up in a rueful smile. "So I think it better if I don't go to church today."

There are certain words that can make the world stand still. Words that root feet to the ground and force eyes to meet. The birds still chirped in the oak tree. The wind still moved its branches. But everything else, things tied to the earth, was held in that moment. There was nothing else but herself, Turner, and what he had to say.

"I thought I could do it," he began. "I thought I could

hate you enough to tolerate your living in my town. Wife to Sir Barty. I'd kept my head in my work long enough that I figured I'd just keep doing that. But you . . . infected everything."

"Infected?" she asked weakly.

"I mean that in the best possible sense," he hastened to assure. "But you did. My mother lights up every time your name is mentioned. We meet in my kitchen at three in the morning and it smells like you for days after. You march into my mill and launch a strategy worthy of Wellington. I cannot separate you from any part of my life, because you've seeped through every layer. And the more and more I saw you, the harder it became to hate you. And if I can't hate you, I have to love you, because there is no in between for me."

No, there was no in between for them. Their last encounter in his little office proved that. Damn him and his presumptuous kissing!

She wanted to scream. She wanted to cry. She wanted so much for this not to be happening. Not now. Her heart couldn't take it now. She . . . she needed him to ignore everything that had happened between them and simply go along with the plan.

She needed him to lie.

But he couldn't. Not anymore.

"I know you don't want to hear this. And I fully realize the folly of it. After all, we are the worst possible people for each other." That corner of his mouth ticked up again, and if her feet had not been rooted to the spot, she was certain she would have closed the distance between them, and . . . she didn't know. Hold him? Slap him? Prove him right . . . or prove him wrong?

"You are hardly one for country life. You sneeze at every passing flower. I'm surprised you didn't go into spasms when you walked into my mill. And you're selfish, and stubborn. So focused on what you want you'll sacrifice what you need to get it.

"And I'm not suddenly going to turn into a prince or a duke. I'm a miller, Letty. I will spend my life turning grain into flour. I don't have the time to sit around writing poetry to your hair, nor the talent for it. I am as plain as they come. I cannot afford a wife who wants to take trips to London every year for the fashions—"

He stopped himself and sighed deep. "But for all that, I loved you from the moment we met. Because you make me feel alive. Life without you was thrown into sharp relief when you stepped out of the door at your sister's house and smiled directly at me.

"And when you're with me . . . I think you're closer to being yourself than even you know." He stepped close to her and risked everything to reach out his hand and cup the side of her face. "When you are yourself? Messy, and honest? You're dazzling."

The heat of his hand on her cheek stole her breath, sped her heart. She closed her eyes, soaked in the warmth.

Stay, she found herself thinking. Willing. Don't speak. Don't act. Just stay here in this moment.

Because when she did speak, did act . . . the moment would end.

And it had to end.

She opened her eyes. He was watching her, sad. Because he knew too that this moment must end.

She had to be the one to do it. There was no other way.

All it took was one step. If she stepped forward . . . if she closed the small distance between them . . . life would change irrevocably.

But instead, she stepped back.

The world rushed back to them. The chirping birds, the

breeze. The bells of St. Stephen's. Everything she had to do today filled her mind again—the calls to pay and receive, the dinners to organize, the letters to write. The ease of a minute life.

The banns to be read.

"The banns. I . . . I have to go." Her eyes fell to the grass beneath their feet. Another step back. More grass. "We've been gone too long. They will notice."

She couldn't risk looking up at his face. She would lose her resolve if she did so. But she could picture his expression perfectly: his eyes becoming hard again, inscrutable. His mouth pressing into a thin line. And no other outward sign that anything was amiss.

She had to do the same thing. Two deep breaths, rolling her shoulders back and pulling herself upright by that invisible string attached to the top of her head. And suddenly, she could see clearly again. She could meet his gaze. And was not surprised by what she saw.

His mask was back up and in place, as firmly as hers. His hands had gone behind his back, his posture stiff. Contained.

"Of course," he said, with a bow. "Please make my excuses to my mother."

"Of course," she replied. "Good day, Mr. Turner."

And she turned and walked into the church. Toward her future.

She did not look back.

18

In the days following Turner's declaration of love, Leticia came to understand a simple truth that many a bride before her had found to be bedrock:

It would have been better to elope.

Her wedding was a week away. Palmer Blackwell's ball in her honor was to be on Thursday. There were a dozen things to do in any given minute.

Aside from what was becoming the usual stream of ladies paying calls, calls to be returned, and shopping on market day, Leticia had daily meetings with Cook, planning the wedding breakfast—which would be held at Bluestone Manor directly after the service next Sunday, and the entirety of Helmsley would be in attendance. Sir Barty was allowing her to expand the menu beyond pork, and had promised not to goggle should a bowl of oranges be produced. Add to that Rebecca, who had been hired to do the cake, coming around almost every day with samples, trying to find the most perfect one for the new Lady Babcock, whom she dearly wished to impress.

Cook mentioned more than once that it should be her

being impressed, since she had a say in all cooking staff hires. But it was notable that she took to those cake samples with a gluttonous glee. She even mentioned the idea of having Rebecca do some tarts for the breakfast as well.

Then Leticia and Mrs. Dillon (who was equally enamored of Rebecca's handiwork) made decisions about decorations. Which was not easily done.

"Flowers should be everywhere!" Mrs. Dillon cried.

"Not unless you want the bride sneezing and her eyes watering throughout the breakfast," Leticia answered, quelling the housekeeper's enthusiasm. "I was thinking we could use the lace tablecloth, with a runner of lavender underneath it."

"But you cannot have a wedding breakfast without flowers," Mrs. Dillon said, dejected. The woman was usually most practical, but the business of planning a party had sent her into an opinionated spiral of glee. It had been quite some time since there had been a party at Bluestone, after all. "Miss Babcock, what is your opinion?"

And she was clever about it too. Because Mrs. Dillon had hit upon the one part of planning a party that Margaret might have some interest in.

"There are some delphiniums in the east garden that would make lovely cuttings. I could go out right now and show you . . ."

"Regardless," Leticia said firmly as Margaret and Mrs. Dillon began to enthusiastically debate which flowers would be best (and forcing a glum Margaret back into her seat), "they will have to be placed far away from me. Any flowers will have to be restrained flowers. Yes, Molly? What is it?"

The new lady's maid rushed into the room, carrying a number of parcels under her arm.

"Oh, my lady!" she exclaimed. "I just couldn't wait. These were delivered for you from Mrs. Robertson!"

"It must be the wedding dress!" Mrs. Dillon trilled with excitement. Leticia smiled weakly. She should have been excited as well. But somehow she felt numb at the thought of seeing her gown.

"We simply must open it!" Mrs. Dillon turned to her with shining eyes. "To . . . inspect it, of course. Make certain there are no flaws."

Mrs. Dillon and Molly both nodded fervently. Even Margaret looked mildly interested.

"All right," Leticia said, waving her hand. "Go ahead."

Molly had the restraint to not tear at the packaging, instead reverently unfolding the brown paper and pulling back the layers of tissue.

"Ohhh . . ." she sighed. "It's the finest thing I've ever seen." With the tips of her fingers, she picked the gown up by the shoulders and held it up for everyone to see.

It was a beautiful piece of work. A warm creamy lace fell over a silk skirt that was almost gold, but lighter, like sunshine overlaid by wisps of clouds. The bodice, in the same buttery silk, was cut in two long V-shaped layers, which would frame her elegant neck perfectly. And the sleeves were barely wisps of fabric, edged with the same lace, but underneath, peeking out from the silk.

It was a perfect amalgam of the polish of town life and the whimsy of the country.

And Leticia felt nothing when she saw it.

"It is indeed beautiful," she said, covering up her feelings, or lack thereof. "Mrs. Robertson does excellent work."

"I can't believe I get to touch something so lovely. Wendra is going to be so jealous," Molly said with relish. Then, remembering herself, she turned with wide eyes to Leticia. "I mean, my lady, Wendra would be jealous, if I told her about it. Which I absolutely will not be doing."

"It's all right, Molly," Leticia said, half smiling. "You

can mention the dress to Wendra." Let the gossiping maid take her information back to Mrs. Emory. Letting her know they were pleased with Mrs. Robertson's work could harm them in no way. In fact, maybe it would soften up the recalcitrant Mrs. Emory to the new order in Helmsley.

"What's that?" Margaret asked, nodding toward the other packages that Molly had laid on the chair.

"I assume that the smaller one is the stockings and gloves that go with the wedding dress," Leticia answered. Then, after exchanging a look with Mrs. Dillon, took a deep breath. "And the last package is for you."

"For me?" Margaret replied, her brow coming down. "But I didn't order anything."

"I know, but when I had Mrs. Robertson measure me for my wedding gown, I ordered something for you as well."

"I told you, I have no wish for a new gown! My Sunday dress will do very well, I am sure."

"For the wedding, yes, but this is for—"

But Margaret, for all her recent going-along, had apparently found a sticking point. For the past week or so, she had done her best to fit herself into the mold Leticia had tried to impart—gently—that she could not bend any further.

"Could you please, please leave one thing well enough alone? I've gone along with everything else." She took the package that Leticia held out to her, swiping it away without any of the reverence Molly had displayed.

Molly squeaked in protest.

"I'm not permitted to tie up my skirts to work, I have to pay calls with you, and agree with everything you say when we are out and I haven't the foggiest idea why! We now have vegetables with our meals, which granted, isn't a bad thing, but it's different."

Margaret tore at the packaging, pulling back the wrapping and tissue paper, again causing Molly to squeak.

"I wish you would listen to me just once! Because I meant it when I said I didn't want another—"

But Margaret's vehemence came to an abrupt halt when she reached into the package and pulled out . . .

"Trousers?" she asked, confused.

"Hmm," Leticia said. "So it would seem."

"You got me trousers?" She fingered the thick brown wool—perfect for hard labor, Leticia had been assured.

"For when you garden. You cannot tie up your skirts, it's far too unseemly, but neither does your smock let you kneel and dig in the dirt as you need to. These will allow you to work freely."

"Ladies don't wear trousers," Margaret said, still staring at them in wonder.

But she simply waved that away. "Margaret, you are a lady. Nothing you do will ever take that away. So if you wear trousers, then yes, a lady does wear trousers."

"Still . . . you said certain things are expected . . ."

"Yes," Leticia said gently. "Certain things are expected. But perhaps, what's expected of you isn't always what is right for you."

Margaret looked up from the trousers, her eyes suspiciously shiny.

"Now, they are only for when you are working, mind. And never to be worn when we are entertaining," Leticia warned. Margaret nodded fervently. Then she sniffled.

"I thought . . . I thought you were going to force me to wear something new for the wedding, or Mr. Blackwell's ball."

Leticia sent a look to Mrs. Dillon, whose eyes were suspiciously shiny as well.

"As you said, your Sunday dress will do very well for

the wedding," she replied, keeping her voice even. "And for Mr. Blackwell's ball . . . there's your blue gown, isn't there?"

"It's too short," Margaret replied, suffocating another sniffle.

"Well," Mrs. Dillon said, taking her cue. "Perhaps that can be fixed. Molly?"

"Oh yes!" Molly said. "We only need a few inches of ribbon to be sewn around the hem. I saw a lovely aqua ribbon at Mrs. Robertson's shop on market day."

Leticia held her breath. Mrs. Dillon did too.

"I suppose . . ." Margaret said, her eyes falling back to her new trousers, "that would work."

Leticia's face broke into a wide smile. "Excellent. Molly, you can have the gown ready by Thursday?"

Molly nodded fervently. Mrs. Dillon winked at Leticia. "But we shan't waste any time. Come along, Molly." Mrs. Dillon picked up the package with the wedding gown in it and brought Molly along in her wake. The words *perhaps don't tell Wendra about the trousers* were whispered to a continually nodding Molly.

Said trousers were still in Margaret's hands, her fingers still running over the twill of the wool.

"In that blue gown," Leticia said, "I think you'll be surprised by the number of young gentlemen who ask you to dance."

"I'm already surprised to be dancing with Mr. Blackwell," Margaret answered. Her brow came down. "Do you think Mr. Turner will ask me to dance as well?"

Turner. Just the mention of his name sent a frisson of attention through her. Its weight sat on her chest, threatening to suffocate her.

"I have no doubt," she said, hiding her reaction with a deep breath. "Margaret, I have to ask . . . are you still reconsidering your philosophy of attraction? Do you still feel that you blush in Mr. Turner's presence or . . . or other people's?"

Leticia hoped that Margaret would say something that would confirm her suspicions about her lack of blushing at Mr. Blackwell. Or something that would mean the girl's heart wouldn't break when Mr. Turner invariably did not return her interest. Because he could not.

But she was to be thwarted on both counts.

"I don't know," Margaret said, a furrow across her brow. "At first, when he tucked the violet behind my ear, I thought that was enough of a sign of affection. But then, his attentions have been so sporadic . . ."

"True," Leticia replied with a sigh. Last week she was livid with Turner for ignoring Margaret, this week she was grateful he did not show up at Bluestone. Luckily, Mr. Blackwell had also had to absent himself from Helmsley, to go and prepare his home for the ball, so they had not had to deal with his attentions either—wanted or unwanted, it was hard to tell.

"But when he does look at me, I feel like he's the only man in the world. Does that make sense?"

Leticia's heart folded in on itself. "Yes," she heard herself say. "I know exactly what you mean."

"But the problem is . . . I don't think he sees me as the only woman in the world."

Leticia's pulse quickened. "You think Mr. Turner . . . has a sweetheart?"

"No. If he did he shouldn't call upon me at all, should he?" She waved that thought away, too innocent to think anything else. "But the other problem is, when I look at . . . someone else, sometimes I see him as the only man in the world too. So how could two men be the only man in the world?"

"That is a conundrum," Leticia had to acknowledge.

"I suppose further analysis is required." Margaret shrugged. "And the ball should afford me ample opportunity to do so."

"That seems a little unfeeling," Leticia said. "To approach a ball as an experiment. Wouldn't you rather just enjoy yourself?"

But a queer look passed over Margaret's face. A disappointment, and then it shuttered.

"I should try these on," she said, holding up the trousers. "May I?"

Leticia nodded, and Margaret, for all her height and determination, practically tiptoed out of the room.

Leaving Leticia to her thoughts. Which was a terrible fate.

Because with her duties and worries compounding—the wedding planning, the upcoming ball, whatever she had just done to cause Margaret to close off again—the only thing her mind wanted to linger on was John Turner.

At first, her entire body felt heavy from his admission. From the truth they had both been denying since she walked into Helmsley. Then, the giddy hysteria began. Because of course he would do this now. Of course—on top of everything else, he had to fling his love at her feet, and not giving her a damn thing she could do about it.

Then came the anger.

Because how dare he? How dare he do this to her now? In the midst of trying to save his mill and secure her future, he decides to make his feelings her problem! How is that kind, or fair? How is that the action of a gentleman?

He had said in the beginning that he would be happy to keep her at arm's length, hadn't he? When he came to her room—heavens, was it just over a fortnight ago?—and they made their bargain. Their first bargain, that is.

But circumstances changed.

She'd changed them. By needing him.

And she had needed him. But not to hatch a plan against Blackwell, like she'd purported.

She found herself again wishing for a confessor—Molly was still too new to be trusted with such an admission, Mrs. Dillon was far too loyal to Sir Barty, and Margaret, for all that they had been negotiating a kind of friendship, this was not for her ears.

She wanted someone she could talk to. That she could lay bare the honest tumult of her own feelings and . . .

She realized with stark clarity that Turner was the only one who fit.

And suddenly she was indescribably sad, because she would never be able to confide in him again.

This entire gamut of emotions was run through in the time it took Vicar Spilsby to read their banns on Sunday.

Sir Barty was beaming, even going so far into impropriety as to squeeze her hand as they sat next to each other in the pew.

Words Turner had refused to hear.

Ever since then, Leticia had been placing concerted effort into moving forward. If that meant burying her rocketing feelings and concentrating on the many details she had to attend to this week, so be it.

She would plan her wedding breakfast. She would go to this ball, discover something nefarious about Palmer Blackwell, and use it to get him away from Margaret and out of her hair. If that got him out of Turner's way as well, she would consider it her parting gift.

Because at the end of the week, she was going to marry Sir Barty and say good-bye to John Turner, and any old dreams she had of him.

Such dreams were folly, anyway.

❧

DR. RHYS GRAY was bored. Again. Hard to believe with all the intrigue and furtive looks going on, but it was true. He longed for a good medical mystery. A strange influenza, an outbreak of consumption . . . hell, he'd even take a curious rash if one presented itself. (In fact, he'd noted that Lady Churzy had a strange reddening on her neck a week or so ago, but it unfortunately cleared itself up before he was able to investigate.)

His purpose in being at Bluestone Manor was ostensibly to spy on Lady Churzy, but she had been in such a distracted state since Sunday there was nothing to spy upon. He'd tried to call on Turner to find out what he'd said to her in the churchyard—because he must have said something to her—and to ask if he was relieved of his spying duty and could go back home. But Turner was far too busy with his mill to see his old friend.

The one he had summoned here. For his help.

Rhys was of half a mind to decamp on his own, to simply declare to Sir Barty that his foot was as well as it could possibly be (although Rhys thought that if the man gave up his beloved pork he might feel a great deal better) and write Turner a letter from the road telling him of his escape. Back to his laboratory, and his studies, and away from any further intrigue that his friends embroiled themselves in.

But he couldn't.

The look that had passed between Turner and Rhys in the churchyard—the one that told him he needed to speak to his countess alone—told Rhys that soon enough, he would be needed.

Not as a doctor, of course. But as a friend.

He'd almost written to Ashby when he saw Turner after

that Sunday—wrapped up in his mill, a fevered determination driving him to work harder and harder, until he collapsed each night from exhaustion.

His mother had pasted a smile on her face and told Rhys that she was certain it was just because the harvest was about to begin. Everything had to be ready. But the worry behind her eyes told him that she had her own concerns.

But other than those vague notions, that creeping feeling at the back of his mind that something in Turner's life was about to come to a head, Rhys had nothing to occupy him.

So, as he waited for something, anything to happen, he found himself again where he felt least in the way: in Miss Babcock's greenhouse.

"Hello?" He knocked on the door, ducking his head in. Over the course of the past week or so, Miss Babcock had gone from being standoffish to being actually rather accommodating.

"Don't come in!" Miss Babcock's voice was filled with panic. Enough that it alarmed Rhys into throwing the door open automatically.

"What is it? What's wrong?" he said as he came through the door.

His sharp eyes saw only a blur of movement as Margaret ducked behind a long table in the center of the greenhouse.

"I told you not to come in!" she cried.

"I'm . . . I'm sorry!" he said, backing away toward the door. "You sounded distressed, I thought . . ."

What had he thought? Oddly, Blackwell had popped into his mind. Or perhaps, not oddly. Ever since that night he had approached the countess, Blackwell's presence had been less and less tolerable. A natural sort of protective instinct came out whenever the man was around Miss Babcock. A silent agreement had been reached between him and the countess—as she could not keep eyes on the girl all the time, and Margaret seemed to be at relative ease in Rhys's presence—that he take up the slack.

And again, he hadn't minded. Margaret, though shy, was an interesting person. He always found people who were interested in things interesting.

Also, he had very little else to do.

"I, ah . . . I apologize, Doctor," Margaret said weakly. "I'm just not supposed to be in company right now."

"Why ever not?" he asked, turning back. "Are you unwell?"

"No," she replied, still beneath the table. "I'm fine."

"Are you certain?"

"Yes. Well . . . oh hang it. Do you promise not to tell anyone that you saw me? Not even Leticia?"

Now he simply couldn't leave. He was too curious. Academically, of course.

"You have my word."

Margaret Babcock rose slowly from behind the table. The table was lined with piles of pots and jars of dirt, formula, and other botanical experiments, so he could only see her from the waist up. But she looked completely normal. She wore a plain blouse with the bib of a muslin apron over it. Her hair was in its normal long braid down her back. Her eyes however, were on the table in front of her.

Then, she stepped out from behind the table.

Interesting.

"Do I look . . . ridiculous?" she asked.

The apron fell to her knees, so it was only from the calves down that he could see she was wearing trousers. Not skin-tight trousers like gentlemen found fashionable, but quite thick and durable. And said trousers fell past her ankles, where they met her sturdy walking boots. For such a tall person, she was much more slim than he had realized. And her legs, now that he had a proper view of them, were quite long. She reminded him of a willow reed. An extremely nervous one.

"No. You look . . . comfortable."

She immediately relaxed, a small smile and blush spreading over her face. "They are comfortable. I can bend and work freely. Leticia got them for me, but with the express instruction that I not wear them in company."

"I understand." Rhys nodded, forcing his eyes to her face. "Your secret is safe with me."

"Good," she said, nodding. "I was about to repot these cuttings. They are outgrowing their current situation."

"I would be happy to assist," Rhys offered. She nodded and he took off his coat and rolled up his shirtsleeves.

They worked side by side for a number of minutes in silence. Margaret had shown him previously how to gently loosen the roots from the dirt so they could grow out in their new space. The sounds of dirt falling to the table and the spade spooning out new earth into the larger pots filled the air, until . . .

"It's odd," Rhys said. "You don't strike me as someone who cares if you look ridiculous. Not that you do," he added quickly. "But most ladies in my experience care deeply about their appearance, at all times. You seem much less concerned."

"I know," she answered flatly. "Most people don't think I care about anything."

"What?" Rhys's head came up. "Why do you say that?"

"It's true." She shrugged. "Because I spend all my time with plants, not people. I would rather approach things scientifically."

"There's nothing uncaring about approaching things scientifically," Rhys said as his brow came down. "In fact, such thoroughness could be construed as incredibly careful."

"Exactly!" she exclaimed. "It makes perfect sense to me. Because how else are you going to be sure?"

"Of course," he replied. Apparently he had hit a strange nerve when he mentioned her lack of concern over her wardrobe.

"Still, they think that since I approach things with logic, that I do not have feelings." Her head stayed down, but he could still hear her whisper. "All I do is feel."

"Something has upset you," he stated quietly. "Can I help in some way?"

"No. Maybe. Leticia said something to me," Margaret admitted. "About the ball. That I should just have fun and not worry about anything else."

"Ah," he said. He was tiptoeing dangerously close to what could be termed "women's issues" and had spent enough time suffocated by ruffles in Lady Churzy's sitting room over the past week that he knew well enough to not make any more comment than that.

"But I have to worry," she continued. "Because it's what I do. And I've never been to a ball before and of course I want to have fun, but I also would like to discover answers to certain questions that I don't know if I will be able to find anywhere else and I don't know how else to do it but approach it scientifically!"

Two things flashed through Rhys's brain. First, that before his very eyes, Margaret Babcock had transformed into a woman. Which, for all her obviously female attributes, he hadn't really classified her as such. But it seemed that beneath that practical, interested exterior lurked the vulnerable center of your average nineteen-year-old young lady.

The second thing was . . .

"You've never been to a ball before?" he asked.

She nodded. "My mother became ill around the time I was to come out, and . . . it wasn't a great interest of mine anyway. I . . . no one will ask me to dance. Aside from Mr. Blackwell, of course, which he did only to be polite, I'm sure."

"Hmm." He thought he understood. She must be worried that she wasn't going to enjoy it. Considering the pressure that she was putting on herself (and that the countess was likely putting on her, albeit unconsciously), it was no wonder that her face was grave and her attention intensely focused on her work.

"I do not often attend balls myself," he said. "But I can promise that you'll have fun—scientific experiment or no. And if you are not having a good time, just come find me and we'll dance together. Although I warn you now, I am not terribly accomplished either. But we can trip along merrily enough."

Miss Babcock's face came up from her work. There was a swipe of dirt across her cheek. Her braid was coming loose around the ears. But as the blossom of color on her cheeks gave way to a wide spectacular smile, something very curious spread through his insides.

Well, he could say this about the upcoming ball: it wasn't going to be boring. Not a bit.

19

*P*almer Blackwell's estate was located approximately ten miles away from Helmsley, across the Wolds and near another of the market towns that ringed the landscape, called Frosham. It was just a hair too far to travel on a daily basis, but for a onetime event of this magnitude, everyone was willing to make the effort.

And everyone did.

The trek to get there was not difficult, and was in fact quite scenic in the late summer evening. Many citizens of Helmsley took advantage of that, beginning their reveling from the time they left their homes, and making their drive as festive as possible, with singing and wine. The Babcock carriage passed more than one cart that had pulled off the road to allow the occupants to enjoy the sunset, the atmosphere, and possibly to sober up.

But while the natural beauty of the Lincolnshire Wolds would impress even the most cynical city dwellers, Palmer Blackwell's "estate" was much the opposite.

The construction was new—within the last few years—and in an effort to impress with size, Blackwell had done away with grace or elegance. His home was a large box framed with columns in the Greek-revival style, on an open expanse of recently cleared ground that was a bald spot on the lush landscape around them. Incredibly overblown and tacky.

At least, that was Leticia's opinion.

But as they pulled up to the front gate, Sir Barty hummed in appreciation, and even Margaret's eyebrows went up, impressed.

"Look, m'dear! Torches lining the walk, and every window ablaze with candles. Must've cost a fortune!" Sir Barty nudged an elbow into her ribs. "And all for us."

Leticia nodded politely. But secretly, thinking about Palmer Blackwell's gauche taste made her far less nervous about the evening ahead.

Because she was nervous.

"I can't believe we are so late!" Sir Barty said, shaking his head as he eyed his pocket watch. "You underestimated the amount of time it would take to drive across the Wolds, m'dear."

She could have simpered, demurred, and told Sir Barty that he was correct. She could have let him pat her hand and say he would take care of it next time, as she shouldn't be expected to deal with things as demanding as time management. But honestly, she had amorphous evidence of perfidy to find tonight and it needed to go perfectly. Her mind was elsewhere.

"No, darling, I estimated it accurately."

Sir Barty's brow came down. "But, I told you, I appreciate punctuality. M'dear."

"Yes, but there are some things you want to be a little bit late for," Leticia answered. "Consider, what would they do with us if we were the very first people to arrive? Mr. Blackwell would want us to stand up with him and greet guests."

And as much as she wanted to spare Sir Barty's leg,

arriving early would also play into Blackwell's hands and harm the Turners, to have Sir Barty seen as such a close friend he did the honors of greeting the guests. Besides that, she thought it remotely possible that if they arrived as early as Sir Barty wished (which was practically luncheon, "to help" as he put it—dear man, he was quite excited), Blackwell likely would have given them a tour of his house. And she needed to be able to claim she had gotten lost, if necessary.

But that wasn't to say that she didn't know the layout of Blackwell's estate. No indeed. Because Miss Goodhue was teacher to the cousin of one of the builders of the house. A quick introduction on market day, fifteen minutes of small talk about possibly having a small pergola built on the far side of Bluestone's orchard, and she was able to ask the man about the layout of his biggest project to date and subtly steer the conversation to the uses of certain rooms. So she knew that the library was on the second floor, but Blackwell's study was on the third. And she was going to have to check both places for any records the man might keep.

Which meant either she was going to have to utilize the servants' staircase to move from one to the other (and it was going to be much in use during a ball, with footmen and maids bearing trays) or she would have to disappear twice from the proceedings.

If only she had an accomplice, things would go much more smoothly.

But she had not spoken to Turner since that day in the churchyard. She could not. Therefore she had never received an agreement to her try-and-find-out-something-terrible-about-Blackwell plan, and she had to assume she was alone in the endeavor.

She supposed she could have approached Helen, but she was counting on the woman to distract Sir Barty during her absences. She could have asked Dr. Gray. But he was such a straightforward, honest fellow, she doubted he could lie convincingly if caught. She even considered asking Margaret—but ever since the girl had tried on her blue silk ball gown with the hem extended by new ribbon, she'd become more excited about the dance itself, more dreamy, and Leticia didn't want to ruin that.

Thus, as she mounted the steps to Blackwell's Box of Garish Plainness, she knew she was alone.

As alone as someone escorted by her fiancé to a ball in their honor, that is.

"Sir Barty! At last!" Palmer Blackwell cried, his face breaking into a wide grin upon seeing them. He'd put a copious amount of oil in his hair and side-whiskers for the evening, turning his already dark hair an inky black to match his evening kit. As he bowed low over her hand, she could swear she saw her reflection.

He would be laughable, if he wasn't so cunning. Cunning and dangerous.

"Mr. Blackwell," Leticia said smoothly as she extracted her hand. "Your home is a wonder."

"Isn't it though?" Blackwell said, no modesty at all. "I did all of the decorating myself. But whatever wife I end up taking will have free rein to put her stamp on it." His brow waggled in Margaret's direction. (Margaret, for her part, seemed oblivious to such brow waggling.) "And Miss Babcock, I am delighted to see you."

"You invited us," she stated.

"Yes," he replied patiently. "But I was becoming worried you would not arrive in time for the first dance. Which I have claim upon."

"We would never have allowed that to happen," Leticia said smoothly, with a wink to Sir Barty. "But Margaret and I must avail ourselves of the retiring room before we begin dancing." Which was true. Even sitting as still as possible, ten miles of travel had crushed their skirts, and they needed a good brushing.

"Of course," Mr. Blackwell replied, indicating. "It's through that corridor on the left. Now, Sir Barty, you have to allow me to show you the refreshments. I know you are a connoisseur of haslet. Interestingly enough, the refreshments table has a view down into Frosham, where you can see my latest windmill construction—six sails, and can handle any grain . . ."

Mr. Blackwell looked over his shoulder at her as he abandoned the receiving line to show Sir Barty his refreshments, haslet, and mill. It was the risk she took, leaving Sir Barty to Blackwell's influence. But if the evening went as planned, it wouldn't matter. She would have the ability to extract Blackwell from their lives entirely.

"Is it all right?" Margaret asked when they were in the ladies' retiring room—which was anything but retiring at that moment. There were a dozen women in what normally must have been a sitting room, placing powder on noses and having maids manage broken hems, laughing and chatting and fanning.

Leticia was kneeling at Margaret's feet, gently shaking out the silk of her gown and letting it fall gracefully into place, minimally less wrinkled.

"I tried to be very careful," Margaret said, a strange sort of panic in her voice.

"And you were," Leticia replied. "No skirt remains wrinkle free when stuffed into a carriage. No matter how careful the wearer."

"Good." Margaret breathed a sigh of relief. Although her hands still had a little bit of a shake to them, something she squelched by gripping her dance card until it bent.

"Everything will be lovely, you know," Leticia said reassuringly. "There is no need to be nervous."

"I know. And I've been assured that I will have fun," Margaret replied, clear-eyed. "It's just . . . I feel that tonight will be important."

They emerged from the retiring room, stepping out into the hall.

Her eyes immediately locked on to Mr. John Turner's.

He was by the mouth of the hallway, where it emerged into the ballroom, standing with Dr. Gray—who, after having once again wrapped Sir Barty's foot, had opted to travel with Turner and Helen, and allow the Babcock ladies more room for their skirts in the carriage.

He looked stunning. (Mr. Turner, although Dr. Gray wore his evening dress very well, indeed.) No, he was stunning—stopping her body from moving, her heart from beating, suspending the world around them like a leaf held in the air on a breeze.

She'd seen him in evening clothes before—the stark black of his suit coat, the crisp whiteness of his shirt and white cravat. This was nothing new—handsome men always presented well when they gave even a modicum of attention to grooming.

But it was the set of his jaw, the crinkle at the corner of his eyes as he acknowledged her with a slight bow of the head that had her holding her breath.

Leticia managed to tear her eyes away for the briefest of moments, and looked over to Margaret.

Who had gone from pale with worry to blushing with fire.

"Yes," Letitia agreed. "I feel tonight will be important too."

∼⋈∽

"ARE YOU ENJOYING yourself, Mr. Turner?"

Miss Goodhue was angling herself between him and the dance floor. Therefore, to look at her he had to see the dancers behind her, swirling in time to the music. And by the hopeful look on her face, and the way she swayed her own skirts, her obvious intention was to find herself a dance partner.

He wasn't dancing tonight.

"Yes, Miss Goodhue," he answered. "If you will excuse me."

He knew her mouth fell open from his rudeness as he walked away, but he couldn't care. He had too much to do tonight. He had to keep an eye on Blackwell. He had to keep an eye on Sir Barty. He had to keep an eye on Leticia.

He needed more eyes.

He'd considered not coming to Blackwell's ball. It seemed a bit crass to attend a party celebrating the engagement of the woman one loved to another man, thrown by one's enemy. Add to that, as his mill was finally complete, and now just awaiting the beginning of the next harvest, he was more and more reluctant to leave it. If something was going to happen, it was going to happen now. But he'd hired three very brawny, loyal, and somewhat dim men to patrol the mill yard while he was away.

He couldn't miss this.

At least, that was what his mother had insisted.

"You would disappoint Sir Barty?" she'd asked, aghast. "Miss Babcock? Leticia told me that Margaret has been very excited about the ball. I should hate for her only dance partner to be that horrid Mr. Blackwell."

He'd told his mother weeks ago that he had no interest in Margaret Babcock. He hadn't shown anything other than polite interest in Margaret Babcock since he'd tucked a violet behind her ear (even though he'd promised Leticia that he would first do less, then do more). But somehow she was still alert to the nonexistent possibility of their union.

He liked the girl, but had no qualms about disappointing her.

He didn't even have much concern about disappointing Sir Barty—he needed him, yes, but if he knew the man, Sir Barty would avoid the topic of business during a party filled with revelry, wine, and presumably food.

But he couldn't disappoint Leticia.

Whether she wanted to see him or not, she would be disappointed if she didn't. And so he drove the knife deeper into his belly and came tonight.

And sought her out.

They'd locked eyes in the hallway, he standing with Rhys and she with Miss Babcock. But really, he couldn't see anyone else.

She'd looked beautiful, of course. She always looked beautiful, but tonight she was transcendent. He'd seen her gown before. She wore it at the ball last year when . . . when he'd first kissed her. It was a cream silk shot through with gold thread. She caught the light, and held it, glowing from within. It made her look both a paragon of elegance and ultimately touchable.

Why had she worn it? Was it in remembrance? To tempt him?

But as with everything Leticia, he had to temper his hopes. She wore her best ball gown because she had to and she could, as the gown retained its novelty and elegance since no one in this town had seen it before.

But it wasn't just the gown that made her transcendent. There was something in the sparkle of her eyes, the flush of her skin. And it made Turner realize two things.

First, that her mask was down. She was as alive as he'd ever seen her. Maybe he was the only one who could see it, but she was shedding worry in this oddly delicate situation and instead vibrating with determination.

And second, that she planned to do something stupid that night.

He knew he was right about the first instance. And he was about to be proved right in the second.

Because, in the short space of time that Miss Goodhue had come batting her eyelashes and swishing her ruffles, Turner lost sight of Leticia.

She'd been standing next to Sir Barty, holding court near the refreshments. Which, since they were surrounded by people wishing to congratulate them and shake hands, seemed like unnecessary torture for a man with a hunger for pork-based treats.

But now Sir Barty was sitting down, a plate of tarts in his hand and a cup of punch at his elbow, and Leticia was nowhere to be seen.

"Where did she go?"

"Who?" Rhys said as Turner reached his side.

"Who do you think? Leticia."

Rhys blinked and looked around. "She was over with Sir Barty."

"But obviously she isn't anymore," he said, his brow coming down. "Dammit, I told you to keep an eye on her!"

Rhys's eyebrow went up. "Two weeks ago, yes. However, I did not realize that my subterfuge was meant to extend all the way to tonight."

Turner sighed in frustration. "Did you happen to see which way she went?"

"No. Perhaps Margaret or your mother did, though."

Rhys nodded toward where Sir Barty sat. Next to him was his mother, and next to her was Margaret, recently relieved from having to dance with Mr. Blackwell.

Where Mr. Blackwell had gone to was also a mystery.

A pit of dread began to pool in his stomach. If Leticia was off doing what he suspected she was, and Mr. Blackwell was also missing . . .

Oh hell.

"Let's go ask them, shall we?" Rhys said as he crossed the ballroom.

He was about to turn on his heel and set about tearing this house apart, but since he didn't know where to begin, he might as well see if his mother did. She'd been near or at Sir Barty and Leticia's sides since they arrived. And while Sir Barty had been proudly presenting his new bride to the local gentry of Frosham, Helmsley, and the Wolds, Turner found it very odd how often Sir Barty would lean over to Helen and say something that would make her snort with laughter.

"There's the man of the hour," Rhys said upon arriving at the group by the refreshment table. "How's your foot? And what's that in your hand?"

"Just a little meat pie," Sir Barty said, wheedling. "Come now, Doctor, it's a party—some celebration must be had."

Rhys indulgently rolled his eyes, letting his patient off the hook for his transgressions, as he turned to greet Miss Babcock.

"Sir Barty," Turner said, bowing, and forcing as much good humor on his face as he could. "Where has your lovely bride-to-be fled to?"

"Letty?" Sir Barty asked, and for a moment an all-encompassing, pulsing red blocked Turner's mind. *He calls her Letty now?* "She's just dashed off to the ladies' retiring room, attending to woman things, no doubt."

Turner's brow went up. No doubt that was what Leticia told him, but since she had been in the retiring room not an hour ago, he highly doubted she had need of it again. No, he knew a vague and convenient excuse when he heard one.

"John, my boy, I have not seen you dancing yet," his mother said. "Truly criminal while so many ladies want a partner."

"I am not much of a dancer," he said pointedly to his mother. "So I think for now I should—"

"There's a lovely girl right there, eager for a turn about the room," Sir Barty said, waving his hand in Margaret's direction.

Margaret for her part was trying very hard to melt into her chair. But then she looked up at him. Her torture was as acute as his, but far more painful.

He had no idea where Leticia was. And he couldn't tear after her without causing a scandal in that moment, as well as deep embarrassment for his mother. So he did the only thing he could.

"As eager as I am, hopefully," he said, turning to Margaret. "Miss Babcock, may I have the honor?"

She blushed readily as she took his hand, and he led her to the dance floor.

It was a quadrille, something moderately paced and with easy steps, thankfully. Margaret seemed glad of it too, until she turned the wrong direction and banged smack into Turner's chest.

"I'm sorry," she mumbled, turning red.

"It's quite all right."

"I'm not much of a dancer either," Margaret said quietly when they came together again.

"You're doing fine," he replied. "I promise, much better than I did at my first ball."

"At least you've had some practice," she commented, giving a shy smile.

He hadn't been to a ball since a year ago, when he'd stood up with Leticia and then kissed her in the middle of the dance floor. But he could keep time to music, he could count out steps. But he'd always lacked grace. She never made him feel clumsy, though. She made him feel strong.

Dancing with Leticia was the only time he'd ever

wished he'd taken lessons. He'd wanted her to see that he could be the gentleman she desired.

He'd given up that notion. And yet . . . the way she'd kissed him back in his little office in his mill told him she didn't care.

But then her answer in the churchyard told him she very much did.

"Oh—I'm sorry!" Margaret said, stepping on his foot and snapping him out of his reverie.

"It's all right," he said, wincing. "You're doing well."

"I wish I could have practiced, but . . . how does one practice without music?"

"I don't know. I imagine you count the beats, and there are books that tell the steps."

"I see," she said, then grew silent again. "And do you like . . . books about dancing?" Margaret said when they stepped close once more.

"I can't say I've read any," Turner replied, his eyes scanning the room, hoping for a glimpse of cream silk and gold thread. Hoping even for a whiff of Blackwell's hair grease. Either would set him at great ease. "Why do you ask?"

"I'm trying to think of things to say to you that you might like."

That brought his head around.

She was biting her lip. Something about her was trying very hard to fit into a new form—the dress, the dance, even her hair was not in its usual long braid down her back. She looked utterly ill at ease, and completely vulnerable.

It made him feel like the worst kind of heel, to be thinking of another woman when he was dancing with her.

But that other woman was on both of their minds.

"Leticia says that one should find common interests with their . . . dance partner. If people have common interests and goals, it gives them something to build toward."

"And you have taken her advice to heart," Turner said.

"It seemed like good advice." Margaret shrugged. "But some of her advice puzzles me."

"How so?"

"That I should show interest in one person to attract someone else entirely. That I should look for signs of interest in unstated ways. It seems like there is always some kind of game being played, and I don't know the rules. When it would be so much simpler to simply say that you like someone out loud."

"Yes, it would be far simpler," Turner agreed. But then, memories of his last meeting with Leticia flooded him. "But also, far more painful if rejected. That's the risk."

"I see." Margaret nodded, her eyes becoming clearer. "So . . ."

"So . . ." he replied.

She took a deep breath. Hoping for him to say something? Hoping for the courage to say something herself? "So . . . do you like delphiniums?"

"I don't know what delphiniums are," he answered honestly.

"Oh." Margaret's face fell.

"I don't think common interests and goals are nearly as important as being invested in each other. As wanting to see the other person happy, regardless of if you both know the name of a flower, or . . . if you come from different places."

"Leticia said that too."

"She did?"

"Yes. I figure it must be like with flowers," Margaret replied.

His eyebrow went up. "How so?"

"A blossom cannot pollinate itself. It needs pollen from a different flower to bear fruit. In fact, plants that are cross-pollinated from other plants very far away tend to thrive best."

"True," he said, thinking over what she'd said. It was like him and Leticia. Their origins were similar but far afield from each other—she'd lived a life quite different from his. But together . . . they just made sense. Pieces fit into place. Even though on the surface she would not fit into his world and he would not fit into hers, when the two of them were alone together, everything found its place.

"She said that as well. That . . . perhaps one needs to look farther afield for . . ."

"For pollination?" Turner supplied, and hoped that she did not understand the unintentional entendre.

"Yes, but I've recently thought that I would find it here. At home," she replied, eyeing him.

He paused. Unsure of what she was asking, he found it impossible to answer. Instead the silence filled the air between them, and her expression fell from probing to quiet.

"Was there any other advice Leticia gave you that you wish to employ?" he asked. "Perhaps I can do better than delphiniums."

"Only if you know something about architecture," Margaret replied.

"You're interested in architecture?"

"Not particularly, but I learned a great deal this past market day." His expression was enough of an inquiry for her to continue. "Leticia and I met with an architect who was known to Miss Goodhue somehow, and he told us all about how he builds houses. This house, in fact."

That put every inch of Turner's body on full alert.

"I daresay Leticia had many questions."

"Oh yes, she wanted to know about the structure, where various rooms were, like the library and the study . . ."

"And where were they? The library and the study."

Margaret blinked twice at him. "I believe the library is in the northwest corner on the second floor, and the study is along the east side of the third."

"Thank you, Miss Babcock," Turner said, stopping abruptly and giving a short bow. "For the dance. For everything."

"But the dance isn't over—" Margaret said, but Turner could not hear her. He was already across the floor, ducking and weaving through the crowd to find his way to the staircase.

If Leticia was anywhere, she was rummaging through either Blackwell's study or his library. And he had to find her.

Hopefully before Blackwell did.

⁓

MARGARET STOOD IN the middle of the dance floor while the music continued to play, and ladies and gentlemen continued to swirl around her.

Actually, said ladies and gentlemen made a concerted effort to stay out of her way. As if abandonment was something they could catch.

A rising panic began to swell in her chest. She had no idea what to do. None of the theoretical scenarios she had envisioned had accounted for something like this. Instead, she'd only planned for (1) Mr. Turner asking her to dance, so they do, allowing her to gauge his interest and find common subjects on which to speak; (2) Mr. Turner not asking her to dance, so they do not, allowing her to realize his lack of interest and not needing to find common subjects on which to speak; or (3) Mr. Turner being coerced into asking her to dance by their parents—which did occur—and having to once again confront the ambiguity of his interest and wonder if her own interest in him would be enough to—

"Did he finally leave?" Dr. Gray asked, his voice filling her ear. "Thank heavens, I could not watch him put you through that misery any longer."

She turned to him. "What do you mean?"

"His terrible dancing. John has always had two left feet, and no amount of practice could solve that. I can see the misery it caused on your face." His voice became just a touch louder, for all those nearby to hear. "Obviously he did not wish to embarrass his partner any further."

"He . . . he didn't leave because he was dancing poorly," Margaret said, fearful that her chin was wobbling. She hated when her chin wobbled. But it wobbled because she knew it to be true. He'd left her in the middle of the dance floor not because of his own ineptness, but instead because . . .

"Nonsense," Dr. Gray said jovially. "He does this all the time. Causes a mess and leaves me to clean it up. Which"— he waved a hand at the musicians. They nodded, and suddenly the quadrille became a fast-paced waltz. Suddenly, Margaret was swept up into Dr. Gray's arms and sent spinning across the floor—"I intend to do now."

As they spun in time to the music, the air catching up around them and creating their own whirlwind, Margaret felt a small smile begin to replace her misery.

"This was not a scenario I had pictured," she said as Dr. Gray guided her through the steps.

"Dancing with me? But I told you we should."

"Yes, but the variables . . ." Oh, how to explain? But then she saw that Dr. Gray was nodding at her, and she realized she didn't have to.

"Unknown variables at an event like this are terribly difficult to account for. There are simply too many possibilities."

"Yes, exactly!" And she laughed as they spun. And spun and spun.

"Now, tell me about all the scenarios you worked through."

"Really?"

"Really. I'm interested."

20

The first thing Leticia realized when she entered Palmer Blackwell's study was that the man was not as fastidious as she'd hoped. There was no labeling of files, documents ordered neatly on his desk. Instead, things were piled on the floor, on the overly ornate desk, on nearby shelves, and strewn about with an order likely only the man himself knew.

The second thing Leticia realized was that Palmer Blackwell, while in no way fastidious, was incredibly secretive. Even going so far as to ban his staff from ever entering his offices. Her first clue was the fact that when she pushed the door open (she entered from the main hallway, only noticing once inside the auxiliary entrance from what must be Blackwell's bedchamber) she inadvertently pushed a pile of books and papers, and oddly a stuffed cormorant, out of the way. The second clue was—

"Ah-*choo!*"

—all the dust she kicked up as she did so.

She quickly shut the door behind her, praying that no one heard or saw her. The initial wave of dust wafted over her, and it was all she could do not to give into the urge to indulge in a fit of sneezes.

This was worse than being in the gardens in full bloom, she thought as her eyes began to water fiercely.

Oh, this was hellish, but she had to find Blackwell's ledgers. She had no idea what she'd find in them, but she needed to know. It was a strange focus driving her, blinkered and yet clear.

She had to do this.

It was not only dusty but deeply dark in the room, but she dare not light a candle and have the light seen from under the door. So once her eyes adjusted enough to navigate (barely), she made her way over to the long windows on the far wall and threw open the heavy draperies.

Causing another shower of dust to be released into the air.

Really, she thought, would it have killed the man to allow one maid in here to at least dust? He could have supervised, made sure nothing was taken or seen.

But then a moment of clarity struck, and Leticia felt that delicious thrill that only ever comes with being right. Because if Palmer Blackwell was this secretive, going so far as to not even allow his servants into his study, that meant . . .

Palmer Blackwell had something to hide.

And he'd hidden it here.

But where to begin?

If she touched any of the piles of papers and books and the occasional stuffed bird, she risked not being able to put them back in the correct order, exposing to Blackwell that someone had rifled his things.

Not to mention, she chanced another plume of dust being released into the air.

She was so caught up debating her next move (and trying to suppress a rather gigantic sneeze) she did not notice when the door behind her swung open silently. However, when a hand came down upon her shoulder, she noticed.

Then she screamed in surprise.

"Oh hell, Letty, it's me! It's Turner!" he whispered fervently, wrapping an arm around her waist, stilling her.

"Turn—ah-*choo!*—Turner?" she asked, twisting herself around. Then, once the shock had faded, relief filled her chest.

Then, annoyance. "You scared me!" she said, swatting at his arm. "And you can let go of me now."

"You're the one holding on to me."

He was right. She had her hand in the crook of his elbow, her body bent into his. Quickly she extracted herself. No need for temptation. Not now.

"You shouldn't be here," she said instead.

"No, you shouldn't be here," he replied. "Blackwell has gone missing from the ballroom. He could be anywhere. We should go. Now."

A shimmer of cold dread ran down her spine. But she squashed and thoroughly ignored it.

"Feel free." She waved, stepping out of his reach. "I'll meet you back there in a few minutes."

"No you won't."

"How well you think you know me."

"Perhaps we forgo the coy responses and for once acknowledge that yes, I do in fact know you. I know you so well that I know you are bent on uncovering something that may not be there, even risking discovery to do so."

"So what?"

"So what?" he repeated.

"So what if I am discovered? I will play it off as having gotten a little tipsy and lost in this ill-designed house."

"Letty." He shook his head. "You're on the third floor. In the family rooms. If I'm not mistaken, that door over there connects to Blackwell's private quarters. Being drunk and lost does not explain how you got up here."

She thought that over. She'd come up to the study first, because she figured that she could explain away being missing from the party for a longer period of time, earlier in the night. There were so many people downstairs, having her missing would not be as noticeable as it would be when a number of people had already begun to take their leave. It was simple math.

But now that she was here, she knew she was in the right place, and rifling the library would not be necessary. She knew it in her bones.

And if Blackwell discovered her, well . . . that was the risk she took.

So, again, she waved off Turner's concerns. "What on earth do you think Blackwell will do to me? I've already made it clear to him that his threats to tell Sir Barty about my late husband are baseless."

"What about Margaret?" Turner asked. "What about his intentions toward her?"

She paused, took that in. "I won't let it happen," she said simply. "Whether or not she responds to his intentions—that girl is impossible to read—once I am her stepmother he will not be allowed anywhere near her. And he won't be able to stop me."

No, he would not be able to stop her, but something strange had crept up Leticia's spine as she'd watched Margaret dance her first dance with Mr. Blackwell. For all the girl's talk of seeing two men as the only men in the world, she hadn't blushed with Mr. Blackwell. Not ever. Not while they danced, and Leticia was beginning to wonder if she ever had, or if her memory played a trick on her.

"Then why are you doing this?" he asked quietly.

She didn't answer, and didn't meet his eye. Instead, she put her gaze solidly over his shoulder, focused on assessing the room.

The task at hand.

"I left Margaret in the middle of the dance floor to come and find you," Turner breathed. "Even if your absence isn't noted, mine will be."

Her eyes flew to his face then.

"Why on earth would you do a thing like that?" she cried. "Margaret must be so heartbroken."

"I did it because I . . . I needed to find you," Turner replied, running his hand through his hair. "I knew you had this foolish plan—"

"It's not foolish."

"And even though you have pledged yourself to another man, you seem intent on thrusting yourself in my business. And I have no idea why—it seems to be almost compulsory on your part."

She blinked at his rush of words. This was no time for an argument.

"Do you think that I'm impulsive?" she asked hotly. "That I rush blindly into things? No. I plan. I plot. All very carefully. I would not be here on a whim. Now, there is something to be found in this mess of a study, and I intend to find it. You can either help me, or you can leave."

He threw up his hands. "And how do you propose to find anything here? Everything's covered in papers and dust!"

"Not everything." Her head cocked to the side as she peered over his shoulder.

The recently opened windows allowed for something other than a proliferation of sneezes. As the light fell on the desk and the piles randomly assembled around it, she could see that there were spots not covered in dust.

The leather chair was shiny from use. On the desk there was a path carved out of the dust to the inkwell and back again. And to the left, a tall pile of papers and leather-bound books were notably absent of dust.

And then she laughed.

"What is it?" he asked, worry in his voice.

Then she sneezed.

"The dust," she said finally. "It's showing us the path. Anything covered in dust is not something Blackwell uses on a regular basis. Those parts that are clean are used often."

She moved around the desk and gently lifted a few of the papers off the top of the nondusty pile.

"Bill of sale, bill of purchase . . ." she said, rifling through them. Then, below all the papers . . .

"*The Production and Uses of Barley,*" she said, pulling out a large volume from the bottom of the pile. She wrinkled her nose. "I could not imagine a more boring book if I tried."

But flipping open the cover, she did not find an index of uses for barley. Instead, she found tightly handwritten entries, with corresponding dates and numbers.

"Hello," she breathed. Then sneezed.

"What is it?" Turner asked, coming over to her. Then, reading over her shoulder, "Twenty shillings for delivery, two pounds six for bottle weight manufacture . . ."

"It's a ledger. A business ledger!" she cried happily. "But why would it be in a book about barley?"

"Because these are his real business ledgers. Ones that he does not want the world to see." Turner just shook his head. "Of course you have this kind of luck. Just skip over a dozen steps and find what you're looking for in the first book you pull from the pile."

"What luck?" she scoffed as she flipped back pages.

"This is all talent and practicality. If I had any luck, I should not have ended up engaged to a man who lives in the same town as my ex-lover."

"We were never lovers," he said, his voice a whisper in the dark. "Unfortunately."

Leticia prayed that her hands were not shaking as she flipped through the book. Begged her eyes to stay down, and her voice to not shake with feeling. "This seems to be a monthly ledger. That is, each page is a month—and it goes back years." She flipped back six years. "Which month was it that your mill burned? The first time, that is."

He told her, and she flipped to the appropriate page. But now, the shuffling of paper had dissipated the tension between them to move his interest from her to the contents of the ledger.

Although it did not dissipate completely.

Instead, she felt his warmth at her back, his arm brushing up against her shoulder, a constant reminder of his strength and presence.

"Everything seems to be quite ordinary," he mused, panning down the ledger page. "Purchases of grain, a contract to hire a worker to repair a sail."

"What about this?" she asked. "There is a payment to a 'Mrs. M,' but no reason given."

"It's not a great sum," he replied, but his brow came down. Thinking. "Not enough to pay someone to commit arson at least. And a woman?" He sounded skeptical.

"A woman is equally capable of striking a flint as a man."

"True, but a woman would be far more likely to be noticed in a mill yard," Turner countered. "And look, it's a continual payment."

Leticia saw as he flipped pages. Yes, every page had an entry for "Mrs. M," all the way until the current month.

"It even goes further back too . . . to a full year before

the mill burned." He shook his head. "This is not what we think it is. This is an allowance. He's supporting someone."

"Out of his business funds?" she mused. "Oh . . . oh, of course! He'd keep it out of the household accounts. He'd want it to remain hidden."

"What?"

"That he has a bastard. He's paying funds to the mother. The child would be about seven now, I suppose. Do we know any women with a last name M that have a seven-year-old?" she asked gleefully.

"Not that I can recall," Turner said. "Surely we would have heard something, though. A child is a secret too big to keep."

"Not necessarily. Men lie, women lie"—she indicated the ledger—"money never lies."

"All right," he conceded, "but I don't see how this is helpful to us."

"If Blackwell has a bastard," she said, "I can take it to Sir Barty—he would never allow Margaret to marry a man such as that. This is proof of his perfidy!"

"I'm afraid Sir Barty might not see it that way," Turner replied, shaking his head. "He might see it as proof of his responsibility. After all, everyone has bastards. Not everyone provides for them."

Her eyebrows went up.

"Everyone has bastards?" she asked.

He blushed. "Well, not me."

She harrumphed. "I'm still taking one of the pages." She began to carefully tear out the page that marked the beginning of the payments to Mrs. M. "Just in case. Perhaps I know Sir Barty better than you."

She delicately folded the page, curved it to her arm, and slid it into her long glove. Then, as perfectly as she could manage, she placed the ledger back underneath the papers, its spine facing out the same way, its title obscured exactly as it had been.

She straightened to find Turner watching her intently.

"Are you ready?" she asked.

"No."

"What's amiss?" she asked. "The pile by the door? I'll move it back as best I can upon exit, but—"

"You still haven't answered my question," he said. "In fact you have assiduously avoided it."

"What question?"

"Why are you doing this?" he asked solemnly. "Why are you trying so hard? Since the ladies in the town toured the mill, my mother has not heard one ill word about it in Helmsley. We've even received some contracts from smaller farmers—we have a chance of success. And even without that ledger page, you were determined to not allow Blackwell anywhere near Margaret. The man is no longer a threat."

"Yes, but now I don't have to worry."

"About him?"

"No—about you." Leticia turned to him. Sighed deeply. He was asking her for the truth, and in this moment—and possibly only in this moment—she wanted to give it to him.

"I can't do what you want me to do," she said simply. "I'm not that brave. But I can do this. I can help you get rid of Blackwell. I can help your business thrive. That's what I can give you, before we . . ."

His hand came out, almost of its own accord, and gently touched her cheek. "Before we what?"

"Before we say good-bye."

His hand stilled.

"Upon my marriage, I won't be your Letty anymore." Until now, she'd refused to allow that she ever was, but in the dark of the study, the moonlight making fireflies of the dust on the air, honesty won out. "Our past will become memory, more and more distant. You'll work your mill, and I'll be Lady Babcock. We'll be friendly acquaintances, of course. Sir Barty and your mother will play cribbage until the end of time, but—"

"But time will separate us."

She nodded slowly. "And someday, you'll meet a young lady who makes you smile, and your mother will be ecstatic. And Sir Barty and Lady Babcock will even attend your wedding, throw flowers, and wish you every happiness on that day. And that is what I want for you. Every happiness. But for that to happen, we have to say good-bye."

"I see," he said, and perhaps he did see. Perhaps he realized that "every happiness" was not something he could attain with her. Perhaps he looked down the road of their lives, and saw their various tortures not ending, per se, but fading away.

His eyes met hers. His thumb began to caress her jaw, slowly. "I suppose you are right," he said. "This is good-bye."

She nodded. Unable to break away from his gaze. Spellbound.

"Then . . ." He leaned forward, and his lips pressed to her forehead. Kindly. Reverently. "Good-bye, my Letty," he whispered.

His forehead pressed against hers, replacing his lips. She closed her eyes and let herself memorize the feel of him. The sharp lines of his face. The strength of his forearm under her hand. The steady beat of his heart. The way his thumb wiped away the tear that had somehow slid down her cheek.

Then . . . their lips were together. It was not her doing, nor was it his. It was simply what happened. His mouth pressing against hers. Her arms winding around his neck.

His hands grasping at the back of her dress, pulling her to him.

The kiss deepened. They pulled each other under, needing this as much as they needed air. The room they were in slipped away, the music drifting up from two floors below became nothing more than a whisper. There was only Turner, and Letty, and their final good-bye.

It was difficult to say who came to their senses first. Leticia only knew that one moment she was lost, feeling the rough calluses of his palm along her jaw, his fingers twisting in the tendrils of hair that escaped down her neck— and then suddenly, something broke them apart. Left them staring at each other, gasping for breath.

"I was wondering where you'd gone."

Leticia's heart stopped as her head whipped around to discover . . .

Helen Turner standing in the doorway of Blackwell's private study.

They leapt apart. Air rushed to fill the void between them, cold against her skin, which had gone hot with shame.

"And I'm not the only one," Helen continued, her unblinking gaze swinging from her son to Leticia and back again. "Your friend Dr. Gray covered for you when you rudely left Margaret on the dance floor, John. I told her you must have had a sudden stomach complaint."

Turner's jaw clenched, but he said nothing.

"Helen, I—" Leticia tried, but any excuse she could make died of improbability before it could be spoken. "How . . . how long have you been there?" she tried weakly.

"Does that really matter, dear?" she said, a pitying smile flitting across her stony expression. Then she turned back to her son. "I think you should go apologize to Margaret, make your excuses, and go home. Don't you?"

He glanced down at Leticia, hesitating.

"I'll stay with Lady Churzy," his mother said calmly. "She obviously got lost on the way to the retiring room. Didn't you, dear?"

"She's right," Leticia added quietly. "Go."

His expression darkened, inscrutable. Then his hand reached out and lightly slid down her arm to grasp hers for a moment.

He nodded at his mother as he passed. He did not look back.

"Helen, I . . ." Leticia began. She tensed, ready for the fury that was about to be unleashed. After all, she was jeopardizing not only her own marriage, but also Turner's standing in the town, everyone's futures. All for a moment of indulgence. A heartbeat, frozen in time.

But time hadn't frozen. It had ticked on, and much to their disadvantage.

Helen's expression was as unreadable as her son's, but as soon as she was face to face with Leticia she let out a long sigh.

And promptly choked on a plume of dust.

"Heavens, you must be dying in here!" Helen said once she was finished coughing up her innards. "Just look at your nose! Red as a beet. Come away, shall we?"

Numb with shock, she let Helen guide her out of the study and down the hall—pausing only long enough to arrange the books behind the door as best she could before closing it again.

"The back stairs, I should think," Helen said, pulling Leticia with her.

"Helen, I . . . I'm sorry," Leticia said. It was the only thing she could think of to say.

Helen pulled to a stop, her hand on the door of the stairs. "Whatever for?" she asked blithely.

"For . . . Helen, I know what you saw, and I feel I should explain. Your son and I met before—"

"There's no need to explain, dear," Helen said, patting her hand.

Leticia searched the older woman's face and found nothing there but kindness.

Kindness and intelligence.

"I've been thinking, Leticia. It would be a crime if you did not get a wedding trip to London, simply because Sir Barty is Sir Barty."

"I suppose," Leticia replied slowly.

"You'll learn this once you're married, but the way you handle that man is that you make plans and then let him catch up. Go ahead and make arrangements to stay in London for a few months. I'll help you convince Sir Barty of the benefits of town. Think of all the culinary delights that await him. Margaret too." Helen looked at her, her eyes sharp and clear. "It's what's best for everyone."

"Yes." Leticia nodded. "Yes, it is."

21

*N*ow, stay absolutely still, my lady. I don't want to rip the lace."

Leticia held in place as Molly knelt at her hem, delicately placing pins in the lace of her wedding gown. Her wedding was tomorrow. But oddly, ever since she came back from Blackwell's ball, she found all the minute tasks she had to accomplish before the big day to be burdensome. Her lethargy had grown to the point that she had put off having her gown fitting until this morning, when Molly practically wrestled her onto the little footstool and forced the dress over her head.

The girl was turning into an exemplary lady's maid.

"Luckily the bodice fit like a glove," Molly was saying, pins stuck between her teeth. "There's so much material of the skirt, I'm going to have to stay up all night on the hem alone."

"Yes," Leticia sighed. "We all realize the sacrifices you have to make due to my delinquent nature."

"I'm just saying, if you'd let me fit the dress yesterday, or earlier . . ."

"It's not smart to admonish the woman who pays you, Molly."

"It's not smart to admonish the woman holding a half dozen pins either," a voice said from behind.

An oily voice.

Leticia turned, a small squeak coming from Molly as she shifted the dress and the girl scrambled to keep the lace from ripping.

"But then again, a countess is forgiven for so much, I imagine," Palmer Blackwell said from the doorway.

"Mr. Blackwell," Leticia said, pulling herself up by the invisible string on the top of her head, looking down her nose at the little man. "Are you lost? Sir Barty should be in his library. Margaret went into Helmsley with Dr. Gray— unfortunately you've missed her."

"Actually, I'm here to see you," Blackwell said, looking her up and down. "You make a stunning bride."

"Perhaps you would consider waiting in the drawing room, then?"

He wandered over the threshold. "I don't think so."

"These are my private rooms. You should not be here."

A smile lifted the corner of his mouth. "Sound advice. But a little wobbly, no? Coming from you, that is."

Leticia's focus sharpened to a razor point. "Molly," she said, her gaze never leaving Blackwell's face. "Give us a moment, please."

"But—" Molly began, the wheels visibly turning in her head. On the one hand, her mistress was still in her wedding dress. On the other, a man not Sir Barty had invaded her private quarters. Both of theses things sat with equal disturbing weight in the girl's mind.

"Please, Molly," Leticia said, nodding at the girl, dismissing her. Molly stood, curtsied, and ducked her head as she passed Blackwell.

"Oh, and if Mr. Blackwell hasn't left in five minutes," Leticia said, calling after her, "send up Jameson with three footmen to escort him out."

"That won't be necessary. This won't take long at all," Blackwell said, winking at the girl. It was hard to tell if a meek servant such as Molly shuddered with revulsion, but Leticia certainly did.

Once Molly was gone, Blackwell gently shut the door behind him.

"That"—she nodded toward the door—"is most improper."

"I didn't think you would want simply anyone to hear what I have to say," he replied. "Don't worry. I'm not here for any reason that your fiancé might interpret as untoward. You can even stay on your pedestal. Simply give me what you took from me, and all will be well."

"What I took?" Leticia blinked at him. "I've taken nothing from you."

"You're not stupid, my lady, please don't do us both the disrespect of acting like it. I knew you had gone into the study the minute you appeared back at the party with your eyes watering from the dust. Your sensitivity to flowers and such is well known."

He wandered over to the window, running his finger along the window ledge. "Not a speck in here."

Damn. And she'd been so careful, trying to hide her presence in the study.

"It took me a little while to discover what was missing, but discover it I did. So, simply return the ledger page, and there is no need for us to part as anything other than friends."

"What—"

"Don't you *dare* say 'what ledger page' like a simpering

moron!" he hissed at her. The veneer of geniality dropped away, revealing his true visage—anger pulsed from the vein in his neck, radiated from the contempt in his eyes. "Don't lie to me, Countess. We are past lies, you and I. Now, I want my ledger page back, and you are going to give it to me, or else."

Leticia took a deep breath. Two. Then rolled her shoulders back. Let the disdain drip from her voice. It was time to do battle.

She hadn't intended to confront him with the ledger page—not yet. Turner had been right, the proof that a man had fathered a child out of wedlock was not exactly the damning evidence they had hoped to uncover (nor was it nearly as damning for a man as it was for a woman, but that was a societal point of contention she simply did not have the time to deconstruct at the moment). However, the fact that he had sought her out . . . the fact that the ledger had been hidden . . . the fact that he was letting his façade of nicety drop and show his teeth . . .

It mattered to him.

And that meant the balance of power was tipped in Leticia's favor.

"Or else what?" she asked.

"Or else I tell Sir Barty your biggest secret," Blackwell replied, a serpent's smile spreading across his features.

"You mean about my late husband?" she asked sweetly. "I'm afraid that won't work, as you well know. Besides, Konrad's sins are not mine, and a two-minute conversation can make that clear, even to a man of such uncomplicated tastes as Sir Barty. So if you don't wish me to show the man proof of your payments to the mother, then you should perhaps remove yourself from the premises." She cocked her head to one side. "Forever."

"Forever?" he repeated, almost amused.

"Yes. Forever," she said, stepping down from her footstool. "Your presence at Bluestone has become quite tiresome. Go back across the Wolds and leave us be. Stay away from me, stay away from Margaret, stay away from Helmsley. If Sir Barty reaches out to you, send no note of regret. Of course, you'll have to resign yourself to the loss of his business, but that's the price you pay."

"The price I pay."

"For trying to blackmail me," she said through gritted teeth, her pleasant demeanor falling away. But only for a moment. Then her smile was firmly back in place, her posture perfect. "Really, when you look at it, I'm being quite kind. Now, I assume I won't be seeing you at the wedding tomorrow, so I'll thank you for the compliment about my dress and bid you good-bye."

She walked over to the door and yanked it open.

And waited.

His eyebrow went up, and he crossed the room to where she stood.

And closed the door.

"That is in truth, a very reasonable list of demands. And I would happily acquiesce to them . . . if only your biggest secret involved your late husband." He bore his teeth, like a predator having found its supper. "But what I was speaking of happened just last summer."

She held her breath.

"Surely you don't need me to jog your memory," he said in mock astonishment. "You were at your sister's house in Leistershire. An earl of some standing came to stay at a house party. He made promises to you, and quite publicly too. And he turned out to not be the earl, but his servant."

"Not his servant," she said automatically.

"Regardless," he said, waving that aside. "You were played for quite the fool. I don't think Sir Barty would like a foolish wife. Or one that would make a fool out of him."

But Leticia, far from freezing in fear as he'd obviously hoped, simply shook her head.

And laughed.

Long enough and loud enough to have the simpering smile drop from Blackwell's features.

"You have very little imagination, don't you?" she said, once her laughter subsided. "Once again, you are trying to visit the sins of a man upon me. It's expected from those of your ilk, that a woman would cower and cover, taking on someone else's shame. But perhaps what you didn't expect was that Sir Barty knows."

One eyebrow went up.

"I told him all about how I was lied to, before we ever became engaged. And amazingly, he still wished to marry me. That's the kind of man Sir Barty is—trusting. And trustworthy. So unless you have something else to add . . . again, I say good day, Mr. Blackwell."

Again she pulled at the door handle. But only managed to open it a few inches before Blackwell took its edge and held it in place.

"You say Sir Barty knows all about how you were tricked."

"I told him all about how I was lied to, yes."

"Does he know it was John Turner doing the lying?"

She stopped. Her triumphant smile slid from her face. And this time, it was she who shut the door.

"I did not think you would be an issue for me," Blackwell said, stepping infinitesimally closer to her. "I thought Sir Barty's bride would be like him—simple, and easy to cull. After all, it only took me a few weekends of sport and revelry to turn him into my boon companion, willing to overlook long-standing friendships in his business dealings.

"But by the time we met, you had already become so close with the Turners, already so decided against me . . . you became a problem I was determined to resolve."

He winked at her, his face far too close to hers for comfort. But she couldn't look down. Couldn't step back. She had to hold her ground. Finally, he realized he was not cowing her, and so stepped away with a little shrug and began examining the little trinkets that adorned her rooms. Nothing exceptional, nothing truly valuable. But all extremely personal.

And he was touching them. Acting as if he had the right. Daring her to stop him.

And damn it all, that creeping, crawling path he traced on her dressing table was being drawn on her skin at the same time, leaving a growing terrible itch on her neck.

"So I did some simple research. And of everything, your humble beginnings, your scandalous marriage, who'd have thought it was your banal sister in Leistershire that would bear such fruit?"

"My sister told you?" Leticia asked, aghast.

"No. My investigator only had to walk into their town—Hollyhock, was it?—and mention your name to hear the full story from so many eager sources. And then they mentioned the name Mr. Turner. And suddenly, everything made sense."

"I can't imagine what you mean."

"That's because you can't see yourself when you look at him," Blackwell replied. "And the way he looks at you—I assume Sir Barty's been cuckolded already? No? Well, I suppose waiting until after the wedding is better politics."

"How dare you—" she bit out, her temper finally flaring. She took two steps away from the door before she stopped herself. Blackwell was watching her, his beetle black eyes alight with triumph.

"I dare because I can. All I have to do is whisper the truth in Sir Barty's ear, and you will be out the door, my lady, and at the mercy of a cruel world. Add to that—do you think he would ever do business with John Turner knowing the man had tupped his fiancé? Do you think Mrs. Turner is going to be invited over for cribbage anymore? No, the Turner Grain Mill will be done. And I'll buy it up for scraps." Blackwell looked aside for a moment. "Actually, come to think of it, my silence costs me quite a bit, in a business sense. You should make it worth my while."

Her voice was ice cold. "What do you want?"

"My ledger page back, for starters," he replied.

"For starters?"

"Oh, I'm certain that as time goes on, I will have other uses for you." His gaze flicked over her body, like it was a possession. She ignored the itch spreading from her neck to her ear and instead settled for a shudder of revulsion. "After all, we are going to be great friends, you and I. But for now, I will have my ledger page back, or else you won't be getting married tomorrow. Which would be a shame. I do love a wedding."

He had her at checkmate. And what was worse, he knew it.

"I don't have the page myself," she said, telling her final lie.

"Safely tucked away at Turner's Mill, is it?" Blackwell clucked. "Leaving your evidence in a location with a history of flammability is a bit of a misstep, but that's neither here nor there any longer."

"I will need some time to retrieve it," she said through gritted teeth.

"Of course. Take all the time you need—up until your

wedding tomorrow morning. If I don't have it in hand by then . . ."

And with that, Blackwell straightened his coat, fussing the wrists into idle perfection. He then gave a short bow and moved past Leticia to the door.

"See you at the church," he said, and was gone.

Leaving Leticia alone, standing in the wreckage of her perfectly constructed, long-sought, and hard-won life.

And there was only one thing she could do.

ceo

"DARLING, I NEED to speak with you."

Sir Barty's head came up from his paper as her voice floated over from the library doorway.

"Of course, m'dear! What is it?" He blinked at her, smiling.

And it made her heart crack.

Because Leticia was about to smash that smile into a thousand pieces.

She could have given in to Blackwell's demands. She could marry Sir Barty, and be comfortable if not happy. However, the entire time, she would be under Blackwell's power. Inviting him to dinners. Catering to his wants. Allowing him to run her life. All because he knew the truth.

She simply would not live in the shadow of a lie.

Not anymore.

Sir Barty had his foot up on its stool, dressed in a fresh wrapping. As she approached, he made a minimal effort to rise, saying, "I'd stand, m'dear, but I want my foot to be in tip-top shape for tomorrow. Nothing is going to stop me from walking with you down the aisle."

"Don't even think of it," she said, waving him back into his seat.

"But I do wish to think of it," he said, his grin coming through beneath his mustache. "We will be presented as man and wife for the first time. I want to do it by your side. Margaret insisted."

"Margaret?" Leticia had to ask.

"Yes," Sir Barty said with eyes as wide as hers. "Margaret. She said something about declaring your intentions, and not hiding behind a game. And since she was demanding it, I thought I had better listen."

Leticia felt a smile breaking through her solemnity. Three weeks ago, when she arrived, Margaret would not have said boo to her father, let alone have an opinion about anything to do with a wedding, unless it was to express shock that there was to be one.

Oh, Margaret. She would have to live with the pain of this too, wouldn't she?

But it would be far, far worse if she learned of it later. If she was her stepmother and the disgrace befell her by association.

Ironic, that.

"Is Margaret back from town yet?" she heard herself ask. Knowing she was stalling.

"Not yet," Sir Barty replied. "She said she had to pick up some lace to match your dress for the bouquet. So . . ." He gave an exaggerated wiggle of his eyebrows. "We are all alone. For the first time since . . . since Paris, almost."

He patted the seat next to him on the wide leather sofa.

"I . . . I cannot," she began, her smile weak.

"Why?" he asked, looking like a hurt puppy. "In less than twenty-four hours we will be man and wife, and a quick cuddle is not against the law." His eyes roved over her, assessing, looking for clues. Then—"Oh, of course! The lace!"

"The lace?"

"Is this your wedding gown?" he said, pointing to her dress. "Don't want it crumpled, do you?"

Leticia glanced down. Yes, she was still wearing her wedding gown, with pins still in the hem. Once she was certain Blackwell had left the building, she had gone directly from her rooms to Sir Barty, without even thinking of her dress.

"No," she said finally. "I mean yes, I don't want it wrinkled, but, darling, I have something to tell you. Something that cannot wait the twenty-four hours to marriage either."

His joviality fell away as he finally realized she was serious. "What is it? Are you all right?"

"I'm fine," she replied. "Physically, at least. But I am afraid I cannot marry you tomorrow."

There was nothing, only the sound of her breath, to fill the silence that had descended.

Then, he laughed. "What is this? Cold feet, I gather. M'dear, don't spout nonsense, everything will be well."

"It's not cold feet." She shook her head. "It's more important than that."

"M'dear, Leticia . . ." He leaned forward, taking his foot off the stool with some difficulty. "If you're nervous about tomorrow—er, after the wedding I mean . . . I am too." He looked at her imploringly. "I know I'm not a young man . . . nor a handsome one. I'm fat and old. And worse, I'm resigned to it. Not exactly what young brides dream of on their wedding night. But I'll do my best by you, know that. I will be as kind and gentle as a man can be. I'll not disgrace you."

He reached for her hand, sitting before her in much the way he had when he proposed. So very eager. And now she had to show him the fool he'd been for asking for her hand in the first place.

"I am not worried about you disgracing me. Rather, if you marry me, I will be the disgrace to you."

He let go of her hand. But kept his eyes on her face. Calm, but not understanding.

"I'm afraid the past I tried to outrun caught up to me," she began, taking a deep breath. "I lied to you. I told you that last summer a man had deceived me, pretending to be a man of quality and courted me."

"He was little better than a servant, you said," Sir Barty said. "And that he had done it to be cruel, to play a trick."

"He . . . he didn't do it to be cruel. It's hard to explain why he did it, but what matters is that he did, and I fell prey to his charms. And he was very charming. You wouldn't know it when you speak to him now, he's so terribly focused on his work, but when he was someone else he was free to be himself. Does that make sense?"

"None at all," he replied. "What do you mean, 'when you speak to him now'? Has he . . . have you spoken with him?"

"Yes, quite often since we arrived," she answered plainly. "The man who deceived me is John Turner."

Sir Barty drew still, a look of complete bewilderment on his face.

"I . . . I don't understand," he finally said.

"John Turner . . . he was secretary to the Earl of Ashby. For a fortnight last summer, they visited my sister's home in Leistershire and they decided to switch places while they were there," she explained haltingly. "It was a wager, which Turner won, and that's how he managed to have enough money to rebuild his mill."

"I . . . I'm still . . ." Sir Barty suddenly stood, needing to pace. "Where the hell is my damned cane?" he shouted suddenly. "Jameson!"

"It's right here, darling." Leticia quickly grabbed it from the arm of the sofa and handed it to him.

"So . . . so he's the one who hurt you," he said, rising and stalking across the room in long lengths. "But you've never—you never said anything. Unless . . ." A dark look overtook his features. "Did you come here for him?"

"No," she replied immediately, but he did not—or could not—hear her.

"Have you two been laughing at me this entire time?"

"No!" she cried.

"I never could understand how someone like you could want someone like me. You're too pretty and refined. I thought you needed someone to take care of you. But if it was just to be near someone else, I . . . I . . ."

"Sir Barty, listen, please. I had no idea that Turner came from Helmsley. When we met in Paris it was a complete coincidence. It was . . . fate."

"Fate," he repeated. "You were fated to come here and pretend to want to marry me?"

"I wasn't pretending," Leticia said, her nose stinging with tears. "I did want to marry you. I do! I thought I would have been very happy to never see John Turner again. He just happened to be here, so I was forced to."

"Forced to. You were not forced to tell me of this when you realized he was here, were you?" Sir Barty spat out. "If it truly was coincidence, why didn't you tell me then? Instead, you kept that secret, so now when people find out, they will look at me as . . . as a fool for bringing you into my house! That poor lonely Sir Barty, taken in by the first pretty face to smile at him. What an idiot."

She took a deep breath, tried to stall her tears. "That's exactly what Mr. Blackwell was counting on."

"Blackwell? What does he have to do with this? Did you make love to him too?"

Her tears dried quickly. "Of course not. Mr. Blackwell is a despicable man. I know you consider him a friend, but you are mistaken in that friendship. He uses people for what he can get from them."

"And you don't?"

That hit her like a slap in the face.

"Mr. Blackwell," she said shakily, "tried to blackmail me with the information about Turner, promising to spread it far and wide, should I not . . . well, I suppose it doesn't matter now. But I won't live my life afraid of him. And if nothing else, I hope this clears up your perception of him. And that you never allow him anywhere near Margaret."

"I'm much more likely to let Mr. Blackwell dance with my daughter now than I am John bloody Turner!" Sir Barty ground out. "Damn it all—he was courting her! You told me so!"

"Yes," Leticia replied, suddenly quite tired. "He was, in a way. It became quite complicated very quickly."

"I should imagine. Holding up lie after lie for you must have been very tiring. Good God, Leticia. You made friends with his mother! Does Helen know?"

"She didn't then, no," Leticia answered honestly.

"But she does now," Sir Barty concluded. "Wonderful. My fiancée has been playing me for a fool and even my oldest friend knew about it."

"I never intended to play you for a fool," she whispered. "But Mr. Blackwell will make certain that you are. That's the kind of 'friend' he is."

Sir Barty turned to her. "Perhaps Blackwell is doing me a favor. Forcing you to tell me the truth before I make a mistake." He shook his head. "I thought this was a story buried in your past. A bit of shame, but understandable and weathered," Sir Barty said, drawing up to his full height. With his size and the cane, he looked imperial, impenetrable.

Her judge, jury, and executioner.

"But to have it be a man we know? A man who you have spoken with publicly and privately, and God knows what else? A man you promoted to my daughter? You bring your shame into my house. And you don't even ask my forgiveness for it."

"You're right," she replied, her voice becoming cool, equally imperial. She was, after all, a countess. "I don't. I was doing what I must."

Sir Barty turned an ugly shade of red, but before he could unleash any of the number of invectives he must have bubbling over, Jameson popped his head in the door.

His timing was far too impeccable. He had to have been listening on the other side.

"You called for me, sir?" Jameson asked, keeping his eyes on Sir Barty.

"Yes. Lady Churzy will be leaving. Immediately. I just . . . I can't have you here right now." Something flitted across Sir Barty's face. Hurt. Confliction. "Er . . . do you need any money, m'd—my lady?"

Leticia shook her head. "No." She still had her sapphire ring. Hocking that would take her to her sister's easily. And give her a little to eat off of for a few weeks, at least. "As you said, I'll find my way."

And she would. As she followed Jameson out the door, she turned back to give Sir Barty one last look. He was pacing, pivoting on his bad foot and crumpling over in pain. But instead of standing tall or being sensible and sitting down, he grunted, and used his cane to strike his footstool, knocking it over in frustration. Sir Barty was lost to his own pain—both from his gout and from what she had caused him.

She would go upstairs and pack her meager belongings. She would go to York, and leave Lincolnshire to let the rumors about her disappearance swirl and the Lie begin to take root again. And once she had recuperated at her sister's for as long as she could stand to be around Fanny, she would fly as far as the wind would take her. New shores. A new life. No longer Letty Price, no longer Lady Churzy. She would start over, and become new once more.

Yes, she would find her way.

She just had one stop to make first.

WHEN MARGARET AND Dr. Gray walked into Sir Barty's library an hour later, they were shocked to discover the footstool overturned. Not only that, but all the papers from the desk were all over the floor, and an overturned inkwell was staining the carpet. In the middle of it all was Sir Barty, a large plate of pork loaf sitting untouched before him.

"Father?" Margaret asked. "We just saw the carriage leaving. What has happened? You're not eating your haslet."

"You shouldn't be eating haslet," Dr. Gray added, but a look from Margaret had him amending. "That is . . . you seem to be upset."

"Margaret, pet," her father said on a sigh. "I've been played for a fool. Lady Churzy has . . . well, we won't be getting married tomorrow. She has been keeping secrets from me. From both of us."

Margaret stood. Then she looked around the room. The mess. Her father's sorry state.

"Father . . . what did you do?"

Sir Barty blinked. "Did you not hear me, child? Leticia has been—"

"I heard you," Margaret said, holding up a hand. "But

secrets don't cause tornadoes. Anger does. So I'll ask again . . . What. Did. You. Do?"

Sir Barty blinked in the face of his daughter's vehemence. She stared him down until he threw his head into his hands.

"Oh hell. I think I botched everything."

22

urner had just locked the door of the mill when someone knocked on it. Chances were it was his mother. And he did not want to talk, or not talk, with her at that moment.

His mother had been not-talking to him since the night of the ball.

Oh, she'd sat across the breakfast table from him. She'd brought the tea tray to his little office in the mill at exactly four o'clock, and sat next to him while he slurped tea and ate sandwiches, working on a bit of knitting while she did so, chatting about innocuous things all the while. Never once mentioning what she saw in Blackwell's private study. Although he could see it in every look she gave him, the words, the questions itching to leap off her tongue.

Instead, she brought him the news that the wheat from Mr. Jenkins's farm was ready to be culled, and since it's a little early, he can't get it into Blackwell's mill immediately. Therefore, he's bringing it to theirs.

Their first work for the season. For the new mill. Come Monday morning, Jenkins's wheat would be delivered and the sails of the windmill would be spinning.

They just had to get through Sunday first.

And that was the reason John Turner really would rather not have a nonconversation with his mother at that moment. Because it was the evening before the woman he loved was going to marry another man, and he had rather hoped he'd be allowed to be miserable on his own. He'd have gotten drunk if he thought it would help, but he knew it wouldn't.

Besides, he resided in a seven-story windmill, with moving parts weighing tonnes. Being unreasonably inebriated while in the building could only cause trouble.

She'd said good-bye to him, and he to her. It was like mourning a death.

He couldn't even tolerate seeing Rhys. His friend had stopped by while escorting Margaret into Helmsley. While she was speaking with Mrs. Robertson at the millinery about the best flower to match to a lace wedding dress, he made his excuses and came by for a few minutes.

Turner had brushed him off. Said he was fine, just busy. Put on the brave face he expected he would be wearing for some years to come. Rhys had hesitated. He was expecting to leave Helmsley and go back to Greenwich after the wedding, but he'd be happy to stay a few days at the mill with Turner, he'd said.

Turner said no.

Therefore, whoever was knocking on the door of the mill could not be more unwelcome.

But the knocking didn't stop. It wasn't loud, but insistent.

And then, a voice.

"I know you're in there."

Her voice.

He almost thought it was his imagination playing tricks on him. Surely, when he crossed the main floor and threw open the door, there would be nothing there but the wind. Surely, it wouldn't even be worth the trouble.

But there was only one way to find out.

"Hello," she said when the door opened. "Would you mind inviting me in? It's rather cold out here."

The sun was setting low behind her, bringing the chill of night. And she stood before him in a slip of a gown, short-sleeved silk with lace. Lovely, and shaking.

He stepped aside and let her in. She hurried past the two large mixing machines on the ground floor, rubbing her arms to force some warmth back into them.

"You're here," he said, unable to believe it.

"Yes," she replied, trying to stop her teeth from chattering. Now that she was inside, it was as if the warm air made her realize that she was colder than she had thought, and the shaking began in earnest. "I have to tell you something—I'm afraid . . ."

"There's a blanket in my office," he said, and before she could say anything, had taken her by her ice-cold arm and guided her toward his little office in the back.

There he set down the lamp in his hand, retrieved the thick wool blanket from his pallet, and threw it around her shoulders.

"Th-thank you," she said, clamping down on her chattering teeth. She took a deep breath, trying to calm her body, but to no avail. "I'll speak quickly. I had the carriage drop me off on the edge of Helmsley—my trunk is still waiting on the side of the road, come to think of it. But I cannot worry about that anymore. I'm going to cause enough of a scandal tomorrow for Sir Barty, my trunk is the least of it."

His heart was pounding, but he waited. Simply . . . waited. Because it seemed to him that everything in his life hinged on the next few moments, and he would be damned if something he said screwed it up again.

"I came here to warn you—tomorrow there will be no wedding, because Blackwell . . . he knows about you and me. He knows that it was you, last summer. And since I did not bend to his demands, I imagine that word is going to spread very quickly. I told Sir Barty, and as expected he was not pleased. Thus the wedding is off."

"The wedding is off?" Turner repeated.

"Yes. Punished again for something I didn't do . . . something we never did." She let out a small laugh, a bubble of sadness. Then she met his eyes, the weight of what they never did thick between them.

She shook her head, her body, brought herself back to the present moment. But Turner could not shake it off so easily. Oh no.

"It's important that you have this." She reached into the neckline of her dress and pulled out a sheet of paper, folded into quarters. The ledger page. She held it out to him, and he took it, warm from her vibrating body.

"The reason Blackwell played his trump was because something in those numbers scared him. If he does have a bastard child, he really does not wish it to be known. So you need to keep this, and keep it safe, because once word spreads about the Lie, and your part in it, you will need it to strike back."

Turner looked at the paper held lightly between his fingers, folded square. Then back to Leticia.

His Letty.

Shaking from cold, wide-eyed with nerves, breathless with anticipation.

He tossed the ledger page onto his small desk. Tossed it aside.

"You said good-bye," he said slowly.

She blinked, drawing her eyes up from where the ledger page had fallen, to his face. He knew it the moment she heard him. Really heard him, and what he'd said. A little gasp was all it took. Her eyes darkening from gold to black with desire. Her lips parting, ever so slightly, without her even knowing it.

"I did."

"But you're here now."

She nodded, never taking her eyes off of his.

"I am."

He took one step, the distance between his present and his future closed in an instant.

"Then stop talking."

It was nothing, nothing at all, for his lips to meet hers. For his hands to cup her face, to thread into her hair. To inhale and take her in.

There was a bare moment of hesitation. But then . . . she let go. She decided to give herself this one night, and to hell with anything and anyone judging her for it. She bent to him, finally free to do so. No longer Sir Barty's bride. No longer Lady Churzy, holding herself at a distance. She was just . . .

"Letty," he breathed, and let her name float on the air.

"Yes, John?" He could feel her smile against his mouth. He kissed her again. And again.

"You're still freezing." His hands drifted to her arms, as the blanket he had thrown over her shoulders fell to the ground.

"Warm me up, then."

He used his skin. Never taking his eyes off hers, he slowly undid the buttons of his thin lawn shirt, pulled it over his head.

There was something to be said for men who worked hard for a living, she thought wickedly.

He came to her, picked her up in his arms as if she was nothing more than a feather floating on a breeze, her body pressed up against his chest.

She sucked in her breath.

"That's a very impressive trick," she said, wrapping one arm around his broad shoulders. "Carrying a lady to your bed."

"It's all for show. Luckily we have a very short distance to cover."

"Still," she said, a little laugh escaping, letting her fingers graze lightly over the hard planes of his chest. "It's an impressive show."

"Ah . . ." he hissed, jumping from the contact. "Your hands are still quite cold."

"Oh." She blushed, immediately pulling her hand back. "I'm sorry."

He laid her gently down on the pallet. "Don't worry," he said, taking her frozen fingertips, kissing them gently, then encasing her hand in his hand completely, warming it. "We'll take care of that."

His eyes were hungry, his mouth more so, taking hers, his tongue tracing a line down her neck and sending a shiver up her spine.

She wanted that tongue to follow that shiver. She wanted . . . she wanted more than she'd ever imagined.

And she wanted it now.

But then . . . he leaned back. And looked.

"What . . . what are you doing?" she asked, her voice shaking. But not from cold. He couldn't abandon her, not now!

But his mouth picked up in that half quirk of a smile, one that spoke of a boy's mischief, but with a man's intentions.

"I've waited too long for this night, Letty. I'm going to breathe in every last inch of you."

"But . . ." she squeaked, but he hushed her with a finger held to his lips.

And then let his eyes roam over her body.

Usually Leticia was a woman of infinite patience. Planting seeds and letting them grow over time, knowing each step in the process toward her goal.

But she wanted . . . oh hell, she wanted to frantically tear at his breeches, rip the lace of her dress, if only to get them closer, as close as two people could be. Not this slow torture. Not his taking in every inch of her, making her skin prickle—not with an itch, no—but rather with a glow of awareness, like a warm breeze dancing over her body, up her calves, to where her stockings were tied. Up higher, and through her, settling into her body with waves radiating out.

And suddenly, she wasn't cold anymore. She was really quite warm. She flushed with each flick of his eyes, heated watching his muscular chest rise and fall with each breath, coming quicker and quicker as his gaze danced and lingered on the neckline of her dress, where silk met skin.

Then, his eyes met hers. And held.

But the slow dance of exploration his gaze had trailed up her body left a path his fingers could trace. And they did.

It began with a light touch on her ankle, his fingers gliding up her silk stocking to the ribbon at the delicate flesh under her knee. She nearly lost her breath when his hands reached her thighs.

And higher . . .

"John . . . please," she begged. "I want . . . Can we please . . ."

"Hmmm . . ." he said. "It occurs to me that you have likely never been worshipped properly. Have you?"

Worshipped? This, this need of two people for each other was never about worship, was it? With Konrad it had always been quick, and her fevered hopes for touch had never been satisfied. All she wanted was . . . a feeling she yearned for. A feeling she knew existed, but never experienced.

"I . . . I don't know what you mean," she said.

"Then you've answered my question."

He lowered his head, pressing his lips to the swell of her breasts, until they came up against the edge of her gown.

Her wedding gown.

"Although, I have to admit, there are some things getting in the way, don't you think?"

Finally. She nodded fervently.

"And while this dress is lovely, I'm not here to worship it."

Slowly, excruciatingly, he pulled down the tiny sleeve of her gown, exposing her shoulder. Then, the tiny buttons at her back were undone with a finesse that belied his callused thumbs. She remembered that about his hands. So deft, and so strong.

His hands found their way to the edge of her hem, gathering it up inch by excruciating inch.

"Ow!" he whispered. "What's here?"

"Pins," she said. "I'll explain later."

"I never knew a gown could be so dangerous," he said, smiling against her mouth.

"Didn't you?" she replied. "A gown is a lady's most formidable weapon."

But then the creation of lace and butter silk flew over her head and fell lightly onto the chair by Turner's desk.

"Looks like you're unarmed."

"That was a terrible pun," she said, smiling.

"I agree, but I work with what I'm given."

They both laughed in the dark at their silliness, at their happiness. Then she took his head in her hands and kissed him again.

His kisses became drugs, lulling her into bliss. Her kisses, however, became fire in his blood, stoked by the little gasps and sighs that escaped her.

Pins fells out of her hair, hitting the hard earth of the floor with dull pings. Her tresses tumbled around her shoulders in a haphazard mess that she couldn't care less about. His fingers found their way to the laces of her corset. Hers—no longer cold to the touch—fell to the buttons of his breeches. She fumbled a bit more than Turner had, but eventually found her object.

And suddenly, all laughter subsided.

"Letty," he whispered, catching her hand. "Wait . . ."

"No," she replied. "I'm done waiting."

The time for reverence and for silliness was over. Now there was only Turner, and Letty, and the fire that drove them, stoked with each breath.

His body nudged her knees apart, settling between them. His hands roamed freely over her soft skin, both becoming slick with heat. She felt the world give way as he stared into her eyes as she opened, and he filled her.

He became as necessary as air. For a flash of a moment, this touch, this contact, was more important than where she lived and how much money she had. It was more important than any name she called herself. It was simple breath—in and out. But it was gentle, tenuous. Too much so. All she wanted was more.

And she had the audacity to ask for it.

"John—I want more."

"More?" his voice was a raw gasp, straining to remain even.

"I want it all."

He found her eyes, gone dark with passion. Her gaze was direct, commanding. Who was he to deny his lady what she wished? With a kiss against her smile, he thrust deeper, deeper, until the space between them disappeared, not even a whisper between them.

This. Oh, this was what had been missing. This feeling of . . . loss and gain all at the same time. Loss, because she was shedding her skin, taking the weight of rigidity and perfection off her shoulders and just being. And gain . . . because of everything else.

She felt glorious.

She felt powerful.

She felt . . . worshipped.

And it was that realization that did it. That stunning moment of wonder that this man in front of her, over her, inside of her, would never judge her. Never hold her accountable for someone else's mistakes. He saw her from a thousand yards away, and still knew her instantly.

He was all that she wanted. And she had him.

It was like air rushing around her body, making sparks against her skin, building up from someplace deep in her center, her body arching against him, begging for it to stop and wanting it to never, never end . . . wanting it all. And for once, getting it.

She moved. She had to. Push against him, pulse in time. Her thighs tightened around him as he pushed and thrust and lost himself in her. He made himself hers in every way he knew how. And she gave him herself in return.

When her breath slowed down enough to feel his collapsed weight against her, she smiled to herself in the dark. She felt his lips find her temple. They were both sweaty, and messy, and glowing. She had given herself this, she realized. Permission. To be sweaty and messy. To have knots in her hair and John Turner kissing her temple. A present, for all the agony she had been through—and oh, all right, caused—in the past year. For one night, she was free.

A low laugh escaped her lips.

"What has you laughing?" he asked.

"You," she said softly. "It's funny."

"What's funny?"

How could she explain? That she was perhaps for the first time fully aware of all her contradictions? How was it possible that she could be burning for him, and be silly with him at the same time? How could he have introduced her to worship but leave her feeling not as if she stood on a pedestal, but as if she'd finally landed on safe ground?

"Just, everything." She sighed, wrapping her arms around his neck. "Being here, with you. Everything."

"And that's funny to you?" His forehead wrinkled in the dark. His body tensed next to her, becoming very still.

"Yes," she replied. "I don't laugh very often." It was true—not honest laughter, at least. She had to be too careful for that. "And the fact that I can—that I am—is funny to me."

"Let me see if I have this straight." His brow unfurrowing and a half smile turning the corner of his mouth up produced a sight Leticia had never seen and that nearly stole her breath—a dimple in his cheek. "You are laughing, presumably because you are happy, a fact that strikes you as funny because of its rarity, making you laugh more."

She nodded once, and smiled at him brilliantly. Openly. Without any calculation.

"Well, then," he growled, his hand reaching between her thighs and causing her eyes to go wide. "Let me see if we can make you laugh again."

23

Turner woke up with the sun to the smell of Leticia in his bed, but not Leticia.

Last night had been a dream. So much so that he thought he'd actually dreamed it. He'd woken himself up in the hours before dawn, relieved to find his arm slung over her warm body. Still in a half-sleeping state, he pulled her tight against him, kissing her neck. She responded unconsciously, turning to him, threading her hand into his hair and pulling his lips to hers. By the time he'd slid back into her, they were both fully awake and panting, the intensity of the feeling only matched by its rightness.

But now, with sunlight painting the walls of the tiny office morning pink, something was deeply wrong.

She wasn't in his bed.

She wasn't even in the room.

Her silk and lace dress—the only thing they had been careful about last night except each other—was still slung over the chair in front of his small desk. But the other garments—her chemise, her corset—were missing.

He found his trousers (inconveniently missing two

buttons—they had scattered on the floor somewhere) and pulled them on before bursting out of the office door and into the mill itself. It was quiet, except for the sound of a breeze whistling through the tower of the mill. Turner knew that sound. It was the sound of the door to the balcony on the fourth floor being left open.

He climbed the spiral staircase two at a time, reaching the fourth floor landing in no time at all. There he saw Leticia, standing in the balcony doorway, wrapped in the blanket that had been so quickly forgotten the night before, and staring out at Helmsley.

"Here you are," he said, letting a lazy smile spread across his face. Then the chill hit him.

"It's brisk out here," he said, rubbing his naked arms.

"It's getting cooler. The days are getting shorter too. Soon enough you'll be inundated with fresh grain."

"Luckily not on a Sunday," he said, coming up behind her and wrapping his arms around her body.

"Yes, Sunday," she said, seemingly realizing. "People will be headed to the church soon."

The church. Where she was supposed to be married today. Was that wistfulness he heard in her voice? Regret? No, it couldn't be. Not after the night that they had shared. Because there was absolutely nothing to regret about last night—it had been everything that was right. So instead he kissed the top of her (extremely disheveled) hair and whispered in her ear.

"Are you going to share that blanket, or are you coming inside with me?"

"I'll come inside," she said with a smile, still staring out at the horizon. Then she turned and they both walked back into the mill. "I just wanted to see it one last time."

"See what?" he asked, as he closed the balcony door.

"Helmsley," she said as she descended the staircase.

It took him a few moments of shock to move again. By the time he caught up with her, she was already on the ground floor, crossing into his tiny office.

"What do you mean, 'see Helmsley one last time'?" he asked.

"Helmsley was almost home. I grew rather fond of it." She threw off the blanket, and picked up her lace gown, grimacing. "Oh, I had forgotten about the pins," she mumbled to herself as she stepped into the gown.

"It still is your home," Turner said, leaning against the doorway. "You're staying here."

She stopped struggling with the buttons at the back and grew very still. Her eyes refused to meet his, instead finding the pallet, rumpled from their cramped and glorious sleep. "No," she said quietly. "I cannot."

"Why?" he bit out the word. He'd had her. Finally. And he didn't mean carnally, although their night had certain qualified. But he'd had her—she'd finally let down every wall and let him in. It was where he belonged.

And now . . . now she was leaving? To hell with that.

"John, you do understand that last night . . . it was the only night."

"No," he said, his eyes becoming fierce. "I damned well don't understand that. What the hell are you talking about?"

She looked up at him then, her eyes wide with disbelief. "Because . . . I left Sir Barty."

"I know, and you came here."

"To warn you about Blackwell."

"You could have done that in a note." He crossed his arms over his chest. "You came here to be with me. You rescinded your good-bye, and you cannot give it again."

"John, I can't leave Sir Barty to be with you," she said, exasperated. "Don't you see? Blackwell is going to tell everyone about you and me because of that ledger page. If we are together, it will just make everything worse!"

"I disagree," he replied, the syllables falling from his mouth like weighted stones. "I want you, Letty. I've wanted you for a year. I want you as my wife, and I want you in my home, in a proper bed and to wake up to you every day."

"Your business would never survive it. Sir Barty and Margaret would suffer. And I'll be the center of a scandal that I can never outrun . . . Now can you please help me with my buttons?" she said, frustrated.

"Not on your goddamned life," he spat, crossing his arms and blocking the door. There was no way she was leaving. If he had to keep her naked and in his cot, then so be it. But he didn't approach her. The fire in her eyes banked to cool ice, warning him away.

"Fine," she said, reaching behind her, bending her elbows awkwardly. "I lived without a lady's maid long enough, I can do it myself."

Oh hell. He swore under his breath and crossed the room to do up her buttons. He didn't want her to leave, but he also didn't want her to dislocate anything in the attempt. "I think that the only way to overcome any stupid scandal—and it is stupid, unbelievably so—"

"It's only stupid to someone who's never had to live through one before—"

"Is to stand together against it. To be together. You love me, I love you, and everyone else will have to adjust around us."

Her buttons done, he spun her around and saw a spark of hope in her eyes. But then it became banked, squashed by fear.

She pulled away from him and shook her head. "You've never heard people whispering about you as you walk past them. You've never dealt with outright scorn for daring to exist."

She began to play with her hair, smoothing it into sections, twisting them up into a simple, sleek bun. It infuriated him that she could care so much about her appearance right now. As if she didn't look goddamned perfect with her hair a mess and tumbling about her shoulders, and now the Letty he knew had to go hide behind the countess again.

"That's not what this is. These are old arguments. The truth is that you're still scared, Letty." He lingered on her name, making her pause for the briefest of moments as she searched the floor for her hairpins. "You're scared of being a miller's daughter again, a miller's wife and not a countess. You're scared that you're going to go back to being insignificant. And you are scared to death of being in love with me. Not because I'm not an earl. But because how you feel about me is something you cannot control."

He knew he'd struck a nerve with that last one. Her cheeks flushed red, livid and frightened. Then, she rose. He watched her straighten her spine, the way she always did when she transformed herself into an imperial goddess who could deflect cannon fire.

"Don't tell me what I'm frightened of," she said, her voice ice. "You're afraid of everything. You're someone who could not confront Ashby for five years, could not confront Blackwell about your suspicions about him. You couldn't even confront Mrs. Em when she went around town telling everyone your mill would fail, your mother and I had to—"

"What did you say?" he interrupted suddenly.

"I said you're scared—so desperate to succeed you get in your own way at every turn—"

"No, not about me. You said I couldn't even confront Mrs. Em?"

"Yes." Her brow came down, and her hands stilled on her hair. "Mrs. Emory. Oh God, she's going to have a field day with this news, Helen will have to work so hard to—"

"Letty . . . Leticia. You didn't say Mrs. Emory. You said Mrs. Em."

"Yes . . ." she said slowly, blinking.

"*Mrs. M,*" he said, practically knocking her over as he crossed to the desk, rifling to find the ledger page he had tossed there the night before.

"Mrs. M?" she said, her mouth dropping open like a fish. "You think Mrs. Emory is . . . Mrs. M?"

"The page you stole—it was the first page with an entry of Mrs. M, correct?" She nodded as he found the page and unfolded it in a rush. "What's the date on it?"

She came and leaned over his shoulder, pointing to the date in the top corner. "Here. See, it's about seven years ago. And Mrs. Emory does not have a seven-year-old. That, I am certain Helmsley would have noticed."

"Oh, I'm not so sure about that," Turner said, his brain turning over the date. "Helmsley can be utterly blind when it wants to. Myself included." Two steps later he was at his shelf, pulling a leather-bound ledger of his own from the middle of the pack.

"What is that?"

"One of my father's ledgers, from when he ran the mill. This one from seven years ago."

"They didn't burn in the fires?"

"No, my father kept his office in the house, where my mother could double-check his numbers. Aha!" he cried, flipping to a page.

Since his head was still in his father's ledger, he didn't see the look that Leticia shot him, but by the way her hands landed on her hips, he could imagine it. "Why did you cry 'Aha'?"

"Because I think I just put the pieces together. But is it enough?" He rubbed his chin in thought. "To hell with it," he said. No more being frightened. He was going to have to bluff, and bluff wildly. But if his guess was correct . . . "I suppose we are going to find out."

"Is what enough?" Leticia asked. "And enough for what?"

"Our conversation about your living situation will have to wait." Turner threw both the stolen ledger page and his father's ledger onto the desk, and found his rumpled shirt in the folds of his pallet. He did up the buttons as he picked up his evidence. "Right now, we are going to be alarmingly late for church."

She was so stunned by his proclamation, he was three steps out into the mill yard before he heard her.

"*CHURCH?*"

❧

IT WAS A short walk from the mill to the main square where St. Stephen's sat proud, but with Leticia dogging his heels asking questions every step of the way, it took longer than expected.

"John, we can't go to the church!"

His long, determined strides forced her to trot beside him.

"It was supposed to be my wedding day!"

He grunted but made no other comment.

"Everyone will be there!"

"That's the point," he replied. Was this what he had to look forward to? The constant arguing? He grinned with relish.

He couldn't wait.

At the churchyard, despite Leticia's running litany, they were relatively early—even with the days beginning later, the sky had only dawned within the past hour. So one might think that most people would still be at their homes, forcing themselves into their Sunday best and gobbling down a hearty breakfast.

Then again, this was no ordinary Sunday.

And Helmsley knew it.

The entire town was waiting in the churchyard. Or so it seemed. When Turner passed through the gates, it was to thunderous applause.

He was momentarily bewildered—especially considering he was wearing little more than breeches with two buttons missing and a fine lawn shirt. Then he realized, Leticia was behind him.

The vicar and his wife leapt down from the steps of St. Stephens, coming forward to greet her.

"Lady Churzy!" Mrs. Spilsby cried. "I should have known you would be so eager that you would precede the groom! Although, I have to admit to some surprise—I should have thought you'd take the carriage."

"Now, now," the vicar chided from beside her, his cheeks rosy with pleasure. "There is a great tradition of the bride and groom walking to the church. And since Sir Barty is . . . not a great walker, his bride is obviously upholding the tradition on her own. Ah, Mr. Turner!" The vicar finally noticed Turner standing there. "Welcome. Run into Lady Churzy on the path into town, did you?"

It took a second before Turner could answer, and it was just enough time for someone else to swoop in.

"Yes, Vicar, we did," his mother said, panting behind him. "John, dear, I know you warm easily, but you simply cannot go into church without your coat."

She had his coat slung over her arm and practically dragged him two steps away to force it on him.

"I saw you out the window this morning. Making an

elderly woman run to catch up to you is not the nicest way to wake up," she whispered fervently. "You're still wearing the same clothes as yesterday."

"Not now," he grumbled as she threw a cravat at him. Instead of tying it around his neck, he simply stuffed it into his pocket. Appearances be damned.

His mother looked horrified. "What on earth do you think you and Leticia are doing?"

"Discovering the truth," he said grimly.

His mother's brow came down. "The truth about what?"

He had already stepped away, back to where Leticia stood with the Spilsbys. But in his brief absence, a veritable gaggle of townsfolk had rushed to fill the void, and he had to wedge his way past half of Helmsley, several of them exclaiming things like, "Mrs. Robertson's dress is beautiful!" "I love how you left it long and trailing, a new style!" (This because in the brisk walk over—or the brisk activities from last night—she had lost a number of pins from the hem.) And . . . "I love your hair—so simple, so elegant!"

Meanwhile, Leticia was paying little attention to the fawning. Instead, she was focused on the vicar and his wife.

"So . . . Sir Barty is not here yet?" she asked weakly.

"Not quite, my lady," the vicar replied, full of oblivious cheer.

"So . . . you have not been told," her voice was little more than a whisper. But absolutely everyone caught it.

Silence descended.

"Told what?" Miss Goodhue asked, squeezing up next to her sister.

Leticia's voice faltered. "That . . . that Sir Barty . . ."

"Ah, there you are, m'dear! Thank heavens!" Sir Barty's voice boomed from across the churchyard. "Thank heavens, we thought we'd lost you."

"Indeed," Margaret replied next to him, and Dr. Gray stood beside her. He moved away quickly to stand at Turner's side.

"When the countess left Bluestone Manor yesterday, I did not expect to see her again so soon." He eyed his friend. "Dare I ask what actually happened?"

"You and my mother are far too nosy for my liking," Turner replied. "However, I'm more interested in what is going to happen right now."

"As to that . . ." Dr. Gray took a deep breath. "I think you should brace yourself."

"Margaret was adamant that you would be here today, and I am glad to see that it is true."

"She . . . she was?" Leticia asked, bewildered. Her eyes flew to Margaret.

"I told him you have nothing to be ashamed of, and you don't," the girl piped up, a wide grin showing her pride in her assertions.

If there had been a single ear that was not attended to the dramatics being played out by Sir Barty and his intended, it was most certainly attuned now.

Everyone crowded around, standing in a circle, angling for a better view.

Sir Barty looked at Leticia with more vulnerability than Turner had ever seen on a man of such size before. It was as if the older gentleman had opened his chest and was ready to expose his beating heart to the air.

"I am so terribly, terribly sorry for the things I said yesterday. I hope you can forgive me. I should have believed you. And . . . I would like everything to go back to the way it was. I hope I can take your presence here at the church and in your beautiful wedding dress as the sign I dearly wish it to be. I don't care about whatever past you have with Mr. Turner. I don't care about your past, full stop.

I simply hope that you will consider sharing your future with an old man who would dearly like some company."

He held out his hand to her. The crowd started murmuring.

Actually, the crowd had started murmuring when Sir Barty had said, "Mr. Turner."

Leticia stared at Sir Barty's outstretched hand. Her mouth tried to make a few sounds, but nothing came out. Then she shifted her gaze to Turner, helpless.

Tell him, he willed her. *Tell him that you love me and cannot marry him.* But she just looked back and forth between the two of them for interminable sentences more. *Damn it, after last night, tell him!*

Turner watched as she found her resolve. As she took those two deep breaths, and straightened her spine, and opened her mouth to speak.

She wasn't going to say it. Oh bloody fuck, she wasn't going to tell him the truth. Shock ran through Turner's body like a wave of pain, cementing his feet like a statue.

"I . . . I . . ."

"A past with Mr. Turner?" came a dark voice from the churchyard gate. "Oh dear, what ever could Sir Barty be speaking of?"

Every head turned to see Palmer Blackwell striding up into the churchyard—Mrs. Emory toting poor Mrs. Robertson conveniently behind him.

Turner's brow came down as he remembered the reason he had marched to the church that morning.

Now the real tornado would begin.

~ ❧ ~

LETICIA FELT HER tongue go dry, her entire body numb with shock. Sir Barty had just . . . had just given her everything she'd ever wanted—the security of his name and the blind faith of someone who trusted her word. She could still be Lady Babcock, the sharp edges of scandal muted by the padding of a title and a wealthy estate.

All she had to do was deny Turner and the night they had shared.

"What kind of past do you mean?" Palmer Blackwell said as he oozed through the crowd, which seemed to part for him. Mrs. Emory was behind him, looking at once apart and still apace with him. Mrs. Robertson lit up upon seeing her gown.

"Oh, your ladyship!" she said, then glanced down. "The hem!"

Mrs. Robertson's protests would have to be ignored for the moment, because John Turner, who until that point had been staring at Leticia most intently, gave his full attention to the new arrivals.

"Mr. Blackwell—and Mrs. Emory. Just who I wished to see."

Mrs. Emory looked quite flummoxed. "You wished to see me? Why? Er, I mean . . . how very obliging, I'm sure."

"How is your son, Harold?" Turner asked. "Have you heard from him recently?"

Before Mrs. Emory could do more than stutter, Sir Barty interjected himself in the scene.

"Blackwell," Sir Barty said, moving his entire body between Leticia and the new arrival. It was the most gallant act of chivalry she'd ever seen from him . . . well, she guessed he was still her fiancé if no one else was made aware of their falling-out—and it made her well up a little bit.

But only a little bit. Because while Sir Barty had wished for everything to go back to the way it was, it seemed that included Palmer Blackwell.

"It's good that you're here," Sir Barty continued. "It seems that you and my intended have gotten off on the wrong foot. Some nonsense about rumors and muck. But since you've come to the wedding, I can assume that you're wanting to make amends."

Sir Barty grinned affably, puffing out his chest. Certain that all would be well.

"I suppose that depends on the lady," Blackwell answered. "Do you wish me to make amends, Lady Churzy?"

Leticia stood, rooted to the spot. Her eyes turned to Blackwell. She saw the hate there, the power.

"If you should be making amends to anyone, Blackwell, it should be to me," Turner said, in a voice loud and clear enough for everyone to hear. "After all, you've been the cause of all my misery."

But Blackwell just smiled, seemingly at a loss. "Mr. Turner, now is not the time for your perpetual sour grapes. I'm a businessman. I refuse to be held responsible for profiting from your misfortunes."

"Even when you are responsible for said misfortunes?" Turner said.

Her heart leapt with fear, and with excitement. John Turner, it seemed, was done wasting time.

Everyone gasped. Only Sir Barty's good nature made him late to the conclusion everyone else had already arrived at. "What does he mean? Helen, what is he saying?"

"I mean that Palmer Blackwell burned down the Turner Grain Mill six years ago. And again, three years after that. And I have the proof."

He held up the ledger page in his hand, still folded, still innocuous. But Blackwell looked at it as if it were a blazing torch.

"There's no proof," he said. "Give me that!"

"Oh, I am sorry, I did not make myself clear. This isn't for you," Turner smiled, then let his gaze fall on Mrs. Emory. "It's for you."

"For me?" Mrs. Emory said, her voice thready, her eyes nervously flicking to the paper. "I'm sure I don't know what you mean."

Leticia, much like Mrs. Emory, was uncertain of what Turner was saying. Mrs. Emory does not have a seven-year-old child, her mind practically screamed. What are you doing?

But she would have to trust Turner. And right now, he was holding court like a master of the stage.

"Well of course you don't. I haven't told you what it is yet," he said, his lips pressing together in a tight smile. "This is a page from Mr. Blackwell's business ledgers. It's a page from the month of August, approximately seven years ago. Of course, you know why that month is important, don't you Mrs. Emory?"

"N-no," Mrs. Emory stuttered. "I haven't a clue."

"It's the month your son, Harold, was hired to work at the Turner Grain Mill by my father."

Mrs. Emory turned as pale as flour. But she said nothing, forcing Turner to continue.

"Harold was never a very good worker. But the war was still on, so workers—good or no—were needed come the harvest. He was paid a good wage by my father. So it leaves one wondering why Mr. Blackwell should be paying your son too."

"He . . . he wasn't!" Mrs. Emory replied, huffing. "I think I should know if my Harold was being paid twice!"

"Actually, you're right, Mrs. Emory." Turner smiled. "He wasn't paying Harold. He was giving the money to you. And according to his ledger, he's continued to do so ever since."

Suddenly, all the pieces fell into place in Leticia's mind. Mrs. Emory hadn't been being paid because she bore Mr. Blackwell's child, but instead because Mr. Blackwell had uses for her child.

They had been right all along. The means was just a bit more convoluted than initially thought.

"As I was saying, Harold was not a particularly good employee. He was always late, always causing errors—"

"Once he even dropped a pail of water into an entire vat of newly ground flour," Helen added, her eyes alight with understanding. "We had to refund the entire price of the wheat."

"Yes. I'm somewhat surprised my father did not sack him on the spot. What's interesting is there was one day that Harold Emory did not show up at all. Slept in, we were told. That, my parents remembered very clearly. Would you venture to guess what day that was?" he asked Mrs. Emory, who had gone from pale to a sort of purplish-blue, like she was holding her breath to keep from screaming.

"It was the day the mill burned," Leticia said quietly. When all eyes turned to her, she shrugged. "Mrs. Emory told us herself."

"Yes, Mrs. Emory," Turner said. "Then suddenly, your son joined the navy—even though the war had by then ended, and the navy has been putting ships in ordinary and discharging qualified sailors left and right since then. Come to think of it, how did your boy purchase a commission?"

"I . . . I . . ." Mrs. Emory's mouth dropped open in her frustration. "This is all rubbish! Give me that!"

She reached for the ledger page in Turner's hand and he quickly pulled it out of her reach.

"Louisa, stop that!" Blackwell snapped.

"Oh, Louisa, is it?" Turner asked blandly.

The crowd *ooh*ed. There was no other way to describe it. "You don't even let me call you Louisa," Mrs. Robertson said, sounding a little hurt. "And I've known you since we were girls."

"Oh, be quiet, Moira!" Mrs. Emory was practically crying in frustration. "Nothing he's saying is true. Nothing, not one bit."

"You know, I had that cousin who said he'd seen Mr. Harold Emory in York a few months ago," Mr. Jenkins of the cabbage farm (and the keen-eyed cousin) remarked, "and you said it couldn't have been because he was in Majorca."

"And he was! Is! He is most certainly not living in York. I . . . I write him all the time. He sends me money, that's how I bought the house on the square. Not because of Blackwell. And, how could I possibly have my locket?" She produced the locket from around her neck, prying it open and showing the tiny portrait of her son in his navy uniform.

"But," Margaret piped up this time, fingering her chin in thought. "A portrait isn't commissioning papers. It's not proof of his joining the navy. It's only proof he sat for a portrait while wearing a uniform."

"Oh, for God's sake!" Mrs. Emory cried. "This is all ridiculous. And none of it is true—Blackwell, tell them!"

"Yes, Blackwell, tell us," Sir Barty said, his thick brow one continuous line of disapproval. "And I'll take this moment to remind you that I am the magistrate in this county. So I would like to know if this is true."

"I'll be happy to show you the paper, Sir Barty," Turner said.

"No!" Mrs. Emory cried.

"Louisa—I mean Mrs. Emory, for the last time, stop! That paper says nothing of the sort." Blackwell rounded on Turner, his back most definitely up. He'd sat there and taken everything Turner had to say, and now it was his turn to attack. "Mr. Turner, I think you are trying desperately to confuse Helmsley, and confuse Sir Barty especially.

Perhaps it has something to do with the fact that your former lover is to be married to him today?"

A cold trickle of dread spread down Leticia's spine. This entire time, Turner had been playing with fire, because Blackwell would retaliate, and he would retaliate against her.

"John . . ." she pleaded quietly.

"Oh, John, is it?" Blackwell sneered.

"You leave her out of this," Turner said, his brow coming down. "She has nothing to do with your crimes."

"I think she does. Because I think you concocted this entire story to hide her crimes," he replied.

"Gentlemen, this is really getting out of hand," the vicar interrupted mildly. "Perhaps we should go into the church—"

"Not on your life!" Mrs. Spilsby said, effectively shutting up her husband.

"Tell me, Lady Churzy, where did you sleep last night?"

Blackwell's gaze bored into her. She suddenly felt that cold dread slide back up her spine, panic rising in her chest. But she would be damned if she'd let him see that.

"That's none of your business."

"But it's Sir Barty's business. After all, he's to marry you." Blackwell was performing for the crowd now, his expression filled with sorrow, his voice filled with pity. "Considering the abject apology he was making just minutes ago, and the trunk with your possessions that I came across at the entrance to town, I would wager that you did not sleep at Bluestone Manor, did you?"

Before she could so much as blink, Turner was between them, his teeth bared and growling in Blackwell's face.

"Get away from her."

"You are simply confirming my theory, Mr. Turner." Blackwell smiled.

"No," Leticia said. The word just popped out of her mouth. But she was tired. Tired of this farce, and tired of lying. "I didn't."

"You were with Mr. Turner, weren't you?" Blackwell said.

The world held its collective breath, waiting for the answer. Blackwell, Sir Barty, Turner. Everyone had his or her eyes on her.

She opened her mouth. Tried to speak. Closed it again. If she told them, told the world she was with John, then her future was irrevocably set. She would be a stain on his character. A scandal in Helmsley. A terrible embarrassment to Sir Barty—and it could even reflect poorly on Margaret, her having been under the influence of an interloper. She would be forever tainted.

But maybe, just maybe . . . she would be happy.

"Of course she was!"

Every head snapped around to find Helen, standing next to Sir Barty, hands on her hips, exasperated.

"Helen," Leticia began, her throat suddenly dry. Heavens, was the air becoming thick in here—er, out here? "That's very good of you, but—"

"Where else was the girl supposed to go after a lover's quarrel?" Helen spoke over her. "I invited her to stay with me. It was so late when she arrived I told her to leave the trunk on the side of the road and my John would pick it up in the morning. Secretly I was hoping that he would be asked to carry it in the opposite direction, back to Bluestone. She stayed in our guest room. Absolutely nothing untoward about it."

"Are you going to let your mother cover up your actions?" Blackwell sneered at Turner.

"That depends, are you going to let Mrs. Emory cover up yours?"

Blackwell hesitated, glancing at the woman in question. Mrs. Emory was working her way through a rainbow of hues on her cheeks, now a firestorm of red.

"Yes, Mrs. Emory." Helen rounded on her rival. "How could you stand by Mr. Blackwell? What kind of pain and suffering have you caused? What kind of terrible person would do such a thing?"

That, it seemed, was the last straw for poor Louisa Emory. Because when she spoke, her voice was a good octave higher than it had been, squeaking in hysterics.

"I . . . I didn't. Mrs. Turner. Moira, you have to believe me. I would never . . . it's just that . . . Harold was always in trouble, and . . . and he offered so much money!"

And then the melee broke out. Everyone erupted in either horror, glee, or horrified glee. Electric energy coursed across the churchyard, charging action into all the principal players.

Blackwell took two steps and slapped Mrs. Emory hard across the face, the crack echoing through the morning air. "You utter bitch, I knew I couldn't trust you!"

Helen gasped, as did Mrs. Robertson, Mrs. Spilsby, and Miss Goodhue.

Turner leapt into the fray, throwing himself in front of Blackwell's fist. His own flew into Blackwell's shoulder, and Blackwell lunged at him.

"Mr. Blackwell! Mr. Turner!" The vicar fairly wailed. "Please, you are in a churchyard!"

"Hit him lower, Mr. Turner!" Margaret said. "I'm told the genitals are particularly painful on a man. Is that right, Dr. Gray?"

"Quite painful," Dr. Gray agreed.

"Blackwell, you are under arrest!" Sir Barty huffed, making the assumption that as magistrate he could arrest people, and leapt forward. He also assumed that his imposing presence would be enough to separate the two brawling men. And it might have been, had he been able to do more than limp to their side with his cane.

"Dr. Gray, Mr. Jenkins, come help me!"

Dr. Gray was already trying to insert himself between the pair (Mr. Turner now had scuffs on his face and Mr. Blackwell was being held by his collar) and Mr. Jenkins inserted himself, managing to pin one of Blackwell's arms.

Meanwhile, all the ladies were gathered around a wailing Mrs. Emory, some supporting and some admonishing. All except Helen.

"Are you all right, my dear?" she'd said, flying to Leticia's side.

But Leticia couldn't answer. Her breath was coming in strange bursts, her vision turning cloudy at the edges. But what focus she did have was on the two men before her, trying to rip each other's throats out.

"How dare you!" Turner managed as his fist flew and struck Blackwell in the shoulder. "You strike a woman, when this is all your doing! You're the one with hell to pay!"

"You had everything handed to you!" Blackwell was raving, spitting mad. "Everything! You inherited your business. I built mine up from nothing! Now you think you can wave around a goddamned ledger page and go home and fuck your countess? You don't get to win!"

Leticia's eyes fell to where the ledger page had landed in the dirt at her feet. But when she looked up, it was to discover that the ledger page was only of interest to herself.

No, everyone else was looking at her.

Even Turner and Blackwell had paused in their fight, finally (mostly) restrained by Dr. Gray and Mr. Jenkins. Sir Barty's eyes were wide enough to see their color beyond his bushy brows, and everyone else just stood there, mouths open in shock.

And then it became clear why.

Because of what Blackwell had just very crudely said.

And everyone was waiting for her to either confirm or deny it.

Therefore, Leticia did the only thing she could think of in that moment.

The one thing she had promised herself she would never do.

She fainted.

24

When Leticia came to, she was in a familiar room, with a familiar voice bursting into her thoughts.

"Good, you're awake!" Margaret said. "Dr. Gray said you would be soon enough."

"What . . . what happened?" Leticia said, blinking up at the ceiling. She recognized it. It was the one in the little sitting room she had taken as her own in Bluestone. How had she gotten from the churchyard to Bluestone Manor?

"You fainted," Margaret said practically, wringing out a cloth from a nearby basin, and slapping it on Leticia's forehead. "Now I know why you said one should never faint if they can help it. You collapsed like a felled tree. Just went down in a giant whoosh!"

Margaret raised her forearm and let it fall, landing with a solid thud against the pillows of the sofa.

"Wonderful. I suppose at least I've given Helmsley something to talk about other than a churchyard brawl."

"Oh no. It's all anyone is talking about," Margaret replied, wide-eyed. "Well, that and your having a past with Mr. Turner. Which I think you should have told us about, don't you? It would have certainly explained some things."

Brilliant. If the molded ceiling fell on her now, she would welcome it.

"It's really not as bad as you think," came the voice of Helen Turner from the doorway. Then she turned a pointed gaze on Margaret. "Right, Miss Babcock?"

But Margaret just cocked her head to one side. "It would depend on how bad she thinks it is."

"Am . . . am I permitted to sit up?"

"Careful now. Dr. Gray said you did not hit your head, so you should be fine with some air and water," Helen was saying as she crossed the room to assist Margaret in pulling Leticia to a seated position. "But I shouldn't wonder that you felt a little poorly. I can't imagine that with all the excitement that you'd had anything to eat since yesterday. Everyone will understand."

"Everyone thinks you fainted because Mr. Blackwell said—"

"Margaret!" Helen said as kindly but firmly as possible. "Perhaps you can pour Leticia some tea?"

Margaret's jaw shut firmly and she went over to the little tray that had materialized in a corner of the room.

"Where is Dr. Gray?" she asked.

"He had some business to attend to," Helen said, wrapping a shawl around Leticia's shoulders.

"He had to go speak as witness to the constable for Mr. Turner, and get him released from his charges," Margaret added, handing Leticia her tea.

Tea that Leticia promptly almost spilled. "His what?"

"Oh, Father was livid after you collapsed in a heap—did you know that your skirt flew up over your knees?" Margaret said. "Anyway—once Mr. Blackwell and Mr. Turner were separated, he had Mr. Jenkins run for the constable, and when the constable arrived, he just arrested everyone. Blackwell, Turner, Mrs. Emory—I believe he dispatched a few men to go look for Mrs. Emory's son in York too. Everyone was brought to the cellar of the church—since we haven't a gaol in Helmsley—and the constable was left to parse it out there. Dr. Gray told Father, Mrs. Turner, and me to bring you back here. So we did." Margaret took a sip of her tea. "Heavens, this is good tea—I wonder if they grew it with lavender in the soil?"

Leticia could only stare at Margaret. There was nothing like fisticuffs to energize a usually quite placid young lady.

"Sir Barty is here?" she asked, and Helen nodded. "I think I should speak with him. I owe him an explanation. Would you mind . . . ?"

"Not at all," Helen replied, rising. "I'll go tell him. And . . . any decision you make, Leticia, I hope you know that at least this Helmsley lady will not judge you for it."

And with that Helen left the room, the door quietly clicking closed behind her.

Leaving Leticia with Margaret.

"I . . . I likely owe you an explanation too," she began, oddly unable to look up from her tea.

"Whatever for?" Margaret asked.

"Well . . . as you said, it would have made things a great deal clearer had I told you about Mr. Turner in the beginning. But I was so . . . surprised to see him, and then you told me you had an interest in him . . ."

"Oh, that," Margaret said, her eyes going wide. "Yes, I suppose you do owe me an explanation for that."

"I was flustered," she replied. "That was really the only explanation that I had. But that your feelings were tangled up in my bad decisions is truly my greatest regret in all of this. If I could turn back time . . ."

"But you cannot," Margaret said. "And it's just as well, I suppose. I've come to the conclusion that Mr. Turner is not at all for me."

"He's . . . he's not?" Leticia asked weakly.

"No. I figured it out on the dance floor at the ball, and then it was cemented this morning in the churchyard. Indeed, my infatuation with him seems to have been nothing more than youthful fancy."

"Youthful fancy?" Leticia replied, letting out a gasp of laughter. "You first told me you wished to marry him three weeks ago!"

"And I was much younger then. After all, there are flowers—beautiful, bright orange lilies—that blossom and die in the space of a week. Surely a love can live and die in three."

"Yes," Leticia mused. Or perhaps it can grow. Wakened from dormancy and brought to full life. "So you no longer care for Mr. Turner," she summarized. "And just to be clear and concise, you do not care for Mr. Blackwell either?"

"Mr. Blackwell? God no!" Margaret cried. "Why on earth would you think such a thing?"

"Just . . . my own stupidity," Leticia said, shaking her head.

Besides, with prison on Mr. Blackwell's horizon, he wouldn't be marrying anyone soon.

"Have you seen his gardens?" Margaret was saying, still stuck on the subject. "Barely a potted plant in evidence. So, I was thinking perhaps you should marry him instead."

Leticia's eyes flew up.

"Mr. Blackwell?"

"No—Mr. Turner."

Leticia froze.

"After all, he meets all of your criteria."

"My criteria?" she replied, feeling a bit like a parrot.

"You told me people who intend to marry should have common goals and ideals. You and he have quite a bit in common."

"We have nothing in common." Leticia practically laughed.

"You have each other in common," Margaret said. "Your shared past."

"It's . . . we knew each other for a fortnight last summer, it's not enough."

"I think it would depend on the weeks in question. I could not tell you what I was doing for two weeks last summer unless I consulted the records of my research. But I imagine you remember those two weeks exceptionally well."

Leticia was silent. That fortnight, even with the specter of the Lie, was indelible in her mind. She knew every conversation, every glance by heart.

"But more importantly, you told me that a man that is worthy of me is someone who cares for me, who will wish to take care of me, and whom I wish to take care of in turn. I think perhaps Mr. Turner would do anything for you. He tried to protect you from Mr. Blackwell. And the way you tried to help him, I should think it's the same for you."

Yes, he had tried to protect her, standing between her and Blackwell, even though she had resigned herself to Blackwell telling everyone the truth when she'd left Bluestone Manor the day before. And even though she told herself she did it for her own gain, the truth was, she'd done everything in her power to help Turner regain his mill, his position in Helmsley. However . . .

"We've had very different lives."

"Doesn't mean you can't have the same one now. Two plants of different species will sometimes cross-pollinate to make something entirely new." Margaret cocked her head to the side, serious. "What's expected of you isn't always what is right for you."

She let the girl's words sink in. It had been second nature to resist this line of thought . . . the whispers in her mind that said she could be happy with John Turner, that she could give up the life of a countess and go back to living in a mill yard.

It's not as if being a countess had treated her very well anyway.

But there was still one consideration left.

"Margaret, I've made a promise to Sir Barty."

"True. However, I find myself agreeing with my daughter." Sir Barty's voice floated quietly through the room. They both turned to see him standing there, hesitating at the entrance to the sitting room. "Are you feeling better, m'd—my lady?"

"Much," she replied. "Margaret, could you give us a moment?"

Margaret glanced from her father to Leticia, then quickly rose with her cup of tea, pausing only to scoop up a finger sandwich or two before exiting the room.

Where on earth to start?

"Thank you so much for taking care of me," Leticia began.

"Of course," he said, sitting next to her. "What kind of person would I be to have left you in the churchyard?"

"Yes, of course. But I meant before." She took a deep breath and met his eyes, which were wide with surprise. "You took me in once when we met in Paris. I had nowhere to go, and no way to get there. But you brought me to Helmsley, made me welcome in your home. You protected me with your good name. And I . . . I have not been worthy of it."

"How can that be?" he asked, fishing in his pocket and bringing out a handkerchief for her. "You knew Blackwell was no good. You brought Margaret out of her shell—I never thought I'd see my daughter dance at a ball. You . . . you're the finest thing I've seen since I lost my darling Hortense." He took her hand in his. "But you're not mine, are you?"

Leticia gave him a watery smile. "No. I'm afraid not. You see, last night, Mr. Turner and I . . . we . . ."

Pink grew on his cheeks as the clock ticked on the mantel, echoing in the silence as he understood.

"That's all right, m'dear, you don't have to elaborate."

She nodded gratefully as he shifted uncomfortably in his seat.

"However, I have to say that the offer to . . . take care of you is still open, if your young man doesn't come up to scratch. But I doubt that is what you wish."

She gave him a watery smile. "I'd rather not disgrace you in that way."

"Even if I decide I don't mind?"

She nodded sadly. "Even then."

"Then that's the way it is," he said with a sigh.

They sat together for a still moment, his hand holding hers. But letting each other go.

"Do you know . . . I don't know what to do now," Sir Barty said at last, staring sadly out the window. "I thought I had a solution. I thought I had a path again."

Leticia's heart broke for the man—so kind, so generous . . . generous in a way that had nothing to do with money. He was everything she'd thought she wanted.

But unfortunately, he was not what she needed.

"Perhaps . . ." she ventured with a spark of realization, "you should ask Helen."

"Helen?"

"I've found her counsel very wise over the past few weeks. She's become a good friend to me, and has always been a good friend to you." She patted his hand. "Helen will know exactly what to do."

Sir Barty considered her words, then his eyes brightened with the idea. "I'm still ahead in our game of cribbage." A slow smile of glee came over his features. "She'll be itching for a chance to even the score."

He rose to his feet, his back straighter than it had been since they first met, his need for his cane almost minimal. Then he turned.

"But what about you, m'dear? What will happen to you?"

Leticia smiled up at her would-be husband. Her eyes were heavy with teardrops, but her vision was completely clear.

"For once, Sir Barty, I know exactly where I should be."

❦

"WHERE THE HELL are you taking me?" Turner called after Rhys as they crossed the mill yard.

"Where do you think?" Rhys replied. "I promised your mother that I would take you home."

"Dammit, man, my mother does not run my life."

"All evidence to the contrary."

Even with Sir Barty's instructions, it had taken the rest of the morning and a good part of the afternoon for the constable—who did have the power to issue warrants and make arrests—to sort out what had occurred. Only after testimony from Dr. Gray, Mr. Jenkins, and the assorted ladies of Helmsley, who vouched for him against Blackwell's repeated accusations of assault, did he declare Turner was free to go.

He could only hope that he was not too late.

"This is a waste of time. I need to go into town, not out of it."

"Whatever for?" Rhys asked as they walked past the house and toward the mill itself.

"To hire a carriage."

"Oh really?" echoed a voice from high above. "Whatever for?"

They looked up. And Turner's heart leapt to his throat upon seeing Leticia—his Letty—standing on the balcony of the windmill.

He'd been so certain she would have gone. That when she awoke after her admittedly less than graceful swoon, she would have made good on her intention to leave town. That she would not want to face the scandal that loomed.

That least of all, she would not want to face him.

"Hello, John," she said, smiling down at them, her hand shading her eyes from the midafternoon sun. "Hello, Dr. Gray."

"My lady," Dr. Gray said with a nod. "I trust your head is feeling better?"

"Quite," she replied.

"What are you doing here?" Turner blurted out.

"Don't you know? This is where I am supposed to be."

His heart, already lodged in his throat, began to thrum like a hummingbird's. "Yes," he declared, a smile spreading across his features. "Yes it is."

And with that, he burst through the door of the mill and bounded up the spiral staircase three steps at a time, his speed veritably setting the sails to spinning.

He reached the landing. And saw her.

She was standing against the sun, a halo of light around her, her dress—the same lace and silk that she had worn when she came to him the night before—dancing lightly around her ankles in the breeze.

"You're here," he breathed. He kept himself at an arm's

length——he was afraid to touch her. Afraid she wasn't real . . . and his skin itching to find out if she was.

"I am."

"I thought you would have left. Gone . . . to find a new place."

She cocked her head to one side. "I don't think I have anywhere left to go."

"Because now word will spread," he stated flatly.

"No, because I've looked everywhere else for my home, so I should think that I'd know it when I found it."

Now he let himself touch her. One hand lifted to gently caress a piece of hair that had fallen behind her ear. For a woman who worked so hard to present herself perfectly, was it any wonder he was fascinated by the imperfections?

"Oh, you think you've found your home, have you?"

She leaned into him, whispering as her mouth met his. "I know it."

Turner felt the world fall away beneath him. It was as if his feet lifted off the balcony, floating on the air. His body sparked to life, his arms wrapping around her body, holding her close, as close as two people ever were and ever would be.

He'd never been so happy. Never knew he was capable of it.

Except . . .

"I'm sorry," he said, breaking free from her arms. "About what happened at the church."

"You are?" she asked, confused. "I'm not."

"I should have stopped Blackwell from saying anything about you." He ran a hand through his hair. "Hell, I shouldn't have confronted him."

"Stop it," she said, stepping forward and placing her hand on his chest. "I knew he would tell the world. By not caring, it relieved him of the only weapon he had over me. Over us."

"There is going to be controversy," Turner warned. "You will face a great deal of scrutiny. The countess and he miller? We all will."

"You once said that if we stood together, weathering the storm would be easier." She smiled at him. "Besides, I think there will be a great deal of controversy from all corners of Helmsley for a little while. With any luck, ours will get lost in the scuffle."

"Your practicality has always impressed me." He smiled as his lips descended to hers again.

After an inappropriate amount of time, she pulled away, but remained in his arms. "Now . . . I need you to tell me if in our current arrangement I'm going to have to learn to bake. Because I really would rather not."

"Bake?"

"Yes. You see that building there?" She pointed to one of the outbuildings to the mill. It was original to the property, having survived both fires. "You own it, correct? But it stands empty."

"It used to be extra grain storage, but I expanded the granary when I rebuilt so . . ."

"Excellent, so you could turn it into a bakery."

His eyebrow went up. "A bakery?"

"This town hasn't one, you know. You have all the flour in the world, you could profit by simply turning it into bread."

"That's not a bad idea . . . I don't suppose you know how to run a bakery."

"Oh, I haven't a clue."

"Not one to get your hands dirty, are you?"

"Not with flour." She smiled at him.

"It's too bad I didn't fall in love with a baker, then," he said as he wrapped his arms around her. "She could have run that side of the business and we could have all been fat and happy."

"Yes. It is too bad," she replied, slapping his arm at his jest. "But I do happen to be proficient at hiring bakers. And there's one who made my wedding cake, which regretfully will never be served. Perhaps she would like continued employment."

"You have excellent ideas."

"Oh, I'm full of them."

"However, you are wrong about one thing. You will see your wedding cake served. We are changing the groom, no other details of your wedding."

Now it was time for her eyebrow to go up. "Not even the day?"

"Well," he hedged. "I imagine we will have to wait for the banns to be read again." At her exasperated look, he explained. "I haven't the ability to procure a special license. You're marrying a poor, unconnected miller, my love. Not an earl. Not even a Sir Barty."

She relented, her shoulders relaxing, her face painting into a smile as she slid her arms over his shoulders.

"I wouldn't have it any other way."

EPILOGUE

$\mathcal{T}$hree weeks to the day after the disastrous events in St. Stephen's churchyard, those memories were replaced by far more joyous ones, when Leticia Herzog gave up the title of Lady Churzy and took on the name of Mrs. Turner.

It was said that Leticia was the only person in the history of the parish to have her name read aloud six times in seven Sundays, and therefore she decided to forgo even waiting an extra week, bending the rules as far as Vicar Spilsby would allow and having the wedding ceremony take place directly after the last banns had been spoken, no week of waiting in between.

She suspected Mrs. Spilsby had something to do with her success.

She also suspected that Mrs. Spilsby had something to do with the minimal amount of gossip that she heard when she walked through town on market day. Mrs. Spilsby, Miss Goodhue, Mrs. Robertson, Rebecca the baker, Molly, her lady's maid, Mrs. Dillon, and Jameson had all come down on the side of support, brooking no ill word and vigorously defending her by playing down the entire situation.

But mostly, she had Margaret and Sir Barty to thank. They immediately let it be known that there were no hard feelings, inviting John and Leticia to dine, for walks in the gardens on Sundays after church, and for public strolls on market day.

Leticia suspected Helen, and her increased presence at Bluestone Manor, had something to do with that success as well.

The Babcocks even went so far as to invite Leticia to stay with them until her wedding day—she was so familiar there now it seemed natural, but here Turner put his foot down. He'd waited a year to have Leticia at his side, there was no way he was letting her out of his sight now, he'd said.

She'd needed very little convincing to see his side of things. But still, she'd let him present his argument. Day and night. Often, and extensively.

Dr. Gray did leave Helmsley as planned, shortly after the fight in the churchyard, but only to return in due course with Turner's other best friend, Ned Granville, the Earl of Ashby.

Who, of course, Leticia had spent the better part of a fortnight last year thinking of as Mr. Turner.

He'd come alone, leaving his bride at home, as she was temporarily not keen on travel—their time on the Continent had been productive.

As for Mr. Blackwell and Mrs. Emory, they were hauled off, facing charges of arson and conspiracy. Mrs. Emory gave a full account, placing all the weight of the deed on herself and Mr. Blackwell, hoping to spare her precious Harold of any blame.

One might say some unkind things about Mrs. Emory, but her love for her less-than-worthy son was never in question.

Later they would hear tell that Mr. Blackwell had been transported to Australia. Rumor had it that he tried to bribe his way off the ship, but as far as anyone knew his attempt was unsuccessful, for they never heard from him again. And his mills, without an heir or successor in place, faltered quickly.

The number of grain mills in the area suddenly reduced from seven to one, Turner Grain Mill found itself with its busiest season in its decades-long history. And no one cared about any scandal attached to the owner, much like no one cared about any worries attached to the new fortuitously installed steam equipment. They simply needed their grain either sold or milled . . . or turned into bread, as the case may be.

Sir Barty's grain included.

It was not long before they found it necessary to expand, first purchasing the remnants of Blackwell's mill in Fennish Moor. There was every chance that they would purchase more in the future.

Since they became so busy, the circumstances of how Mr. Turner acquired his wife faded from collective memory faster than otherwise. To the town, Leticia simply became Mrs. Turner, the savvy and improbably stylish miller's wife, her countess origins forgotten as soon as the townsfolk of Helmsley forgot to use the "my lady" honorific when addressing her.

Surprisingly, she did not miss it.

And to Turner, Leticia became what she always had been—Letty. The maddening woman who could recognize him at a thousand paces, whom he loved and who loved him back.

She asked him once how he'd decided that he loved her. And he, amazingly, had an answer.

"Because you unbalance me."

"I unbalance you?" she replied.

"Yes, every time I think I've reached an equilibrium

with you, you do something to throw me. It's not even anything direct. It could be as simple as a mischievous look. A practical sigh. A vulnerable posture. Everything about you breaks my heart and pieces it back together at the same time."

"Heavens," she replied, concerned. "That sounds uncomfortable."

"Oh, it is . . ." He smiled, rolling over on top of her. "I often ask myself, is this what it's going to be like forever? Or will I be able to ever see her without feeling the floor going out from under me?"

"And what is your conclusion?" she replied, shifting delightfully beneath him.

"That I'm doomed," he said. "This is how it is for me. This is my truth."

He kissed her nose.

"I love Leticia Herzog."

He kissed her eyes.

"I love Lady Churzy."

He kissed her mouth.

"I love you, Letty Turner. And not a damned thing is going to change that."

ear Reader,

I love research. Not only does it help fill out the world my characters live in, but sometimes it helps fill much larger plot holes.

From The Game and the Governess, I knew that John Turner had a family mill, but I didn't know what kind, or what they milled precisely. I knew only that the mill was in Lincolnshire—a pleasantly named county I'd yet to explore in any of my books. So when I was researching Lincolnshire (oh, those Wolds!) and discovered it was populated with windmills back in the Regency day, suddenly John Turner's entire history—and his place in Helmsley—clicked into place.

Besides, Cervantes isn't the only one who finds windmills romantic.

Unfortunately, I don't live near any working windmills, but my research led me to the Maud Foster Mill in Boston, Lincolnshire, on which I based the Turner Grain Mill. I tried to stay as close to the specs of a working windmill as I could, but I didn't find a single one that had a space for a bed. Thus I did some judicious rearranging of the blueprints, so John (and Leticia) could enjoy some privacy away from all the flour.

I hope you enjoyed the story of the miller and his countess, and the whimsy and majesty of spinning white sails. . . .

Sincerely,

Kate Noble

Because the best
conversations happen
after dark . . .

ANNOUNCING A BRAND-NEW SITE FOR ROMANCE AND URBAN FANTASY READERS JUST LIKE YOU!

 *Visit **XOXOAfterDark.com** for free reads, exclusive excerpts, bonus materials, author interviews and chats, and much, much more!*

XOXO **AFTER DARK**.COM

31901056705579